MAIN
AF-MYS.

U.W.

# Murder in
# the Rough

Also by J. S. Borthwick

# Murder in
# the Rough

## *J. S. Borthwick*

ST. MARTIN'S MINOTAUR ✹ NEW YORK

Note: The Ocean Tide community, its residents and visitors, and the events described are entirely fictitious.

www.minotaurbooks.com

Chapter illustrations by Alec Creighton

Map by Mac Creighton

Library of Congress Cataloging-in-Publication Data

Borthwick, J. S.
    Murder in the rough / J. S. Borthwick.—1st ed.
        p. cm.
    ISBN 0-312-28829-8
    1. Deane, Sarah (Fictitious character)—Fiction. 2. McKenzie, Alex (Fictitious character)—Fiction. 3. Women detectives—Maine—Fiction. 4. Golf courses—Fiction. 5. Maine—Fiction. I. Title.
    PS3552.O756 M87 2002
    813'.54—dc21

                                                          2001048747

First Edition: March 2002

10  9  8  7  6  5  4  3  2  1

To four golfers. Three of fond memory: my grandfather, William M., who claimed to have invented a better baffie; my father, Luther Edmonds, who once upon a time qualified in a tournament two strokes ahead of Bobby Jones, and my father-in-law, James Alexander, who never met a sand trap that he couldn't get the best of. And finally, number four, the Gump, a man whom neither snow nor hail nor gloom of night can stay from his appointed round.

# Cast of Principal Characters

SARAH DOUGLAS DEANE—Assistant Professor of English,
  Bowmouth College
ALEX MCKENZIE—Physician, husband of Sarah
ELSPETH MCKENZIE—mother of Alex, wife of John
JOHN MCKENZIE—husband of Elspeth, father of Alex
FERGUS MCKENZIE—uncle to John McKenzie
BETTY COLLEY—wife of Ned Colley, mother of Brian and Dylan
ROSE BINGHAM—mother of Betty
BRIAN AND DYLAN COLLEY—sons of Betty and Ned
SHERRY MOSEBY—wife of Albert, mother of Nick, Matt, and Tim
ALBERT (AL) MOSEBY—husband of Sherry, father of Nick, Matt,
  and Tim
NICK MOSEBY—Manager of bike rental shop; Yale student
MATT MOSEBY—Grounds crew member at Ocean Tide
TIM MOSEBY—youngest son

JOSEPH MARTINELLI—Manager of Ocean Tide community
CARLY THOMPSON—Executive assistant, Ocean Tide
NAOMI FOXGLOVE—Social hostess, Ocean Tide
PETE SALIERI—Assistant golf pro, Ocean Tide

GEORGE FITTS—Sergeant, Maine State Police CID
MIKE LAAKA—Sheriff's deputy investigator
KATIE WATERS—Deputy sheriff

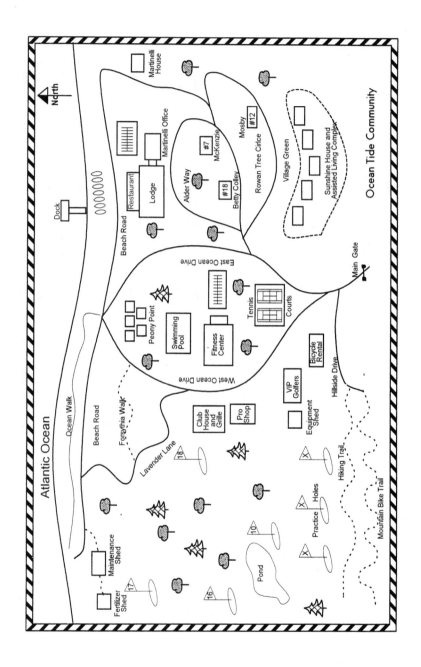

# Murder in
# the Rough

# 1

Accidents will happen in the best regulated families.

—Charles Dickens, *Pickwick Papers*

MIDCOAST Maine. The month of May. Rain, northeast winds, fog. Chill. Temperature moving between upper forties and lower fifties. General misery.

But rotten weather only figured in one of four apparently unrelated events. The first was the departure on the first day of the month from Cambridge, Massachusetts, of Professor John McKenzie and his artist wife, Elspeth. Heads down, muffled in rain gear, bucking sheets of rain, the two closed the door for the last time on their rather dilapidated Victorian house, and behind a heavily loaded moving van, followed Interstate 95 north to its junction with Route 1. Three and a half hours later, visibility worsening by the minute, the couple arrived at their new home, a one-floor, two-bedroom cottage complete with attached garage at 7 Alder Way in the recently opened Ocean Tide community in the township of Rockport, Maine.

This "architect-designed hometown community"—to quote from the brochure—offered "a variety of cottages, semide-tached houses, apartments in the Lodge, as well as an assisted-living complex set among a grove of birch and young maples, this last being surrounded by an attractive picket fence (since the assisted residents might be given to wandering about). Meals and guest rooms could be had at the Ocean Tide Lodge and many splendid facilities for all ages circled the property: swimming pools, indoor and outdoor, tennis courts, croquet for the "young in heart," and an eighteen-hole golf course.

Manager Joseph Martinelli made it a point of honor to personally greet each new arriving resident and assure them that when the rain finally gave up and a nurturing sun came out, they would find a feast of gardens, pleasant shaded walks and woodland trails. "Also," said the enthusiastic Joseph as he greeted the McKenzies on their front steps, "everyone has beach privileges for picnics, family outings, special occasions." Here Joseph waved at the fog-bound shore, and, after calculating the combined age of the new residents, added, "Facilities for everyone. Stairway and ramp so that our beach is wheelchair and walker accessible. Easy up and easy down is what I say. So welcome from all of us at Ocean Tide." Of course what Joseph Martinelli did not say and the Ocean Tide Welcome brochure did not mention was that the "beach" on that particular stretch of coast, except for a patch here and there of imported sand, was composed almost entirely of rocks and led into a frequently turbulent section of the Atlantic Ocean.

Then with the two new residents standing in dripping rain gear Manager Martinelli handed Elspeth a small potted azalea with a blue ribbon around its throat, and pulling the collar of his yellow slicker tight around his neck, splashed down the walk and departed in his official blue Ocean Tide Explorer.

The second event—a few storm-filled days following the

McKenzie arrival—involved another wet departure and relocation to the Ocean Tide community. The Colley family— Grandmother Rose, her daughter Betty, and her eleven- and thirteen-year-old sons, Brian and Dylan—had left behind a large and unprofitable farm on the sparsely populated hills of Appleton township to move to a three-bedroom cottage at 18 Alder Way, a site close to John and Elspeth McKenzie's cottage. The Colley family, too, received a potted azalea and the personal best wishes of Manager Martinelli.

The third happening on the next Saturday that May saw Mr. and Mrs. Albert Moseby and their three sons detach themselves from a small ranch house that bordered the family garden supply and greenhouse business set on outer reaches of Union, Maine—a township close to Appleton—and with umbrellas, slickers, and rain hats in place, with smiles fixed on all five faces—accept their azalea and start the business of settling into a four-bedroom number at 12 Rowan Tree Circle, a move that put the Mosebys within spitting distance of the Colley family (their close relatives) and to John and Elspeth McKenzie.

The last and binding event occurred almost two weeks later on Friday, the twenty-sixth of May, after yet another week of unnatural cold and what the television weather person cheerfully called "windy with persistent intermittent rain showers." This was the early evening discovery on Ocean Tide's western flank of the rain-soaked and partly decomposed body of a young adult male lying in the rough just off the last of three practice golf holes. These practice holes, adjuncts to the regular eighteen-hole course, bordered two parallel trails, one for hiking, the other for mountain biking. After superficial examination by the forces of law and order, this distressing object was pronounced a probable victim of homicide—a chain encased in a plastic sheath being wrapped tightly about what was left of his neck.

*    *    *

"Aw, Jesus, what a god-awful mess he is," said Sheriff's Deputy Investigator Mike Laaka, who had just arrived on the scene after a call from the Maine State Police. He spoke with tightened lips and tried not to take a deep breath of the heavy moist air that hung about the corpse. Mike, a tall blond man of Nordic aspect, was usually able to take his job for better or for worse without much apparent angst. But Mike, whose hobby was focused on thoroughbred racing and placing bets through a family connection in New York, had recently seen a rerun of the PBS *Civil War* series. And today, standing in the ankle-deep mud on the bike trail and seeing the man's gray sodden body in its smeared wet clothes, its limbs awkwardly twisted, he was powerfully reminded of some of the photographs taken in such places such as Bloody Angle and the Sunken Road. And the immediate effect was one of an overpowering nausea that threatened Mike's ability to keep his last meal down. For a few moments he turned away, struggled, breathed hard through his mouth, and then getting a grip on his digestive system, straightened his shoulders and turned to the man in charge, Sergeant George Fitts of the Maine State Police CID.

"So, do we have any idea about an ID?" demanded Mike. "Hasn't anyone around missed this guy? I mean, for God's sake, this is right next to a golf hole. Next to hiking trails. Bike trails. Part of the Ocean Tide outfit. Why didn't one of the residents, someone anyway, get a whiff of him? Or why didn't a dog track him down? Because it sure looks like he's been here for days."

George Fitts, a play-it-by-the-book character, a bald-headed steel-spectacled man of few words and no tolerance for the free and often breezy ways of Mike Laaka, frowned and stripped off a pair of surgical gloves. "Use your head, Mike. I'd bet no one's been through here lately. The weather's been lousy and the grounds and paths too muddy for biking. Or for hiking. Or walking a dog."

"Except the murderer. He made it through okay. Maybe with a corpse on his back. Brings in the body from somewhere else because who in hell would plan a meeting here with a nor'easter blowing."

"Forget about a meeting," said George. "With the steady rain and no one around it was a good place to dump a body." And then, sharply, "Back up, Mike. Move it. We don't need your footprints messing up the scene. The mud is bad enough. We'll wait for the medical examiner. And I've sent word for forensics."

"But you checked his pockets, the guy's wallet?"

"No ID on the body, no wallet," said George shortly. "And we won't monkey around with the body until the pathologist gets over here. Meanwhile, put a call in for missing persons. See if they can come up with something."

"Some of the guys on that list, they should stay missing," grumbled Mike. He backed up another few feet and reverting to the diction of his fishermen ancestors shook his head. "My Gawd, don't he stink, though."

"Get on the horn and do as I say," said George. He turned around and raised a hand indicating an approaching group. "Here come the crime scene guys, so look busy."


The following Saturday morning brought clearing and dry air. The McKenzies, wife Elspeth and husband John, sat at the breakfast table which being set by a front window gave out on a view of Alder Way's curving brick sidewalk. Both had rejoiced at the appearance of the sun, the temperature had risen into the high fifties and they were now at the breakfast table occupied with sections of the *Boston Globe*—a subscription to which had been continued after their removal to Maine. Both were unaware of the previous night's grisly discovery on the far margins of the Ocean Tide property.

"Family parties," announced Elspeth McKenzie to her husband, John, "can be absolutely lethal. They should be forbidden by law. Or at the very least there should be a marriage counselor and a riot squad standing by."

John McKenzie lowered the sports section and looked re-proachfully at his wife over the top of his half-glasses. He didn't like being disturbed by breakfast chatter until he had checked out the Red Sox news, the editorial page and the latest Dilbert cartoon.

Elspeth usually agreed with her husband in this matter. She, too, avoided conversation until she had scanned for pre-viously unreported world calamities, checked the fine arts sec-tion—she was an artist of considerable local repute—read Ann Landers and Dear Abby and had a go at the crossword puzzle. In fact, throughout almost forty-five years of marriage, both McKenzies had maintained an agreeable rule of silence during the breakfast hour until it was time for the second cup of coffee.

"What have family parties to do with anything?" said John.

"Just that there was this party in Acton, a family reunion, and one of the sons tried to strangle his grandmother and an uncle threw a pork roast, platter and all, at his fourteen-year-old niece. And the mother went and got out her husband's shotgun from the laundry room and general hell broke loose."

John McKenzie put down his section of the paper and, using the marmalade jar as a marker for a report of dissension in the Yankees' management ranks—always welcome news to a Red Sox fan—prepared to listen to a tangled tale of domestic violence that in some mysterious way connected with the lives and times of the McKenzie family. When his wife broke the sacred silence of the breakfast table, there was usually a rea-son, even if that reason seemed undetectable by the listening partner.

Elspeth shook the paper, found the continuation of the Acton story, skimmed it, and put it down. "The family was just asking for trouble. Three generations—no, four, there's a great-grandfather—all staying under one roof and some of them haven't seen each other for years. A son turned up who was AWOL from the army only no one knew it. And there were twins from L.A. They'd joined some sort of a cult that used four ounces of cognac for Communion and toasts. Anyway, some people got drunk and things went to pieces."

John McKenzie tried to keep any impatience from his voice. "Elspeth, please make the connection. I'm sorry for the family from Acton, but what on God's green earth has it to do with us? We have enough to worry about. We have a new house with not enough room in it—my books are still in cartons because there aren't any decent book shelves in this place. And you have your studio to set up and you want to get ready for a show in the fall."

"John," said Elspeth with some exasperation. "Listen. Please. This party in Acton reminded me. Hit me over the head, really. Because I've been thinking about us giving a party. A family party. To celebrate our move. And your uncle Fergus, it's his ninetieth coming up. And your birthday a day later on June twenty-eighth. You'll be sixty-five whether you like it or not. And since we were married on your birthday, it will be our anniversary."

"But we never make a fuss about our anniversaries," John remarked. "Go out for a nice sail in the cove, have dinner. Nothing fancy."

"This is the forty-fifth," said Elspeth.

"That's not like the fiftieth."

"But add it together, plus the fact that Alex and Sarah have a week off around the end of June. And Sarah's got her doctorate last fall. So I thought we should do something. A kind of triple event. Or is it quadruple?"

"That sounds like a heart bypass and about as much fun."

Elspeth ignored the remark and soldiered on. "Well, Angus is coming in from Colorado for a visit, and Kate and the children from Hartford. Maybe Ellen if she can get loose."

"So you're saying it's an opportunity for one of our children to nail someone else with a roast pork and maybe one of the grandchildren will try and strangle Uncle Fergus. Which actually sounds like a good idea."

Elspeth put down her coffee cup with a clank. "You are

beginning to sound like Uncle Fergus himself. But a family party shouldn't be that hard to manage."

"We haven't even finished managing this move." John's arm took in the circumference of a dining-cum-living room whose windows not only gave a distant view of west Penobscot Bay but also, in his opinion, entirely too close a view of his neighbors on Alder Way.

"I feel like a refugee," he grumbled. "A displaced person. And there's too much light in this place. Big windows and no privacy what with people going by the windows all the time. We're bugs under a microscope. I don't know how I'll get any work done. I thought I'd never miss Cambridge, but now that moldy old house of ours looks pretty damn good."

Elspeth, her face troubled, pushed her chair from the table and went to stand at the window. She was a tall angular woman with unruly white hair tufts and curls today held in place by a bandanna. Age had long since left its mark in a network of wrinkles around her eyes and the corners of her mouth. But the planes on her face were sharp, her mouth strong and thin, her gray eyes hooded like a hawk. A woman of humor, pride, and intelligence, given to devious solutions and unorthodox ways and means. An artist of skill and imagination. In short a woman to reckon with.

And she had her match in tall John McKenzie, white-haired, black eyebrows like shelves, a thrusting chin, a booming voice designed not so much to shatter glass as to cleave rocks. Short-tempered about the small things of the world, long on patience if some beloved person or cause was involved. Now a retired professor of English—Old English epics and ancient linguistic forms—and with his wife, one of the new residents of Midcoast Maine and the Ocean Tide community.

Summers the two senior McKenzies shared in an ancient shingle cottage on Weymouth Island; winters in Cambridge. Now it was going to be full-time in Maine: winter on the mainland, summers on Weymouth. The choosing of Ocean Tide had been due not just to the view of Penobscot Bay and the gray shingled cottage but to the trails, especially the bicycle trails. Both Elspeth and John McKenzie enjoyed bicycling, for years had wheeled around Cambridge—often at great personal hazard—and John had become a familiar figure riding to and from his classes on his ancient three-speed black Raleigh, his briefcase strapped behind his saddle. These bike trails had been a management's hooks to catch not only the senior citizen on his recreational bicycle—or tricycle—but the serious biker of all ages. A generous number of level or undulating bike paths wound around the perimeter of the cottages, and followed a sea route on the lip of the ocean cliff. Besides these, for those who had the muscle to enjoy rough riding, a series of mountain bike trails had been set into the hilly west side of the Ocean Tide property.

Of course there had been a conflict of conscience. When the idea of moving to Ocean Tide's "protected living" had been brought up by concerned family members, the McKenzies, bird-watchers and nature lovers, had protested vigorously. John had thundered from the distance of Cambridge over the destruction of unspoiled habitat, Elspeth had spoken with feeling about the use of fertilizer and the sterile uniformity of planned communities. But time went by, the bulldozers departed, the houses and cottages rose from the ground, the swimming pools were filled, the beach front cleared, the golf course shaped. And the McKenzies had succumbed.

"I think we're just too old," said Elspeth sadly. "It would have been fun thirty years ago to homestead in the north woods in a cabin we've built with our own hands. But now there's no point in buying an old house in the country where we'd have to worry about the septic system and have to plow the snow and cut the grass. Here it's all part of the deal. So let's be nature loving hypocrites and move in. Go for it. Make an effort."

And they had.

Now Elsepth, peering out at a stout gray-haired jogger

thumping by the window, shook her head at her husband. "I suppose we'll get used to the place but it's going to take time. The problem is our things looked fine in Cambridge in dark rooms with the dark wood walls and dusty windows. I mean, nobody could really see anything. And now everything looks threadbare. Like a secondhand store. Just look at that rug." She pointed accusingly at a threadbare, unevenly fringed Persian carpet of blues and dark reds that had been laid in a lumpy way over the wall-to-wall pale beige carpet that came with the cottage. "It's faded and worn through and you can see the dog pee stains. And all the walls are so white that you and I look embalmed. At least I do. And even the dogs"— Elspeth pointed to a pair of snoozing Sealyhams by the kitchen door—"they look dirty."

"We can buy some dark curtains," said John. "But please finish what you were saying because I want to read my paper. Eat my breakfast. If you want my advice, you'll kill any party plans before they start to come true. Besides, you're forgetting, we'll be out on the island by the middle of June and we can't have a big whoopee-do there. Not enough room. All the ferry reservation problems. So forget it."

Elspeth turned and faced him. "You're the one who's forgotten. We're reroofing the cottage. And fixing the porch stairs and painting our bedroom. Nothing will be finished until after the Fourth of July. We can have the party after I get back from the week in Provence."

"Provence?" John scowled at his wife.

"You know. I've been invited there for a week. Painting. But I'll be back for the party and we can't disappoint the children. They've been talking about a 'celebration.' "

"They can have that after we're dead. Celebration for the life of."

"I've checked with the Lodge. They have rooms for our guests. We can have our big dinner right there in the Lodge and lots of picnics down on the rocks."

"Are you talking about a party lasting a week? You're out

of your mind, Elspeth. And I think," said John, returning to his paper, "that if you go on with this we'll outdo that family in Acton. Go ahead and order the pork roast. No more party talk. I'm trying to keep my sanity and stay busy. What do you think about my doing a volunteer teaching gig this fall? Try and sell the community college on a survey of Anglo-Saxon literature."

"That might be a hard sell," observed Elspeth.

"You never know. I can stick to the battles and swords and shield walls and the ravens circling over dead bodies. Anyway, if you want a party, my dearest wife, on your head be it. I don't want to hear another word on the subject. Not until there are live people actually walking up the driveway."

"Of course," said Elspeth, "there will be all our new friends."

John, who had picked up his newspaper, lowered it again and glared at his wife. "New friends! What new friends? Hell, we don't have any new friends. Except the mailman and the oil delivery man. I don't want any new friends. We have too many old ones as it is."

"Don't be such a grouch. I met the Moseby family at the convenience store yesterday. They've just moved in. Around the corner, Rowan Tree Circle. The big house with the gray shutters. There's a getting-to-know-you reception thing today at the Fitness Center. We have to go or everyone will think we're a couple of snobs. You know how old-time Mainers feel about newcomers from away, particularly the ones from Massachusetts. So behave yourself. People will think you don't want to meet them."

"They'll be right," said John. "I don't. I hate receptions. All that standing around with strangers."

But Elspeth had picked up a section of the *Rockland Courier Gazette*, a new subscription because, as she insisted, "It's time to pay attention to what's happening right here in Knox County."

John looked at her over his glasses. "I'm thinking of joining the local nature preservation group to try and stop any future

Ocean Tide developments. And then perhaps we can really move to the northwoods and build a log cabin with our bare hands. And die with a clear conscience."

Elspeth, who had heard these sentiments before, picked up her newspaper and retired behind it. And for a moment, all was contentment with only the sound of the soft rustling of turned pages. And then Elspeth frowned and exclaimed.

"What now?" said John in a resigned voice.

"A body. A dead body."

"Bodies are usually dead."

"No, listen. A news bulletin. The body—it says an 'unidentified male' has turned up yesterday evening—and guess where?"

John leaned back in his chair, tipped it on two legs, teetered perilously, and returned to earth. "Our garage?"

"Well, almost. On the edge of the Ocean Tide property. Over by the one of the practice holes. Near the trails. It says here that 'The death does not appear to be from natural causes.' "

John paid Elspeth the compliment of appearing moderately interested. "On the golf course itself?" he asked.

"No, off on the edge of the green. It says in the heavy grass. We'll have to call Alex. Since he's one of the county medical examiners, he might know something. Maybe he was called in."

"In which case you, my dear love, will not bother him. It's Saturday, and it's either his day off or he's at the hospital. So he doesn't need to be beeped by his mother."

But John's warning fell on deaf ears; Elspeth had already reached the telephone and was punching in a familiar number.


Elspeth's son, Alex—for Alexander—was not at home that morning. Nor at the hospital. All for the simple reason that he was meeting with Mike Laaka and George Fitts in George's depressing office at the state police barracks in Thomaston.

Depressing not only because it resembled most such spaces—gray metal desks, vinyl seats on metal chairs, gray metal file cabinets, but also because George had not allowed even the dullest black-and-white calendar from the local oil supply company to decorate his walls. No framed photograph of a family member, a loved one, a deceased grandmother, a respected mentor from the state police academy stood on his desktop. As far as anyone in the constabulary knew, George had no family, no attachments. His life was his work and his work was his life and heaven help any slipshod person who tried to mess it up by being late with reports, not turning up promptly at a homicide scene, not appearing in court ready with every relevant piece of information on the tip of his tongue.

Alex, arriving two minutes ahead of time, took a seat in the office and waited for George to finish skewering—by telephone—some unhappy subordinate. George, seated, looked to the discerning eye like nothing so much as a neatly dressed storefront dummy. Or perhaps an alien trying to pass himself off as human—a figure from a Ray Bradbury story. Besides the bald head and glasses, his lips were pale, his eyebrows faint, his bald head the shape of an electric lightbulb, his arms long and hairless, his body slender and apparently unmuscled—a misconception that had caught several miscreants off guard.

And, thought Alex, waiting for the telephone conversation to end, the contrast to the now arriving Sheriff's Deputy Investigator Mike Laaka was unnerving. Mike, the tall fair type, was one of Maine's many descendants from the numerous Finns who had lived and worked for a hundred fifty years along the coast. Mike, striding in, his almost white hair ruffled with the morning's breeze, his cheeks reddened, made George look positively unhealthy. A fact that George was only too aware of.

George put down the telephone. "Mike, you're late. I haven't got all day. Alex made it on time. Let's wind this up."

Mike, who regarded George as a hair shirt, an impediment

to surviving his day's work, gave George a shrug. "I'm within your three-minute allowance. And what do you mean, wind it up, we've just begun to fight."

"We need to look at Alex's report. Then he can go and we can get back to work. Alex?"

Alex produced a folded form and slipped it over to George's desk. "Unattended death—apparently. If your team comes up with footprints in all that muck, then maybe it was attended, probably by the killer. A likely homicide if that plastic-covered chain around his neck means anything. There was also head trauma to consider. Maybe not severe enough to cause death but you never know. Anyway, it's over and out to the forensic people. They can fool around with time of death. And cause. The chain may be decoration, but the swelling, the contusions around the neck, everything else suggests a good old-fashioned throttling. My guess is the body's been there for a while. A week maybe. So thanks and good-bye. I have the morning off."

"Hold up," said Mike. "We've a possible ID. From Missing Persons. Came in late last night. Eighteen-year-old. From the Appleton area. Lived in a trailer by himself, or sometimes with a couple of buddies. Dropped out or was kicked out of high school. The DNA match will take a while—the labs are really stacked up—but the dental records ought to confirm the guy."

"Okay," said Alex, standing up. "So get to work, you two."

"Wait," said George. "This may interest you. Probable victim's name is Colley. Jason Colley. Probably a relative to some of those Colleys that live all over the Appleton-Union area. Half brother to the two kids belonging to Betty Colley."

"Hey," said Mike. "I know Betty. She and her mother and the two kids just moved in to that new Ocean Tide affair in Rockport. Just like your folks, Alex. They may be neighbors."

George looked mildly interested. "Alex, have your parents met the Colley family? Or know them at all? It might be useful if someone in that community did."

Alex stopped at the door and frowned. "Useful? What do you mean, 'useful'?"

"George is saying that if your mother is like my mother," said Mike, "she will have weaseled information about all the neighbors and could probably write up a life history of any of them. And could point out any black sheep they're trying to hide."

"Mother knows Betty Colley," said Alex. "She used to buy eggs from their farm. But my mother and father are new at Ocean Tide. They'll have been too busy getting settled to have met anyone."

"Bunch of crap," said Mike, who had grown up in Rockport in close proximity to the McKenzie family before their remove to Cambridge. "Your father's not much of a mixer, but I remember your mother always used have her fingers in everyone's pie. Everyone's yard sale, everyone's wedding, funeral service, you name it. I'll bet that in a week she'll know more about the Colleys and their neighbors at Ocean Tide than George will be able to find out in a year."

"Okay," said Alex. "You want me to find out if my mother's been over there with a plate of brownies?"

"Nah," said Mike. "Just drop in. Be natural. Hi, Mom, did you know Betty Colley's one of your new neighbors? You should run over and say hello—in case you haven't. And Mom, it'd be a good idea to have a real chat with her. Won't hurt for us to get some background info."

"There's no point in alarming the Colleys," said George, "until we get dental confirmation. If it is Jason Colley, I'll go over to see them. After that we'll go public with the ID."

"Betty Colley, she hasn't been beating the bushes to find this boy?" asked Alex, now interested in spite of himself.

"She filed a missing person Wednesday, asked around informally," said George. "But Jason—if it is Jason—wasn't exactly staying in touch with the family. He'd been living in that trailer for over a year after a row with Betty, who's actually his stepmother. We've had several complaints about Jason over the past year. He's got kind of a reputation. And an attitude. Firearms sounding at odd hours. Kid picked up a couple of speeding tickets and lost his license. His car turned up abandoned about two weeks ago. Burned out. The trailer was a rental. Nothing of any value in it. Except a very nice bicycle in a shed in the back."

"Expensive as hell, that bike, special mountain job," put in Mike. "I took a look at it early this morning. Kid could've bought a decent secondhand car for the same price."

"I was going to drop in and see my parents today anyway," said Alex. "So, okay, I'll ask a few general questions. But I don't want to encourage my mother into anything like snooping. She's almost as bad as my dear wife. Finds trouble where there isn't any."

"Love to Sarah," said Mike. "And no one could be worse than she is. She's like flypaper. I think people deliberately fall dead at her feet to drive us all crazy."

George opened his notebook and ran a finger down a list. "Do you know anyone called Moseby?" he asked. "They're apparently related to the Colleys, and they've also just moved to Ocean Tide."

"I know 'em." said Mike. "Different types. The Colleys are sort of basic, backcountry types. Farm folks. Down to earth. The Mosebys have delusions. Or illusions. Not exactly grandeur but they're more on the upscale side. I've heard that the oldest boy got a big scholarship from Yale."

"So good for him," said Alex. "If I hear anything, I'll let you know. Then I'll try and steer very clear of the Hatfields and the McCoys."

"That's Mosebys and Colleys," said George, who didn't like anyone playing fast and loose with the verities of a homicide investigation.

Alex stood up. "As long as the McKenzie tribe doesn't get sucked into it. My mother and father are still in moving shock. Heads are still in Cambridge and their bodies are in Maine.

They've got enough to do deciding where to put the living room sofa and my father's desk. And I'm up to my hips with some very sick patients and the usual hospital crap. And don't you even think of asking Sarah to chat it up with anybody, especially the Colleys. She's busy hunting for a summer job and has given up homicide. For life. Forever."

# 2

THAT same Saturday morning in which Alex McKenzie met with Sergeant George Fitts and his assistant, Mike Laaka, found Sarah Douglas Deane, recently anointed Ph.D., rattling around in their old farmhouse on a Union hillside. Unemployed. Yes, she could fiddle about with her dissertation with an eye to getting it published. But she also needed at least a part-time job. Out of the house. She had just finished a demanding semester as a fill-in English teacher at a girls' boarding school in Massachusetts and would not begin teaching English at Midcoast Maine's Bowmouth College until fall. So what to do?

The trouble was that June was not looking like a time to settle into a job. Her mother-in-law, Elspeth McKenzie, had been sending up small trial balloons about a birthday for the dreaded Uncle Fergus to be combined with John Mckenzie's birthday plus an anniversary. But if this circus was really going to be taking place then she couldn't start working until the party plan had been wrestled into shape. Sarah had promised to help Elspeth in the matter of food, amusing presents, and in particular a present for Uncle Fergus. "A first edition of something," suggested Elspeth. "He went to Amherst, you know, and then taught at Cornell. And he collects old golf clubs. So do your best, you know what he's like."

Oh, God, Sarah had thought. Something for Uncle Fergus. Ancient Uncle Fergus Arthur McKenzie. About to be ninety. A dried-up man of sinew, phlegm and canker. A lighthearted jocular offering would not be acceptable. Uncle Fergus thought very well of himself and the present would have be something in the nature of a tribute to his wisdom (this seriously questioned by his family) and most certainly to his remarkable powers of survival. Maybe she could check the family photograph archives and have several of those sepia photographs of Uncle Fergus enlarged and framed. As a youth on the Andover baseball team scowling at the camera; as an Amherst student, and later a graduate curmudgeon at Yale; as an older curmudgeon teaching at Cornell. As a curmudgeon emeritus lecturing hither and yon on the history of the Plantagenets—his specialty. So perhaps a print. A portrait of Bolingbrook or Richard the Third yelling for his horse? A college scene, spires, Doric columns. Cayuga's Waters? An ancient golf club, or a framed picture of an ancient golf club?

Sarah looked at her watch. Almost noon. She would grab a bite to eat, do some errands, and then go and inspect the McKenzies' collection of family albums filled with glued-down photos, six to a black page. Uncle Fergus as an infant on a fur rug, a child in knickerbockers. Photos under which someone with white ink had carefully printed legends such as "Fun at the Beach," "Sailing down the River," "Out for a Drive in the Pierce Arrow."

She changed her jeans for lightweight chinos, checked herself in the mirror and saw, without thinking about it, a thin face with high cheekbones, disheveled dark hair in a short chop, gray eyes, an undistinguished nose, and a firm mouth. Not as firm a mouth as her mother-in-law, Elspeth's, but adequate. It neither drooped nor smirked. She wiped a smudge from her forehead, brushed her hair, and began reconsidering her aversion to nailing down a full-time job, an eight-hour, half-day-on-Saturday sort of job. Hadn't she worked like a galley slave all winter at that very disturbed girls' boarding school? Didn't she deserve a little space before she locked herself into the fall semester at Bowmouth College, into classrooms packed with undergraduates who didn't want to take the compulsory Intro English Lit? Considering this new idea of a modified workload, Sarah crossed into the kitchen and snapped a leash on the collar of her slumbering Irish wolfhound, Patsy. And then stopped by the radio, which had been dealing out the usual Saturday classical fare from Maine Public Radio. Only now Brahms had been overtaken by the local news.

And for no reason that she could possibly explain, instead of switching the radio off, Sarah halted and listened. Had she caught a name? Was it Laaka? Well, there were a lot of Laakas in Knox County, but only one might be connected with the police, actually in this case with the sheriff's department. Alex's grammar school buddy, Mike Laaka, now a friend of long-standing of hers as well as Alex's. She frowned and turned up the volume. And the words, "Medical Examiner Alexander McKenzie" came out loud and clear. She let go of Patsy's leash and bent to listen as if leaning closer would drive the news away. ". . . apparent victim of foul play," said the announcer. And then, "From an unidentified source it has been learned that an identification of the deceased is expected soon and will be made public after members of the family have been notified. Residents and visitors to the Ocean Tide community are advised that there will be no access to the bicycle and hiking trails or the practice three-hole golf course on the west side of the property as the police have cordoned off the area where the body was discovered yesterday evening by a man walking his dog."

Oh, God, Sarah thought for the second time that morning. So that's where Alex went last night. She had thought it was just a routine hospital call, had turned over in bed and hadn't quizzed him when he'd come home. And then he'd left early, before she got up, for, she presumed, a morning of bird-watching. After all, he'd been going on about the need to catch some of the spring warbler migration—an annual event that pretty much left Sarah where it found her.

Poor Alex. Well, that's what you get for agreeing to be one of the county medical examiners. You get dead bodies. And Sarah most fervently hoped that this particular body was no one anyone knew, not a child nor yet any worthy citizen. And since it obviously had to be *someone*, she hoped that it might turn out to be the remains of a particularly vicious and dangerous escapee from the state prison.

And thank heavens she had not stumbled on the corpse while walking Patsy. Since Ocean Tide had opened and her in-laws had moved in, Sarah had looked forward to hiking around the trails with Patsy. But because of the month's foul weather she had put off exploring, especially the more rugged up-and-down trails of the western edge of the property. But if the weather had been fair, she knew with an absolute certainty that Patsy would have sniffed out the corpse in nothing flat, and she, Sarah, would have been faced with another dead body.

And Sarah had given up, had abjured, had forsworn finding bodies. Several incidents in her past had brought her, or Alex, or both of them, face to face with these melancholy objects and she wanted no more of it. And her luck held. She did not find this one. Had in fact been nowhere near the area in the past few weeks. And Alex's role in the matter was simply an official one. He would have declared the victim dead, signed a report, and retreated. End of involvement.

She turned off the radio and with Patsy in tow headed for the shopping district of the small coastal city of Rockland, Maine.

The weather had really turned. The sun was shining, a pleasant breeze ruffled the waves in the harbor, and Sarah completed a number of tasks in record time, hit the Second Read Restaurant for soup and a slice of French bread, and a secondhand copy of an Inspector Morse mystery she'd missed. And she came to a firm decision. No full-time job. She wanted only bits and pieces of a job, flexible hours, with plenty of spaces for summer time reading in a hammock. Sailing. A visit to the McKenzie compound on Weymouth Island. Swimming in Weymouth Island's ice-cold water. And with these blessed breathing spaces she could spend a little time organizing her fall teaching schedule, send in her book order promptly for once. And just as Sarah took the last bite of bread, the last swallow of her iced tea, and paid for her book, the perfect answer had reached over and knocked on her head.

She would tutor. Reading, writing, grammar, the art of taking exams, of surviving multiple choice or essay questions. The comma, the semicolon, the sentence, the paragraph. *Great Expectations*, *The Red Badge of Courage*, *Lord of the Flies*, *Native Son*, One of Zora Neale Hurston's books. Even Shakespeare. Or for the lower grades, *Tuck Everlasting*, *Tom Sawyer*, a Cynthia Voight novel, *The Hobbit*. One of the Harry Potter books. You name it, she'd tutor it. Right now, today, she'd bait the hook, put an ad in the local papers and wait for some worried parent or guardian to decide that Assistant Professor of English, Sarah Douglas Deane, was exactly what Heather or Hillary or Michael or Joshua needed to make it safely into sixth grade, into high school. Or out of high school. Whatever.

Sarah began working on the wording. English teacher, secondary school and college, experience, blah, blah, blah. She only needed a few students, three, at the most four. She could meet them at odd hours, give them writing and reading assignments. Low key. Informal sessions. Payment? She would check around and charge the going rates.

An hour later with ads left off at the offices of the local newspapers, Sarah climbed into her elderly Subaru and headed for the senior McKenzie headquarters.

The small minicolonial structure that housed the guards and the white wooden swinging gates that opened, or barred, the way into the new community were deceptively modest. The wooden planters filled with red and white petunias, the painted welcome sign gave visitors the sense that Ocean Tide was holding out its arms and rejoiced in their arrival.

Nothing could have been further from the truth.

Built into the security system was an active sense of managerial paranoia—Ocean Tide had come into being only after a series of protests by environmentalists, oceanfront preservers and the like. And this paranoia had spawned not only two guards at all times on duty at the gatehouse but a number of roving plainclothes persons who tried to keep an eye out for untoward activities or persons who might appear to be lurking with ill intentions.

Sarah, however, was the possessor of a white sticker in the shape of a lighthouse which proclaimed her (or rather her vehicle) as either belonging to a resident or an approved visitor to Ocean Tide.

This being so, she and Patsy, sitting upright in the passenger seat, sailed through the opening gates receiving a welcoming flick of a salute from a stout guard in the Ocean Tide uniform, light gray with navy blue facings.

She drove slowly down the entrance drive (more petunias ranging down a median strip, a sign planted among them proclaiming a fifteen-mile speed limit, and saw that Hillside Drive—the road to the western hiking and biking trails and the practice holes—was neatly blocked by a blue-and-white squad car and two uniformed sheriff's deputies.

And then, as if her Subaru had taken charge, Sarah found herself swinging left toward the blocked road, pulling over and stopping. Without warning, her bump of curiosity had released its noxious juices and communicated itself to the steering mechanism of the car. So what could she do?

It wasn't as if she were looking for trouble. It had nothing to do with that dead body. She had given up dead bodies. It was Patsy. He needed a walk. The poor dog had spent the morning being toted around the Rockland shopping district. And she could hardly arrive at the McKenzie house and allow Patsy to pee on all the newly planted shrubbery.

She reached for Patsy's leash, disembarked and walked up to the two uniformed men—neither of whom she recognized. Fortunately. If one had been old friend Mike Laaka, he would have removed her bodily and sent her away as a well-known hazard to orderly police procedure.

"Goodness," said Sarah to the first uniformed deputy—it was an expression completely foreign to her but somehow in her role as innocent-woman-walking-dog the word came naturally.

The deputy, a red-faced, bristle-haired man, held up a hand the size of a first baseman's mitt. "Sorry," he said. "This road is closed. For now, anyway."

"Oh, but I only want to walk my dog. Along the hiking trails. I won't bother anyone." Even to Sarah's ears this sounded foolish to the point of idiocy.

But apparently the deputy, one Steve Upham, was used to meeting up with idiot citizens. "Sorry," he said again, in a gruff and very firm voice. "Road's closed. All the west trails are closed. If you'll get back in your car and turn around, you can walk the dog some other place." And in the way the man pronounced the words "other place" Sarah could tell he had absolutely no use for upscale "hometown" architect-designed communities.

"Can you tell me what's going on?" asked Sarah, still the naive visitor.

"Accident," said the man. "Now if you'll get back in your car . . ."

"Serious accident?" asked Sarah holding her ground.

A wave of exasperation rippled over the man's flushed face. "I wouldn't know," he said. "I'm just doing my job. Now if you'll get back in the car."

And Sarah, seeing from the corner of her eye the approach of a police van turned her car and headed for number 7 Alder Way and the senior McKenzies. *It's as if I have a multiple-personality disorder,* she told herself. *It's the evil twin syndrome. One half wants nothing to do with accidents and sudden death, is appalled by it. Stays away from it and goes about its proper business. And the other sticks its nose in anything nasty it smells.* Well, it was all a matter of discipline. She would force her evil twin to yield to the better sensible, law-abiding twin.

And as she entered the main road, Ocean Drive, she decided to take the long way round to get a better sense of the community. Ocean Drive turned and twisted past the play area, the bike shop, the tennis courts, the swimming pools, along Forsythia Walk, past Peony Point, and along Beach Road, and then around toward Alder Way. And as she maneuvered her way through the winding roads, she decided not for the first time that this was a foreign world. Pale gray shingle cottages, white clapboard colonial houses with green or gray shutters, trim little saltboxes, the Lodge—a pale yellow hybrid by Queen Anne out of Mount Vernon, and a number of semidetached "town houses" that actually looked like Siamese twin colonials. Everywhere the white picket fence, the tidy green square of front lawn, the new-planted yews and cedars. Hollies and lilacs. Groups of just-dug slender white birches, roses and clematis climbing trellised entrances to public gardens and paths. The honeycomb of blue mailboxes at each road entrance. Everything ship-shape, spruce, spit-spot. It was in fact so spanking new that for a moment her evil twin surfaced, and Sarah was overwhelmed by a desire to throw a handful of mud at something. To accelerate her car and lay a patch of rubber.

Somehow she couldn't see the redoubtable Elspeth McKenzie—she with her often frazzled white hair, clad in paint-spattered jeans and old washed shirts—and forceful John McKenzie with his booming voice, wearing equally disreputable trousers and worn shirts—fitting into the scene. Wouldn't they be outcasts in this community of a replica New England village?

But of course the two were getting on, heading toward their seventies. John wore a pacemaker, Elspeth had arthritis. They needed someone to take care of their grounds, shovel snow, cut grass, dispose of garbage, fix the roof. They needed to live in a place that gave them a chance to exercise safely— by bike, swimming pool, golf course, and trail—and yet was set in a larger surrounding community that offered art galleries for Elspeth, and perhaps volunteer teaching opportunities for John. Plus a whiff of salty ocean air and a place to have meals if cooking became too much of a chore. *So keep my lip buttoned and be enthusiastic*, Sarah instructed herself. Tell them how wonderful, how convenient, how very well kept the whole place was. Sentiments that for the most part were true. She would pull in her horns and be positive.

These resolutions in place, she pulled her car into the small drive in front of the McKenzie's attached garage, and with Patsy in hand, climbed out and found herself confronting her husband and erstwhile medical examiner, Alex McKenzie, standing at the open front door.

He looked up with relief. He had just arrived, and in response to his mother's questions, had begun a verbal two-step around the subject of his father and mother's near neighbors, the Colley family.

"Hello there, Sarah," called Elspeth, who with John now emerged from behind Alex. "We're so glad you came. Alex is making no sense at all. Going on about the Colleys and being neighborly and simply ignoring the accident. That body on the Ocean Tide property. Which, I'm sure, he knows all about but won't admit it."

Sarah climbed out of the car and went through the ritual greeting of kiss and hug and then addressed herself to Alex, who to judge from his expression was prepared to say only so

much and no more on the subject, maternal pressure not re-
garding.

"Let's go out on the deck," Elspeth said. "Have something
to drink. Put our feet up. Have a nice get-together."

"Which means you can jolly well fill us in," said his father.

"I'll get lemonade," said Elspeth. "Or tea. Or beer."

"Beer," said John McKenzie and Alex in one breath.

Settled on the small deck that overlooked a modest garden
area protected by a four-foot white painted board fence, sup-
plied with fluids and a plate of rather gritty oatmeal cookies—
Elspeth was a slap-dash cook—Alex gave his family a strictly
edited version of the event. He was a black-haired man with
a thin mouth, taut faced, with gray eyes, black rather formi-
dable eyebrows and a notable jaw. In many ways he was his
mother's son with the exception that while the mother's nose
and hooded eyes suggested the hawk, Alex's nose was straight
like his father's and his eyes a darker gray. Today he wore
khaki trousers and a long-sleeved blue work shirt—a costume
chosen for the bird-watching hike that had been postponed.
Or scrapped.

Alex now addressed his listeners. "You know I can't talk
about the accident."

"You mean the murder," put in Elspeth. "That's what the
*Courier-Gazette* said."

"Off that practice hole," added John McKenzie. "Next to
the trails.

"They've got the whole west side road system marked off,"
Sarah contributed.

"Practically speaking," said Elspeth, "it's happened right on
our doorstep. As if we'd never left Cambridge. Ambulances
and yellow tape."

"I suppose it livens this place up," said John. "Police cars
whizzing around. Although we could have done without a
corpse. A simple burglary would have sufficed."

Alex drew a weary breath. "Look, listen, and let me speak

my piece. Because a small effort on your part might be useful. Sergeant Fitts has asked me what you know about the Colleys. Betty Colley. Her family. He would like you to share what you know. Give me a summary or call him. For a case he's working on."

"He wants us to be neighborhood spies," said Elspeth. She shook her head. "We always want to help, dear, but as snoops, I don't think so. I've bought eggs from Betty Colley for years. But here we're trying to get along with our neighbors. I've been telling John we mustn't act like clams. Or is it snails. Anyway, not hide in a shell."

At which interesting point, the telephone sounded loudly, Alex rose, disappeared, mutterings were heard, and he reappeared.

"That was George Fitts," he announced. "I'm to put you in the picture. At least partly. The information is confidential, but George needs a little help. The pathologist has not yet made positive identification of the body—dental records still to come. The probable victim is Jason Colley. Eighteen years old, didn't live at home. If a positive ID is made, George will be notifying the Colley family—your neighbors—sometime later this afternoon that the body is Betty Colley's stepson. He's asking around trying to find out if Betty or the grandmother who lives with them—her name is Rose Bingham—has a church. If there's a minister who could stand by. And, oddly enough there's a family called Moseby who are Colley relatives and are also your neighbors. Right on the corner of Rowan Tree Circle. Betty Colley is Sherry Moseby's sister. But George says the Mosebys seem to consider themselves a cut above the Colleys in the social scheme of things. But since the Mosebys are close relatives they should be brought into the picture."

"It's very sad," said Elspeth uncertainly, "but I don't see what we—"

"Hear me out," said Alex. "No one is sure that Betty Colley will be completely thrown by the news. It might be something she's been expecting. Jason Colley was something of a problem kid. Dropped out of high school at sixteen. Went in for motorcycles, party life, smoking dope, and hanging around. Has been living in a junked-up trailer somewhere on one of the hills near the Union and Appleton town lines. Only known possession was a very expensive mountain bike."

"You want us to rally round and offer sympathy," said John, eyebrows rising. "We don't really know Betty Colley except for buying eggs. It would be pretty presumptuous if we went over there."

"Betty," said Elspeth, "is a very nice person. Forthright. Speaks her mind. I used to talk about crop problems with her when I stopped at her farm stand. When I came off island for shopping."

"The one who might need support," said Alex, "is Grandmother Rose. She's a patient of mine, a tough lady, but probably not about her grandson even if he's an ax murderer."

"I know," said Elspeth. "It's hard to find fault with grandchildren."

"Well, Jason wasn't any major criminal. Small-time nuisance really. Said to be personable. Betty Colley is a single mother now since husband, Ned Colley, drifted off a few years back. He and Jason seem to be two of a kind. I've seen Betty once or twice in the office when she brought Mother Rose in, or about some medical problem of her own when her regular doctor was away. What I know about Rose and Betty is that they're not into what we call 'patient compliance.' If they don't like your advice they damn well don't listen."

"She ought to get along with John," said Elspeth, looking fondly at her husband.

"Right," said Alex, grinning at his father.

"Enough palaver," said John in a loud voice. "What does Sergeant Fitts want the McKenzies to do about all this? From what you've told me, George Fitts hates civilians messing with his cases."

"He hates 'em," said Alex. "But he uses 'em. Like now. He wants you to go to this getting-to-know-you affair at the Fitness Center this afternoon and see if you can get a sense of the Colleys. As people. And the Mosebys. Because even if the Mosebys don't happen to mix with the Colleys, young Jason was buddy-buddy with Matt Moseby, the middle son, a while back. Both boys about the same age, even shared living quarters in that trailer for a while. Went ice fishing together. And, George has found out that Matt split with Jason in a very noisy way this winter. Had a row at some local eatery."

"So," concluded Elspeth, pushing back her glasses until they perched atop her white hair, "George wants us to be spies but he won't use the word."

"He hopes you will achieve—and now I'm quoting—'some social interaction that may provide the police with informal insights into family dynamics.' After all, even George can't come to this cocktail reception thing and pretend he's a resident of Ocean Tide trying to make friends. To borrow an expression, George would freeze the balls off a brass monkey."

"George," said Sarah succinctly, "doesn't have friends; he has witnesses, suspects, accessories, and informers."

"But," objected Elspeth, "while the Colleys are enjoying themselves at the reception, the state police are making ready to pounce on the family with the news that Jason Colley has been murdered. That's pretty brutal."

"Repeat," said Alex. "The ID isn't definite. The corpse was in lousy shape—lying out there in that rain and mud last week. There's no point in not letting the Colleys have a normal afternoon until the police are sure. If there's no confirmation, well, no harm done. You'll have made some new friends, that's all."

"No harm," said John in annoyed voice, "except we'll have tried to make friends with a bunch of people who probably don't want us as friends. Who wants a couple of old farts like us around anyway? That's what I'm saying."

"And I," said Elspeth, "would like to point out that Ocean Tide is home to a lot of old farts so we shouldn't have any trouble making friends. John's been an academic too long. It's poisoned him. We're going to this reception and try and be part of this community. Come hell or high water."

"Which," said John McKenzie, "is probably a good description of the entertainment."

# 3

ELSPETH raised her eyes to Sarah. It was a look that said in a clear voice: time to rally round the family.

Sarah understood. The two McKenzies senior needed dilution by other family members so that their appearance at the get-together would cause only a minor wrinkle in the social fabric. John McKenzie, when pushed into alien situations by his wife, was all too likely to express opinions in the voice of a sergeant-at-arms bellowing at recalcitrant troops. Or, to be exact, like a tenured professor faced with an ill-prepared group of students. And in this case it was quite possible that most of the guests thus confronted would shrink into the woodwork muttering about academic tyrants from Massachusetts who thought they could throw their weight around. And Elspeth would have to make reassuring noises at those still close enough to hear, would pluck at John's sleeve and steer him in the direction of anyone whose deafness prevented him from hearing what John was saying.

"You will, won't you?" said Elspeth to Sarah. "Alex can

keep his cool and you leaven the loaf, if you know what I mean. You have that harmless orphan look sometimes. It's your hair and being so thin, and having those dark eyes so no one's afraid of you and that works to cancel out any damage John's done."

Sarah nodded reluctantly. She knew that no matter how hard she tried for the tough professional woman-of-the world look, people meeting her for the first time found the words "waif" and "stray" floating into their heads. It was not only being thin—or positively skinny—but it was the thatch of unruly dark hair that no hairdresser or personal effort had ever been able to make look as if its owner were in control. Plus she had the sort of eyes and eyebrows that needed no heavy-duty liner and eye shadow because if she had indulged in these beauty aids, she might have been taken for some sort of underfed vampire. But all in all, in the past when in a tight corner, the waif look had served her well. Like George Fitts himself, she was a person whom a perpetrator—or perp, as he was known in police circles—tended to discount as an observer. Or an adversary. Which mistake had frequently undone the perp.

Elspeth now turned to Alex. "You know how your father is in strange places. I have this theory that he's pathologically shy so that he has to raise his voice. Kick up dust. He's compensating."

"My father," said Alex smiling, "is about as shy as a crocodile, but you're right about the party. Sarah can defuse the confrontations, and I'll mingle and hope not to run into too many of my patients who've been kept sitting for hours in my waiting room. And I'll look around for the Colley family. Have a word with Betty, introduce her to Dad. She ought to be a good match for the old man. Let those two go at it."

"And," added Elspeth, "let's hope that this murder has nothing to do with Betty's family. That George Fitts is way off base."

"Anyway, Mother," said Alex, "you can hover and flutter or

do what you're very good at. Infiltrate. Into the rest of the Colleys and the Moseby clan if they turn up. Give you ten minutes and people start telling you about their gall bladders and their misunderstood cousins in the Maine State Prison."

"My purpose at this party, dear Alex," said Elspeth, "is to show the good people of Ocean Tide that the McKenzies are community-spirited people. Of course not too community spirited because I don't want to arrange flowers for ladies' luncheons. Art shows and classes for children, yes, luncheons, no. And John can offer to give a talk at one of those lecture series the Ocean Tide brochure mentioned. They want volunteers. John can talk about Anglo-Saxon wars. Teenagers ought to love it. Battlefield scenes, blood everywhere, and thanes drinking themselves senseless in the mead halls. He has some wonderful videos—reenactments—that he used for his freshman classes."

"What you're saying," Alex put in, "is that you can't focus entirely on the Colleys."

"I've always liked Betty," said Elspeth, "so it won't be a chore. As for the Mosebys, I'm not going to force myself down their throats to please George Fitts."

"Do what you can," said Alex. "And if George appears bearing bad news, then maybe in the first hour or so—but only if it seems appropriate—you could be part of Betty Colley's family support system. They're new to this place, too, so you may be one of the few people who have actually known them. Later, close family members, the clergy, a counselor can take over. Sarah, you don't have anything on for tonight, do you?"

Sarah shook her head. "No, but should I change? Run home and find some smashing costume?"

"No, dear," put in Elspeth. "Come just as you are. I'll lend you my black linen shirt and that shell necklace. Simple and not threatening is the look we want. But as I've said, no one would ever be frightened by you."

"Someday," said Sarah irritably, "I'll shave my head, dye my skull purple, pierce my body parts, wear spurred combat boots, and pack a Smith and Wesson model 15 Combat Masterpiece that'll make everyone turn to jelly when I come through the door."

The manager of Ocean Tide, one Mr. Joseph Martinelli, had gone all out for the first getting-to-know-you gala of the season. The so-called final "settlement" phase had been completed. The Lodge was almost full, the cottages had been variously leased or bought outright, the villas, the semidetached "town houses," were settled. Even the Village Green (the assisted living sector) complete with walk-in clinic and Sunshine House for those with memory loss, had been 80 percent subscribed. And, another triumph of planning, Camp Ocean Tide for children and teens had a waiting list.

Joseph Martinelli had been born in Genoa, made landfall in Boston at the age of fourteen, and never looked back. He was a man gifted with the energy of sixty and he had a dream. And his "dream" was of a semi-Eden of a community, a living space for all ages, all races, religions, all interests, all passions spent or still burning. In short a true-blue neighborhood—something, Joseph claimed, that in America had almost been destroyed by the heavy hand of commercial greed and overdevelopment. But now he, Joseph Antonio Rosario Martinelli, was prepared—due to a number of successful investments in concrete—to show the world that in Knox County, Maine, true community was possible. That Ocean Tide would be something like the warmhearted extended Italian family he had grown up in. Or by Jesus, Mary, and Joseph he'd damn well know the reason why.

So, as he often told his staff, to hell with all those environmental types who complained that he'd bulldozed acres of what people called habitat—useless alder thickets and brush—to create his community, his golf courses, his bike trails. God knows, he'd used nothing but organic products, the kind of fertilizer you could have for lunch, the insect spray that a baby could suck up in its bottle, he'd put up bird feeders and swallow houses, and offered fat-free, and vegetarian, and Kosher choices on the Lodge menu. "Eggs from free-range hens," he had yelled. "Honey from bees that spend the winter in Florida. No mad cow beef from Europe. I mean, Holy Mary, Mother of God, what more do these people want?"

Joseph Martinelli was short and stout, with receding dark hair that he clutched into a nest when excited. His hands were busy, his feet were busy, he rushed here and there, eyebrows elevated, tongue wagging. He extolled, cajoled, exclaimed, pushed and pulled and unrolled maps, charts, architects' drawings, and somehow through the strength of his convictions plus his bountiful supply of energy had gotten Ocean Tide off the ground and moving in the span of a little over two years.

But like all humans, Joseph had faults. He had never been a facer of unpleasant facts nor could he tolerate opposition to his rosy but sometimes muddled ideas. These, if possible, he swept under the first available rug. Or he diverted, circumvented, and often through sheer and unfounded optimism had disarmed new owners' complaints as various as a leaking roof, a malfunctioning toilet, a fractious neighbor, or a territorial dog. Often a session with an owner would begin in tempest and end with a latte, a cappuccino, homemade biscotti (flown from Genoa by loving relatives) in the Ocean Tide Office. As the brochure "Welcome to Ocean Tide" stated: "Mr. Martinelli is ready day and night to serve you and resolve any difficulties you might encounter."

Joseph believed in the hands-on approach. He was ready with the hug, the shoulder clutch, and if need be, the plumber, the roofer, the social hostess, the veterinarian.

This all being so, anything that ruffled the community peace was anathema. And a decomposing body with a plastic-sheathed chain around its neck, the coming and going of police vehicles, the conspicuous yellow crime scene tape that disfigured the entrance to the western practice holes and the hiking and bike trails, the questioning of residents and visitors—all these he took as a personal affront.

"Oh, goddamn, goddamn," said Joseph to his administrative aide, Carly Thompson, that Saturday morning. "Wouldn't you know. A corpse. A goddamn dead body on Ocean Tide property. Another twenty feet north and we'd have been in the clear."

"It would still have been a corpse," said Carly reasonably.

"But no lousy publicity for Ocean Tide. No police crawling around like lice. So I ask you, Carly. Where do bodies belong? They belong in bars, on the sidewalk, in a ditch. Out on Route One. But not by our new mountain bike trail. Our new practice course. It's like they've been polluted. These are our special 'attractions,' for Chrissake. Parents and kids don't want to think they're going to be bumping into some dirty old corpse when they're out enjoying the trails or practicing their approach shots."

Carly, a sturdy fuzzy-haired blonde with wide-open blue eyes and a wide smile, often felt she had been put on earth to keep Joseph's feet, if not on the ground, at least at treetop level. Fortunately, she was fearless and at the drop of a hat told her employer exactly how she felt about the running of the manager's office. Today, as on all business days, she wore the dark blue slacks and light blue polo shirt with the Ocean Tide logo (pine tree against sea and sky). This was the friendly sporting look Joseph liked. For more formal moments, Carly had to wear a white skirt and navy blue blazer.

Now she prepared to pour water on the flames. "Hey," she said. "It happens. All over. We're not immune. You're not the Wizard of Oz and this isn't the Emerald City even if you think it is. Besides, no one's come charging into the office to complain and no one's canceled his lease. You should be grateful. Finding this body, it's sort of bringing people together. Gives them something to talk about. A way to get to meet your neighbor. Now they've all got something in common."

"That," said Joseph in a sour voice—in a tone unusual for him—"isn't what I want them to have in common." He circled the air with pudgy hands. "Community, diversity, being neighborly, that's what they're supposed to have in common. Not the body of some sleazy character on our property."

"You don't know if the body was a 'sleazy character,'" Carly pointed out. "It might be the cable television guy, a UPS delivery man. Or some Methodist minister."

Joseph drove these suggestions away with a flip of his hand. "I have a feeling for this type of thing. That corpse, you'd better believe, he's some sleaze. Just you remember what I said when the police come and tell me he's got a record a mile long."

"About the party," Carly reminded him.

"Yeah, that's what I'm saying. This party. It's for getting community feeling off the ground. Making it fly. Activities, a nice ambience, everybody happy. That's what we want. Have you checked with Naomi? She's been primed, right?" Naomi Foxglove, the Ocean Tide social hostess was, along with Carly, the other pillar of Joseph's support system.

"Naomi's got it under control." said Carly. "The party's still a go. The Fitness Center's stuffed with balloons. The chef says cakes are decorated and the punch is made. And we've got a clown for the kids. Naomi's seeing about name tags and favors and special hats."

Joseph moved into fast forward. "Make it champagne along with the fruit punch. And prizes for the kids. Get on that right now. Send someone over to the shopping plaza. Souvenirs of the occasion. Maybe those new T-shirts with our logo."

"Ashtrays?" suggested Carly. "Like the ones in the 'smoking-permitted' Lodge rooms."

"No ashtrays. We're pushing a total smoke-free environment. We have to keep a few rooms for smokers but I'm not about to encourage it. See what the Lodge Gift Shop can do for you price-wise. It's a concession but tell 'em it'll build goodwill. Make new customers. And get candy. Good stuff, not five-

and-dime. And beef up the music. The trio's okay but find a piano player. That guy, what's his name, we stole from the Samoset Resort. The one we're using for the Sunday brunch. Have him stick to oldies for the goldies. You know, 'Dancing in the Dark,' 'Me and My Gal,' old stuff like that. And games. Find the camp counselors. Have 'em set up games. Check that Security's going to keep an eye on the teen scene. No joints and no spiking the fruit punch, no little baggies with white powder. Got it? And cross your fingers none of the cranks show up."

"You mean like old Mrs. Hodge, the one who waves her cane around? Or that retired football coach with the Russian name. Dimitri somebody. And Professor John McKenzie," said Carly, who had already stubbed her toe on these citizens over a variety of maintenance problems.

"I'll have Naomi ask one of the hostesses to keep an eye out for the first two. But as for McKenzie, he'll be okay if you handle him right," said Joseph. "A fine man. A real asset. But you know academic types. Kid gloves."

"Professor McKenzie wants more bookshelves in his cottage," Carly went on. "On every wall and in the two bedrooms."

"And he shall have them," said Joseph grandly. "We're in favor of teachers at Ocean Tide—I think we've got six of 'em, one sort or another. And I know teachers like John McKenzie. I had one in Business Methods at Boston College. Professor Hazeltine. Barked up a storm but didn't bite."

"So hope McKenzie only barks," said Carly.

"He's got that wife to cool him down. Elspeth McKenzie. A charmer. Real artist without being snooty. Had a two-man show at the Farnsworth a few years back. So, Carly, get on your horse. Time's a-wasting."

And Carly, her brain whirling—Joseph Martinelli usually had that effect—left the office ready to create an even warmer and fuzzier event than had been planned.

\* \* \*

The getting-to-know-you party was set in the big new Ocean Tide Fitness Center. The walls were strung with streamers, the chefs and sous-chefs sweated over barbecued, roasted, deep-fried, and broiled tidbits of fish, fowl, and good red meat, while waitresses circled back and forth with trays of cold vegetables and assorted dips.

Also among the throngs floated Naomi Foxglove. Naomi was another of Manager Martinelli's triumphs. While Carly Thompson was wholesome, blond, curly-haired, a straight shooter, someone who made residents think of a women's soccer captain, Naomi was all mystery and grace. Tall, long armed, lean and lithe, she swam from social crisis to household emergency to committee meeting of anxious residents without a ruffle in her smooth brow, without a sharpening of her husky voice. Wherever she went she soothed, she calmed, she explained, and made all well. And so handsome too. Coffee-colored skin, slightly Oriental dark eyes, glossy black hair pulled back and fastened with a silver barrette.

"I don't know where on earth Martinelli found her," Elspeth had said to Sarah as they walked to the Fitness Center for the party and saw Naomi whisking around the corner holding a basket of gift-wrapped favors. "I mean with all his going on about ethnic and racial diversity, he's somehow gotten hold of a woman who's apparently part Native American, part African American, with some sort of a Vietnamese uncle and a Mexican grandmother. She's a sort of walking United Nations, and besides which she's amazing. Seems to get along with anyone."

"So what's wrong with that?" asked Sarah, who detected a note of disapproval in her mother-in-law's description.

They paused just before the Fitness Center entrance to watch Naomi, wearing a spectacular black-and-tan printed silk tubular affair that came to her ankles, glide over to an angry-looking elderly man, smoothly slip her arm through his, smile, murmur a few words, and ferry him safely through the entrance.

Elspeth eyed the retreating couple. "Naomi is just too perfect. She reminds me of something sinister. One of those women in mystery books who keep daggers up their sleeves or deadly powders in little papers ready to slip into a cup of tea. And that dress of hers, which I admit is something else, it reminds me of a boa constrictor."

"And people accuse me of being suspicious," said Sarah.

"Of course," admitted Elspeth, "from all I've heard this place wouldn't function without Naomi. Or Carly. It's just that I react to perfection. I suppose I'm jealous. Anyway, let's try and mingle with the crowd and have perfectly normal thoughts."

"You mean about someone strangled on the bike trail?" said Sarah, grinning at her mother-in-law.

But now they were at the door and in the line moving forward to greet Joseph Martinelli. For the festive occasion Joseph had chosen a Gay Nineties costume with striped shirt, sleeve garters, pasted-on handlebar mustache, straw boater, and was altogether in fine fettle. He presented the adult arrivals with matching boaters, the blue ribbon marked with Ocean Tide in silver letters; for children, Camp Ocean Tide baseball caps. And then with expansive gestures directed the newcomers to a long table presided over by Carly, who handed out paper name tags fashioned like horse-show ribbons with Ocean Tide printed down the vertical and the name of the wearer in the middle of a rosette.

John McKenzie, walking in behind his wife, did not take kindly to being hatted, named, and decorated, but with Elspeth saying that he could refuse the hat, but if he didn't stand still for the ribbon she would stab him through the throat, she succeeded in pinning the ribbon on John's seersucker jacket—a remnant from the early seventies. Then Sarah, knowing her job, took hold of her father-in-law's elbow and steered him toward a distant table that seemed to promise liquid refreshment.

Elspeth, relieved of her husband, joined a group of very

much older women, most of whom seemed to be having trouble with locomotion, and pointed out a cluster of comfortable chairs set along the east wall. Elspeth would bring them some punch and some cake. No, it was no trouble. And she was looking forward to sitting down for a few moments, meeting neighbors.

This act of benevolence left Alex free to hunt down Betty Colley. But not before he had reviewed what he knew of the family. There was Betty's mother, Rose Bingham. Someone who always struck him when her saw her for a medical appointment as a very much with-it old soul despite being quite deaf and slowed up by arthritis. And Betty? Forthright and demanding. But sensible. Knew her own mind. And Ned Colley, the husband who wasn't around. Not dead, just not there. Maybe not even divorced. And Betty was Jason's stepmother, Ned his father by Ned's first wife who, according to research done by George Fitts, lived in Iowa with her third husband. But for the last few months had been spending time for shoplifting so was an unlikely candidate for strangling her son in Maine.

What an unholy mess some families could be. Everyone hiding something, ducking something, or out to get another member of the clan. Alex, who had threaded his way through some of his patient's family tangles, was not very sanguine about finding the Colley family—or even the Moseby branch—a hive of love and caring persons. But one could always hope. He paused in the middle of the now crowded gymnasium floor and scanned the edges of the room.

He'd know Betty if he saw her. But then it had been almost a year ago since she'd last turned up in his office. In his mind he ran through a series of middle-aged female patients sitting in examining rooms holding their too-short, imperfectly tied hospital gowns together. Yes, he thought he had her. Carrot red hair, blunt chin, face as square as a brick. A body built for large size overalls, tractor driving, delivering calves, and hoeing vegetable rows. A problem with high blood pressure, wasn't it? And acid reflux. But what was such a healthy down-to-earth character doing in this sanitized community? But perhaps Betty, after years of hard farm work thought it was time for something easier in a place where lawns and heat and general maintenance were someone else's worry. Where her children could find friends that weren't four miles away across the next ridge. And her elderly mother could get around on one floor, make friends of her own age.

Alex worked his way through knots of men and women—straw hats in place, bright summer clothes, blue jeans and sandals for the young, polyester and New Balance for the elderly. T-shirts beyond counting. Ocean Tide logos, the Bruins, the Red Sox, the Celtics, the Maine Mariners. GAP, Save the Whale, the Forbush Lousewort, the Cougar, the Black Rhino, the Parthenon—the Parthenon?—the Yosemite Wolf. One purple shirt with Save Sex in silver. Circling about, waving now and then to a familiar face (patients, the Maritime Oil delivery man, a hospital volunteer, a librarian) he kept moving, pausing only for a second to hear one teenage boy in regulation oversize pants and a back-facing baseball hat pulled over his green hair tell another such that the whole place sucked, they needed to scare the shit out of everyone.

*God*, thought Alex, *I feel old. Antique. What I want to do is to turn on those guys and scare the shit out of them. If I could.* But then he saw Betty. Back to the wall, one hand on the arm of a wheelchair. In which sat a thin white-haired woman in a tomato-colored pantsuit and with a face that always reminded Alex of Lil' Abner's Mammy Yokum. Same sharp chin, same miss-nothing eyes, now taking in the scene with an expression of curiosity mixed with annoyance. Grandmother Rose Bingham.

Betty Colley looked up. "Hey, it's Dr. McKenzie," she cried. She jostled the woman in the wheelchair. "Mumma, it's Dr. McKenzie. You remember. You've been stuck in his office for hours." She stretched out a hand made of leather—the hand of someone who dealt with the countryside, with soil, bush, and rock, not tennis courts and swimming pools, and bicycle paths. Yet here she was, big as life and grinning from ear to ear.

Betty put one hand protectively on her mother's shoulder. "And, Dr. McKenzie, you know my mother, Rose, only she's usually not in a wheelchair. Had a bad fall in the kitchen the other day. Knee all swollen up. I was going to bring her to see you but she wouldn't go so I put ice on it instead. Mumma hates doctors."

Alex leaned over and extended a hand to Rose. "Hello there, Mrs. Bingham."

"Call me Rose," she said. "Everyone does. And I know you as Alex because I remember you when I used to work in the grade school cafeteria. What an awful kid you were. Trouble and more trouble. You and that Mike Laaka. Couple of no-good kids, if you ask me. And yes, I hate doctors. But don't take it personally."

"Aren't you one of the Montville Binghams?" asked Alex, for lack of anything positive to say about his behavior in past school days.

Rose shook her head. "I'm not a Bingham except by marriage to Frank Bingham and he's been dead since '85. Not that he was that much of a loss."

Alex moved to divert Rose from a family recitative. "So how are you liking Ocean Tide?"

Rose gave him a sharp look. "Don't know what we're doing at this fancy-pants hideout, but I've got my own bathroom and I haven't been mugged yet, so I won't complain. Not yet, anyway."

"Mumma hasn't quite adjusted," said Betty. "I mean she's been living by herself since Papa died. Basic living, if you know what I mean. Woodstove and a backhouse and a chem toilet upstairs. But then she had a couple of bad falls last year. That's when we went to that orthopedic guy in Belfast and he said she needed more help. So now she's moved in with us and we're making out okay."

44

Here Rose cranked her body around in the chair and shook her head at Betty. "She always gets it wrong. Back home I never liked to complicate my life with gadgets any more than it was already complicated. But then I'm an old bat so here I am. Living the life of the kind of people you see on TV."

"My mother," said Betty with a certain pride in her voice, "acts like she went out West in a wagon train. She was born in Portsmouth, New Hampshire, not on the Oregon Trail."

"But what made you leave Appleton Ridge?" Alex asked Betty. The Colleys, from what he'd heard, had fair stretch of farmland that gave a view of distant mountains. The farm, his mother had told him, not only supported a small dairy herd, produced vegetables, but as an added bonus owned a stretch of rolling blueberry barrens that provided a fair income when the berries were ripe.

"Time to move on," said Betty. "I'm tired of fixing storms and replacing gutters and dealing with sick cows and trying to get a crew together to rake the blueberries every year. The boys miss the place, though."

"The reason," said Rose in her cracked voice, "was money. Money pure and simple. Someone came along and offered Betty a bundle and she gave in."

"Okay," said Betty cheerfully, "a good price for the old farm made the decision pretty easy. But it will take some getting used to, this place. I keep checking to make sure my clothes don't have holes in them. But you know, a single woman, that's me since Ned Colley took off for the wild blue yonder...."

"He didn't join the air force," said Rose. "He walked off. Farming is tough work and Ned never went for tough work. Being a husband isn't what he did best even though he could be a real charmer if he put his mind to it. And now we're missing Jason. That's Ned's son. Another charmer. Like he was born to it. You haven't bumped into anyone called Jason Colley—about eighteen, tall, dark hair—have you?"

"I don't think so," said Alex, stalling for time. The question had come out of nowhere. And then, since it was not his place or assignment to throw premature clouds over the Colley family, he answered keeping to the narrow truth. "I haven't bumped into anyone called Jason Colley. That I know of." Not "bumped," he told himself. Maybe knelt next to, helped roll into a body bag, loaded into an ambulance. But not actually bumped.

"We're getting pretty worried," said Betty. And her cheerful freckled face creased with worry. "It's not like Jason is a homebody or we got along that well. I mean, when he left school—as a junior, he wanted out of the house. Out of the family, off the farm. But even if he could be a real pain, well, I kind of miss him. He could always make me laugh even when he was driving me out of my skull."

"But you do have other children?" asked Alex, again moving the talk to a more positive avenue.

Betty brightened, her face smoothed. "Two boys. Dylan, he's the oldest. Thirteen. And Brian, he's eleven. And they're both going to finish school if I have to take them there in leg irons."

"Good," said Alex, thinking it was time to say good-bye before he was pushed into a real corner about the missing Jason.

"And," said Betty. "I'm planning to switch to you. As my doctor. Since Dr. Gould is retiring. Your secretary said you weren't taking any new patients but I told her I'd come to you before and Mumma was your patient—when she feels like it— so I'm being let in. And even if you keep your patients waiting until midnight, well, we know you. What's the old saying, better the bad things you know about than the ones you don't."

On that upbeat note, Alex said good-bye and began to snake his way through the throng with the idea of rounding up the members of his family. Maybe go out for an early dinner. Some quiet restaurant off the tourist track. Surely he had done what George Fitts had wanted and covered the Colley family as far as it went. Betty and Rose were worried and thought of the missing Jason with some irritation. But also with affection. Now his parents and Sarah were off the hook as far as hunting down the Colleys went, and Betty and Rose could be left in peace.

But as often happens, Fate, that unpredictable presence in human lives, had decreed that Sergeant George Fitts of the Maine State Police had at that very moment turned off the Old County Road in Rockland onto Route 1 and was pointing his olive green Ford sedan toward the Ocean Tide community.

# 4

WHILE Alex mixed it up with the Colley family, Sarah had played the dutiful daughter-in-law. Not that she minded. John McKenzie was usually a humorous and an articulate man who, beyond his special field of interest was a mine of information on such disparate subjects as handmade canoe paddles, the running of the Iditorod, Flemish painting, the history of certain small villages in the border country of Scotland (from whence some of the McKenzies had sprung), and doings of the Raleigh Bicycle Club of Cambridge.

And John in the proper circumstances could show himself to be an amiable soul, especially when focused on known objects of his affection, i.e., members of his family, his own academic community, a number of favored friends who had met come hell or high water for killer bridge every Tuesday night in Cambridge. These last made up of lifelong associates (male and female) included a local pharmacist, a retired fireman, a YMCA board member, a patrolman, a geophysicist, and a long-retired Red Sox third baseman.

But with his roots cut by the removal to Ocean Tide, John had become irritable and impatient. Even after retirement he had thought to stay in the city for the winter months. But Elspeth, encouraged by their children, had overcome his objections citing easy housekeeping, problems of health, the proximity of number one son—a physician—plus the closeness of his Weymouth Island summer cottage. "No more long hot drives down Route One from Boston with a packed car, all those books and journals, the two Sealyhams—usually carsick—jammed into the car," Elspeth had pointed out. "Now when summer comes, we get on the ferry and forty minutes later we're there."

It all added up, Sarah knew, to a possible season of discontent. So she steered John away from the more boisterous knots of partygoers, found him a flagon of beer—he wasn't a champagne drinker—and tried for an upbeat conversation on the arrival of the McKenzies at Ocean Tide.

This effort produced only disconnected answers, and even when Sarah pointed out that the bicycle paths of Ocean Tide were a lot safer than the streets of Cambridge, John remained indifferent.

"Oh, I don't know," he muttered, looking out the oversized Fitness Center window and letting his gaze wander over the beds of alyssum and petunias that edged the entrance path, over the velvety green lawn, the white fences that circled the tennis courts.

"Don't know what?" asked Sarah. And then seeing that John's brow remained furrowed, his eyes now fixed on the distant view of the Assisted Living complex, added that she had seen quite a few bicyclists circling around. Not just kids bombing around on mountain bikes."

"You mean, Elderhostel types," said John. "Like us. Senior citizens, golden agers—how I loathe those expressions—scooting around on their tricycles."

"Well, damn it," said Sarah, exasperated. "Give them credit, John. Scooting around on a tricycle means they're not just sitting in a chair staring into space or watching some brain-rotting TV game show. And a lot of people your age are riding fancy-looking bikes with a thousand gears, and they're wearing bike clothes and helmets and they're entirely real. And some of them might even prove to be interesting people who know a hell of lot about early English literature and can recite *Beowulf* at the drop of a hat. So there." And Sarah grinned up at her father-in-law to ease what was beginning to be a deepening frown and clenching of teeth.

"Besides," she added, "you could show everyone a thing or two. You've been putting the fear of God into pedestrians for years. Start a Raleigh club if there isn't one already. And if Elspeth won't ride with you—I know she's working on her art show—I will. We can pack lunch and guzzle Gatorade and you can recite *The Seafarer*. I never could get the Old English accent right."

John smiled to mark his appreciation of Sarah's efforts, but then gave a lusty sigh and lapsed into silence.

Really, thought Sarah, seeing his black eyebrows drawn together, it might have been better—even with their medical problems—for the two of them to have found an old house out in the country. One with a pond or a small stream. Something like the farmhouse she and Alex were trying to fix up. The McKenzies could have occupied themselves for the next few years with putting it into shape, building bookshelves, digging a small garden. But it was too late. They were moved even if not settled, acquiescent if not contented. Resettling took time, especially for the long in tooth. Sarah, too, avoided the soothing euphemisms for the aged beloved by the publishers of *Modern Maturity*.

But she couldn't let the man stand there staring out of the window. Elspeth had told her to take him, by the hand if necessary, to look around and make himself familiar—if not at home—in the place.

"Come on," said Sarah, pulling at John's seersucker jacket sleeve. "See those paintings over there." She pointed to a series of three murals that ranged down the length of three walls, each featuring different aspects of the ocean.

These were examined, and Sarah was pleased to see that her father-in-law inspected them with some interest.

"Not bad, are they?" she said. "The ocean in a storm, the ocean at peace, and the ocean at dawn. Whoever did them didn't turn them into postcards."

"You're saying he hit a happy medium," chuckled John, enjoying his joke.

Sarah laughed obediently. "He could be a she, but it doesn't matter. They take away the gymnasium look. And now there's the golf pro. How about asking about the course. You used to play golf didn't you?"

"Used to," said John. "Gave it up. Stupid game. Trying to put a little white pill into a hole. I always had a terrible slice. These new courses, they're all too tidy. If I ever played golf again I'd go to Scotland. Real golf courses with gorse and traps six feet deep. A real rough. No pandering to weaklings. Hauling your own golf clubs, too. Or using a caddy and walking. None of these motorized carts."

"John," said Sarah. "I'll bet you'd love a golf cart. I tried one once. They're fun. Why not give the game a try?"

"Well, I'm not going to be the family wet blanket. So I might give it a whirl. Or a shot." Here John chuckled again.

"Your puns are in good order, anyway," remarked Sarah, happy that her charge was, if not mellowing—too strong a word—at least making a modest effort. Perhaps another beer and then time to circulate. Find the golf pro. Or, better yet, with any luck, someone from the class of 1956 of Bates College, John's undergraduate alma mater.

But John had turned and cocked his head at a man standing alone near the end of the refreshment table. "Good God!" he exclaimed.

"What is it? said Sarah, alarmed.

"Jacob Houghten. Lawyer. Looking into my pension plan for me. Something funny about the deductions. What in hell is he doing here? Well, I'm not going to let him get away. You know lawyers, he's been sitting on my stuff for ages. I'll go and put a burr under his tail. Sarah, enjoy the party. Or go meet some of these Colley people Alex seems so fond of." And with that John McKenzie strode across the floor and gripped the shoulder of the man. Who flinched and looked around for possible rescue.

Sarah, delaying an invasion of the Colley family space and aware of a rising hunger, decided to try the food. She worked her way over to the long refreshment table and was reaching for a triangle of rye bread and a slice of ham when she found herself surrounded by two teenage male shapes. They were hitting the feeding trough with a vengeance. Noisy, elbowing each other, they reached for hunks of meat, stacks of bread, fistful of sandwiches. Their topic of conversation, judging from random remarks, seemed to be aimed at "that asshole" Manager Joseph Martinelli.

"Who's he think he is?" said one young man with a wedge of turkey in his mouth.

"Thinks he's God Almighty," said youth number two. "Saying we can't use the pool today. What'd he think, we're going to pollute it or something? Piss in it."

"We'll piss in it tomorrow," said the first. "Show the guy."

"Pool's got too much chlorine. Chlorine's no good to swim in," said number two.

Sarah couldn't resist. "Neither is piss," she said sweetly, and took her plate and moved away. *Probably*, she thought with a sigh, *those two will turn up in my English classes next year*. And then she became aware that she had backed directly into a young man who seemed to be listening to the two boys with an expression of admiration and agreement. He was a tall, handsome youth with very blue eyes and his brown hair cut in a short military style that would certainly win the approval of every grandparent in the room. A walking Ralph Lauren ad. Blazer, open polo shirt, khakis, polished loafers. And socks! Sarah could only think that he was a plant put there by

Joseph Martinelli to reassure the older generations that all teenagers were not lost to the niceties of dress and decorum.

Before she could speculate further, the boy shrugged out of his blazer, dropped it behind a large ficus tree—a decorative item no doubt dragged in for the occasion—loosened his tie, pulled his shirt out of his trousers, and approached the two.

Sarah couldn't hear what he said, but youth number one let out a guffaw and said loudly, "What the fuck do you care, Matt?" and the trio walked away from the table and headed for the door.

So much for the model community and the token model youth, Sarah told herself. It would take more than a Joseph Martinelli to restructure the teenage crowd.

What next? Sarah skirted a posse of ladies in flowered pant-and-shirt costumes, an infant in a stroller with a Mickey Mouse balloon tied to its wrist, and at length found Elspeth and a sturdy sunburned woman gazing at one of the sea murals—"Penobscot Bay at Dawn."

Elspeth reached for Sarah's arm and made the introduction to Betty Colley, "Our new neighbor," praised the Colley farm produce through the years, and said she didn't know where she would go for fresh eggs now that the Colley farm was no more.

"You'll go to Shop 'n' Save or one of the other supermarkets like everyone else," said Betty Colley. "I don't think our eggs were anything special, but we took good care of our hens. They had a good life and so did we. While it lasted."

"What's happened to John?" asked Elspeth to Sarah. "I thought you were going to bird-dog him. See that he didn't leave too soon."

"He's run into a lawyer who apparently knows something about his pension plan. He seemed quite eager to talk to him."

"He'll probably end up terminating whatever pension we're getting," said Elspeth. "And now," she added in a voice Sarah recognized as being something more than casual. "Did you know that Betty's cousins, the Moseby family, have moved into

Ocean Tide? They're going to be almost across from us on Rowan Tree Circle."

"Don't have a clue why they moved in here," said Betty. "Gave up a perfectly good setup, nice ranch house outside of Union near Al's greenhouse business. I mean, I know why we're here in this place. Sherry was comfortable, but then she always liked new things. New places. Upward and onward. Not that I mind," Betty said hastily. "Sherry's okay. She's my little sister, when all's said and done, and we get along when we see each other. Family picnics, anniversaries, funerals, that sort of thing. She's always there with some sort of fancy casserole from a French cookbook. And she's a pretty good cook."

"Maybe the Mosebys wanted a maintenance-free life," suggested Sarah. "Sometimes I think Alex and I are crazy to spend so much time and money keeping an old building from falling down. Besides, here it's a safe place for the children. Trails, recreation, that summer camp. Things like that."

Betty shrugged. "Well, I never thought Sherry was that hung up on safety, so I guess it's the style of the place."

"Well, I hope the Mosebys are having luck meeting people," said Elspeth still in her disguised voice.

Sarah took the hint. Find the Mosebys and chat it up. Take care of George Fitts's request to check the families of possible victim, Jason Colley. Right. Sure. But, she was damned if she was going to spend much time on the project. She took her leave, wondering what the Mosebys looked like, where to start the search. But almost as soon as she began working her way through the thickening clumps of guests she was confronted by Naomi Foxglove. She, under instructions from Joseph, was circling around keeping an eye out for anyone with a lost or puzzled expression.

Sarah qualified as the latter.

"Are you looking for someone?" asked Naomi. "Or would you like to join the tour of some of the facilities. We have a group just starting out." Naomi spoke in a reassuring, soft velvet tone. Not unlike the purr of a large cat, thought Sarah.

"The Mosebys," said Sarah. "I heard they were new, and, well, I know their relatives. The Colleys. So I thought I'd say hello to—Sherry Moseby isn't it?"

"Sherry and Al Moseby and their children—they have three boys, Nicholas, Matt and Tim," said Naomi, who was apparently one of those persons with a perfect memory for names. "They're going off on the tour of the whole place." Naomi stretched out a graceful arm and pointed at a far door where a line had formed. "The bus is just loading, so why not join them. Mr. Martinelli is doing the honors, pointing out the sights. When they get back we'll be having the games and drawing for prizes."

Sarah ignored the possibility of games and prizes. "Which ones are the Mosebys?" she asked.

"Near the door. Sherry's in the blue skirt. Al is next to her, and behind are the boys. The ones in jackets. With shirts. And ties. Mr. Martinelli is very happy to have a few teenagers who don't look like they're going to start a gang war."

Sarah squinted into the distance and noted with interest that the boy who had shed his blazer and joined his pals at the refreshment table was now back, jacket on, shirt tucked in, and submitting to being herded toward the door.

"Interesting," said Sarah, who unexpectedly found herself turned off by the sight of well-dressed teenage boys. They didn't look natural. She turned to Naomi, who in her black-and-brown dress with its reticulated pattern reminded her not of Elspeth's boa constrictor but a presence far more exotic, more beautiful. Someone from a temple or a palace in the Far East.

"Thanks, but I'll skip the tour," Sarah told her. "I can catch up with them later." No point, she told herself, trying to make overtures to the whole family on a crowded bus tour. With that decided she moved briskly toward the door, free of the need to mingle and ask thoughtful questions of strangers. Free to get some fresh air in some open space. Walk down by the shore. Sniff the salt, perhaps wade a few feet into the ocean.

She wandered down a small service vehicle path that wound behind Lavender Lane—all the roads and lanes were named for some form of vegetation—and found herself on a seaside stretch of gravel path punctuated at intervals by park benches. Benches, Sarah noticed with interest, chained to a small concrete pylon with an iron ring.

So much for trust in the perfect community, she thought. Well, Joseph Martinelli wouldn't have reached his position as Ocean Tide's Lord High Pooh-Bah without keeping an eye on his pocket book. He'd paid good money for the benches—they were strongly made of wood slats on a metal base—and he was damn well going to hang on to them.

She slowed her steps and then turned and surveyed Mr. Martinelli's kingdom. What was it about this place that kept reminding her of a movie set with a camera man moving in for a close-up? She shook herself. She was too damn critical. After all, the place was amazing. Coherent, completely in synch with itself. The landscaping was tasteful even if, as Elspeth and John claimed, the spraying of possibly toxic substances might have taken place. And, it certainly wasn't comfortable to think that maybe robins and warblers were dropping dead along with mosquitoes, black flies, and mealy bugs, mice, and rats.

But these doubts aside, the variations of New England shingle and clapboard architecture at Ocean Tide, though dull, were not displeasing. In fact, the place could have been a lot worse—fake Tudor or plastic hacienda and Santa Fe adobe. Abe Lincoln log cabins and rough-hewn fencing. As for setting, what could beat the Maine coast on a late spring afternoon? Sarah walked on, the party clamor and music fading into the distance, and came presently to a winding beach path.

Peace. Only the sound of the small waves ruffling against the rocks. Herring gulls crying as they soared overhead. A couple of grackles quarreling by a stand of fir trees. The sun low in the sky sending shadows over the shore and a soft late afternoon breeze rising. She could stay here by the shore forever.

Well, not forever. A few hours perhaps. As a respite from bodies and the possibly bereaved Colley family. At a remove, the possibly bereaved Moseby family. A respite, too, from the fact that she would have to work up tutoring plans for whoever happened to answer her ad. She would have to be versatile. She might attract anyone from a six-year-old with attention deficit disorder to an angry adolescent whose parents—or parent—thought a D minus in English was not an acceptable grade for a high school junior. And since she'd been teaching college students, she would have to research new grade school strategies, curricula. But for now, not to worry. Think about it later.

Sarah found a bench, curled up on it, pillowed her head with Elspeth's soft white sweater and closed her eyes. And drifted. And slept.

And woke to a screech.

High-pitched yells. A door banging. Or a piece of wood hitting something.

A soft thumping sound. Getting louder.

Running feet.

Running feet coming closer.

And closer.

The screams turning to an incoherent string of words centering on Jesus. As in, "Jesus, Jesus, Jesus Christ, oh, Jesus."

A boy's voice. Squeaking up and down the scale. Breaking with excitement.

Or terror.

# 5

MUZZY headed with sleep, Sarah, blinked, shook herself, and then scrambled to her feet. Where had that voice, those frightened cries come from? Somewhere beyond that little patch of woods. On the other side. Over by the golf course?

And now she saw him. Bursting out from the shadows of the trees. A boy. Yellow hair flopped over a white face. Running, panting, arms and legs pumping. Then tripping across that big tree root. Falling. Down. Flat on his back. A sneaker off—untied shoelaces across it. Gasping. Wind knocked out.

The boy began to struggle for breath. Succeeded in taking one long shuddering gasp. Fighting for a second breath. And another. And another.

Then the boy, with Sarah now supporting him, pushed himself into a half-sitting position. A thin, wiry boy, around twelve or thirteen. The mop of straw hair almost covering his eyes.

"Hey," said Sarah, trying to hold him in a sitting position. "Take it easy. I think you just had your wind knocked out. You fell smack on your back."

"Oh, God," he gasped. "Get me out of here. Let me go. Get away from me. I gotta get out of here." He shook loose from Sarah's grip and scrambled to his knees.

Sarah clutched the sleeve of his T-shirt. "Hey, wait up. What's the matter?"

But the boy, still gasping, shook her off, wriggled free and was on feet. "Oh, God. It was awful. I gotta go. Let me go."

Sarah reached out and fastened her hand around the boy's elbow. "Listen. Hang on a minute. You took a terrific fall. Went absolutely splat. Get your breath and then tell me what's the matter."

"Back there," sputtered the boy, his chest heaving. He paused, struggled through three more breaths. Then reached down, shoved his foot back in his sneaker, tied it, hesitated for a second. Then, without warning, like an animal caught in a trap, he twisted his elbow free and without looking back began running back up the grassy incline toward the nearest building—one of the houses on Lavender Lane.

Sarah hesitated. Which way to go? What had the boy meant by "back there"? Should she look? Or run after him? Yes, chasing him down would at least promise further information. She threw herself into forward motion after the now diminishing figure of the boy. Telling herself as she ran that what had frightened him might be something no one would want to tangle with. "Back there" might mean a rabid skunk or raccoon. A fox. After all, a rabies epidemic had spread to midcoast Maine and people were becoming jumpy on the subject. And if it was something that dangerous, people had to be told.

One thing, she told herself, now beginning to puff but gaining on her object, it would hardly be another body. That was sure because the police had just been over the entire resort property and Mr. Martinelli's security troops were everywhere. This was not Sarah's evil other self in action; this was Sarah Douglas Deane, responsible citizen.

Think. What else beside an obviously rabid animal would

send a twelve- or thirteen-year-old boy swearing and running away as if chased by the furies? A fire? An out-of-control brush fire on the edge of the new golf course—or in one of the equipment sheds that dotted the various recreation areas. A drunken player waving a golf club in a threatening manner; the boy may have popped out of nowhere and ruined his tee shot, his putt. Or, how about a golf cart wreck? A collision. Golfers hurt, blood spattered around, and the boy had freaked out. Should she go back? See if she could give hands-on aid. CPR? No, she was too far committed to the chase. Trying to breathe through her nose, dig in deeper, take longer strides, she ran on and up the slope away from the beach.

And she was gaining. But now he scooted past the clumps of white birches. Rounded the end of Lavender Lane, crossed the lawn, passed by the swimming pool enclosure and headed straight toward the main entrance of the Fitness Center.

At which point two things happened. First, the boy slowed his headlong plunge, hesitated, and turned suddenly toward a side entrance of the building. Reached the door, flung it open and disappeared. Probably right into the middle of the getting-to-know-you party.

Oh, damn. Sarah skidded to a halt. Could she even identify the boy in that crowd? A straw-haired boy in a white T-shirt with some sort of logo, baggy over-the-knee shorts, and big clumping sneakers. A generic twelve- or thirteen-year-old kid.

But she had to give it a shot. Try to track him down. Find his family—if he had one at Ocean Tide. But then the second thing happened. Or arrived.

Coming slowly down the drive from the direction of the entrance, a car. The elderly olive green unmarked Ford Escort, a vehicle known by 90 percent of the county's residents as belonging to Detective Sergeant George Fitts of the Maine State Police Criminal Investigation Department. This vehicle was followed closely by a more recent model gray Chevy Cavalier, which pulled into the parking place behind the Escort. George climbed out, followed by his associate, Sheriff's Deputy Investigator Mike Laaka, who carried a brief case. These two were joined by the man from the gray Chevy, a person so obviously a "man of the cloth" that Sarah didn't need the sight of the white collar and black book in the man's hand to identify his calling.

George Fitts and Mike had obviously come to rain on the parade. Spoil Betty Colley's party, the Moseby's party. It was bad news—as the police, as Alex, had expected. The body found in the long grass by the practice hole must have now been positively identified as that of Jason Colley. And the minister—the priest—was there to do what he could in the matter of prayer and consolation.

But now what? She couldn't go hallooing into the Fitness Center asking if anyone had bumped into a breathless boy in a white T-shirt. Not when the implications of George Fitts and company's visit became clear to the crowd inside—something that would take about fifteen seconds. Betty Colley, the other Colleys, the Mosebys would be discreetly removed and driven somewhere. To their houses or to the police station. And the remaining partygoers would mill about speculating, guessing, and quite possibly relishing the excitement.

And the boy? By now he must have found his family. His friends. Someone from the Ocean Tide staff, and perhaps, if he were not too frightened, told his story, whatever it was. But Sarah wasn't going to settle for this uncertain conclusion. The boy was undoubtedly safe here at the Fitness Center. But a good citizen—Sarah's new identity—doesn't shrug off a scene with a frightened boy. Something had happened back there in the woods and it was time to find out what it was. Then find the proper help. Should she go in and extract Alex to help? No, he would probably be functioning as part of the consolation team for the Colleys and the Mosebys. Explaining the medical part. Prescribing sedatives, telling them that Jason probably didn't suffer—isn't that what doctors often assured families after the fact when there were no clear signs of protracted torture?

Sarah turned around, broke into a trot, accelerated to a run, around to Lavender Lane, down to the beach path. Headed for the bench on which she'd had her brief nap. From that vantage she could try to orient herself to the place whence had come the boy's first cries of distress.

She skidded to a stop by the bench. Occupied. Leaning back, his eyes closed, breathing softly, his hands folded over his stomach: John McKenzie.

Sarah reached out a hand to shake him by the shoulder. To wake him up and enlist his help; two might be better than one when looking into dubious circumstances. And then, inches away from his rumpled seersucker jacket, she stopped. Let the man sleep. He looked so peaceful. And she would be cautious. Approach slowly on silent feet. If something vile or nasty lay beyond the path leading through the grove of trees to the golf course, she would turn tail, alert John, and they would, like the responsible people they were, inform the authorities.

But being cautious also meant being ready. She took several steps along the path and then paused. And decided that whatever had scared the boy had not been a fire or collision of golf carts. Other golfers would have long since come along and dealt with these events. But a rabid raccoon or a drunken golfer or skulking lowlife remained a possibility. Sarah picked up a fallen branch found at the edge of the little grove of trees, a good stout piece of wood, almost four feet long, which when swung through the air gave a satisfying swoosh.

Thus armed, she walked slowly, one foot, then the next, lifted and put down carefully on the leaf and pine needle floor and in a few minutes' time found herself in an opening. Green turf, two sand traps, a raised green velvet surface with a flag bearing the number seventeen sticking out of its middle. A non-threatening scene if there ever was one. Two golf carts bearing four men were just spinning off down a small asphalt path marked with a sign TO 18TH TEE while down the seventeenth fairway another two carts had halted.

Sarah stepped cautiously toward the nearest bunker and looked around for anything untoward. Then trying to appear casual, just a golfer with a lost ball, she clambered up to the green, across, and walked around the far side bunker. And was rewarded not with a dangerous presence but with a rousing cry of "Fore!" And a white ball landed with a plop on the edge of the green and rolled into the sand trap. She retreated hastily, backing into the shelter of the surrounding bushes and clumps of birch and pine, and as she turned caught sight of a substantial shingled hut with a green door on which Maintenance was writ large. And the door stood open. Inviting entrance.

*Well, I'm not that much of a fool,* Sarah told herself. *I'm not going to go marching in and find myself clobbered by a rake or shovel.* Or face a raccoon with foam on its jaws. A disheveled skunk. That open door suggested that perhaps someone—the boy?—had departed in a hurry, leaving the door open. But what about the banging she'd heard? Maybe the boy had slammed the door as he left but being frightened had not lingered to see if it stayed closed.

But there was a safer route to take. A dusty window was fixed into the left side of the building and a large rock stood obligingly at the base. She could case the interior in safety. If all was clear, she would go in and have a look around. With stick in hand. At the ready.

The light wasn't all that great; the shadows had now lengthened over the area. But by pressing close to the window, squinting, and shielding her eyes Sarah was able to make out a number of innocuous objects fastened against the wall: rakes, metal and bamboo, undoubtedly meant to deal with leaves on the green or to smooth out sand traps. A number of shovels. Two heavy-duty weed whackers. A clutch of aerators, little rolling machines with spikes. A brush hook, several small scythes, and two long-handled ones—the kind described by Tolstoy in *Anna Karenina*. Sarah had a sudden vision of the greens keepers attired like Russian peasants, swinging their scythes as they marched down the rough in perfect unison. Then, in the corner of the hut, she made out a long-handled kind of drill—an auger—perhaps for replacing the cups on the green. But.

But no lurking figure. No sodden or spaced-out person slumped against the wall, splatted out on the floor. No visible animals, rabid or otherwise. Nothing.

Almost disappointed, Sarah stepped down from her rock and, walking to the door, stick still grasped in her right hand, pushed it open a few more inches. But the interior of the maintenance building was as she had seen it through the window. Full of neatly placed implements suitable for the care of a golf course. But how about the feeding? Didn't golf courses eat quantities of fertilizer, special turf-feeding mixtures, weed-killing compounds? That would mean bags and bags of the stuff. But she had seen no sign of such a supply. And then, peering out the window, she saw the corner of a smaller hut, or, really, a large shed situated to the rear of the larger structure.

Sarah, looking warily over her shoulder, slipped out of the maintenance building, noted through a gap in the clump of trees that one golfer of the foursome was whacking away without effect at his ball from the trap while his friends waited, leaning on putters. And with these four lay safety. Sanctuary. If something untoward happened. And if, of course, she reacted quickly. Taking small quiet steps, she worked her way around the building. No helpful window in this little shed. Only double wooden doors on the far side of the shed, these reached by a wooden ramp. A cautionary sign to those persons dealing with toxic chemicals such as fertilizers and below the sign a small hose with a spray attachment and a small sink. The doors to the shed were closed. But not locked because an open combination dangled from a heavy hasp.

She hesitated. No sound other than one explosive "God-damn it" from the sand trap. Surely no malefactor would be crouched in this small place with golfers coming and going like clockwork. She stepped to the right-hand door, lifted the latch free of the combination lock, and gave a small push. Five inches open. Cautiously she poked her stick inside the building and tapped the floor lightly, ready to sprint for safety at the slightest sound—the safety that lay only fifty yards away on the golf green. Not a sound, not the smallest rustle. Not the slightest shift of movement from something alive.

She waited for a full minute and then pushed the door open another few inches and fixed her eye on the crack. A dim interior with shadowy piles of rectangular objects. She hesitated. Then, oh, what the hell. Sarah gave the door a shove, reached in, found a light switch and pushed it. A dim—bulb lit up the square space. She walked—or rather sidled—in, stick held firmly. No one. Just a number of bags arranged in bins and on shelves. As she had thought: fertilizers, turf builders. Grass seed, weed killers. Heavy economy-sized bags, thirty-, forty-, fifty-pound ones. She took three more steps inside until she stood in the middle of the room. And stopped. One entire set of floor-to-ceiling shelves seemed to have up-ended their entire supply of something called Gro-Green so that the bags lay in an untidy pile across the far corner of the little room.

And under this heap of what must have been hundreds of pounds of bags protruded a pair of heavy work boots. Soles facing her, toes up. With legs attached. And, beyond, one hand, fingers curled. The hand being attached to a wrist showing the cuff of a checked shirt.

Sarah took a long deep breath and closed her eyes. But as she did she was overtaken by a sudden vision of the Wicked Witch's feet sticking out from under Dorothy's house. Then after another long shuddering breath, she clenched her teeth and opened her eyes. Whatever it was, it was dead. Gone. Six or eight feet deep of filled Gro-Green fertilizer bags on top of a body would not permit life. Even in that dim light the curled hand appeared slate blue.

In four strides, she was out of the shed, had slapped the

door shut, jammed the combination lock closed. And beat it. She didn't scream as the boy had because, perhaps, she didn't have enough breath to scream. Just enough to run.

Not to the seventeenth green, which if she had taken time to think, was the obvious, the quickest way to help.

But she didn't think. After the single act of locking the shed, she just got the hell out of there. Just as the boy had. Because that must have been what he'd seen. Must have found the door open and went snooping.

She plunged back through the small patch of woods, back to the bench and was about to hurl herself up the grassy slope when the tall white-haired figure of John McKenzie rose from the bench and confronted her.

Sarah skidded to a halt. She'd forgotten John.

"Whoa, whoa, there," he called.

"John. John, I can't stop."

But he reached for her. Took hold of her hand. Just as she had tried to hold the boy.

"Stop," he ordered. "Stop, get your breath. Explain."

And somehow the old voice of authority—as well as good common sense—exerted itself. After all, those dead feet and that dead hand weren't going to come alive or get any deader if she did the two-minute mile and arrived at the Fitness Center in an incoherent state of collapse. So, gasping—like the boy before her—she told her story. Starting with the boy charging out of the woods, her pursuit of him, the arrival of George Fitts and company, the boy's disappearance, her decision to take a look. And what she had found.

"Pounds and pounds of fertilizer bags just piled on top of him."

John held up his hand. "Him? You're sure it's a him?"

Sarah, her breath now slower, considered. "The boots looked pretty big, but I suppose I shouldn't guess."

"Okay. Here's what I think we should do."

Sarah looked up at the sun-reddened face, the tufted white hair. "I" had become "we." And he was over sixty-five with a heart problem, a pacemaker. "I don't think you should do anything, John. Come on back to the Fitness Center. We can call Security or see if George Fitts has a policeman to spare. Without upsetting the Colley family scene."

"Yes," said John. "I suppose they'll be breaking the news to Betty Colley. And to that other family, the . . ." He paused.

"The Mosebys, the mother, Sherry Moseby, is Betty's sister." Sarah said. "And I certainly don't want to throw this business—a second dead body—into what's going on with those two families. Maybe we should wait until George takes the family wherever he's supposed to. Or we could call someone else, though I don't quite know who."

"I think," said John quietly, "that I should walk—walk, not run—over to that shed and keep an eye on it. You know all the fuss police make about evidence and the scene of the crime. You said you locked it. But the police wouldn't want any of the grounds people coming in, unlocking the shed, and start throwing fertilizer bags around. Or the boy comes back."

Sarah nodded. It made sense. Except. "What if the person who did it, dumped the bags on the body—or the live person if he was alive—" Here her syntax became hopelessly tangled. She started again. "What if someone is waiting around to nail anyone who's being too curious?"

"You seem to have survived," said John dryly. "I'd say that whoever did the thing is in another county by now. I'll stay by the seventeenth green in sight of all the golfers but keep the shed in view. Warn anyone who goes near it. And in a short time you'll have alerted the police, someone from Security, and they'll come down here on the double."

Sarah nodded. And frowned. "But take it easy, John. Use my stick. You can use it as a walking stick. Because, after all . . ."

"If you say because I'm old and fragile I will club you with that stick."

Sarah gave a weak grin. Then said, "Okay, I'm off," and began a modified trot back for the second time up the slope toward the entrance to Lavender Lane and the Fitness Center beyond.

She arrived at the corner of that building near the entrance just as George Fitts, the priest, a man in the sheriff's department brown uniform, Alex, two unidentified civilians, and a bunched procession of Colleys and what must be Mosebys—the rear being brought up by the boy with the blazer as well as a young man in a blue polo shirt and chinos—were all being escorted into three waiting cars. Sarah hesitated by the corner. She couldn't leap into action and grab George Fitts. Or the deputy. So it had to be Carly or Naomi or Joseph Martinelli himself, any of whom would goose the security system into motion. But then, walking out of the entrance, carrying his briefcase—Mike Laaka. Mike from the Knox County Sheriff's Office. Old buddy, Mike. Thank God.

Sarah sprang away from her watching place, ran to Mike and planted herself in front of him. "Wait up, Mike. I need you."

Mike looked at her, expression serious. "Not now, okay? I've got to follow up George. See if he needs any reinforcements. Maybe a nurse. We've got a homicide to explain to two families. And to make arrangements for statements to be taken."

"You need me," Sarah almost shouted. "Or you need what I've found. What some boy found. Someone dead."

"I know," said Mike. "Didn't Alex tell you? It's been confirmed. The body is Jason Colley. No question."

"Goddamn it, Mike. Listen, will you? Not Jason Colley. I know about him. And I'm sorry for the family. Or families. But there's a body down there. Another body." Sarah waved in the general direction of the ocean front and the seventeenth hole. "In a shed. One of the equipment sheds. It's very dead, and under pounds of fertilizer bags."

Mike came to. "What! What in hell are you saying?"

Sarah, her audience focused, explained. Described.

And Mike went into action. By phone and then in person at a run, Sarah puffing behind him, trying to explain about locking the combination, about John McKenzie standing guard.

Mike stopped in midstride, swiveled his head. "Jesus, Sarah, John McKenzie's got a cardiac thing, a pacemaker. You knew that."

"Damn it, Mike, of course I knew that. But John does what John wants and it made sense. There was no one else around. Everyone's at the Fitness Center party."

And there was John, just off the seventeenth green, leaning against a white pine, holding a small book of verse in one hand. "I always carry a book," he explained, closing the volume and slipping it into a back pocket. "Just in case. Hello, Mike. No one has been near the shed. But I've seen a hell of a lot of lousy golf."

The machinery cranked up. Mike by cell phone activated the constabulary, the scene-of-the-crime team, the forensic team. And Sarah and John by request stayed sitting on a bench by the eighteenth tee—all approaching golfers and maintenance personnel having been held up on the sixteenth hole and sent back—the golfers complaining mightily—to the clubhouse, there to leave names, addresses, telephone numbers and given notice that they would be asked to account for the times of their play, their companions, and what or who they had seen during their round of golf.

As luck would have it, state pathologist, Johnny Cuszak, happened to be around the corner watching his daughter Jennifer pitch in a Little League game in Rockport. Called to the scene, he arrived in minutes and reported that the victim, when unearthed in a flattened condition, had probably been killed—broken, smothered, squashed by means yet unknown—some four, maybe five hours ago.

"Never can fix the time on the nose," said Johnny. "That's for detective stories. The lab will have to come up with the details, stomach contents, blood, tissue, then we'll fiddle with a more exact time of death. Cause? Well, you can see the guy was bonked on the head. Then stuffed under those fertilizer bags. All of which you know, Mike."

"Yeah, okay, I know," agreed Mike in a tired voice. Gloved in latex, dressed in a coverall, he had helped in the removal of what seemed like a million bags of fertilizer and grass seed from what was left of the man. Sarah had been right, the boots, approximately size eleven, belonged to a man.

At which point, Alex arrived, having come from prescribing mild sedatives to the Colley family and putting the Moseby family in touch with their family physician, Dr. Joe Foxe, as well as their minister, Pastor Bob Killey.

"What's going on?" he said. "There was a call in for the medical examiner."

"I found Johnny at the Little League game, right around the corner," said Mike. "But if you want to pronounce the victim dead, go right to it. He's in there."

"You haven't fooled with the body, have you, Mike?" said a crisp voice. George Fitts had arrived.

"I never fool with bodies," said Mike. "That's Johnny's job."

"We just started," said Johnny. "He hasn't been dead all that long. Rigor just established. Legs, arms broken, skull smashed. Most of the damage postmortem."

"Not taken any evidence from the corpse?" asked George, and when Mike shook his head, he nodded his approval. George wanted a supervised collection from the body's person. Either by himself—the one person he really trusted—or by an evidence team whom George would watch with the eye of a jealous serpent. George, to use Mike's phrase, had seen too many bodies, their clothing, the whole evidence scene fatally compromised, totally screwed up by hasty police examiners.

"Photographer's about finished," put in Mike. "Area's taped off, more or less secured. I mean as far as anyone can secure part of a golf course and a patch of woods, which no one can. And then there's the beach. Just beyond the seventeenth green, you've got the beach. Or the shore rocks; not a real beach, just some imported sand. Couple of paths leading down. Figure the guy who did this may have used the shore, coming and going. Or just going."

"Don't figure anything yet," said George. "But we'll send a couple of men on down to the beach with evidence bags before the tide comes back in. It's about dead low now."

"Dead low. Nice way to put it," said Mike.

George ignored Mike. He knelt down and pulled on his surgical gloves. "Let's see what we've got." Gingerly he slipped his hand into a front jeans pocket—jeans that covered the lower half of the pancaked torso—and pulled out a small pocketknife, which he slipped into a waiting paper bag.

"Label the bag for me," he ordered Mike. "Time, location, description."

Then from that pocket, he extracted a crumpled pack of Marlboroughs—the cigarettes mashed to fragments—some odd change, and a couple of toothpicks.

"Another guy who still smoked," remarked Johnny, who stood watching. "You know, more'n half of my bodies, they're still smoking up a storm. I think it goes with the territory."

But now George, with the help of Johnny's elevation of the hip of the corpse, had moved to the rear jeans pocket and between forefinger and thumb had pulled out a darkened leather wallet, which even the weight of the fertilizer bags had not been able to change its shape, curved to fit a back pocket.

George opened the wallet, bent down to examine a driver's license complete with picture—license expired, he noted—and gave a soft whistle. This from George who tried never to react visibly to what he found. Mike had claimed that George, finding his own mother with a sword sticking out of her chest, would have only nodded soberly. Not whistled. Nor used profanity.

Now George did both. First the whistle.

Then the oath.

"Christ," said George. "Look at this, will you?"

Alex, Mike, and Johnny bent over the wallet.

And Alex whistled next, and then shook his head. "Edward Colley," he said slowly.

And Mike swore in his turn. "Jeezus, I'll be. That's Ned Colley. Betty Colley's husband. Left her a long while back. Been gone for a coon's age."

"Well," said George, "he's come back now."

# 6

MIKE stared down at what was left of Ned Colley. Or to be exact, Edward Joseph Colley, husband to Betty, father of the deceased Jason by his first wife, father by way of Betty of sons Bryan and Dylan. Mike had known Ned, in the way that people who live in small rural communities know each other—or know people who are related by birth or marriage to each other. Who have shared school classes, high school sports, work experiences, have fished and hunted together.

But apart from these tenuous connections, Ned Colley had with some frequency attracted police attention by what might be described as a disorderly lifestyle. Even as a boy he had had occasional brushes with the juvenile court, but police wisdom had it that from his earliest years Ned could pour on the charm, could be counted on to show the proper amount of repentance when faced with a judge. Result: charges dismissed, sentences suspended. Fines, yes, but in Ned's own words, no big deal.

And he'd been a handsome son of a bitch, Mike remembered, looking at the distorted and darkly mottled face. Never without some woman. His first wife, beauty that she was, had been what is generally called a piece of work, and their split could have been predicted from the day of their wedding. After this Ned has been seen with any number of very willing partners and then Betty Colley had married him. She'd been the last of his string—as far as anyone knew—and the best of the lot in most people's opinion. He'd been damn lucky to get her. During what would later be thought of as the "Betty Colley period" Ned had seemed to settle a bit. Helped out at the farm, worked part-time at a local Exxon station, later spent a few months at a lumberyard, then almost a year working as a mechanic at a machine shop. And then, just like that, he'd sauntered away from home one fine August day about three years ago when a job on a trawler out of Portland had turned up. A couple of returns home followed, Ned as affable and humorous—and as unreliable—as ever. But for the past two years, not a sign of the man.

As for Ned's deceased son, Jason, the boy had announced that he had no plans to finish the last two years of high school and had left home for a life of independence at about the same time that Ned had taken off. But since the two hadn't been seen around together it was assumed that these departures had not been related.

Mike, standing behind George, wiped his forehead. The shed was small and airless and the fading day now combined warmth with dampness—a fog bank that had hovered offshore had begun drifting landward. Mike was wrestling with some knotty questions. How could corpse A—Jason Colley—dead for almost two weeks and found on the outer reaches of the Ocean Tide property near a practice hole have anything to do with corpse B—Ned Colley—dead probably for five, maybe four hours and found in this fertilizer shed fifty yards or so from the seventeenth green? Under everyone's noses, for God's sake. Yet a link there had to be. One link: Colley father to Colley son. Lowlife senior to lowlife junior. The second link? Easy. To Betty Colley and her family. And maybe to the Mosebys, but that was at one remove: Jason was only a cousin and a nephew to the Mosebys; Ned a brother-in-law to Sherry Moseby and Al an uncle by marriage to her three boys. So how on earth . . .

"Move it, Mike," said George. "They're taking him away, so how about you hanging around and make sure your gang has secured the scene. I want tape marking the woods, this part of the golf course, along the shore, all off limits."

"Come on, George," protested Mike. "You can't fence off the whole blasted ocean. Someone can just row in and sneak ashore. Snatch away a piece of evidence before anyone can find it."

"We'll do our best," said George stiffly. "So when you finish securing the area around this shed, go on down to the beach. It's the logical get-away place."

Mike tried again. "Jeezus, the beach, the rocks go forever. Where do you aim to stop? Or," Mike moved into sarcasm, always a dangerous route to take with George Fitts, "do you want to head on into the Atlantic Ocean? How far? Couple of feet? Couple of nautical miles? To the international line? Monhegan? Cape Cod? Prince Edward Island? Come on. Why wouldn't the guy leave by way of the golf course?"

George Fitts regarded his associate coldly. "The golf course is possible but it's very public. So you hit the beach. Both directions. Take specimen bags and keep your eyes open. We're interested in any possible weapon, the oddball pipe or stick. Maybe buried in the sand, tossed in the ocean. Jason Colley may have been first banged on the head before the murderer did his finishing job with that chain. And Ned was brained before fertilizer bags were dumped on him."

"You think the same guy did both jobs? A week apart?"

"It's a reasonable guess. Victims related. But if two murderers or ten murderers are involved we'll still have to look for weapons."

Mike shrugged. His evening time off, even ten minutes for

dinner and coffee, was disappearing fast. "Okay, you're the boss. But I'm serious about the water. Where do we stop? Low tide line? Or wade in."

"Wade in about six feet past the low tide line. I'll get some people to help and we'll try for a couple of guys with wet suits to go out about a quarter of a mile and if nothing turns up maybe we'll call on the Coast Guard to try some dragging."

"Don't forget," said Mike, "you've got an entire resort community, an eighteen-hole golf course, a three-hole practice course, buildings and houses and hiking and wilderness bike trails to cover."

"Thank you, Mike," said George. And he turned on his heel and started back through the patch of woods. Stopped, and returned. "On the beach, watch it that you and the others don't step all over footprints. Cover your shoes. Take casts if you get good prints. Even a good partial."

"Footprints," snorted Mike. "Ninety percent of the so-called beach is just a bunch of rocks with some sand dumped around. Calling it a beach is Joseph Martinelli's idea."


Manager Joseph Martinelli had established his offices in an annex to the Lodge: the top story a conference room, complete with private stairway and private elevator; the first floor, Joseph's own office and reception room, was set in what might be called the heart of Ocean Tide complex. From large windows fore and aft the manager could survey the comings and goings of three major roads, the Camp Ocean Tide complex and beyond that the beach and ocean. For other scenes and up-to-date information, Joseph depended on a number of television screens and an elaborate double computer setup that fed statistics, daily events, personnel information, upcoming strategies—in fact the whole Ocean Tide world to the manager.

But now, slumped in his reclining office chair, Joseph was the picture of despondency. It was getting on toward seven o'clock, his secretary, Mrs. Alice Eisner, had crept gratefully home after a pro forma offer to stay and keep a finger stuck into the leaking dike called Ocean Tide. And Joseph, too, wanted out, wanted his house on the edge of the Ocean Tide property, wanted to sit by his own living room window looking over the ocean and have someone from the Lodge bring over a steaming platter of *pollo con pesto Genovese* made by the inspired hands of Chef Paulo Cellini. And most of all he wanted to recover the happy tranquility of three days ago when, as the emperor of Ocean Tide, he had sat on his throne and all the world rejoiced to do his bidding.

But instead of domestic warmth Joseph faced a double homicide supported that evening only by the resilient Carly Thompson since Naomi Foxglove was now busy dealing with residents' questions and generally calming waters at the Lodge. It was all too much. The herding by the police of the Colleys and Mosebys to the police station for statements had been bad enough—"I mean, it's just not fair, like it's a put-up job," complained Joseph to the long-suffering Carly. They had retreated to the sanctity of Joseph's inner office, a place whose tributes from the Chamber of Commerce, photographs of Joseph shaking hands with civic leaders, the gold-framed oil painting of a tranquil slice of ocean shore titled *Morning at Ocean Tide* usually gave him a glow of comfort.

"My God, Carly," he went on, "those two families are *our* families. They're Ocean Tide people. We can't afford to have our residents on the front page of the *Courier-Gazette.*"

"Make that the *Portland Press Herald,*" said Carly. "*The Bangor Daily News.* All the local rags. And TV. The phone's been ringing off the hook, reporters knee deep. Naomi Foxglove's had calls from the *Boston Herald* and the *Globe* but she hung up on them."

"Hound dogs," said Joseph. "How did they find out about this second body? Don't tell me we've got a bunch of spies on the payroll."

"You know how it is," said Carly. "One body, not that big

a deal. Two bodies found within forty-eight hours—very big deal. Like those serial murders. One body, then another. Then bodies all over the place. Murder USA."

"Carly," said Joseph between his teeth. "Can it. Ocean Tide, it's just getting off the runway, about to lift off, and now, what are we having? Two bodies. Don't you even think about more bodies. Don't open your mouth to the media creeps. It's 'no comment' all the way. You, me, Naomi, all of us. We regret, we are shocked because Ocean Tide is a peaceful community. A God-fearing civilized community. Don't give the news guys a single straw to chew on."

Carly tapped the folder marked Prospects on Joseph's desk. "We couldn't give them anything to chew on because we don't have anything."

But Joseph had been thinking. "Maybe I'll suggest it's a gang thing happened accidentally on our property. By people not from Maine. That usually goes over big. People not from Maine are usually suspect. I could hint at a gang from . . . say, Chicago."

"Chicago's a little out of the way," observed Carly.

"New Jersey, then. Boston. Lots of gangs in New Jersey and Boston. Or Hartford. I've heard Hartford has real problems."

"I suppose," said Carly thoughtfully, "that some people moved to Ocean Tide to get away from city gangs."

"Mother of God," said Joseph, for lack of anything else to say. He shoved the Prospects folder away from him. And then focused on the title and brightened. "You know, we sold two more units late this afternoon. On Lilac and Tulip. Even after the police had roped off the seventeenth hole. And we added four names to the waiting list for Sunshine House."

"I've had inquiries about the attached cottages on Peony Point," Carly said. "If you ask me, the publicity isn't going to hurt that much. It's not like some child's been hurt. Or some upstanding person or one of our seniors. Jason Colley was a sort of drifter, left home a while back. Maybe no one's going to have a major scene over his being dead. And that might include his family."

"Maybe," said Joseph doubtfully, "but what about this body in the golf equipment shed? What if it's the body of some high-profile type? A TV personality. An important lawyer. Not just a teenage kid on the loose."

"If it turns out to be a lawyer there might be dancing in the streets," said Carly. "Anyway, I don't think you need to get into a flap just yet. I read an article that said things like this put spice into life. It's like people being attracted to fires and ambulances."

At which point, Naomi Foxglove appeared at the office door. "Just reporting in, Mr. Martinelli," Naomi said in her low soft voice. "It's quieting outside, we've closed down the party at the Fitness Center and have put on a movie for the children. *Toy Story III*. And Sergeant Fitts, he wants a word with you."

"Chrissake," said Joseph. "What's he want?"

"He'll probably tell you," said Carly reasonably as Naomi on soundless feet slipped from the room.

Joseph straightened his shoulders, ran his hands over his hair, and assumed the look of a much-tried executive. And George filtered into the room and took the blue leather chair next to the desk offered by Joseph.

"Shall I leave?" asked Carly in a barely audible voice. She very much wanted to stay. Two bodies in forty-eight hours had certainly ratcheted up her interest in the job—a job that often had its tedious moments.

"Please stay," said George. "I've just asked Ms. Foxglove for any assistance she can give us about anything out of the ordinary that happened during the past week or so. And you, too, Ms. Thompson. Now, about these two events . . ."

"Oh, go ahead and say it," prompted Carly. "Not events, two dead bodies on our doorstep."

"No!" Joseph almost shouted it. "Not on our doorstep. The Colley boy was barely on the property and this other one, that shed is away from the living areas."

"We've had a positive identification of the second victim," said George, ignoring the outburst.

"Oh, for God's sake already," said Joseph. "Who is it? I mean who was it? An accident? Tell me it was an accident. Something that could happen to anyone. Like a heart attack. No one's told me a thing. Only that this guy's turned up in an equipment shed."

George decided to take the last questions first. Mr. Martinelli might fly into pieces when he heard the victim's name and George hoped that competent-looking Carly Thompson could keep Joseph's lid on. Keep him functioning in a useful—useful to the police—fashion.

"Indications," said George, "are that the victim sustained head injuries and then was disposed of. In the shed. Fertilizer bags pulled on top of him."

"So you mean murder," said Joseph, grasping this essential without difficulty.

"We are treating this as a second homicide. Possibly related, possibly not related, to the first."

"Who, who?" sputtered Joseph. "Why related? I mean the other person . . . the Colley boy . . ." He came to a halt and simply shook his head back and forth, looking to the watching Carly like a large puzzled bear.

"The victim from the fertilizer shed is Edward—or Ned as he was called—Colley. He was Jason's father by his first wife and Betty Colley's husband, the father of her two boys. The Moseby family members are, of course, related by marriage."

Joseph, eyes bulging, started to cross himself, hesitated, thought better of it and instead reached into his desk drawer and pulled out a wadded-up handkerchief, and wiped his brow. Reached back in the desk and brought out a small silver flask and unscrewed its top. "Brandy," he announced. "In case I'm faint or something. I keep it on hand. You never can tell. Like now." At which he tilted up his head and took a long swallow. Shook his head back and forth, and again Carly thought of a bear. A bear in a zoo perhaps. Behind bars and not sure how such a thing had happened to him.

There was a moment of silence; George consulted his notebook and Joseph replaced his flask. To keep the conversation going, Carly spoke up. "Well, doesn't that make it easier? I mean it's all in the family now. Maybe it's one of those family revenge things. Dad kills son and then shoots himself."

"Ms. Thompson, thank you. No speculation. We want to keep a low police profile here, but we will have to do a thorough search of the premises. Starting with the golf course and the beach area. We'll use plainclothesmen as far as possible and try and not disrupt your day-to-day operation."

"Disrupt!" Joseph's voice rose again in a shout. "You might as well come in with a bulldozer and a forty-piece marching band."

George gave him a thin and wintry smile—a George Fitts specialty. "Please, Mr. Martinelli. Cooperation is the route to go. Stick to whatever schedule you have planned for the coming week. As long as it doesn't interfere with our investigation. I suggest that you issue a bulletin to the residents and visitors. Say if anyone has any questions, they can come and see us. We're setting up a small field command post—borrowing your utility equipment shed and what you call the VIP Golfer's Cottage. And we'll be keeping a staff there for the present. And now, thanks for your help." And George was gone.

Leaving ruin behind him.

Joseph Martinelli let his body slump into his office chair like a punctured balloon. He gave a great whistling sigh and let his head drop onto his arms. Then he raised a reddened face to Carly, who stood ready to administer either more brandy or to start putting together a reassuring bulletin to the effect that Ocean Tide—or at least its management—was saddened but standing firm.

This last thought she shared with Joseph. Who mumbled it about in his head and then went for it. "You're right. That's it," he said. "We're standing firm. Like a rock. Tempests may blow and storms may storm, but Ocean Tide . . ."

"Well, it's not World War Three," said Carly. "Or the bubonic plague. You just talk about troubled times and how Ocean Tide is an oasis."

"Some oasis," said Joseph bitterly. Then, bouncing back, he added, "A port in a storm. I like that. Not an oasis. We're not in a goddamn desert. We're in a storm and we're a port in a storm. The storm of incivility."

"Murder's a little strong for incivility."

"Disturbing incident, then," said Joseph.

"Incidents," corrected Carly.

"All right, all right. Incidents. Have something on my desk in half an hour.

"I'll try," said Carly. "But a couple of things need your okay. No, nothing to rattle your teeth. Requests before body number two came on the scene. A recorder group wants to play at the Sunshine House and the Lodge dining room. During the lunch hour. Its free. No charge, bunch of volunteers, so Naomi asked me to check with you. I mean, you can't turn down a freebie. I've written them in next Tuesday. It's a good distraction."

"Okay," said Joseph. "As long as it isn't loud. No rock. No obscure medieval stuff. Nothing about being killed. Being shot or hung. Folk songs, maybe hymns. 'Amazing Grace,' 'The Yellow Rose of Texas,' 'My Old Kentucky Home,' maybe add in a sing-along."

"The first line of 'My Old Kentucky Home could start a riot," said Carly. "You know, 'It's summer, the darkies are gay.' "

Joseph scowled at her. "So check out the lyrics. What's next?"

"Call from the Colleys. Before they heard about Jason being dead. Betty Colley and her sister-in-law, Sherry Moseby. They want to find a tutor for three, maybe four of their boys.

Seems they're not doing so well in English. I thought of Professor McKenzie."

"He'd be a tough nut to work with. You're talking teenage. Not college, university. Professor McKenzie probably won't put up with any teenage horseshit. But I'll ask around. Now get moving on the bulletin. And use the word 'profound.' Like we're profoundly sorry, or like 'it is with profound regret. Like you gotta sound dignified."

"Like I hear you," said Carly, turning on her heel and making for the door.


Night fell but repose was not available to a number of members of the community of Ocean Tide as well as certain representatives from the Knox County constabulary.

Mike Laaka spent a dismal evening with several henchmen crawling over the three-mile stretch of stony beach. Their progress or lack of it was assisted with large battery lamps and handheld flashlights. But the rewards were few.

"Goddamn rocks, goddamn seaweed," said Mike to his assistant, Deputy Katie Waters. "I'm going to break my neck or my leg." He reached into a crevice and extracted with a pair of tongs a sodden cotton glove (a common wash-up from the lobster boats in the area) and a condom in poor condition.

"For an upstanding community, there's a lot of fornication going on down here," Katie remarked. "And," she added, "it must be pretty uncomfortable. Who wants to make love with stones biting into your back?" Katie was a tiny redhead with a small square head with a determined small square chin who, having recently been promoted to the investigative branch of the sheriff's department, was one of the people best able to talk back to Mike.

Now she rotated her flashlight on a trio of boulders and centered on a piece of splintered wood. "Looks like a piece of an oar," she announced. "Something you missed, Mike. Probably been here since Maine belonged to Massachusetts."

"Aw, let's leave it," said Mike. "Otherwise we'll be bringing in a ton of useless flotsam."

"George said anything unnatural. For all we know the murderer came down here in the dark, did a bit of beachcombing, and came up with this as a weapon. Look, he slams the victim over the head with a piece of an oar and later throws it back where it came from. Where someone like you would decide it was part of the usual beach collection and leave it. Tide would take it out. End of weapon."

"Enough already," said Mike. "We take it. Stow it and move along. Times-a-wasting."

"Your word is law," said Katie with a slight edge to her voice. "I'll put the oar in the big paper bag and then in the sack."

At which point one of the uniformed deputies, rubber boots to the knee, waded in to shore holding something bright in his gloved hand.

"Lock," he announced.

"A what?" said Katie.

"Lock. Combination lock. Looks new. In about eighteen inches of water."

"Okay, bag it," said Mike. "Probably from one of the stolen bikes."

"Stolen bikes?" queried Katie. "What stolen bikes?"

"You know," said Mike. "Regular industry. All over for the county. The state. Wherever. Bikes are big business. Some of those suckers cost a fortune."

"You're saying stolen bikes are part of the Ocean Tide scene?" asked Katie. "Listen, combination locks are all over the place. Every shed and toolhouse and summer cottage has a few. And I doubt if a combination lock will make George jump for joy."

"George has never jumped for joy in his life, and hey, the bugger may turn into a weapon after all. Put the thing on the end of string and zing it around your head and whambo! Into the skull and some poor guy's out like a light."

"You, Mike," said Katie, "could be writing some really lousy detective books. You're wasted here."

But Mike wasn't listening. He had bent over and was carefully extracting a 5cc syringe complete with needle from a small fissure in the rock by his feet. This he held up with gloved thumb and forefinger. "In cities," he said to Katie, "you find this on street corners. In the gutter. Stairways. Down drains. Here we find them in clean wholesome family-friendly beach sites. Cute, huh?" And Mike, securing the syringe in a protective tube, slipped it into one of the evidence bags at his feet and returned to topic A. The combination lock.

"That little baby," he said, "needs attention. It just may have something to do with this second body affair. Maybe the murderer got away on a bike, left the bike with a bunch of other bikes on the Ocean Tide property. But threw away the combination lock because it might identify the bike and who rented it. Or owned it. This place is crawling with bikes."

"The rental bikes, most bikes, I think," said Katie, "have IDs stamped on the frame."

"So he filed off the ID."

"You, Mike, are impossible. What do you think the murderer did? Hoisted this unconscious guy who had been banged on the head onto the back of the bike, pedaled along until he came to the seventeenth green. Saw the equipment shed. Broke open the combination lock, but left it hanging on the hasp. Then he opened the shed, dragged in the body, dumped a pile of fertilizer bags on the body, pedaled away. All this while golfers are going up the seventeenth-hole fairway and then hanging around the green while the players hole out and never notice a thing."

"Go on," said Mike, "you've got me hooked."

"Then," finished Katie, "the person who has this mysterious combination lock in his pocket runs down to the beach and tosses the thing in the water. Gets back on his bike and mixes with the crowd. And no, I'm not being sarcastic. That's what you think, isn't it?"

Mike paused in the process of freeing piece of seaweed from yet another rubber glove and shook his head. "Make up what you want, but as far as I'm concerned this lock is as good a weapon as a lot of weird stuff people use."

"Like that plastic-covered chain you guys found around Jason Colley's neck?" said Katie. "I've got a chain like that one for my bike. With a combination lock attached."

"So," said Mike grinning, "right now, Katie, you're the best suspect we've got. Shall I read you your rights?"

But Katie, shaking her head, had moved ahead toward the tide line.

# 7

THE question of hardware used in a lethal manner had been raised by a report from forensics only a few minutes before the discovery of the combination lock in the ocean. George Fitts picked up the phone in the newly established field evidence building, formerly an equipment building for the Pro Shop inventory. Here tables and metal storage shelves, two large refrigerators had been brought in, telephone lines and computer capabilities established, water lines and a sink put in place. The interior of this structure was about as cheerful as most of its kind: an enlarged claustrophobic shoe box.

On the line, Johnny Cuszak. "Howdy, wrangler," said Johnny, who sometimes liked to adopt a rider-on-the-lonesome-trail approach. "Want some news? Somethin' to kinda chaw on. Somethin' a little pecu-li-ar."

"Johnny," said George. "It's been a long day and it's getting longer. We all know you were born in Skowhegan, Maine."

"Hey, a guy's gotta get away from the small town sometime. . . ."

"Not on my watch," said George. "What have you got?"

"Know that chain around the neck, the first victim? Plastic-covered chain about sixteen inches. Remember?"

"I remember," said George with irritation.

"Standard item," said Johnny.

"What'd you mean 'standard'?"

"Standard because it's what half the shops for miles around sell for locking up bikes. A plastic sheath covers the chain so the metal won't abrade the paint job on the bike. Some of those bikes cost a mint. No one wants 'em scratched up."

"Go on."

"Plastic cover is kinda stiff. Heavy-duty. Chain's heavy, too. They make 'em so not just any old pair of wire cutters can slice through them. The thinner cables are easy to cut. Anyway, the one around Jason Colley's neck was the heavy kind. Not so easy to use as a garrote."

"And?"

"I'm saying it might have gone like this. The bang on the head probably knocks the guy out. He goes down. And then whoever did it got that chain around the neck and began twisting. It'd have been awkward. Chains in plastic sheaths don't do a job like rope. Or wire."

"Which means?"

"Not my department, but for what it's worth maybe the murderer hadn't planned to kill the Colley kid. Or hadn't planned exactly how or with what he was going to kill the guy. Say it just happened, a fight, a row. Things get out of control. Guy gets conked and the murderer looks around for a weapon. Sees his bike. Or someone's bike, grabs at the chain and presto! Around the neck. The scenario is your business. All I'm saying is that a plastic-covered bike chain sure wouldn't be my weapon of choice when it comes to strangling. Unless maybe a stick was fixed into the twist to tighten the thing. Would've been easier if we'd found the combination lock. Chains like that usually have a lock hanging from them. Then maybe you could trace the sale."

"Did you get anything off the chain? Hair, fluff, lint? Bits of grass, turf?"

"Bit of a thread from a piece of heavy cloth. A few rubberlike fragments. Lab seems to think that they might have come from one of those coated gloves fishermen wear. So, over to you, George. Start beachcombing. I'll bet you find more'n a hundred stinking gloves." And Johnny Cuszak, whistling the first bars of "The Streets of Laredo," hung up.

At which point the door was simultaneously knocked on and shoved open. Mike Laaka had arrived, followed by Katie Waters. Each bearing a clutch of plastic and paper evidence bags.

"Put the stuff here?" suggested Mike. "Until we can call the lab for a pickup."

George looked with disfavor at the bags, smeared with seaweed residue, reeking of a combination of salt, seaweed, and dead fish.

"Anything?" he asked, tilting back in his chair, rubbing a stubbly chin with one hand. An action that Katie Waters watched with interest. She had long held the view that baldheaded George didn't grow hair; and the sight of a shadow along the Fitts jaw line threw her picture of the sergeant askew.

Mike ran through a summary of the findings. Beginning with the multiple number of fishermen's canvas and rubber gloves, going on to the condoms, the syringe, the child's sneaker, the broken bits of Styrofoam lobster buoys, smashed beer and soda cans, pieces of plastic baggies, candy wrappers, empty oil quarts, all the detritus that comes in with the tide and that kept Joseph Martinelli's beach-cleaning team busy all year round.

Mike kept the best until last. "One more thing," he said, keeping it low-key. "The guys came up with a combination lock. Kind of lock you use on sheds. And bikes. Maybe clothes lockers."

And within seconds of absorbing this information, George got onto the lab team, summoned them forthwith, fast. And then eyeing Mike and Katie allowed them a small measure of praise.

"Not bad," said George. "Might even be useful. Johnny called about that chain around Jason's neck. We decided what was missing was the combination lock. We might just have gotten lucky."

*You mean,* said Katie to herself, *Mike and me, we got lucky. Not you guys.*


It had been for the McKenzie household an endless afternoon. John had spent a good deal of it fending off several curious neighbors who thought they'd drop in and say hello, and then he went with Sarah to answer police questions. Elspeth, dressed in what her husband called her "sympathy outfit," navy blue with white shirt, had spent time with Betty Colley. Betty had certainly not come to terms with Jason's death, how she felt about that death, even how she felt about the boy himself beyond an overwhelming sense of regret for what might have once been.

"Damn miserable mess, the whole business," Betty told Elspeth, who had arrived with two turkey pies from the nearby Brown Bag restaurant's catering department. "Thinking about it won't help me get my mind straight and it might rile it up more." Here Betty sighed deeply. And sank back on one end of an old sofa covered with a blue-and-red afghan and shared by a small brown dog and larger black shaggy one, both of no particular breed. Betty Colley, sensible woman that she was, had seen no reason to throw away comfortable old furniture just because the family had moved into a spanking new cottage.

She pushed the dogs to one side and patted the seat beside

her for Elspeth to sit down. "You stay for a minute. I'm just sitting here useless. There's a whole gang in the kitchen cleaning up and putting supper together. The minister—that's Father Dapple—rang up to say he was coming back, although I can't see why. He's done his thing. But those pies of yours are welcome if he decides to hang in here for a late supper. We'll just have to get used to the idea that Jason got himself in a hot spot and couldn't get out. No point in going on about how we'd warned him. Told him to stay in school. To graduate. Not to hang around with a lot of scum. But he always knew best. And he was pretty persuasive if he wanted anything. Ned gave in to him, of course. Mostly to aggravate me. But," she added, shaking her head sadly, "that Jason, a funny kid, great sense of humor even when he was up to his hips in trouble. And he surely was one of the nicest ball players I've ever seen. Threw straight as an arrow. Could hit, too. Short stop for Rockland High. Varsity when he was only a freshman. Before he dropped out. What a hell of a waste." And she wiped her eyes.

Elspeth expressed her sympathy, offered to help in any capacity, but then just as she was leaving, the news arrived by means of Father Dapple that body number two was that of her long-disappeared husband, Ned. No mistake. He had been identified by his wallet, identification papers, and by Al Moseby, Ned's onetime brother-in-law. And this news, no matter how gently delivered, took out whatever starch was left in Betty. Stunned into silence, she slumped against the wall, then stumbled over to the sofa and sank her head in her hands. Then looked up and shook her head back and forth, and said over and over, "Who'd have thought it? Who'd have thought it?"

"I'm so sorry, Betty, shall I get Alex?" asked Elspeth. "He could get you a sedative. Something to tide you over."

"He's already left something," said Betty's son, eleven-year-old Brian, coming out of the kitchen. "Mom just won't take it. And Dylan's taken off somewhere. On his bike. I thought we were supposed to hang around."

"Oh, God, I'll have to start tying him down. He's always gone when I want him. I'm just at my wits ends so I don't need medication. I need my wits about me . . . if I have any left," said Betty, her head beginning to sink again.

At which point Father Dapple took the seat beside her and began a low comforting mumbling. And Elspeth left them to it, tiptoed out the door and walked the half block to her own cottage around the bend on Alder Way. There she found her husband, John, and their daughter-in-law, Sarah, both just returned from a session with George Fitts.

"A quick go-round, but we have to go back," said John, sleeves rolled up, busy at the dining room sideboard with bottles and an ice bucket. "So Sarah and I need a snort. Keep our blood moving."

"All we had to do," explained Sarah, accepting a rum and orange juice, "was say that we'd found the body—or I had. And give George an idea of the time I saw it. And whether we heard anyone else. Or saw anyone. And how I told John about the body and how he stood watch at the seventeenth green as I ran to call the police."

"Oh, Lord," said Elspeth. "What a day. Poor Betty Colley. I was there when the minister came with the news. Father Somebody. Betty looks like she's been hit by a truck. First her stepson and then her husband. Even if both of them weren't entirely admirable, in fact real troublemakers, well, it's all too much. In fact, when all is said and done, I'd say she'd kept a real fondness for both of them."

"Scotch?" said her husband. "Straight, or ice? Soda?"

"Soda," said Elspeth. "And have we come to the end of it? For tonight, I mean. Surely George Fitts has better things to do than to call you in again. Or come over here. I mean, you two have done your bit." She reached for a glass, dropped in two cubes of ice, splashed in the scotch and filled the glass with soda.

"I've got some Gouda and crackers," she said. "Let's sit

down and regroup. Alex called and said he'd be along in a few minutes. We can at least end the day in peace.

But it was not to be. Footsteps crunched up the short gravel drive, sounded on the doorstep, the door opened, and Alex and George Fitts stepped into the living room.

"Sorry," said George. "This won't take long. Something I forgot to ask Professor McKenzie. And Sarah. Things have been happening so fast that I'm getting careless."

"That," said Alex, "will be the day." Then to his father, "Are you low on scotch or shall I go for the beer?"

"Drink," said his father. "It's what we're here for. To drink and not be merry. Just to settle back. Sergeant Fitts, please accept some alcohol. It will make the evening seem shorter. And sit down. You're making us nervous."

But George, who had never been seen to drink anything but a glass of ale once at a policeman's benefit, shook his head. "I don't need to sit. This won't take more than a minute. This is really for Sarah. I know you found the body under the fertilizer bags. But why did you find it?"

"Good question," said Alex. "I think it was magnetism. My wife is drawn to these things."

"Oh, do shut up," said Sarah. "I was just in the area."

"But," said George, "those two buildings, the big maintenance shed with the tools and the small fertilizer storage shed. They were just behind the eighteenth green. Do you play golf?"

Sarah stared at him. "No, I don't play golf. What are you getting at?"

"He's wondering," said Alex, "what possessed you to take a sudden interest in golf course maintenance equipment. And grass fertilizers. And since you're not a golfer, you couldn't have been looking for a lost ball."

Sarah wrinkled her brow. Then light broke. "You mean, George, I didn't tell you?"

"Tell me what?" said George, who having refused a drink, stood over the party like a bird of ill omen.

"Why I looked in the shed."

"No," said George, tight-lipped. A man whose patience had been badly tried.

"The boy," said Sarah. "That boy. He came yelling back. Screaming."

"What boy?" Alex and George and Elspeth spoke with one voice.

"The boy. John, I told you about the boy. Didn't I?"

John shook his head. "You may have. Probably did. Slipped my mind. Important thing is you found a body."

"Go on," said George in a metallic voice, "about the boy. From the beginning."

And Sarah described the almost hysterical boy, his fall, his rising up and running back toward the Lodge. How she chased him, how he disappeared. How she hadn't seen him since.

"And you told this to Professor McKenzie?" demanded George.

"I think so," said Sarah uncertainly. Had she? Hadn't she? "Things were happening pretty fast, so I'm not sure."

"His name?" asked George, without much hope.

But Sarah hadn't gotten his name.

"Description?"

Here Sarah was more helpful. "White T-shirt, baggy pants. Khaki, I think. White-faced, scared looking. And yellow hair. Flopping all over his face. And he was skinny."

"That's it?" said George.

"Sneakers. Dirty. You know those clumpy ones kids wear. Laces untied, I think. As I said, everything went by so fast. When I saw I couldn't catch up with him, I went back in the direction he'd come from. The boy hadn't told me why he was frightened, and I thought maybe it was a rabid skunk. Or a rabid something. Or some drunk who'd scared him. Anyway, I found a little path behind the seventeenth green and saw that it led to two sheds."

"And you looked around," said Alex.

"And I looked around," said Sarah. "In the window. The

big shed had tools, you know, shovels and rakes. Nothing else. But the combination lock was open on the little shed. So I went in. I had a stick with me in case I needed to protect myself from something, and, well, you know the rest."

"The rest might have been," said Alex, voice rising, "that you, too, would have been found under a pile of fertilizer bags. That stick you carried could have worked as an incentive, red rag to a bull. You were asking for it, my beloved."

"Okay, okay, but I didn't get stuffed under fertilizer bags," said Sarah with asperity. "I was careful. I looked over my shoulder. No one followed me down the path. The big shed was empty. The little shed behind it was open. And no one was in there either. No one alive, I mean. All I was doing was trying to prevent some golfers—or anyone else—from being bitten by a rabid skunk. Or mixing it up with some crazy jerk. And I was worried about the boy. Maybe somebody had been after him. Child abuse. You remember child abuse."

George gave a thin smile. "You win, Sarah. Yes, after the boy came out yelling, something had to be done. Something like you first calling the police and not going into that shed by yourself."

"Remember, George," said Sarah sweetly, "that half the police in Knox County were crawling around looking for clues connected with Jason Colley's murder, and you and Mike were probably busy upsetting Betty Colley, the poor woman. And her family. *And* the Moseby family."

"All right, Sarah. I'm glad you remembered about the boy. We'll try to locate him." said George. "And we will be grateful if you keep an eye out for him."

Sarah shook her head. "There must be a lot of boys around who look just like him. Only the floppy hair stands out and there are probably ten others with just the same sort of look. Besides, I don't live here. I just visit Ocean Tide. To see Elspeth and John."

"Visit more often, then. Be casual, walk around, look in on the playground. Camp Ocean Tide property. They've got a soccer field and baseball diamond. And if you happen to see the boy, don't grab him. We don't want him frightened. He's probably plenty frightened as it is. Call us. Don't ask him for his name. Ask someone else who he is. Above all, whatever you do, don't stalk him."

"I don't stalk people, George. And I don't scare them. It's the boy who scared me."

With which George Fitts had to be content. He bowed out, first inviting Alex's attendance tomorrow on Jason Colley's autopsy in Augusta, urged John McKenzie and Sarah not to indulge in idle chatter. Or any sort of chatter about either case. Good night.

"I do not chatter," announced John, after the door had closed behind George. "He's treating us like a bunch of infants."

"That's George's way," said Alex mildly. "But he's Mr. Efficiency. Not lovable, but good at his job."

"And George on his job," added Sarah, "gives me a good case of the creeps."

Then, after a brief discussion on the subject of scrambled eggs for dinner, these declined by Sarah and Alex, the senior McKenzies wearily settled down for a late meal, and Alex and Sarah agreed that going home for a bowl of canned soup and an English muffin sounded like the promise of heavenly peace, and went their way.


Eight in the morning of Sunday, May 28, brought to the Ocean Tide community a greater police presence, the adding of more electronic equipment to the VIP Golfers Guesthouse, which had been taken over for the purpose of informal interrogations. The last nine holes of the golf course and the practice holes had been kept off limits but a number of plainclothesmen had not confined their efforts to these holes and swept the course from the first tee to the last green, causing general confusion and shouts of "Fore!" as the team wove back and forth across the fairway clutching their evidence bags.

At the same time, Mike Laaka returned to the beach scene with two men in underwater gear and a small skiff. The finding of the combination lock had seemed to George Fitts a good reason to do some further nosing around underwater. Fortunately for these efforts, the wind hovered between five and ten knots from the southwest and the ocean remained unruffled.

Twelve-thirty brought Sarah and Alex, at Elspeth's urgent request, to the community's famed Sunday brunch. Elspeth was urgent because she said it was time—recent murders aside—to start talking about the Uncle Fergus birthday bash-cum-anniversary party she'd been thinking about. She reported that she'd been to the Ocean Tide nondenominational, all-purpose chapel for a brief memorial service for the two victims, that interment and a proper funeral would come when the victims' bodies were released, and that she'd looked in on Betty afterward.

"Betty's getting her feet back on the ground," said Elspeth. "Her family, the Mosebys, that is, have rallied around and at least two ministers seem to be in attendance. And George Fitts's henchmen have metastasized, so there's not much we can do today. Except retire and deal with our own domestic affairs, which are still in a muddle."

"As I've told Elspeth, this Uncle Fergus affair," said John McKenzie, "is over my possibly dead body. More important, I have an idea for Sarah. A summer job."

"Oh," said Sarah, faintly. "How interesting." She struggled to keep her face straight and as if welcoming the news. But a sudden horrid vision rose of herself loading onto a computer an entire manuscript dealing with some arcane part of the Old English syllabus while John paced about the room, shouting corrections for words using the eth, the ash, and the thorn.

But Alex, reading his wife's reaction, changed the subject. "We're looking forward to the feast, but we can't stay all day.

Sarah has to get back and I've got to look in at the hospital and then drop in on the autopsy, actually both autopsies, one after the other, at four o'clock."

Joseph Martinelli's Sunday brunch was a triumph from the word go. Pâté, lobster in various forms, clams, roast beef, ham, jellied this and that, salads, flaming desserts, cold desserts, kosher and vegetarian selections from special tables, all these were crowd pleasers.

"I suppose," said Elspeth, as she, John, Sarah, and Alex made their way into the dining room, "that there'll be a lot of empty tables. Everyone talking in whispers. I mean, you can see at least two police cars from some of the windows. Two bodies don't make for festive brunches."

"Wrong," said John looking over her head. "The place is stuffed. Could have told you. People go for things like this. Moths to the flame. Feeding frenzy."

"Not quite so bad as that," said a voice. "It's sort of what I told Mr. Martinelli. I think people do react to excitement, even if it's murder." It was Carly Thompson, who then walked with them to their table and helped them pull out chairs and sit.

"I'm not your waiter," said Carly. "He'll be along in a minute. We are a bit shorthanded because the police are taking statements from all the staff. What I want to know, Sarah, has Professor McKenzie told you about the job?"

John McKenzie raised a hand. "Not yet. But I'll tell her now. Miss Thompson thought I might be just the person to tutor some young brats who are failing English. Bring them up to speed. Not my cup of tea. I've done my bit with freshmen and I've too many battle scars. Kids are for people like Sarah. She's young and strong and needs a job."

"You mean summer school," said Sarah, puzzled.

"A tutoring job," said Carly. "Two, maybe three times a

week. Couple of hours each session. It's particularly important that we get someone with experience."

"These are hard-core cases?" asked Sarah, "From some youth correction home, out on parole. On probation. Something like that?"

"No felons. Four boys who might need a bit of managing."

"Sarah," said Alex. "Am I right, you want a part-time job, but not anything that will blight the whole summer?"

"Just blight part of it," said Sarah. She looked up at Carly. "Out with it. What do I have to do, use chains and whips? Join the Marine Corps?"

"The families are what you call troubled. Troubled as of yesterday. And the day before."

"You're saying . . ." Sarah began.

"I'm saying that it's Betty Colley's two boys and Sherry and Al Moseby's boys. The two Colley kids are okay, I think, but kind of wild. All over the map. Betty's always hunting them down. The youngest Moseby reminds me of Eddie Haskell sometimes, sometimes a perfectly normal kid. The middle Moseby thinks he's pretty cool. And maybe he is."

"I don't know," said Sarah stalling. "But I did just leave an ad with some of the local papers about tutoring."

"So here's your chance," said Carly. "The boys are clean. No suspensions from school for bomb threats. No drugs. Nothing weird. I asked around."

Sarah considered. The timing was right, the place was familiar. She could handle the preteen and teen set; she'd done it before. As for the money . . .

Carly read her mind. "Above the going rate for tutors. The parents want the tutoring to start the minute school's out, mid-June, which means in about two weeks. So let me know tomorrow and I'll set up a meeting with the Colleys and the Mosebys."

"Won't they be tied up with the police? The investigation. Funerals to plan?"

"It won't hurt a bit if they're distracted by a perfectly normal plan to help their boys pass English courses."

"Which I suppose they hate," said Sarah. "You have no idea how many adults come up to me, and after they hear that I teach English, tell me how much they hated it. How it ruined their high school days. Or college years."

"But you," said Carly with her broad smile, "will be the one to shine a light into their dim little heads. So I'll be hearing from you."

Carly departed and the McKenzie tribe settled down to their Sunday brunch. And as Sarah worked her way through fresh slices of cantaloupe, the salmon salad, the buttery croissants, she decided that Carly had it all wrong. The inhabitants of the Ocean Tide community may have come on the crest of excitement, of curiosity, but now the sense of one big party was gone. The atmosphere had turned edgy. Every now and then a laugh would sound, but it would be a lonely sound in an empty space, out of tune. Intrusive. Murder, no, two murders, did make a difference. Each diner faced with his loaded plate seemed to be inspecting it without enthusiasm. It was as if each were thinking that his next-door neighbor, the member of his golf foursome, his or her bridge partner, the man or woman over there at the next table, one of the waiters now decanting the wine, bringing the coffee, pushing the dessert trolley, had perhaps sought out two living persons and, for some unspeakable reason, beaten them, strangled them, suffocated them by dumping large bags of fertilizer on them.

Sarah gave herself a mental slap, told herself to come out of it. Make an effort. Because no one else at her table was. John McKenzie was scowling at a thick slab of roast beef that resisted his efforts to cut through it, Elspeth had laid down her fork and was staring at a large watercolor of pink peonies hanging on the opposite wall, and Alex had twice in the last few minutes looked at his watch.

"So," said Sarah to the group in general. "What do think about this tutoring job? I should take it, I suppose. It's exactly what I had in mind and leaves part of the week free. . . ." She stopped suddenly, sat up straight and stared out of the window.

"Free for what?" asked Elspeth, bringing her attention back to the table.

But Sarah had half risen, her napkin falling to the floor. "Excuse me," she said. "I have to see about something." And she was gone, twisting past the diners, the waiters, the dessert trolley, past the piano player by the triple window, brushing his arm so that "Smoke Gets in Your Eyes" missed a whole beat, and then she was out. Down the front steps, around to the back in a fast walk. "Don't frighten the boy," George had warned her. Well, she wasn't going to frighten him, but after that flash of a yellow head of hair bent over the handlebars of a bike had passed the dining room window, she knew she might never have such a good chance.

And there he was, some fifty yards ahead. Heading for one of the bike trails that circled the children's play area and outdoor swimming pool.

Sarah increased her pace. To a jog, to a run. He wasn't going very fast. She might be able to catch up, just to get another close look at him. Perhaps, ask him—no, not his name—something harmless. The time. The make of his bike. Where the bike rental shop was located. And she was gaining because he had stopped, put one foot on the ground. Seemed to be fiddling with his gears. And then Sarah, taking an awkward step, stumbled. The boy jerked his head around, hesitated for a second, then stamped on his pedal, threw his leg across the bar and took off like bolt of blue metal. And was gone. Around a small outcropping of pines. Out of sight in seconds.

# 8

SARAH, fighting the urge to shout "Come back" at the top of her lungs, stood for a minute gazing at the clump of pines as if the act of watching would force the boy to reverse direction and come riding back into view. Then she reluctantly turned around and walked slowly toward the Lodge. Toward her unfinished meal.

Back toward the curious McKenzies. To listen to questions, to reminders that she mustn't approach, chase, scare the missing boy. "Remember what George told you," Alex would say. Well, she'd done a real job of it. She had chased him and then by stumbling had called attention to herself. And if the look of surprise—or was it terror?—on the boy's face when he saw her meant anything, she had scared the daylights out of him. Which in itself was curious. What had she done during their earlier brief meeting to make him be afraid of her? Had he just then even recognized her? To him she might just have been a generic adult back when he'd stumbled, and now he was jumpy about anyone behind him? Certainly any boy who had found a dead body would be jumpy.

Sarah put this question into the back of her mind and reviewed what she would say to her critical audience. Had she accomplished anything by the pursuit? Did she now know any better than before what the boy really looked like? When he wheeled by the dining room window it was the sight of the shock of unkempt yellow hair that had grabbed her attention. The hair like a flag that had levered her out of her seat and after him. But what else? Well, for what it was worth, his T-shirt was not white, but blue this time. Medium blue. And his bicycle? Dark blue, she thought. Not helpful. His face? His shape, his figure, his frame? Nothing new there. Just a skinny kid. If he and two similar yellow-haired boys turned up in a police lineup, she wouldn't have had a single mark, mole, freckle, snaggle tooth, to distinguish him from the others. When she had first seen him, she hadn't even noticed the color of his eyes. The shape of his nose. Everything had happened too fast. One fact she remembered now, when he came shouting out of the woods, his voice went up and down. Mostly up. Conclusion: his voice was changing but hadn't finished the job. As she had told herself after their first encounter, he was an ordinary twelve-or thirteen-year-old boy. Fourteen or fifteen, but that was a stretch.

Sarah rejoined her party in time to refuse anything on the dessert trolley that was rolled up for her inspection. In fact, the idea of forcing an éclair or a custard tart down her throat was a disagreeable one. Instead, forestalling questions, she gave the three listeners a hasty run-through of her departure and pursuit, and then, chin up, confronted the three.

"So, yes, I may have screwed up. Scared the boy who will now avoid any adult female coming up behind him. Anyone he thinks might be chasing him. He'll probably go into hiding. Put on glasses or dye his hair purple."

"I think you're missing the important point," said John

McKenzie, looking more animated than Sarah had seen him in some time. "Just why is this boy afraid, why was he running away? I don't think from you, Sarah, because we all agree you're not a threatening-looking human."

Sarah frowned at him. "You all make me feel like a complete blob. But okay, you have a point. Since I didn't do anything except tell him to take it easy when he fell, there was obviously another reason for his taking off."

"His running off suggests," said John, "that he was already half scared to death when he ran away."

"Well," said Sarah, "finding those legs sticking from under those fertilizer bags is pretty scary.

"Or was he frightened for some other reason?" asked Elspeth. "Doing something he shouldn't have been doing. Aren't children that age always doing something they shouldn't be?"

"Let's leave all that for the experts," said Alex. "It's something I find myself saying a lot, little good that it's done."

"Alex," said his mother. "Don't be boring. And don't go on as if you're giving a lecture to idiots. It's something a lot of doctors have trouble with. Try to work on it."

"Amen," said Sarah, grinning at her husband.

Alex shook his head at the two women. "I'm driven to lecturing because of the excesses of my wife. And sometimes of my mother. And probably my father's up to something I don't even know about. But now I've got to get over to the autopsy. Actually, two autopsies."

Elspeth sighed. "Oh, dear, I'd forgotten. Well, I suppose you must, but we haven't even talked about the party. The end of June isn't that far away and I'll be away for ten days in Provence so I need everyone's input as soon as possible. There's so much to do. John and I need to start planning."

"No," corrected John. "Elspeth plans, not John."

"For now," said Elspeth, "we'll head back to our cottage. Or house. The dwelling. Whatever it is. Actually it's neither fish nor fowl."

"Semi-assisted living," said John, standing up. "Sarah, if you need a backup about your little chase event, I'd be glad to face George Fitts if he gets mean. He reminds me of my college physics teacher. A reptilian man who could strike and recoil before you could start to defend yourself."

"George is okay, really," said Sarah without conviction. "He's just too damn focused. No time for chitchat."

"An excellent thing in a state police detective," said Alex. "I admire George. I could use him to cut down on my patient load. Now good-bye, all, and Sarah, if it makes you feel better about your coming confession, George will be at the autopsy; you'll be dealing with Mike Laaka. Or someone similar."

Sarah smiled and rose. "Good. Piece of cake."

It was not a piece of cake. She found Mike returning to the evidence building from yet another trip to the beach. His trousers were muddy, his shoes and socks wet and filled with sand and small stones, he had not had lunch and was altogether irritable. He heard Sarah's story with narrowed eyes and then allowed himself the luxury of swearing.

"Christ! Christ in heaven. What a screwup. Here's this kid we're trying to find. Maybe a witness even. A kid who may have seen more than two feet sticking out from fertilizer bags. May have seen someone leaving, sneaking off. And there you go scaring the bejeezus out of him. Twice, yet. First chasing him to the Lodge and then, by God, today you do it again. Talk about subtle. You shouldn't be allowed out."

Sarah, controlling herself with difficulty, said through clenched teeth that they wouldn't even know about the boy if she hadn't spotted him coming out of the woods. "It was luck, I know, but I was in the right place at the right time. And he shouldn't be so hard to find, even if he's scared of me. And it's probably not me, he may be scared of anybody. Most of all the police. I mean, finding a dead body does have an effect on the nervous system."

But Mike, having blown his fuse, settled back. "Okay, okay.

At least we know the kid is still around, meaning he might be a resident, not some visitor brought in for the Fitness Center affair."

"Or," said Sarah, "he and his family—assuming he has one—"

"Which we don't assume these days," said Mike.

"Is here for the weekend. Or a week. Rented one of the condos."

"Which means," said Mike, grabbing a notepad and scribbling, "we'd better get a move on and find him fast. Okay, Mrs. Poirot, any details you picked up in your most recent pursuit?"

"More like Inspector Clouseau," said Sarah ruefully. "But yes. Blue T-shirt, navy blue bike, and, something I just remembered: his voice is just breaking."

"Big deal," said Mike. "That the best you can do?"

"There's that mop of yellow hair. And he's skinny."

"That description takes us almost nowhere. And listen, Sarah, for all this kid knows, you're part of the murder event. Or the perpetrator himself. Herself. You're the first thing he comes to when he runs yelling out of the woods and then he sees you. And he doesn't want to have anything to do with anyone so close to the body. So he splits."

"Heads for safety. For people he knows. A place he knows. In this case, the Fitness Center party scene. All of which means," Sarah added unhappily, "that as far as finding this boy is concerned, it won't be easy. He'll be looking over his shoulder for evil spirits. Or murderers. Or me in case I'm one or the other."

"He may have recognized you today. Sneaking after him. So now maybe you're double danger." Here Mike sighed and shook his head. "Having you around is beginning to make my head hurt. More than it does already. Lucky you don't live at Ocean Tide. My advice would be to stay away. Visit the McKenzies by telephone. E-mail."

"You should know," said Sarah, "that I've just accepted a job tutoring four kids in English. Which they're apparently failing. Tutoring here at Ocean Tide when school gets out in June."

"Well, shit," said Mike. "Maybe you'll be holed up in some house on the edge of the property. Then you won't be able to chase this kid and mess up these two cases we've got on the stove."

"As a matter of fact," Sarah replied, not meeting Mike's eye, "I'm tutoring Betty Colley's and the Moseby boys."

Mike shook his head slowly back and forth. "All I can say is double shit. What is it about you, Sarah? You're like a piece of Velcro. Everything sticks to you. Can I interest you in applying to the Maine Police Academy? Dress you in uniform, put you on the streets, night shift. Inner city. Vice squad."

Sarah turned on her heel, headed for the door, which she intended to slam. But was called back.

"Hey, wait up," said Mike. "I didn't mean some of that. I'm just about wiped out and I laid it on you. Look, you know me well enough to know I shoot off my big mouth a lot. We need you. You've seen the kid, we haven't. And forget this crap about the kid being scared of you. You personally. He was scared period. You're the most harmless-looking person I know."

"Thanks a lot, Mike" said Sarah, still bristling. "If I hear once again that I look harmless, I'll throw up. Someday I'm going to start a riot and scare the bejeezus out all of you."

"Sit down. Cool down. All I'm saying is that kids and dogs don't naturally run away when you turn up. Listen, that kid, he'd probably have run if Santa Claus or the Easter Bunny or the Tooth Fairy started after him. Did he get a good look at you when you chased him just now?"

"No," Sarah admitted. "He just gave a quick glance and took off."

"Were you wearing the same clothes you had on Saturday?"

"No," said Sarah. "Very different."

"Okay. So it wasn't personal. The kid had a knee-jerk reaction to someone running behind him. If you see him again, please, please let us know first. If you bump into him face to face look your usual wholesome and friendly self. If he wants to chat, okay, but don't push it. And on second thought, it's probably a very good idea that you're going to be around Ocean Tide this summer. If you're tutoring the Colley and Moseby kids, well, you may pick up something useful. Keep your ears open. Kids pick up a lot of stuff. George doesn't want anyone to step on his official shoes, but he never minds a little helpful gossip. You know, even if he'd flat out deny it, George might even like you. As much as George likes anyone. Which isn't saying much."

With those cheering words in her ears, Sarah departed and headed for the McKenzie homestead intending to pick up Patsy and head home. To regroup and examine the possibilities for the coming weeks. Set up a tutoring program, keep a low profile but a sharp eye out for the boy. Get some exercise, do some energetic biking when the mountain bike trail was reopened. And stay well clear of any of George Fitts's team of investigators.

But instead of a quick good-bye, Sarah found Elspeth McKenzie in something that would have been called in Victorian novels, "a state." Fury mixed with tears. Tears that Sarah saw with surprise and concern. Her mother-in-law looked all of her sixty-two years, standing there by the garage door gesturing at Carly Thompson. "It was right in the garage," she was saying in a high, overwrought voice. "And I locked it. At least I meant to. A long black cable. And a combination lock."

"Was the garage door open?" asked Carly.

"No," said Elspeth. "Not usually. Because we have all sorts of things in there we don't want taken. Some things we haven't sorted out yet. Some of John's books. And his old Raleigh. The lawn mower. A canoe."

"But the door wasn't locked?" persisted Carly.

Elspeth hesitated. "Well, no. Sometimes we leave it a little way up. Sometimes we close it. And lock it. Or don't lock it.

But my bicycle must have been taken while we were over at the brunch. I didn't actually check this morning. But Ocean Tide is supposed to be a place where you don't have to lock everything up. Next thing, you'll tell me we need bars on the windows and radar."

"No, no," said Carly in a soothing voice. "What you need to do now is to call Security to come and then give them the details."

"John's called them," said Elspeth. "I just grabbed you when I saw your car coming around the corner. Sarah, there you are. My bicycle has been stolen. The new one. John bought it for my birthday. From that bike shop in Cambridge just before we moved. It was a surprise. It was because of all the bike trails here, and it cost a small fortune."

Sarah put her hand on Elspeth's and pressed it sympathetically. It was pretty certain that she and John were sliding into a state of deep fatigue. Both were still worn out with the move. And Elspeth had been rushing about trying to bolster Betty Colley. Well, someone needed to bolster Elspeth. And John, who had that tricky heart condition.

"It's a safe community," insisted Carly. "About as safe as you can get. But bike theft is very big. It's a regular growth industry. Especially the touring, the mountain bikes. The ones for racing. And we do ask people to use locks. Leave them in locked garages."

Sarah broke in. "Just how many bikes have been taken?"

"You mean in Knox County?" asked Carly. "The police probably know, but I don't. We've lost about twenty or more here in the last month. Mostly the rentals. People leave them lying around, leaning against a tree. Forget to use the locks. And of course some of the special rentals cost mega-bucks. The bike shop features high-class bike rentals, not just heavy-duty clunkers. Mr. Martinelli claims resorts all over the country that use rental bike systems lose a lot of inventory every year."

"And bikes," added Sarah, "are such an easy steal. Take

off a wheel and toss it in the back of your SUV or pickup or van."

"Or hop on it and ride away," said Elspeth. "It's all anyone has to do. Well, here's Security. Thank heavens." This as a Ocean Tide Ford van with a logo on its flank rolled up and parked, and a uniformed man emerged.

"At least," said Carly, with an attempt at distraction, "you didn't find a body in your garage." She paused, struggling. "No, I didn't mean that, and I wasn't trying to be funny. But everything has been a bit much. It must be getting to me."

"Your remark, Ms. Thompson," said John McKenzie, emerging from the house, "was not in the best taste, but I sympathize because it's exactly like something I'd say."

And Sarah, finding her offer to stay refused, that Elspeth had pulled herself together, slipped into the house, fastened a leash to a somnolent Patsy, and departed, promising to turn up in the morning. Ready for any task Elspeth might devise. Unpacking, sorting, bike hunting. Or any distraction John might find agreeable.


At nine o'clock that evening Alex found Sarah half-asleep in the living room of their partly fixed-up, partly falling-down farmhouse set into long sloping Sawmill Road close to the little town of Bowmouth, home to Bowmouth College and the Mary Starbox Hospital, Sarah's and Alex's places of employment. She was lying on the sofa, Patsy at her feet, a television remote control held loosely in one drooping hand while a nature program on the tube featured close-up shots of the home life of the prairie dog.

She struggled into a sitting position. "God, what time is it? I've just been sacking out. How did the autopsies go? And have you had dinner? I haven't. Didn't have the energy."

"I picked up Chinese on the way home." Alex put a large brown paper bag on the table and began to separate small white cartons. "Come on, we'll eat first and then I'll give you the news."

"Keeping the gruesome parts out."

Alex nodded. They settled with heaped plates in front of the television, ate silently, and watched the prairie dog life give way to that of the diamondback rattlesnake, to the coyote, the scorpion, and finally, in a burst of background music, to a soaring bald eagle.

"That's the thing I like about nature programs," said Sarah, putting her chopsticks together on her plate, "They do try to end on an upbeat note and not leave you with a snake swallowing a baby bird. Or some lion tearing a zebra into pieces." She thrust her thumb into her fortune cookie and pulled out the slip of paper. "I'm going to have a happy encounter at time of full moon. How about you?"

"I will meet person of my dreams when the snow falls," said Alex. "That obviously gives me time to find someplace to stash you."

"With a heavy financial settlement and all the furniture," said Sarah, making a face at him. "Okay, back to topic A. Tell me what happened. Jason was murdered, wasn't he?"

"No doubt about that. A blow on the head probably knocked the boy unconscious. Then that chain around his neck finished the job. The real question is *where* was he killed. According to Johnny Cuszak, even allowing for all the wet and mud there wasn't a sign of a scuffle, or a fall near the practice golf green nor on any of the trails. He thinks the body was brought in and dumped."

"But why on earth would someone go to the trouble to transport a body to a well-patrolled, inhabited area like Ocean Tide? I mean, wouldn't it have been easier to leave him off in the backcountry, in the woods? Or dump him in a pond? Plenty of unpopulated places where no one would find the body for ages."

"Agreed. It's an oddity. George is thinking maybe Jason

was murdered pretty close to Ocean Tide, maybe on the other side of Route One. The parking lot behind one of those fast-food places. If that happened, then the eastern end of the Ocean Tide property was the closest thing around to a wilderness area."

"Hardly a wilderness area," said Sarah. "Bikers, hikers, joggers. Golfers."

"Remember it'd been raining for a week. Cold. Windy. Nasty weather for anything outdoors. The police think he was probably dumped at night. Not too much risk."

"Okay, I'll accept that. So what about the father, Ned Colley?"

"Blow to the head. Dead when the fertilizer bags were dumped on him."

"You mean someone toted a dead body down the golf course and dumped it? Talk about stupid. Golfers coming and going. Hunting for balls. That shed was just off the seventeenth green where any minute, if a golfer didn't turn up, someone from the green-keeping crew might walk in for fertilizer."

"I don't suppose," said Alex, "there's a guidebook called *Best Places to Leave a Dead Body*. Think of those bodies that are packed into the trunks of cars, stuck in closets, fitted into freezers."

"All right," said Sarah reluctantly. "But somehow I think that next to a practice hole or in a shed are just plain dumb choices."

"So you're dealing with a murderer who makes dumb choices. Or was in a panic. Short of time. Or, just maybe he wanted the bodies to show up. Cause a commotion."

"A political statement for reasons not yet discovered?"

"Or a gang statement. Time to erase a couple of rats. Who knows."

"You're saying the murdering mind moves in mysterious ways—which sounds like the first line of a very bad poem."

"Let's leave it at that for now," said Alex. "Time for bed."

"One more thing," said Sarah. "Your mother's upset. Besides trying to get settled, your mother's been running around, trying to help out at Betty Colley's house. And now her bike. It's a sort of last straw."

Alex sat up straight. "Her bike! What about her bike? Dad just bought it for her. It cost a bloody fortune. The way they talk about it you'd think she had a Bentley. Or a BMW at the very least."

"I forgot to say. It's been stolen. Right out of the garage."

"What! Her bike stolen! I convinced Dad she needed a new bike. He won't give up his Raleigh, but my mother was riding around on an old cast-off of my sister's."

"She's really frazzled about it. But admitted she left the garage door half-open. Might not have locked the bike."

"She never did, not even in Cambridge. But no wonder she's frazzled. And Dad, too, probably. That's all those two need."

"Poor old dears."

"My mother and my father would not like being called 'old dears,' " said Alex.

"We can both check on them tomorrow," said Sarah. "I'll be going over anyway to see about this tutoring job at Ocean Tide with the Colley and the Moseby boys."

"Speaking of the devil. Or the devils."

"It may be a bit touchy. I don't know how close any of the boys were to Jason. Or Ned. I gather that neither has functioned as a family member for the last few years, so maybe the kids won't be that upset. But I'll tread softly. See how the land lies."

"So good. That settles your summer job, doesn't it? Leaves you some free time. But not free time to get mixed into George and Mike's scene. Please, my darling, wonderful, most cherished wife, don't let your remembrances of any previous snoop work you've done contaminate this tutoring job."

"Never," said Sarah stoutly. "And I don't know what you're talking about. That was my evil twin. She's in Tibet this summer. Making yurts."

"Good place for her. Well, damn again about my mother's bike."

"Carly gave me a lecture about the fact that bike stealing is a very in thing. So I guess no community is immune. Unless it's the Maine State Prison with guards and barbed wire. And I for one," Sarah said virtuously, "will lock my bike when I ride around Ocean Tide. Even though my bike's six years old and no one would want it."

"But they might want you, my love. I can live with bike theft—even my mother's bike theft. But not with two murders in one community and you riding in remote places. Don't bike alone. I'll say the same to my parents."

"I'll take Patsy. No one would dare to challenge an Irish Wolfhound."

"Bike with people. Patsy *and* my father. Or my mother. Or even your loving husband."

Sarah smiled, slipped her arm around his neck, kissed him behind the ear, and said, "That's it, a bicycle built for two. We can pedal into old age."

"Right now," said Alex, "it's a bed built for two I want."


That night, some time after his family had finally settled down after a long and generally miserable day, Dylan Colley slipped out of the lower half of his bunk bed, crept on stealthy feet to the kitchen, opened a drawer, withdrew a pair of utility scissors, returned to the bathroom next to his bedroom, turned on the light, closed the door quietly. Then, stripping off the T-shirt that did service as a pajama top, leaned over a wastebasket and began handful by handful to cut his hair down to the scalp. This operation took some fifteen minutes. The pieces of straw-colored hair were then carefully picked out of the basket and flushed down the toilet, the light turned off, the scissors returned, and Dylan, resembling nothing so much as an inexpertly plucked chicken, returned to his bed and slept soundly.

# 9

MONDAY morning on May 29 found at least one member of the Ocean Tide community experiencing a modified kind of hell. Driving around the back side of Alder Way intending to give support to her mother-in-law in the matter of the stolen bicycle, Sarah spied Betty Colley sitting on her small front porch, looking like a person in the grip of some powerful emotion. Betty sat bolt upright, her hands gripping the arms of her rocking chair, glaring at the world beyond her porch. Where, Sarah wondered, slowing her car, was her support group, neighbors, the minister, her children? Probably inside dusting and dealing with dishes and beds, activities that might have helped Betty's state of mind. After all, vigorous action could sometimes do wonders for those low moments that lie in wait for most humans.

But Sarah, as the car crept toward the house, saw that Betty was not exactly in a black funk; from her posture and the set of her chin, she looked like a woman in a state of rigid fury. Betty, Sarah had concluded from the first moment of meeting her, was made of tough material. However, she had received a double blow and might like a few sympathetic words, even from a comparative stranger.

Sarah pulled to the curb, climbed out and waved. She saw that Betty had chosen a black pair of slacks and a long gray cotton shirt as an attempt to honor—or at least acknowledge—the recent events. Her face, now that Sarah was closer, looked swollen, her eyes puffy. But her red hair was pulled back in a fierce knot, her lips tight, and Sarah would have bet that Betty could hold her own even with the likes of George Fitts at his sharpest.

Sarah walked over to the porch, climbed the three stairs and extended a hand to Betty who started to get up.

"No, don't get up, please," said Sarah. And, as Betty lowered herself again to the rocking chair, Sarah began a rather confused introduction: "I'm Sarah Deane, I met you with my mother-in-law at the party. Elspeth McKenzie and I are so sorry about all this and if there's anything I can do—" She was cut short.

"I remember you," said Betty, "and thanks for stopping. But there's not a blessed damn thing—pardon my English—anyone can do. We've all got to get through this business as best we can. I suppose I'm still real upset—yesterday I was knocked off my feet. But today I'm feeling like Ned just has himself to blame because he never looked for trouble even if he was up to his hips in it. Thought he could talk himself out of anything, and he usually could. It was his specialty, and he always had buddies egging him on. Now, that's not nice of me, but I'm not feeling so nice. First Jason and then Ned. God Almighty, they were a pair."

Here Betty turned and gazed out beyond the porch in the direction of the ocean as she expected to see two ghosts moving toward her. Two irresponsible ghosts. Then she shook her head slowly. "I knew in my heart Jason was probably going to end up at the wrong end of the stick, get himself destroyed somehow. And Ned, after I married him, pretty fast I saw he wasn't going to be anyone's prize husband and father for more than a few years. Oh, but he could be a real joker. Fun, games, and a bottle of beer. But steady, it just wasn't in him. Jason, the same. Talk about your chips off old blocks. So I thought I was prepared for anything. Anything bad." And now Betty's voice became thick, she paused, and almost angrily pushed a tear that had started down her cheek.

"But you can't be prepared, really," Sarah put in.

"That's it. You're never that ready." She paused again, struggled for words, and then, sitting up even straighter, said in a firm voice. "We'll get through it, all these police statements. All of us. My sister Sherry and Al Moseby's family. But it's hard on Sherry. She lives such an organized life. Everything just so. Goes to pieces when something messy happens. But for me, I hate the idea of the police poking their noses into my life. Especially Mike Laaka."

"But Mike's a sensible man," Sarah began.

Betty interrupted. "Trouble is, I've known Mike all my life. Even baby-sat him a few times. So I don't like him asking a bunch of personal questions. As to that ice cube, George Fitts, my life is none of his damn business."

Since there was little point in trying to defend the police, Sarah switched gears. "It must be terribly hard on your children."

"Well, yes. The boys, they're that upset and excited all at the same time. Dylan couldn't sleep last night and cut off his hair—I suppose it was some sort of crazy reaction to it all. Kids do things like that. I remember being mad at my math teacher once and painting my face green. And this morning Dylan got Brian to chop *his* hair off. Neither of them were fit to be seen and with my having so much to do, I could have wrung their necks like I used to wring my chickens. I mean, what a pain. But I got out the clippers, cleaned the boys up and I suppose short hair is good for summer. Dylan claims buzz cuts are in, but I think it's kind of a reaction to these murders. They had to do *something* and at least they didn't get into alcohol or break some windows. Steal someone's bike."

"Stealing bikes!" Sarah's voice went up in a squeak. "Are the kids, I mean not yours, but a lot of the kids around, are they stealing bikes?"

"It's the new thing," said Betty. "One of Dylan's friends and one of the Moseby boys—Tim, he's the youngest—they were talking about it and I overheard and gave them the devil. Sort of a game. Seems what you do is jump on a bike that someone's left around, ride around for a while, and dump it somewhere else. They claim it isn't stealing, just borrowing and using. I told them it's stealing plain and simple and to cut it out."

"My mother-in-law's bike was taken last night," said Sarah. "Maybe it's been tossed down on another street. I'll take a look after I've seen her. And, Mrs. Colley—"

"Oh, call me Betty, for God's sake," said Betty. "And here's the police car coming down the street. They said they'd pick me up. And Mumma and the boys. Didn't trust me to make it there myself. Like I'd take off for Bermuda or something. I'll have to go inside and warn everyone." And Betty heaved herself out of the rocking chair, straightened her shoulders, pulled down her shirt. "You know what Father Dapple says when he's trying to get the congregation to get off its butt and do something about something. 'Gird up your loins and smite them hip and thigh,' which always makes me laugh even though I don't know exactly what it means. Anyway, I won't gird up my loins, which wouldn't be a pretty sight, but dear Lord, I'm ready to smite hip and thigh. Police hips and thighs. And their thick skulls."

With which Betty started for the door. And stopped. "Nice of you, Sarah Deane, to stop by. Your husband called this morning and said he'd sit in on the police scene. Keep an eye on Mumma. Her blood pressure's been spiking all over the place. I have a machine and a cuff, so I know."

And Sarah watched Betty open the screen door and dis-

appear, heard her shouting, "Dylan, Brian. Mumma," and then Sarah returned to her car. She had wanted to bring up the matter of tutoring Betty's two boys, suggest that after things settled down a bit they could arrange a meeting with both families. But time had run out, and a police car, like a cruising shark, slid into place by the curb behind Sarah's Subaru. And Sarah, putting her car into gear, headed for the senior McKenzie homestead with the intention of mixing tea and sympathy and so missed the opportunity to scrutinize the two boys with their buzz cuts and imagine one of them with a thatch of yellow hair.

George Fitts waited with Alex at his command post, the VIP Golfer's Cottage. Like so many of the nonresidential buildings around Ocean Tide the architects had tried to cross-breed genus New England Village with an Important Building Look, the result being a sort of bastard Virginian colonial. The VIP House featured aged red brick, frontal columns outside and in the front hall a scenic wallpaper hung with nicely framed vintage prints of VIP golfers from yesteryear: James Braid, Harry Varden, J. H. Taylor, Walter Hagen, Bobby Jones, Gene Sarazen, Ben Hogan, and the like. Of course, Manager Martinelli had not yet lured any genuine VIP golfers to Ocean Tide but the guesthouse stood ready and he had hopes of putting on a big-money tournament in August. Tiger Woods was of course too much to hope for but surely there was someone, perhaps from the senior tour, who could be talked into coming.

George Fitts, mindful of interfamilial contamination in the form of shared stories, had arranged for the Moseby family— Albert and Sherry and their three sons, Tim, Matt, and Nicholas, the twenty-year-old Yale student—to be toted over to the Maine State police barracks in Thomaston for their session with assistant sheriff's investigator, Katie Waters.

George was not looking forward to the session with the Colley family. Initial statements had been taken from Betty,

but Grandma Rose had not been questioned. Nor had the boys, and he was not looking forward to debriefing two eleven- and thirteen-year-old sprouts. Children were not George's cup of tea; they represented a special form of disorder, a veritable black hole. Adults playing games could often be managed or nudged unwillingly back to the straight and narrow. But kids were something else. Often didn't know the difference between truth or fact, or if they did, would spend enormous amounts of their creative juices evading it, embroidering it, or hiding any frightening event they may have witnessed. Or participated in.

"Take this boy Sarah claims she saw," George said to Alex who was sitting to one side of the Sergeant's desk, a polished mahogany item over which hung a photograph of Jack Nicklaus in his Master's jacket. The room was the Jack Nicklaus Library of the cottage and like the other rooms was named after a noted golfer. George, after examining other possibilities, had chosen the most handsome and best furnished.

"What do you mean, 'claims'?" Alex interrupted. "She wasn't hallucinating."

"Figure of speech. What I'm saying is this kid may have been so scared that we'll never get anything out of him. If we ever find him, that is. Or the boy may not have seen a thing. More likely he may have been up to something he shouldn't have been and someone caught him at it."

"Like swiping a bicycle," suggested Alex.

"Exactly," said George. He pushed a paper across at Alex. "Talking of which, here's another report. The middle Moseby kid, Matt, claims his bike was taken last night sometime. He left it leaning against the side of the house. The boy says the bike wasn't top of the line, whatever that means. A Mongoose NX 7.1 mountain job. Only about seven hundred bucks. But it was new and a Christmas present."

"Are you adding bike theft to your portfolio?" asked Alex. "I'd have thought that was something for the locals, the Rockport police."

"It may be part of the package. We've had an ID on that combination lock Mike fished out of the water. Seems a few bike shops keep track of who has what combo number. Because so many people forget the numbers."

"Don't keep me hanging."

"The lock was sold to Jason Colley. Along with a chain covered with a plastic sheath. Apparently for the new bike we found at his trailer. Seacoast Bike Shop in Camden sold it to him, made a note of the combination. So it looks like Jason may have been strangled with his own bike chain and the lock was thrown away. Into the ocean. Murderer didn't want to get caught with it."

"But why take the lock all the way to the beach just to get rid of it?"

"Who knows. Maybe he was going down there anyway. Maybe he—or she—lives at Ocean Tide. Visits here. I'm asking Mike to look into the bike angle. Me, I don't think it's that pertinent but I'd like to put it to rest. And the oldest Moseby boy, Nicholas, works in the bike rental shop. We can pick his brains."

"You're not suggesting he's got a side line in bike theft and murder."

"I'm not suggesting a thing. But it will be useful to talk to someone who knows about the bike rental business. Different bikes. Cost and make. Who rents them. What's the average inventory depletion."

Alex shook his head. "I don't see how an expensive bike could make it out of the Ocean Tide area. The place has a gatehouse. Guards. Security people running around like ants."

"Offload them on the beach. Boat comes into shore at night," suggested George. "Or, better, ride them up the mountain trail, right onto Route One."

"Okay, that would work for a few bikes. But Mike was talking about a lot of bikes missing from Ocean Tide as well as the whole area. You can't hide bikes under your shirt."

"Vehicle. Any good-sized vehicle," said George.

"You mean perhaps six or seven at one time? That wouldn't be, what's the expression, 'cost effective.' You'd need a big truck. A moving van."

George took a handkerchief from his pocket, removed his rimless glasses, huffed on them, replaced them. Then he picked up his pen, clicked it, pulled his notebook in front of him and looked back at Alex. "The bike business is probably a distraction. A red herring. Right up Mike's alley. He likes distractions."

"But," objected Alex, "red herring or not, how could a kid like Jason Colley, who apparently didn't have a nickel to his name, come to have a very high-class bike? How expensive was the thing?"

George reached for his notebook. "A Schwinn Straight Six. Price well over four thousand. Bought with cash. Who knows where the kid got the money. But I want to stay on track with these two murders. We've got to find Sarah's so-called witness. The boy who screamed. I wonder if she'd meet with one of our police artists, see if we can get a sharper idea of what he looks like?"

But the question went unanswered. Under the escort of Mike Laaka, Betty, Grandma Rose, and the two boys arrived, squinting as they came into the semidarkened room, only George's desk light doing the job of illumination. The ladies, Alex noticed, looked weary in their somber clothes. Rose in a tentlike black dress that might have fitted her once, but that once was long past. The two boys, Brian and Dylan, were marginally clean in jeans and T-shirts and both were sporting close-cropped heads that would have passed muster in a marine boot camp. And the two, almost of a height, were close enough in looks to pass as twins.

Betty waved at the boys. "It's the buzz look. They look like sheared sheep. And here's Grandma Rose,"

Alex pushed forward a sturdy upholstered chair, Rose settled and gave a long whistling sigh. "My acid reflux," she explained. "Took my pill so I'll be all right. Stuff you gave me, Dr. McKenzie. "Acid something."

"Prevacid," said Alex.

"Expensive is what I say. Cost an arm and a leg. Hello, Sergeant Fitts. Good name for someone who gives me fits when I lay eyes on him." And Rose gave out with a hoarse laugh and nicked Betty in the ribs. Then sobered. "Yes, that's a joke, but I always say there's no rule you shouldn't laugh even if people are dying or sick all around you. Otherwise, we'd all go crazy."

This great truth being duly acknowledged, Betty settled down next to her mother, the boys were handed comic books—George had thought ahead—and escorted to the Gary Player Sitting Room to await an interview with Mike Laaka.

An hour later, George, relentless in his questioning, with Alex as a listening post and support party, found Rose flushed with the excitement of being in on the action, Betty alternately close to tears at the fate of Ned Colley and her stepson, Jason, and angry at the past irresponsible behavior of both victims.

"I hope I'm not speaking ill of the dead," exploded Betty, after giving a long and rambling account of her marriage with Ned and her trials with Jason, "but the two of them—oh, my word, trouble, trouble."

"You're saying both men deserved what they got?" asked George in a mild voice.

At which Betty reared up, shook her head vehemently, snapped her mouth closed, folded her arms. And George, who knew when enough was enough, closed the interview and the entire Colley family departed with Mike again as the escorting member.

"So what do you think?" said George, who was rarely interested in what any layman thought about an ongoing case. But Alex as one of the county medical examiners was semi-official, and had been mixed in with George's affairs before so he was occasionally allowed to give an opinion.

"For what it's worth," said Alex, "I think Betty was surprised. Shocked at what happened. Can't come to terms with the terrible idea that she might be somehow to blame for both Jason and Ned going off the rails and ending up dead. She undoubtedly knows that isn't true, but people who lack reasonable explanations for something happening are apt to blame themselves."

"There are times," said George, patting his notes into a neat rectangle and slipping them into a folder, "that the police, I myself, lack a reasonable explanation, but I don't go off into space by blaming myself."

"But," said Mike, looming in the door, "that's because George can always dump blame on my head if someone screws up. What's the word, 'whipping boy'. That's it. Me, and the rest of the underlings."

"Sit down, Mike," said George. "About Grandmother Rose. I'd like to hear what you—and Alex—think about Rose Colley."

"She's a patient of mine," objected Alex.

"I'm not asking about her blood pressure or cholesterol level," said George. "Mike took her statement, but Alex knows her as a person. Mike, you first."

Mike considered. "Rose is like my own grandmother, Sadie Laaka. Rose seems strong. Says what she wants. Doesn't seem to care what other people think. She told me on the drive back she hadn't run into Jason for at least five months, and then only at a convenience store where he avoided her, ducked behind a display case. She called him out, gave him a lecture, and bought him a couple of Mars bars. Ned she hasn't seen since he walked out on Betty, except once at a gas station. Shook her fist at him as he drove away. She came right out and told me she had always thought they'd both end up in a ditch, and now she refuses to have a breakdown about their being dead. But her voice trembled a little when she said this. So I think she does have a soft spot for Jason. Maybe even for Ned."

"Alex?" asked George.

"I think the same. Rose Colley gives it straight from the shoulder. No nonsense. Has a sense of humor about herself. I remember that once, when I was filling in for her regular physician, she said she thought old age was ridiculous. What a stupid thing to have happen to you. That we'd all be better off without it. 'I don't need any Dr. Kevorkian,' she told me. 'When the time comes and I'm too bad, put me in a skiff and I'll row out to sea and roll over the side. You'll be rid of me and I'll be rid of myself. It's a good way to go.'"

Alex shook his head and gave George a grim smile. "You just don't forget remarks like that."

George nodded. "I agree. And I wish all witnesses were like Rose. Okay, Mike. What about the kids?"

Mike had endured much from the "kids." The boys had kept their eyes on their open comic books, stuck to monosyllabic answers. Even on such subjects as baseball and soccer or summer plans they had wiggled around in the green leather arm chairs, twisted their feet in the fringe of the oriental carpet (no expense had been spared furnishing the VIP Golfer's Cottage), had hunched their shoulders, scratched their newly shorn scalps, and chewed their lips.

"I couldn't get them to meet my eyes," complained Mike. "And when I thought Brian was about to open his mouth on some dumb question like what TV program did he like, Dylan would given him a kick and he'd close up. Like those monkeys that see no evil, hear no evil, speak evil. Whatever one said—which wasn't much—the other repeated. Lots of 'okays' or 'not okay.' I said I was sorry about their stepbrother, Jason, and you'd have thought they'd never heard the name Jason Colley in their life. I asked them about the Moseby cousins, did they hang out with those boys, and I could have been asking about George Washington or Marco Polo."

"In other words," said George, "they're holding out."

"Hiding, holding out. Or don't know a blessed thing, haven't seen a blessed thing but won't admit it."

"Scared," suggested Alex. "Or worse, someone's told them, made them keep their mouths closed."

"We'll try again," said George. "I'm having the Colley and Moseby homes watched. We don't want any more bodies. As for the boys, later on we might have them in again without Mom and Grandma in the next room. If it seems worth the trouble. In the meantime, Alex, I hear Sarah's going to be doing a tutoring job at Ocean Tide. And Brian and Dylan along with two of the Mosebys will be her students."

Alex grinned. "You hate having us amateurs in your soup but you won't hesitate to use us."

George opened his briefcase, dropped in his manila folder, snapped the briefcase closed and faced Alex. "What's that song from the musical?"

"George," interrupted Mike, "you'd never do anything so frivolous as listen to music."

George stood up. "There you go, Mike. Generalizing. I listen to musicals at night sometimes. On video. You know that song, something like 'I've Grown Accustomed to Your Face.' *My Fair Lady.* Well, I've grown accustomed to Sarah's face and her incursions into police work. I don't want her but I'm used to her. So I'll be glad to hear what she has to say about the boys."

"Like Alex said, you're glad to use her," said Mike. "Warm and fuzzy old George. Born in uniform with laced boots and a badge in his mouth."

"You're right," said George, turning toward the door, "I was a Cub Scout, an Eagle Scout, and a lieutenant in the National Guard. Mike, get to work. Alex, good-bye. I'll be going over statements for the next hour if you want me."

Mike, walking down the cottage path, turned to Alex. "Do you mind George using Sarah as a source of information, or to put it bluntly, as a spy?"

Alex shrugged. "Sarah's quite capable of telling George to stuff it. She swears up and down she won't do any probing, questioning of her students, but if something lands on her lap, she may share."

But Sarah, driving slowly toward the senior McKenzie compound, and remembering Elspeth's distress at losing her new bicycle, had reached a decision. The two murders, the missing boy, they were police problems. Her duty in the matter was done, her statement given. It was time to prepare for her tutorial class with the Colley and the Moseby boys.

But for extracurricular activity, she would focus on a matter close to the McKenzie happiness. She would start today to look into bicycles. Bicycles lost, bicycles strayed, stolen. Or taken—as Betty had described—for a joy ride. In this she would engage Elspeth McKenzie; it would keep her mother-in-law busy, from feeling out of sorts. And John, he might like to snoop about, take notes about bikes. Makes of bikes, favorites models chosen by the thieves. Wouldn't becoming bicycle vigilantes, bicycle sleuths do wonders for their mental health? *I am,* Sarah told herself, *someone who can come up with solutions. I understand older people and their needs. What John and Elspeth need is a little benign excitement with just the tiniest hint of, well, not of danger but of the unexpected.*

Smiling broadly, Sarah slowed her car at the Alder Way residence of the senior McKenzies, jumped out of the car and ran up the steps.

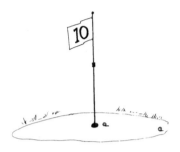

# 10

SARAH found Elspeth McKenzie recovered from her slump of the night before. Now, like Betty Colley, she was ready for battle. Battle the security team of Ocean Tide and by extension the bike-thieving population of the community. Or the outside world. Or both.

Elspeth was standing on the porch in a patch of warm sunlight as Sarah drove up and even at the slight distance her posture—hands on hips, shoulders back—suggested an Elspeth on the warpath. She seemed to be listening with a certain amount of impatience—if a tapping foot was a symptom— to what might be commiseration over the bike theft incident from the beautiful Naomi Foxglove, the social coordinator extraordinaire Sarah had last seen swanning through the throngs at the getting-to-know-you party. They made an incongruous pair: Elspeth all sharp angles, with her white curly mop tied back with one of John's neckties, wearing her paint-splattered overalls, her hawk eyes narrowed, her beak nose thrust up, her hands chopping the air; Naomi with her perfect circle of short brown curly hair, her rounded smooth face the color of café au lait, her gestures smooth and flowing, slim as an eel in a long moss green tube of a dress. (Naomi had somehow escaped from the mandatory Ocean Tide uniform.) Sarah climbing out of her car could hear their voices, Elspeth's high, excited, angry, Naomi's low and soft as smoke.

Sarah was greeted with pleasure by both parties.

"Ah, Sarah, just the one I need," called Elspeth.

"Hello, Sarah Deane," said Naomi. She glided two steps forward and extended a beautiful hand, the fourth finger embellished with a single polished turquoise ring circled in silver. "How nice. Your mother-in-law is upset about her bicycle, which she certainly should be. I walked over to tell her how concerned we—the whole management team—are about the matter. We've got to get a grip on this business, it's epidemic in the whole area—not just Ocean Tide."

"I heard one of the Moseby boys is missing a bike," Sarah said.

"Yes, I have the report. Carly Thompson is going to check on it. But with the children, we usually wait twenty-four hours. They race around and drop them wherever they feel like. But it's a shame. The Mosebys and the Colleys have enough problems without this."

There was the briefest of silences in honor of the Moseby's and Colley's "problems" and then Naomi said briskly, "About Mrs. McKenzie's bike. I think she should talk to the bike shop people. And, of course, the Ocean Tide employees will keep their eyes open. And, Miss Deane—or are you Dr. Deane, Professor Deane? . . ."

"Sarah will be just fine," put in Sarah.

"And I'm Naomi. But please help me, won't you? I'm trying to persuade her to help our senior citizens—"

"Of which I'm one," said Elspeth curtly.

"Yes, but a special one," said Naomi. "An artist that everyone in the Midcoast area knows. We're thinking ahead to a fall art class for our Village Green community—that's our assisted-living complex," she explained to Sarah. "And we're planning an Ocean Tide art show in the Lodge in December and we'd like your mother-in-law to perhaps teach a class, act as a judge for the show."

"I'll think about it after I get my bike back," said Elspeth. "When we've finished moving in, which may take the rest of my life. And after I've survived a family party that I'm trying to put on at the end of the month. But thank you so much for asking, Miss Foxglove, and now Sarah and I have things to do. And we're late as it is."

And Miss Foxglove, no one's fool, smiled at the two, and floated down the steps and disappeared at a swift walk—or glide—down Alder Lane in the direction of Tulip Park.

"So what are we late for?" asked Sarah.

"Nothing," said Elspeth looking after Naomi as she disappeared around the bend. "It's that woman. She makes me nervous."

"I think she's gorgeous," said Sarah. "And she's asking you to help run the art scene. You might enjoy being the art guru here. But now I have an idea."

"So do I," said Elspeth. "We're going bike hunting."

"My idea exactly," said Sarah. "But how do we start?"

"On bikes," said Elspeth firmly. "We'll rent bikes. Get a fix on this bike rental and bike-stealing business that seems to be going on. And maybe even find some wretched child riding my bike."

"Do you think John would like to join us?" asked Sarah, looking over at the McKenzie cottage.

"Later he might love it. Oil up the Raleigh. Now I've badgered him to go over to the Pro Shop and see about taking a golf lesson. Or trying a round. My hope is that he'll meet four or five men just like him."

"That," said Sarah, "I doubt. Let me stick Patsy in your house and then we can hit the bike shop. Looking around for your bike can't possibly annoy the police. Mike Laaka thinks I want to get into this murder business, but I don't."

"Even if you see the boy who was running away from the body."

"If I see him I'll call George or Mike. And that will be that," said Sarah taking Patsy by the collar, pushing though the door of number 7, and rejoining her mother-in-law."

"We can walk over to the bike shop," said Elspeth, "and bike back on our rentals. It will be good for us."

Sarah looked at her mother-in-law's spattered and loose overalls. "Can you ride in those? They're sort of baggy."

"I'll hitch them up," said Elspeth firmly, striding ahead. "I'm not living in this place to make a fashion statement. If that Joseph Martinelli thinks I'm lowering the tone of the place he can go . . ." She hesitated.

"Exactly," said Sarah hustling to catch up. Elspeth had long legs and a long stride and when on a mission she moved like a steam engine.

"When we get our bikes," said Elspeth, "we can cycle around to see if some kid jumped on my bike and dumped it somewhere else."

The Ocean Tide Cycle Shop stood at the beginning of the entrance to Ocean Drive, a road that wound past the Pro Shop, the tennis courts and swimming pool cabana—each area decorated by a series of interlocking beds of flowers that changed with each passing month, purple and white petunias now replacing the spring displays of narcissus and tulips and hyacinths.

Elspeth led the way to the bike shop, another pastiche of the colonial and the pretentious, with a dark green paneled door complete with a brass knocker in the shape of a whale. She stopped and shook her head. "I know I should be ashamed to be complaining about a stolen bike with half the world living in mud huts or under trash bins or ducking bullets. I should shut up and be a good citizen."

"Being a good citizen," said Sarah, nudging her mother-in-law into forward movement, "doesn't mean you can't ask about your bicycle."

Which Elspeth did. At length. The counter in the bike shop was manned by a tall, rather handsome young man, dark hair flopping over his forehead, open blue eyes, suntanned face (and it was only late May). He tried several times to insert a comment into Elspeth's flow, but finally had to wait, arms folded, a smile fixed on his face, until she wound down.

"I'm so sorry," said the young man, "and I know Mr. Martinelli is very unhappy about it. He says it's sort of like an epidemic. Bikes are so portable."

The young man paused, his smile widened, and he thrust out a hand, a hand with only a small smear of bicycle oil. "I'm Nick Moseby," he said. "And I can really sympathize. One of my younger brothers, Matt, his new bike was stolen last night and he's having a major seizure about it. Of course with all that's been going on with our family no one was paying attention to people coming and going, and Matt just left the bike leaning against the side of the house. I suppose it was taken at night. Do you think yours was taken after dark?"

Elspeth—and Sarah, on Elspeth's behalf—both found themselves taken aback. Here was a Moseby, a cousin and nephew of the murdered Ned and Jason Colley. A son of—as the local paper put it—"one of the stricken families." And here they stood crabbing about a mere stolen bicycle.

"I'm so sorry," Elspeth began. "You must have more on your mind than lost bikes. Your whole family. The Mosebys and the Colleys. What a terrible thing."

Nick Moseby lifted his shoulders slightly and grimaced. "Yes, everyone's pretty upset. But I have this job to do and it won't help anything if I skip out on it. Mom has a lot of support, my dad's been staying home from the greenhouse and Aunt Betty—she's Mom's sister—they've been helping each other. But, look, a bike stolen in this place is pretty serious. Mr. Martinelli wants everything perfect here, perfect right down to the kind of bike oil we use, the type of golf balls they sell at the Pro Shop, the temperature of the water in the swimming pool. . . ."

"Perfect is impossible," said Elspeth, shaking her head. "How about settling for excellent?"

"Or even very good," put in Sarah. And then, "You're the oldest Moseby, aren't you? You're at Yale. What year?"

"Junior next year," said Nick. "It's a really great place. And tough as they come. But never mind Yale. It's your bike we should worry about. I'll put up a notice about it in the shop, but I can't put Stolen signs all over the place because Mr. Martinelli wouldn't allow it."

"You mean," said Sarah, "image is all."

"You bet," said Nick, grinning. "I mean he cares right down to every detail. He made me change my Ocean Tide shirt yesterday because of a loose button. And now," Nick settled to business, "you both want to rent something. For the week or just by the day? You get a better break on the price if it's by the week. And do you want anything special? We've got everything from super mountain bikes to tricycles or tandems."

Elspeth and Sarah refocused their attention, and after a certain amount of hands-on inspection each chose identical touring bikes named Road Wizard which promised to be easy to handle, all-terrain, with user-friendly gear systems, comfort saddle, aluminum cross frame—in short, the works.

Wheeling their Road Wizards down the path, Elspeth turned around briefly to stare at the Cycle Shop. "That young man should head straight into politics where he should do very well. Or perhaps the credit should go to Mr. Martinelli because of a great training program for summer employees."

"I'll bet on Martinelli," said Sarah. "Guys who have visions are pretty tough characters. The don't leave things to chance. He's going for the Garden of Eden. . . ."

"Without snakes," put in Elspeth.

"Yes, but he's bound to stub his toe. I mean the scenery's great here, ocean views are terrific, the facilities here are first-rate, but humans will be humans and go around stealing bikes. . . ."

"And throttling other humans and leaving the bodies near golf greens or in equipment sheds."

"But," Sarah went on, "I'll have to give him a big E for effort. Look at the staff—at least the ones I've met. Carly Thompson, she could manage a country in the Balkans. And Naomi Foxglove. Juggling the whole social apparatus with one hand. So why are we surprised at this Nicholas acting like an Eagle Scout."

"I never knew an Eagle Scout, but you know, it's like altar boys, sometimes they end up as serial killers," began Elspeth.

"I thought you were going to think positively," Sarah reminded her as the two women peddled their way back to the Mckenzie cottage, had a quick lunch and took off for a trial spin.

All went smoothly, the day was shining, the bikes were well tuned, but as they headed for the second tour of the community, Elspeth was suddenly diverted. She gave a hoot and gestured ahead at a turn in Lavender Lane. "Look, look down there. That boy. In the red shirt. He's just picked up that yellow bike off the lawn and is taking off."

"It's probably his bike."

"Much too big. He can hardly reach the pedals. He's stealing it. Listen, Sarah, I'm going to chase him down." With which words Elspeth bent forward and gave her bike a push and then accelerated after the boy in the red shirt.

Sarah threw herself into greater effort and in a few seconds had caught up with her mother-in-law who had streaked past a man who backed up with alarm on seeing a wild eyed white-haired woman apparently fleeing from some pursuing force. "We can't chase every kid we see on the wrong bicycle," she shouted, coming abreast of Elspeth.

Elspeth swiveled her head. "No, but maybe we can catch a small fish who can lead us to a larger fish. It may be a gang." And Elspeth bent lower over her handle bars and accelerated, followed by Sarah, and they both swept around the curve of Forsythia Walk and visibly gained on the red-shirted boy.

Who turned around, saw Elspeth and Sarah, grinned widely, hurled himself off the bike, which clattered to the ground, galloped into a back garden, gave a yell for someone called Josh, and disappeared behind a hedge.

The two women ground to a halt, panting, and then, as they stared at the bike, a second youth, taller, black shirted, appeared, pulled the bicycle off the lawn, flung his leg over it and took off as Sarah and Elspeth stood openmouthed.

Sarah spoke first. "Forget it. Kids can keep this up all day, but we can't. It's a game. Not an international theft ring."

Elspeth nodded slowly. "All right. I give up. Let's go back to the cottage and I'll comfort you with iced tea."

But iced tea would not be forthcoming. As the two women circled sedately toward Peony Point and the path toward the beach, a blue sedan with the Ocean Tide logo on its flank slowed. Naomi Foxglove leaned out of the driver's window, one arm extended, the hand waving.

"Hello again, Sarah Deane," she called. Then, "Good afternoon, Mrs. McKenzie. May we borrow Sarah? In about fifteen minutes, Sarah, if you have the time. Mr. Martinelli wants you to meet with Betty Colley and her boys."

Sarah frowned. "I don't see why—" she began.

"The tutoring proposal. Mrs. Colley saw you this morning and thought since you were already at Ocean Tide it might be a good idea to meet with her boys, that's Brian and Dylan, and talk about your ideas."

"And the boys' ideas," put in Sarah, "which I don't suppose will be entirely favorable."

"You can't expect two boys facing their summer vacation to be crazy about more school," said Naomi smoothly. "But Mrs. Colley thought that having you discuss your plans would distract the boys from what's been happening."

"How about the Moseby family?" asked Sarah. "I should talk to Mr. and Mrs. Moseby."

"If you're agreeable," said Naomi, "we'll try and get hold of Mrs. Moseby and two of her boys to meet with you after you've seen the Colleys. And, Mrs. McKenzie, I see you and Sarah have your bikes. What handsome ones. So good-bye again and have a wonderful day." Sarah and Elspeth watched as Naomi Foxglove swung her car back into the road, a hand raised in farewell.

"That woman," said Elspeth, "I want her to fall into a mud puddle."

"You're jealous," said Sarah grinning at her. "And now I've got fifteen minutes to ride back to your house and then turn up at Martinelli's office with a tutoring plan in my head, not to mention a list of suitable reading. For kids who may be reading for all I know on the first grade or on a college level. Come on, let's saddle up and head for the barn. No more sleuthing right now."

Sarah arrived in Joseph Martinelli's waiting room with seven minutes to spare. Escorted into the room by Mrs. Eisner, his secretary, she settled in a leather chair with a view of the ocean and a table of magazines by her elbow. On the walls hung a series of pastel prints showing nineteenth-century scenes that might have gone under the label "Olden Days on the Maine Coast." In matching narrow gold frames the room was ringed with views of lighthouses, surf, antique-looking sloops and schooners, children in sunbonnets and bathers in long dark dresses or one-piece suits. All in all, the room reminded Sarah of that of a well-heeled physician or dentist who, by means of decoration, hoped to soothe the waiting patient.

And Sarah was waiting. And waiting. She checked her watch. Ten minutes late. Where were the Colleys? Had the day's events proved too much, Betty's brain had become scrambled, and she'd forgotten? For the tenth time she swiveled in her chair and peered out of an adjacent window overlooking Mr. Martinelli's parking lot. And saw Betty climbing out of her car.

And saw a young boy with a shaven head climb out and join her.

And saw a second slightly taller boy with a similar haircut

follow him, hesitate, look up at his mother and then turn and with a sudden jerk, twist away from her reaching hand, duck behind a parked car, and without looking back, speed off into the shrubbery edging the parking lot.

Sarah watched Betty start out after the boy, hesitate at the edge of the parking lot, raise both arms into the air, hands rolled tight into fists, in a tableau of frustration. Then she returned to the smaller boy still standing by the car, grasped his elbow and steered him toward the door of the office. It was, Sarah thought, one of those scenes painted by Norman Rockwell that used to be featured on the covers of family magazines. It would show a mother wearing an apron, her sleeves rolled up, her face red with exasperation, grasping the arm of one all-American small boy, his hair in what was then called a summer brush cut, while a second runaway boy would be crouched in the bushes, his face illuminated by a wide triumphant grin. The title would be something like *The Truant*. Or perhaps, *Meeting the Tutor*.

Sarah was still meditating on the possible titles when the real thing—Betty Colley and son Brian—came through the door, Brian wiggling under Betty's grasp, Betty breathing heavily.

"That Dylan," she exploded as Sarah rose from her chair. "Just like his Dad, God help them both, and Brian would have gone off if he'd thought of it." Here she tightened her grip on the boy's elbow. "I think it's genetic. And with all we've just been going through, the police, the memorial service, for them to behave like a couple of wildcats. And Dylan and Brian taking off every time I turn around. And all I'm trying to do is get the boys to read at their age level. And write a composition their teacher can read. What I'm saying is this . . ."

And Sarah allowed Betty to wind down but her meaning was clear. She was sorely tried, her two sons reminded her strongly of a terrible combination of charming and useless Ned Colley and his son, Jason Colley. "And God help all of us," said Betty again. She wasn't going to stand for it another minute.

And now Brian here was going to shut up and listen to Miss Deane and then go home and do whatever assignment she was going to give him and meet with Miss Deane all summer or there'd be no Camp Ocean Tide, no picnics, no swimming, no Union Fair, no nothing. The same went for Dylan when she got her hands on him. So there.

Sarah through all this had experienced not only a rising sympathy for all parties but a certain pricking of her thumbs. The boy, Brian, standing head down, one sneakered foot rubbing against the other, was he The Boy? Sarah, half listening to Betty, tried to imagine a yellow thatch of hair on Brian's shaven skull because the boy certainly met many of the other requirements: knobby knees, thin face, adolescent. He was almost right.

"And so what do you think, Sarah?" demanded Betty.

"What? I mean what does Brian think?" asked Sarah, dodging a question the beginning of which she had tuned out.

"You mean," said Betty, "about giving him an assignment right now? Before school is out? It's time for Brian to start taking responsibility for that D-plus in Language Arts, which is a stupid name for English in my opinion."

"Brian?" said Sarah in an encouraging voice.

The boy looked up. And transformed himself. He looked Sarah full in the face with wide open blue eyes. And smiled, the wide smile of a boy who knew how to use it. "Oh, sure," he said. "I don't mind. It might be kind of fun. Could I read about animals? Or write a story about my cat? His name is Charlie and he's really weird." The smile grew wider. And Sarah suddenly knew what Betty meant by the ability of the Colley males to manipulate their world.

"I think we can dig up a book about animals," said Sarah. "And I'd like to read a story about Charlie. Why don't you work on that, and after school is out and we start the tutoring program you can bring it in. One or two pages. No more. And I'll be looking for some animals stories. Have you read *The Red Pony*? Or *Old Yeller*?"

"No," said Brian, the smile still fixed on his face.

"Good," said Sarah. She turned to Betty. "Tell Dylan he can write a story for me, too. A topic he chooses. Animals would be fine. Outer space, sports, aliens, an adventure. Travel. Fishing."

"No crime stories," announced Betty in a firm voice. "The boys can leave blood and guts and crime alone for a while. We've had enough of that. Brian and Dylan will be seeing a counselor soon to work out some of their feelings about what's happened to Jason and Ned."

"I'd be glad," said Sarah with feeling, "to leave blood and guts to the psychologist." She turned to Brian. "Say hello to your brother and tell him I don't bite, okay?" And Brian cranked his smile open another inch, blinked his eyes, and nodded.

After mother and son left the room, Sarah went back to trying to fit the face—without the smile—into the face she saw coming out of the woods, tried to imagine again the mop of yellow hair fitted onto Brian's buzz-cut head, tried to match Brian's voice to the gasping of that terrified boy. She frowned. He was so almost the right boy. But why had brother Dylan taken off like that? Had Dylan remembered her better than she remembered him? Had he recognized her from that day when he took off on the bike? Maybe he'd stalked her, found out her name. And now wanted no part of this tutoring scheme. She, Sarah, meant danger. Meant a dead body. Meant the police. Or were both boys in it together? Unlikely. But which one? Dylan running away didn't prove much because Betty, after losing Dylan, got a grip on Brian.

She'd have to see both boys together. And when she finally met both boys—providing Dylan didn't leave town—she could hardly start the tutoring session by showing the boys pictures of equipment sheds, scenes of the seventeenth green, piles of fertilizer bags. And even if one of them turned out to be "it," what was she going to do, haul the kid off to George Fitts and

Mike Laaka so they could run him through the interrogation scene again? Oh, shit.

Sarah pushed herself out of the leather chair. Even her evil twin, Sarah the Snoop, wouldn't stick her nose into this buzz saw. This boy, if he had been alone at the shed, most probably had had enough of a scare to last him through the summer. And yet—

And yet, two god-awful murders might just move an inch or so toward solution, toward community peace, if the mystery boy actually had seen something more than a pair of work boots sticking out from a pile of fertilizer bags. Right now all she could do was hope that Betty Colley's sons had been miles away when Ned Colley's body was found. Let Mike and George find the right boy, do the dirty work. Her business was to teach, to support the senior McKenzies, to find some quality time with Alex, walk her dog, balance her checkbook, see her dentist about that loose filling, send in her fall book order, refill that allergy prescription because the hay fever season was looming. All those were her business; it was not sneaking around trying to finger some hapless kid.

"So there," she said aloud, echoing Betty Colley, a role model if there ever was one. She marched to the far window and glared down at a croquet game in progress behind the Lodge. Croquet was one of the many activities offered to the citizens of Ocean Tide, and Sarah had overheard Mr. Martinelli recommending it to a group of white-haired ladies. "A friendly game," he had said, "and not too strenuous." But Sarah had never found croquet "friendly." Lethal was more like it, and she had spent many angry childhood moments with her mallet raised, shouting "You're cheating" at assorted cousins who raised their mallets in turn, yelling, threatening. The next murder at Ocean Tide might well take place on the croquet lawn.

Then Sarah, appalled at the way her unruly mind reverted to moments of disorder, gave herself a mental shake. Shape up, she ordered herself, because in a few minutes she would have to face the Moseby family, have to give the false appearance of a focused teacher who could help two young Mosebys pick their way over the shoals and rocks of the English language.

And right on time the door opened and the Mosebys stood on the threshold of the waiting room.

# 11

IN came the Mosebys. First Sherry. Waved through the door by Mrs. Eisner. Midroom, Sherry hesitated. Took two steps back, tightened her grip on a yellow linen handbag that perfectly matched her yellow cardigan, her yellow sneakers, and looked at Sarah. And swallowed hard.

Sarah stepped forward, introduced herself, gestured at a chair, and asked about the children in question.

"Oh," said Sherry. "They're right outside. I wanted to see if it was okay to bring them. I didn't know how you wanted to do this. My husband—that's Al—he wanted to come but he's playing golf and then he's got to go back to work this afternoon. The greenhouse. It's the time of year that people are getting into the planting and buying peat moss and compost and all that. You know how it is with the garden business."

Sarah hadn't thought much about the springtime crunch in the garden business, but she nodded her head in agreement, shook Sherry's hand, and asked about her prospective pupils. "Don't you want to bring them in?"

"You see," said Sherry—and Sarah could hear the tension in her voice—"they're not exactly wild about the idea of summer school. I mean, beginning practically the day vacation begins. And Matt, he's sixteen so maybe he could meet with you separately. You know how it is, Matt thinks he's an adult, which he isn't, but after he got his driver's license and the job with the golf course crew and, well, you know . . ." She trailed off uncertainly.

Honestly, thought Sarah, this is going to take all day. And this woman is a nervous wreck, she's in worse shape than Betty. With a lot less reason. Unless . . . but Sarah let the unfinished thought trail off. "Bring the boys in," she told Sherry in a firm voice.

The boys, one after the other, entered, stood still, extended hands, inclined their well-brushed brown heads, said "Hi" (Tim), and "How do you do" (Matt). Waved to two of the leather chairs, they sat upright, looking straight ahead at a particularly vapid print depicting a child in a straw hat sitting under a beach umbrella. The two were dressed in clean chinos, blue polo shirt with the Ocean Tide logo (Matt) and white T-shirt with a harbor seal on a rock (Tim). Both had clean—clean!—white sneakers. In Sarah's opinion, neither boy looked quite real.

It didn't take long. Sherry Moseby sank into a distant chair, hands folding and unfolding in her lap. Sarah assumed command, and first Matt was assured that he could do independent study, meeting her at times compatible with his golf course job, and Tim was given the same assignment as Dylan and Brian. Then Sarah, glancing over at Sherry, said, "I know it's been a terrible week for your whole family. And, Matt," she added, "I was so sorry to hear about your bike. That someone made off with it. Has it turned up?"

Matt, who like his brother Tim had been sitting fixed in

his chair in a robotic state, came to life. "No," he said. "We've had Security and everything. It's probably some scumbag from Rockland or Rockport who came in here—"

"We don't know that," said Sherry.

"Jeezus, Mom," began Matt, but was stopped cold.

"Language," said Sherry in a high-pitched tremulous protest. She turned to Sarah. "I don't allow swearing at home."

And Sarah, quick to the ways of students, saw the glimmer of a smile, the merest up-bending of lips on the face of each boy. Swearing she was sure, was part of the daily bread of both. But it was time to call a halt to the visit. Sarah rose. "My mother-in-law's bike was stolen, too," she told Matt. "And she's spending a lot of time looking all over Ocean Tide for it. She could keep an eye out for yours. What make was it?"

Matt became alert. Sarah had hit the right button. "Custom Schwinn Aluminum 2000 MOAB frame. It's got a replaceable deraileur hanger, coil springs, and a Shimano twenty-four-speed drive-train with Shimano V brakes. And a lot of other stuff like great tires, Panaracer Fire XC tires, and—"

"Color?" said Sarah who knew squat about the finer points of bicycles.

Matt gave her a look of pity. "Color isn't that important," he said.

"It is if you're looking for something," said Sarah crisply as she moved to the door.

"Okay," said Matt. "It's mostly green with some white and it says Schwinn and the tires have a red rim."

"Good," said Sarah. "And you can keep an eye out for Mrs. McKenzie's. She's got . . ." Sarah paused, trying to remember what Elspeth had said. "A blue bike that says Mass Bike Shop somewhere. And it's brand-new."

Matt looked at her with something like scorn. "You don't even know the make? Mass Bike Shop isn't a make."

"Just keep an eye out," said Sarah. "And thanks for coming. Call me if any of you have questions. Boys, see you in a couple of weeks."

And she was alone. Sarah blew out a heavy breath. It had gone fairly smoothly. Of course the two boys were under heavy wraps, so who knew what they'd be like when out from under mother's eye. And it wasn't a bad idea to suggest that Matt play detective—with emphasis on "play"—and keep an eye out for the two bikes. And now, off to the McKenzie household. Perhaps take out the rental bikes for a spin. Drag John McKenzie with them. What the man needed was exercise and to get away from those unpacked boxes of books.

But it was not to be. At least not yet. Sarah was stopped at the outer office door by the ever-watchful Mrs. Eisner. "Oh, Miss Deane. It's Mr. Martinelli. He wants to see you, just for a few minutes. Right now if you could." Tiny Mrs. Eisner reminded Sarah powerfully of a female version of Stuart Little—alert, lively, resourceful, qualities that would be needed as one of Joseph Martinelli's minions.

"You can go in right now," repeated Mrs. Eisner in her high whispery voice, as Sarah hesitated.

"I really have to leave . . ." Sarah began, but the secretary had ducked her head down and fixed her eyes on her computer screen.

Joseph Martinelli rose from his desk as Sarah stepped into the room. His round face was set into a welcoming wreath, and he came around with both hands extended, took Sarah's in his—it was like being clasped by two junior-size catcher's mitts—and propelled her into a chair, one of those leather chairs into which the sitter sank as into a bowl of Jell-O.

Sarah grasped the arms of the chair, trying for an upright position, and became aware that Joseph was pointing out the wonders of his inner sanctum: the relief maps (the mountain bike trail looking like the Andes), the plaques and awards, the local racing bike team he was helping sponsor, and as the pièce de résistance, a table model of Ocean Tide as it might look by the year 2010.

"Gotta look ahead," said Joseph. "We'll need to expand. Maybe some nearby land will come available. Another well-known resort, a nearby golf course might turn up, and what an opportunity. . . ." He paused, seeming to realize that these raptures might not be grabbing his guest's attention. He returned to his desk, picked up a folder, tapped it lightly shaking down the papers inside, and beamed at Sarah.

"We're so happy. This tutoring thing. Just what the community needs. Keeps the focus on education the whole year round. And a faculty member from our own Bowmouth College in Camden."

"Yes," said Sarah, not sure where this was tending.

"You don't think," said Joseph, "that you'd like to expand your services. Have a real class. Perhaps arrange for credit with the local schools."

Sarah held up her hand. "No, absolutely not, Mr. Martinelli. I don't want a full-time job. Four boys is just fine. I need time off and I have fall classes and . . ."

Mr. Martinelli waved fall classes away. "Just a thought. Think about it. We're glad you're taking the Colleys and the Mosebys. What a terrible thing. Murder at Ocean Tide."

Sarah couldn't help herself. "That's a title," she said. "For a murder mystery. Or a TV special. An Angela Lansbury thing. Or even a western."

But Joseph was not able to make the leap from the disgrace of two local bodies to a drama waiting to be scripted. "It's been a dreadful experience for our whole community family. I can't make light of it even if you can, Miss Deane." And Joseph eyed Sarah reproachfully. And then he brightened. "I'm going to share an idea. It's about what's gone on here. Like maybe these murders are an inside job. Our Ocean Tide staff is specially selected. Researched. But you never know, some of the groundskeepers. Temporary kitchen staff, waiters brought in for the parties. I heard from the grapevine you've done some amateur detective work, so what about a job on our staff? Part-time."

"Part-time what?" said Sarah warily.

"Looking around. Eyes," said Joseph rubbing both hands together. "We need more eyes. More people moving around watching things. People who no one would think had anything to do with Security. The law."

"You want me to be a policeman?" Sarah squeaked, not believing her ears. What family member had been blabbing about any of her previous snoop activities, activities she had now renounced?

"Plainclothes. As a visitor. A friendly visitor. Visiting her father and mother-in-law. But one that keeps her eyes wide open. Sees things. Sees something suspicious."

Sarah took a deep breath and looked at Joseph Martinelli with narrowed eyes. No, he wasn't Mr. Friendly Santa Claus, just another sleaze turning everyday life into a pond of big fishes eating, chasing, spying upon little fishes.

Joseph, reacting to the sudden drop in temperature, held up his big hand. "Hey, no. Now don't go getting the wrong idea."

"You mean," said Sarah icily, "you'd like to hire me to spy on the Ocean Tide people? The McKenzies' friends, Betty Colley and Sherry Moseby's family and anyone else I bump into?"

"No, no." Joseph's voice rose. "It's just we need help. Security's a real problem. Any place like this. Humans are humans. They take things. Kill people. Ruin communities. People will stop signing up. Bottom line, you want your mother-in-law's next bike lifted? You want her mugged when she's taking a walk in the evening. Down on the beach?"

But Sarah looked at the manager with narrowed eyes. When she answered her voice was level but with a hard edge. "No, Mr. Martinelli. I don't want anyone mugged or strangled or raped, but that's something you've got to stop. This place is your baby, so you have to take care of it. I am not available so please ignore whatever you've heard about my past life. People talk too much. I'm just here to visit my in-laws. Or for tutoring. Period. If I see someone in trouble I'll try to help like any common citizen, but not as any part of your security system force. Are you clear on that? You understand what I'm saying?"

Joseph Martinelli, who had sagged visibly during this lecture, looked at the door as if expecting the efficient presence of Carly, the soothing face of Naomi Foxglove, to materialize in the manner of the Starship *Enterprise* crew. Now he exhaled slowly and as Sarah turned to go, stumbled out from behind his desk and clutched, unsuccessfully, at her sleeve.

"Please, Miss Deane. Dr. Deane. Sarah Deane. Don't go. I didn't mean what it sounded like. I misspoke myself. I'm not trying to hire you to do anything you don't want to do. I meant it all as a compliment because I'd heard so much. I value your family. The McKenzies are a wonderful addition. We need people like Mrs. Elspeth McKenzie with all her art experience, and I hope she'll be willing to help out with one of our programs. And Professor McKenzie, too." This said with less conviction. "Please sit down. Just for a minute. And forget the security idea. We are so very happy to have you help the Colleys and the Mosebys. . . ."

"Which I'm very happy to do," said Sarah, halting in her trip to the door but eyeing the manager with suspicion.

"All of us, the Ocean Tide team, our whole executive staff. Kids like Nick Moseby in the bike shop and Matt Moseby on our greens crew. All of us are happy to have another good person working here. The Colleys are, what's that expression, from the Bible, is it? The salt of the earth. And the Mosebys, just the sort of family we want at Ocean Tide. Their kids don't look like rockers or gang types. Anyway, please accept my apologies, Miss Deane. Professor Deane. I'm just so worried. The trouble is—" Here Joseph Martinelli looked quickly out his window as if expecting to see a microphone hanging on a tree and then lowered his voice. "The trouble is," he repeated, "I really think it has to be an inside job. Someone, a temporary, who works here, who's out to get the Colley family. Maybe the Moseby family."

"Inside job? You mean a temporary worker related to the Colleys killing Colleys? Or the Mosebys? I think that's crazy," said Sarah, staring at the manager with surprise. Oh, Lord, she thought, now he's going to start playing detective.

"I wasn't born blind and stupid. It can't be an accident. Two people from one family killed at Ocean Tide."

"It may be a coincidence," said Sarah, without conviction. Then with more energy, "It just might be someone trying to ruin Ocean Tide. Someone who's got it in for you. An old enemy. I'll bet you've got old enemies around, Mr. Martinelli. Left over from whatever you used to do which must have been making a lot of money to put this place together."

A deflated Joseph, shoulders hunched into his neck, his mouth drooped, and he spread both hands wide. "Okay, Ms. Deane. So who makes friends in the construction business? And okay, someone out there might think he's got a grievance, like I've cheated him somehow, which I never did, so help me God. But there might be someone sneaking around the area who thinks I'm a sort of mafia type. Because of my name. It's Italian, you know."

Sarah nodded. "Well, yes. It sounds Italian."

"So you're making me think it's personal. Not about our residents. Just because the two Colleys were accidentally available. Where they shouldn't have been. Easy to pick off. Get back at me. So maybe it's someone who's got a job here on purpose. Right now is going around in a blue Ocean Tide jacket with our logo on it. Maybe won the Employee of the Week Award. Has a photo right up there on the Lodge wall smiling with a big fat grin. Saying, I gotcha."

"Or," said Sarah, despite her resolution not to get involved in this speculation, "it might be a resident, someone who's bought one of the apartments, one of the cottages. On purpose. To ruin you."

But this last idea was too much for Joseph to contemplate. He shook his big head like a bull getting rid of a tormenting insect. "No, no way. We don't want to investigate our guests.

Our guests are family. I tell you it's one of the staff behind this. Riding a lawn mower. Cleaning the swimming pool. Servicing the golf carts. Someone from a union. I had a lotta trouble with the unions. And Miss Deane. Sarah, if I can call you Sarah, forgive me. I didn't want to get you riled up. But let me say it again, our Ocean Tide residents, they're family. Today, I'm just not myself. Okay? Say it's okay."

And Sarah looking at the puffed-up reddened face of Manager Martinelli, felt her annoyance spill out like sawdust from a rag doll. The man's brain, she decided, was muddled, overheated, confused. She nodded at him, albeit without much enthusiasm, and said it was okay.

But as she left the manager's sanctum, Sarah found the idea of a double murder done as an insider job, whether aimed at boss Martinelli and his Ocean Tide empire or at the Colley-Moseby family, strangely compelling.

Heading now for the McKenzie cottage, driving slowly around the curving roads, seeing but not taking in the fact that the tree leaves were almost fully out, lilacs showed blossoms, the tulips, the daffodils had gone by, the forsythia was history. This heartwarming evidence that June was around the corner left Sarah untouched. Her head was filled with double murder, inside job, outside job, or family revenge.

So why not? she asked herself as she mulled over Joseph Martinelli's notion of the two murders as inside events. Weren't the usual suspects from the neighborhood, the community, the family? The homicidal stranger, the random act of violence, contrary to what the public seemed to think, was the oddity. Coastal Maine from time to time yielded its homicide victims, but it certainly wasn't in the same class as the Bronx, Roxbury, the projects of Chicago, angry sections of L.A. The same with terrorism. No way could Ocean Tide be thought of in the same light as the West Bank, Uzbekistan, an unstable part of Africa or the Far East.

So what were the facts? A father-son homicide happening a week apart. Jason and Ned Colley. Drifters. Charming. Totally unreliable. Not living together or even hanging out together. But even taking into account that both men had cut the ties that bind, they were father and son and both had roots in two local families. Death by the practice green, death in the Ocean Tide fertilizer shed—weren't those events just good old-fashioned homegrown cases of homicide? But how homegrown? Betty Colley—vengeance shall be mine—on the prowl with a bike chain and later slipping the body of a most unsatisfactory husband under a load of fertilizer bags? Forget it. Or the Mosebys, at least Mom and the boys—Sarah hadn't had a clue about Dad Albert—climbing the ladder of social success, humiliated by tomcat Ned Colley, and scuzz-ball Jason, had taken steps to keep the Moseby escutcheon clean.

Then Sarah, braking suddenly for a tortoiseshell cat that streaked in front of her car, slowed to a crawl and gave herself a vigorous mental shake. What on earth was she doing? It was Sarah, the evil twin, at it again. Messing in murder. Stop it, she ordered herself. Remember what she'd said. Said publicly. Watch for bike theft, support of the McKenzie seniors, tutoring—just tutoring—these were her things. Her proper business. Even the mystery boy, if finally identified, would be pointed out to the police, and Sarah would pass from the picture. Wipe her feet, wash her hands, keep her nose clean. Sarah the Good and Proper would be in charge.

Resolve in place, she picked up speed and found that she had somehow passed the entrance to Alder Way and was approaching the Golf Pro Shop. And as it loomed by her left flank she was struck by a splendid idea. Golf. Golf for John McKenzie. Elspeth was pushing the idea. So would she. Sarah had never been much interested in the game. Nor, judging from John's remarks, was he enthusiastic. But never mind. He had, at one time, played golf. And he needed to do something besides trying to resurrect some Old English lectures for the local historical society. He needed recreation. People to do something with. He was adrift, but golf—foursomes, twosomes—would bring him into a social circle. And the beauty—

or disadvantage of golf, depending how you looked at it—was that the game went on and on. For hours. A popular golf course teeming with players meant that sometimes five hours were swallowed in playing eighteen holes. Then add to those hours, there was the warm-up on the driving range, a sandwich and a drink midway, and then the obligatory beer and snack or meal after the round, the rehash and replay of every hole. Why, golf could, with proper management, consume an entire day.

Sarah knew all this from having a golf-playing father, and she, her brother, Tony, and her mother had spent much time numbly listening to golf talk. The whiff, the shank, the hook, the slice, the out-of-the-bunker, the into-the-water shot. The choice of the club. The missed putt, the sunk putt. All familiar subjects. But now golf as therapy for her unsettled father-in-law seemed just the proper medicine. And Sarah could take action. With this resolve she turned into the parking area by the Pro Shop, climbed out and headed for the door. What would it be? John had clubs. Sarah had seen the golf bag, dusty from disuse, leaning against the wall of the garage. She would buy him a golf-related present. But what? A polo shirt, the striped kind Tiger Woods favored? A golf glove? No, something closer to the game. Golf balls. Yes. Some state-of-the-art golf balls. Whatever state-of-the-art was these days.

She opened the door and went in. Not just a simple sport shop. A department store. Trousers, shirts, shoes of every hue and degree of cleating. Jackets, windbreakers, umbrellas. Plaques with mounted golf balls. Framed pictures of famous golf courses here and abroad, distant figures swinging away at tees, exploding from bunkers, hunched over putts. And golf bags of every size and shape, clubs by the dozen. Prices— Sarah peered unbelieving at several small price tags around the shafts of a quartet of graphite woods.

And then she saw the balls and walked over to inspect the supply. Good God, some were over forty dollars for a box of twelve. And they seemed to offer everything that a ball could offer: soft feel, cut-proof, increased distance, maximum spin, all with mysterious inner ingredients that made them sound like small atomic bombs. Sarah hesitated, looked around for a clerk who could tell her about some good, medium-priced balls. But the place was empty. And as she peered around, she became aware of what could only be called a rising grumble of noise coming from a back room behind a closed door. Voices raised in anger, murmuring, more voices, a thump as something like a fist struck a table or a counter.

And then the door burst open and a wedge of men pushed through. Headed by one Albert Moseby—a face she'd seen at a distance at the Fitness Center party, a handsome face of the dark-haired hero type, but now a face distorted in what could only be called rage. Albert looked as if he were about to sink his teeth into someone's leg, or shove a fist into someone's face.

"Goddamn it, I'll show you," he shouted. And followed by his three cohorts—each in golf costume—he marched over to the display of clubs.

"These," he said, seizing three irons from a display container. "These, just like these. A set just like these. Callaway Steelhead Irons X-14. Over nine hundred goddamn dollars."

More murmurs, soothing, sympathetic from the Albert Moseby's companions.

"I take today off. First time in months. For a round of golf. Want to try out my new irons. I tell my partner and the two other guys to wait on the tenth tee, and I pull my cart up near the Pro Shop because I need a new glove. Leave the damn cart near the door. With my bag and my partner, Joe's bag, too. I go in, back door. Back door. Buy a glove. Go out. And gone. Gonzo. My three new irons are gonzo. Stolen. Lifted. Not Joe's clubs, just mine. Like my boy's bike lifted last night. As if my family didn't have enough on its plate what with the Colley murders. Jeezus H. Christ, what are you Ocean Tide guys going to do about it? I'm asking and I'm not getting any answers."

At which interesting point, Manager Joseph Martinelli,

Carly at his heels, pushed open the front door and almost ran up to Albert Moseby.

Sarah melted away. Out the door, into the car, out onto Route One, over to the closest shopping center, where she was able to buy a package of twelve Top-Flite golf balls, marked for the "average player" for a mere $16.95. Driving back to the McKenzie cottage she tried to put the scene out of her mind. She was not going to add stolen golf clubs to the search for stolen bikes. Keep it simple, she told herself.

# 12

ALEX, responding to a call from Mike Laaka to meet him at five in George Fitts's VIP Golfer's Cottage, arrived after an irritating afternoon of seeing a number of patients who wanted their rights but weren't sure what those rights were, wanted a second, a third opinion, wanted to change their medication and be given a pocketful of free samples to try out, or cancel their appointment for a colonoscopy. "I mean," said Levy Harmon, an eighty-year-old curmudgeon in perfect health, "who needs a cable up his tail if you're going to die next year anyway?"

Now, Alex looked on his appointment with Mike and George as something like an anodyne to daily life, an oasis away from the hospital, and it must be admitted, a postponement of his visit to his parents—especially his father, who seemed to daily become more irascible.

"Shoot, Mike," he said. "But I can't see how I can help you. The pathology report is pretty simple. Blow to the head, then strangulation for Jason. For Ned Colley, severe head trauma, fatal, followed postmortem dumping of fertilizer bags on the body."

"Listen," said Mike, "I can't be calling Johnny Cuszak every five minutes about some dumb detail on the medical report, but hell, you're around and you probably owe me a couple of favors anyway. I don't understand why they can't pin down time of death with Jason. I mean, okay, it was cold and raining all week, but wouldn't digestive fluids, rigor, skin condition, bruising on the neck, stuff like that give you some kind of idea of when he was killed, strangled? Johnny's backing away from any commitment. What I'm saying is unless we can pinpoint time of death a little better, how in hell can we go around asking people where they were? Who they saw hanging around the bike trail?"

"But everyone agrees that the rotten weather probably meant no one would have been playing a practice hole or using the trails," observed Alex.

"Except the guy, or guys, who were dumping Jason. Okay, but again we'd like a reasonable time frame for when he was killed."

"Mike," said Alex with some exasperation, "I'm not a forensic pathologist. Grab hold of Johnny and express yourself."

"What we both thought, Alex," said a familiar voice, "was that you could grab hold of Johnny and dig into the medical details." It was George who had filtered soundlessly into the Jack Nicklaus Library and now slipped behind his desk, opened a folder, and began tapping a page with his ever-present ballpoint pen.

"Johnny will let you squeeze him dry," said Mike. "Doctor buddies together. He gets impatient with the likes of us."

"Time of death is crucial with Jason Colley," said George. "We've got to zero in on the people in Ocean Tide and find out what they were doing approximately five, six, seven days before the body was found. But "approximately" isn't good enough. We'd like it fixed at one day, two at the most. Or we'll be stuck all spring and maybe half the summer trying to cover a seventy-two-hour period for everyone in the place. Residents, visitors, potential customers, employees, maintenance people. Delivery drivers. Not to mention delivery waiters, cooks, housekeepers, night personnel, nurses at Sunshine House and the staff at the assisted-living units on Village Green, most of whom live elsewhere and have a permanent pass to come and go."

"Just think," said Mike. "It's bad enough asking a crowd of people what they were doing between ten and midnight. Three days would be a nightmare. Amnesia, confusion, what was I doing, let me see, where was I? No one remembers too many details of a three-day stretch of time, unless there was an earthquake going on. A revolution. Or their uncle died and left them money."

"Wait up," said Alex, who was trying to coax a small kernel of information from the conversation. "You're saying you want to get a fix on time of death—within reason—and you're going to limit the interviews to people connected to Ocean Tide?"

George hesitated, tapped his pen in a quick staccato on the desk, and then nodded. "Not limit exactly. But we need data on Ocean Tide residents, look for contradictions, get a handle on people's routine. See if anything leads anywhere."

"What George is saying," interrupted Mike, "is why screw around with the whole of Knox County, especially in summer tourist time, when you've got the victims tied in with two families at Ocean Tide.

George nodded reluctantly; he disliked agreeing with his subordinate. "The Colley-Moseby connection is hard to ignore. We've been checking out Jason Colley's trailer park and the Moseby greenhouse operation. Nothing out of the way so far."

"Go back to Ocean Tide," said Mike. "Someone might have seen something. Everything is so damn open in the place. Open roads and trails, cut lawns, open gardens, shaved golf course. Unless you're hiding out in a building, you're in view. I could stand almost anywhere, turn my head, and I'd see the people go by. Isn't like the murders happened off the trail on Mount

Katahdin or on the Allagash. Or a crowded city."

"Of course," added George, "there's the matter of the bicycles. I just learned that the oldest Moseby's bike—that's Nick—was also stolen. A racing model. Apparently Nick was training with a local bike-racing group, the Penobscot Wheelers. And Albert Moseby's extremely expensive set of irons have gone missing."

"Well, damn," said Mike. "This is turning into a sports story."

"It is and remains two cases of homicide," said George. "However—" He paused and a shadow passed over his face. George's face was possessed of only a small repertoire of expressions: usually it went from shadow to gloom to irritation. Rarely to pleasure. Now irritation settled in.

"Do you think it's a case of hit the family when they're down?" asked Mike.

"But," objected Alex, "isn't the Moseby family a side issue? Betty Colley is the one who lost a husband and a stepson. Sherry Moseby is her sister, yes, but Jason was a stepnephew; she wasn't really related to Ned. Same with Albert Moseby, just a connection by marriage."

"You think we have a couple of Colley homicides and some Moseby sports equipment thefts and they may have zip to do with each other?" said Mike.

"Possible," said George. "But for what it's worth, Jason paid cash down for that expensive mountain bike of his. Bought it at that Camden Techno-Bike Shop. Bikes there start over four hundred bucks and go up from there. Jason had a Schwinn model selling in the low thousands. That's where his combination lock Mike found in the water came from. As we know, because that shop just happens to keep track of the combo numbers. So where'd Jason get the money? He was last working as a dishwasher in a Camden restaurant."

"Back to time of death," said Mike. "That's the numero uno need."

George ignored this. He disliked being prompted. "Alex,

see if you can make some headway with Johnny Cuszak. He never wants to put himself out on a limb, doesn't want to end up in court being cornered by some slippery defense lawyer. But if you push . . ."

"Not just push, grab him by the balls, make him talk," said Mike.

"I get the point," said Alex standing up. "I'll give Johnny a ring. Soften him up over some friendly baseball talk. He told me he's a Detroit Tigers fan and no one shows any sympathy to him here in Red Sox land."

"You'd think it was against the law to root for anyone but those Red Sox losers," said Johnny over a glass of predinnertime beer at the Rockland Diner. They sat in a corner under a large print of a four-masted ship under full sail with the name Maritime Oil imprinted on its mat. Alex had caught up with Johnny as he came out of the sheriff's department in Rockland. "Catching up on local paperwork," he said with a heavy sigh. "Been a long day. A DOA at the hospital, guy shot on both sides of his head, just above the ear. Different caliber weapons. I mean what kind of scene was that? A two-gun assault, a double-handed shoot-up, Smith and Wesson in my left hand, Glock in my right."

"I can take your mind off the problem," said Alex. "George and Mike want a closer fix on the Jason Colley murder. Think you can give it to them but are holding out to drive them crazy."

"The day I drive George Fitts crazy will be the day I'll send up balloons and hand out free ice cream," said Johnny.

"So what about it?" said Alex. "Right now time of death is anywhere from mid-Friday, May nineteenth, to late Sunday night, the twenty-first. Could you shrink that for us?"

Johnny Cuszak looked around the restaurant and its occupants as if expecting to see a bailiff, a robed judge, or worse— one of the county defense team having an early dinner. "Off the record?" he said, lowering his voice to a husky whisper.

"Off the record. The police just want a place to start."

"What I don't get," complained Johnny, "is why somebody's dog didn't find the Jason kid earlier. Make my job easier. I mean, there was this body in this high-class packaged-living community. Ready for any dog to sniff out."

"Steady rain for almost a week," Alex reminded him. "No one walking his dog. And the place has a leash law. No loose dogs to run around finding bodies. People have electric fence systems, dog runs, but no loose animals. My parents were warned about letting the two Sealyhams out."

"What I'm saying is," Johnny went on, "I don't want George and company to hold me to a set time. It's a tough call. Corpse hardly had a chance to decompose properly. Not like it would in an ordinary warm spring week."

"Wait up," said Alex. He rose from the table, disappeared behind a counter, returned in two minutes. "Called them. George won't hold you to it. His word. They want a 'suggested' time period. A 'possible' time period. Not signed in blood and notarized."

"Okay, okay," said Johnny, putting down his glass. "Cases like this Jason kid, they're a pain in the ass. If I had my druthers, I'd get to see the corpse within an hour or so after death or find it after fifty years frozen into the ice."

"So," said Alex. "since this one wasn't frozen into ice, what's a fair guess?"

"Based on the whole picture, skin breakdown, some presence of gas, fluid leaks, well, maybe I'd go for Sunday. Saturday night at the very earliest, early Monday morning at the latest. But my money would be on a twenty-four-hour period covering Sunday. There, does that box it in for you? I won't put it in writing. Time of death, it's not like an algebra formula. Too many frigging variables. But I've got another gift for George. I'll be calling him when you leave. Microscopic fragments of dark green paint found on Ned Colley's clothing. Also spots of some lube oil. Or grease. Grass stains. The lab's working on all this, but with the paint, it's like the kind used on metal work, bikes, railings, garden equipment. Now the police can run around scraping up samples of green paint, grass, and checking out oil samples."

Alex rose to his feet. "Since Ned Colley might have been dragged in from the golf course to that equipment shack, it's not surprising about the grass stains. And the paint, well, he could have picked it up anywhere or sat down on a bench. And from what I've heard of Ned Colley, I'd be surprised if his clothes didn't have grease stains."

"Wherever the stuff came from, it should keep George and Mike busy and off my back," said Johnny with satisfaction.


Elspeth was standing on the doorstep of the McKenzie cottage when Sarah pulled up. With a big gesture she waved Sarah into the living room and then exploded with information.

"You'll never guess," she said, and Sarah was hard put to tell if Elspeth was in a state of outrage or just simple excitement.

No, she told Elspeth, she couldn't guess. Here she fended off a greeting from Patsy that involved paws on shoulders and a face licking. Then, confronting Elspeth, she gritted her teeth. "Not another body, is it?"

"No, for heaven's sake, Sarah, you have a fixation on bodies. But it's another bike. A bike theft. A neighbor, Bill somebody, just told me."

Sarah swallowed hard. Not bodies. Not even golf clubs, another bicycle. She sighed in relief. Bikes were okay, they were in her—and Elspeth's—sphere of interest. "You mean here?" she asked Elspeth. "At Ocean Tide? Another bike? But who?"

"It's unbelievable but it's a Moseby. The oldest boy, Nicholas, the one we met at the bike shop. He was out riding, doing some kind of training run. Needed to fill his water bottle, left the bike against a tree at a friend's house, came out, and no bike. Right here, on that stretch of road over on Peony Point.

He went into the kitchen, filled his bottle, went back out and it was missing."

Elspeth removed a sleeping Sealyham from a soft chair covered in a faded floral pattern and sank into it. "Two Moseby bikes," she repeated. Then, "Maybe someone hates the Mosebys. Or loves their bikes."

Sarah, in her turn, sat down, patted Patsy on the head, accepted the indignant Sealyham, settled him in her lap—it was either Stupid or Seymour; they were identical—and confronted her mother-in-law. "Actually it's golf clubs, too. Albert Moseby is missing three golf clubs. Another hit on the Moseby family. Or I should say, the Moseby-Colley clan."

"Those two families," said Elspeth in a wondering voice. "It's as if they had a curse on them. An ongoing curse."

"You mean," said Sarah frowning, "first dead bodies, then bikes, then golf clubs. In sort of a reverse order of importance."

At which interesting point John McKenzie entered the room. Dressed for the outdoors. The heat had retreated, the air was turning brisk with a north wind and he wore an ancient canvas jacket, much worn and mended. His white hair rising like a cloud off his head and his face ruddy from either exertion or the wind.

"I just stopped in at the Pro Shop," he announced. "It's in an uproar."

"I've been telling Elspeth," said Sarah, "about Albert Moseby's golf clubs."

"Yes," said John. "Some fantastic make I've never heard of. Martinelli's there along with that nice Carly Thompson. They're trying to calm things down, offer a new set of clubs, but it's like pouring kerosene on a bonfire. Moseby's going on about nothing being safe."

"It's because the Mosebys have expensive things," put in Sarah, who along with Elspeth wanted to nudge the conversation away from the idea of Fate at work with two related families. "You know, the attractive nuisance idea. Who wants to steal an old bike, old golf clubs? A beaten-up Subaru like mine or a five-year-old Ford. They'd rather help themselves to an MG or a BMW, super-duper bikes and golf clubs. I mean, aren't those things just asking to be lifted?"

"What an awful view of the world," said Elspeth. "As if we have to have junk in order to be theft free. I should have known better than to get a new bike. Let that be a lesson to me. From now on it's rags and tatters. Secondhand all the way."

"So, John," said Sarah, still trying to move the McKenzies into a forward gear. "Just what were you doing in the Pro Shop? Thinking about golf? Did you sign up for a starting time? Find someone to play with?"

"Well," said John reluctantly. "I left my name but now I think it's a pretty stupid idea. My clubs are ancient. And we haven't finished this moving business and I have all my papers and books to sort and—"

"I think golf is a terrific idea," said Sarah. "Fresh salt air and zooming around in a golf cart. And I have a present for you." She rose, walked into the front hall, picked up the box of new golf balls and presented them. "Now you have to . . ."

"Follow through?" finished John, chuckling.

"You took the words out of my mouth," said Sarah, thinking that a man in love with his own puns could not be beyond rescue.


Alex climbed back into his Jeep, plugged in his car phone, got George on the line and gave him the news. "Off the record, Johnny's got it down almost to thirty or so hours so you can begin working around Sunday." With that Alex stepped on the accelerator, made it to the Ocean Tide security gate in record time, and then, obeying the fifteen-mile speed limit, crept around to 7 Alder Way.

There to find that something other than homicides, stolen bikes, and golf clubs now occupied his parents. He found

Sarah, holding Patsy, lingering in the background, as John and Elspeth stood in the middle of the living room. Arguing. Gesticulating.

"Good news and bad," called Elspeth as Alex walked in.

"Start with the good and work down," said Alex.

"The good," said Elspeth, waving a letter she had been clutching, "is Phoebe Sachs, my friend in France who has a house in Venasque. Well, she's had a guest cancel out, and I can push my trip ahead, which leaves more time for getting this family party under control. Provence in June is heaven on earth. But not so much heaven for John. Leaving him here."

"John," said John, "can be left perfectly well. It's what's going to be left *with* John. That's the bad news."

"Out with it," said Alex. "Not my cousin Giddy and a druggie boyfriend."

Elspeth shook her head. "Worse. Much worse."

"A drugged boyfriend I would welcome with open arms," said John.

"It's Uncle Fergus," said Elspeth. She reached into her overall pockets and produced a second letter. "He wants to come. A longer visit. Not just a few days for his birthday."

"Two weeks at least," said John. "Maybe more. Sees no use in short visits. A waste of time. His words."

"Oh, God," said Alex. "Call him off. Ring the alarm. Set the dogs. Sound the claxon."

"The man," said Elspeth sinking down in a chair and gesturing with Uncle Fergus's letter, a large white sheet with a black spiderlike writing scratched across its surface, "is not reachable. He's on a sort of bus tour. College towns of New England. And, he says, he can get off here. In Rockland. Land right on our doorstep."

Sarah, seeing the consternation on the three McKenzie faces, tried to put together her last memory of Uncle Fergus. Two years ago? A visit to Weymouth Island and the McKenzie "cottage"—for cottage read large rambling shingle affair with porches, dormers, uneven steps, furnished by a multitude of odd furniture in wicker and oak, with iron beds, and sagging horsehair mattresses. Uncle Fergus had arrived, dressed in white rather like the Kentucky Colonel, and had taken up the attention of the entire family and half the neighbors. His diet required things like coddled eggs, twice-strained orange juice, steamed cabbage, puréed prunes, vanilla junket, and bread made with stone-ground oat flour. His comfort demanded the big chair by the fireplace (usually John McKenzie's chosen spot); the front guest room usually reserved for Alex and Sarah, who moved into back area bunk beds; meals served at the exact hours of 7:30, 12:30, and 7:30. Blood pressure checked and medications reviewed (by Alex); and the delivery of the *Boston Globe*, *The New York Times*, the *Wall Street Journal* within ten minutes of the morning ferry landing on the island. Visits to the Weymouth library had taken on the aspect of a royal progress ending with Uncle Fergus denouncing the gaps in the collection and, after borrowing a book, returning it with a number of misprints marked in ink. The visit ended with Elspeth close to collapse, John in a thundering temper, and Alex and Sarah leaving to spend several restorative days in the northern Maine wilderness.

And why did the McKenzies put up with it? Sarah had asked herself. But Uncle Fergus was, she decided, one of those lifelong burdens that many families take on, almost unwittingly, and bear to the grave: either to their own graves, or if fortunate, the grave of the family termagant. Sarah herself, her whole family, had been dealing with a modified female version of Uncle Fergus for years. Her own grandmother Douglas had tried to rule over her family through Biblical injunctions and veiled threats from a musty Victorian house in Camden and now at ninety-one was still going strong.

Sarah came out of her reverie to find that Alex had taken charge.

"Not staying here," he announced. "The Lodge. If you can't stop the old bird, you can at least keep him at a distance."

"But," protested Elspeth, "he knows we have a guest room.

And a pull-out sofa in John's office. And a rollaway in my studio over the garage."

"How," demanded John, "does Fergus know these things."

"I write him," said Elspeth apologetically. "It's one of those things you do. I mean, he's all alone. . . ."

"With good reason," said John. "And he's my uncle. I should be writing him."

"But you don't," said Elspeth. "So I do. And I never know what to say so I just ramble on with stupid details. I described Ocean Tide. Our cottage. The layout."

"Mother," said Alex, "that was noble of you. But as of today, this place will not have room for anyone. We'll move Dad's books—all those boxes in the garage—into the guest room. Fill the place up. Dad's office, too. More boxes. And Mother pack more stuff in your studio so there's no room for the old goat. So now I'll go and reserve a room at the Lodge. Uncle Fergus can eat breakfast and dinner there. Remember what Dear Abby, or was it Ann Landers, said, 'No one can take advantage of you without your consent.' "

Sarah, getting into the swing of things, interrupted. "There's a senior citizen table; I'll could sign him up. There are probably a dozen other Uncle Ferguses—or would it be Uncle Fergi?—at Ocean Tide."

"And," went on Alex, "sometimes Dad can have soup and a sandwich at the Golf Grille with him, and Sarah and I will come in and take him out to the local eateries. And as I remember, Uncle Fergus can still dodder around the golf course. We'll sign him up for a string of starting times. And you, Mother, can go to Provence and paint to your heart's content and forget about Fergus until the birthday-anniversary bash, which Sarah and I'll help put together."

There was a moment of silence while the elder McKenzies digested these statements. And then a general letting out of breath, an exhalation of relief.

"Perfect," said Elspeth. And then, "All right, not perfect.

Nothing about Uncle Fergus is close to perfect. But it's manageable."

"And I," said John, "will sign up for golf starting times at a different hour from Uncle Fergus. We can wave at each other from different fairways."

"Perhaps," said Elspeth, ever hopeful, "he's had a change of personality."

"That I doubt," said Alex. "But I will be on hand from time to time to bolster your backbone. And on a weekend I'll take the old boy out for bird-watching."

"I don't think he watches birds," put in Elspeth.

"He will now," said Alex grimly. "And now, Mother, start packing and find your passport. Dad, let's go down and arrange the golf schedule."

"To change the subject," said Elspeth, "how does the search for my bicycle continue if I'm in Provence and Uncle Fergus is on the premises? That was what Sarah and I—and John, too—were going to do, look for my bike."

"Don't worry," said Sarah lightly. "Maybe we can rent a tricycle for Uncle Fergus and he can help us look."

"You, my dearest love, and you, my respected parents," said Alex, "may look around for Mother's bicycle. And by all means take Uncle Fergus. But, no one is to go looking for the bikes—or golf clubs—belonging to the Moseby clan. Those things may be connected, for now, anyway, to the homicide scene. Interaction with the Colley and Moseby families should be limited to taking over loaves of bread or dishes of shepherd's pie."

"Don't be such a bore, Alex," said his mother. "You're always pontificating about what we shouldn't do."

"That," said Alex, "is because you and Sarah are always doing what you shouldn't do. And this doesn't come from me. It comes straight from Sergeant George Fitts, Maine State Police, CID, with a seconding motion from Mike Laaka, sheriff's deputy investigator, sheriff's department, Knox County."

"Actually," said John, "no one's told me not to be involved. I may start reading up on forensic medicine."

"The point is," said Elspeth, looking brighter, "that, with a little planning, I think we can get a stranglehold on Uncle Fergus."

"Interesting remark," said John. "Wasn't that Colley boy strangled?"

# 13

THE last days of May and the first weekdays of June brought friendly temperatures in the low seventies and soft southwest wind, which not only eased the usual plague of black flies besieging anyone out of doors but created new problems for Manager Joseph Martinelli. People wanted to go to the beach. After a long bitter winter, they wanted out. Shore and ocean. That's why they moved to Ocean Tide, wasn't it? Not necessarily to swim—the Maine waters were not swimmer friendly until almost July—but to walk, to collect shells, to have picnics, sit under an umbrella with a book, launch a skiff, a kayak, or a small sailboat from the Ocean Tide boat dock.

But the police had declared the entire shoreline out of bounds. The coast offered a possible ingress—or egress—to the small equipment shed near the seventeenth green where Ned Colley's body had been found, *and* Jason Colley's combination lock had been discovered in the shallow waters off a prime stretch of the shore. And added to Joseph Martinelli's grief over the closing off of the beach was the yellow tape surrounding the seventeenth green, a stretch of its fairway, the rough, and surrounding bunkers. This action had caused a makeshift green to be created adjacent to the eighteenth green tee, which caused great confusion, approach shots to the seventeenth green often ending up on the eighteenth tee.

But Joseph was a fighter. He sent that upbeat character, Carly Thompson, out into the golf and beach world to manage, explain, suggest hiking, bicycling (this another sore subject but not a prohibited activity), a swim in the outdoor pool, a game of tennis—complimentary tennis balls for the next two weeks. And Naomi Foxglove went forth as the understanding ear, the soother of the angry. The planner of distracting social events. The Midcoast Community Band was imported to present an evening program of popular numbers from well-known musicals.

"We've just had Memorial Day," announced Joseph to Carly. "That should stop the whining about beaches and the golf course. Make people think about our soldiers and sailors. Our marines. Air force. Lost over there." Joseph gestured in the general direction of Europe. "Or this country, Gettysburg, Antietam, those places. Lexington and Concord. The Alamo. Vietnam, Korea, The Middle East. Everywhere," he added, lest some area of the fallen be neglected. "Keep the flags flying on all the public buildings for the whole of next week," he instructed Carly. "Refreshments after the music program. Ice cream, quality stuff."

"You have a message from the Midcoast Audubon Society," Carly told him. "They think that all the grass and golf course mowing and the tree trimming have upset the warbler migration and now are disturbing the nesting birds. And all the police buzzing around is making it worse. Also they want to know what Ocean Tide is using for fertilizers and insect sprays."

Joseph made a gargling sound in his throat, which was interrupted by good news from a just-arrived Naomi. The Sunday buffet with its two kosher tables was a great success and the menus with foods suitable for Muslims and Hindus and vegetarians, including vegans, should be worked out by next week. "And," she added, "the police will not be coming into the Lodge dining room to eat, they'll be sending out for food."

"Best of all," added Carly, "a call just came in from gate security. A van delivering baked goods to the Lodge kitchen was stopped—routine, the driver looked nervous—at the gate and two of our rental bikes were found in the back."

Joseph's face broke into a wide and happy smile. "Mother, Mary, and Joseph, thank you. Good news for a change. Two homicides I gotta live with but we don't need those bike thefts." Here he paused, his round face creased again with worry. "Too much to ask, I suppose, that Al Moseby's golf clubs turned up in the van. Or Mrs. McKenzie's new bike."

"Security's calling the police," said Carly, "so I guess they'll be bringing the driver in and doing a search. The van, the guy's house. We can only hope."

On the McKenzie home front, by dint of much labor, John's boxes of books from the garage had been added to the guest room and overflowed into his study, which was also augmented by several odd pieces of furniture no one had been able to place. Elspeth also achieved the crowded look by scattering a number of large old canvases about her garage studio and adding two folding beach chairs so that by the first of June the fortress was complete and the McKenzies were as ready as they would ever be for the invader.

"I feel as if I'm committing a sin against hospitality. Against family values," said Elspeth while she and Sarah, as a finishing touch, set up a long disused standing easel in the center of the studio.

"If Uncle Fergus was going to stay with you for two weeks or even more," said Sarah, "you'd be committing something else. He doesn't care about other people's sensibilities let alone proper guest behavior. The last time Alex and I saw him he went on about doctors bleeding the sick and why wasn't I staying home having babies instead of taking jobs away from qualified academic males."

"Oh, dear," said Elspeth weakly, "I didn't know he'd sunk his teeth into you two."

"The point is," Sarah answered, "that Alex and I can protect ourselves, but you two are sitting ducks. Cannon fodder. Now with Fergus at the Lodge, John can take him in small doses, Manager Martinelli can hover around acting deferential—it's something he does very well—and we can all celebrate Uncle Fergus's birthday without wanting to cleave him in two with an ax."

"And I can think about packing," said Elspeth. "June fourteenth. I'm on an American Airlines evening flight from Logan. And best of all I have a ride all the way to Boston. That racing-bike team, the one that Nick Moseby's with, they're on the same flight to France to race next week. Mr. Martinelli is underwriting part of the team. And poor Nick. Imagine having your racing bike stolen before the race. Even if he has a whole string of bikes, it must have been upsetting."

Sarah opened her eyes. "A bike race in France. That sounds like a major event. Not the Tour de France? Even I've heard of that."

"This isn't a big-time event," said Elspeth. "But pretty exciting for a local Maine team. Anyway, I'll get a ride in the Ocean Tide van. All the comforts."

"It all sounds wonderful for you," said Sarah, trying to focus on Elspeth's trip. The trouble was that after Uncle Fergus had been dealt with her mind began turning to subjects closer to home. Although school was not out, Betty had insisted on beginning as soon as possible. So Sarah was summoned to spend time that afternoon in Betty Colley's living room during which Sarah would go over the assigned essays. Then, as soon as school was out in the middle of June, formal times and dates would be arranged.

But Sarah, visiting Betty the day before to plan a schedule, found that the shock of Jason and Ned's death, rather than receding had somehow intensified.

Sarah had been met at the door by a flushed and tearful Betty, looking disheveled in worn slacks and a large faded man's work shirt hanging almost to her knees. What had happened, Sarah saw at once, as Betty waved her to the porch swing, was that guilt with a capital *G* had kicked in. Betty had begun to find reasons for her own complicity in the two deaths. It was, Sarah had heard, what happened to families and friends. In the face of evidence to the contrary, the victim's nearest and dearest tried to play the "if" game. What if I had been more thoughtful, caring, loving, sharing? What if I had paid attention that day, that night, that month, that year? Why didn't I see the signs, listen more carefully? Tell him not to have that third drink, tell her not to light another cigarette, make him slow down to sixty? Fasten their lifejackets properly? Why didn't I say something, try to stop something? Do something? Anything.

Betty said all this and launched herself on a complete post-mortem rehab program of Ned Colley and Jason Colley from early days to their last grim appearance. Perhaps, Sarah reasoned, sitting next to Betty on the swing and patting her hand, it was human nature to bestow on the two men virtues they didn't have, and so validate their lives and deaths. Which in an odd way, made Betty's increasing grief and mourning legitimate.

Of course, Ned and Jason, being the characters they were, chameleons, turncoats, even in death they could get the best of Betty. They both had shared that wonderful ability to apologize, weep, promise and swear at the crucial moment, and then to make an uproarious joke of the whole business. They had, Betty told Sarah in a voice muffled by a combined laugh and a sob, this crazy, almost magic way about them, that wonderful smile that turned you right around in your chair.

"Like we were all in a movie or down at the local bar

whooping it up," said Betty. "Goddamn Irish, even if they've lived here all their lives, it's something genetic or the DNA or something. They could get away with anything and leave me laughing." Betty then went on to tell Sarah about Jason's short but brilliant baseball career—"played the game like an angel from heaven, balls dropping in his mitt, pitched right into his bat"—and Ned's singing, all those old songs—"made us all, even Mumma, break down and cry."

But with Sherry Moseby it was a different matter. If she had felt grief, it had been fired in another furnace. She had come over that afternoon, dressed for summer, her dark hair smooth and swept back, her white slacks and navy shirt, her white canvas shoes unmarked by wear. Like the perfect guest—or sister—she had brought a still-warm coffee cake to share with tea or lemonade, so they had all settled down in Betty's kitchen, a space in disarray with dishes, cereal boxes, half-eaten bananas, a frying pan under a dripping faucet giving a sense of unhappy confusion.

Sherry had gone right to the matter. That Jason, Sherry had insisted, was no good from day one, so stop eating your heart out. He was a flake, a druggie, made for trouble. And Ned was nothing more than a two-timing slime you couldn't trust to make change from a dollar bill. He got into bed with any woman who walked by him. Her sister was lucky—yes, it was a terrible thing to say but she, Sherry, was going to say it—Betty was lucky to be rid of them both. "And," Sherry ended, "this is such a wonderful community to live in, you can't let this spoil it all. I've been so upset thinking that those two sleazes might have ruined Ocean Tide for all of us. Not just Betty but me and Alfred and our boys. We care, too, you know. We really do."

Sarah, listening to Sherry, watching Betty shrink back in her chair, thought that if Betty was close to meltdown, Sherry was going to break into a hundred sharp pieces. She seemed even more nervous than she had been when they had met in Manager Martinelli's office, and she kept looking around as if expecting some unnatural apparition to come out from a utility closet. Asked by Sarah about her own boys, Sherry confessed that she didn't know whether they were bothered about the murders. "It's best not to go on and on about it. Betty here, if she won't stop agonizing over it, she'll have Dylan and Brian jumping out of their skins, which they already are if you ask me."

But Betty had made an heroic effort, pulled herself together. Taking deep breaths, she wiped her eyes, and helped herself to a piece of the coffee cake. Sarah then summed up her hopes for the tutoring program and departed, uneasy about the support system in both families. Betty on a guilt trip, Albert Moseby and older son Nick both absent and busy with their jobs. Sherry a jittery mother, and at least one boy, Dylan, wasn't it? who had wiggled out of the first meeting.

And now the day after this scene, leaving Elspeth reassured on the score of Uncle Fergus and ready to look to her packing, find her portable easel and watercolor boxes, her passport, Sarah, briefcase in hand, walked up to Betty Colley's front door and knocked.

Four boys sat opposite Sarah. Two on a sofa, two on adjoining chairs, Mosebys together, Colleys together. Thin faced, knobby kneed, they looked all of them more like brothers than cousins, even the older Moseby who sat somewhat apart— Matt, wasn't it?—fitted into the picture. This uniform impression was enhanced by the costume of baggy khaki trousers, enormous sneakers, and white T-shirts with logos. Then, as she opened her briefcase a cold tickle ran down her back. One of the Colley boys she was certain was going to be the boy she, the police, was looking for. The trouble was that the room was dark, curtains pulled possibly in deference to recent events. The four boys sat in the darker part of the room, the only light a standing lamp behind Sarah. Furthermore they each wore, pulled tight over his head, a baseball cap—Red Sox caps for Brian and Dylan and Tim; Dallas Cowboys for Matt. And each boy kept his head lowered as if contemplating the state of his sneakers or the Colley living room rug.

The session was not a success. All four boys stuck to monosyllabic replies. The assigned essays were produced and read aloud—or muttered aloud—and all showed minimum effort and inspiration. Short sentences, little action, no description. "A Day Fishing" by the youngest Moseby, Tim. The weather was good, the wind wasn't strong, the fish weren't biting, they went home early. They didn't catch fish. Maybe next time they would.

So it went. Brian Colley wrote, as Sarah had expected, about his cat, Charlie, who didn't come when he was called, had sharp claws, and sometimes threw up his dinner. End of essay. And Dylan Colley, keeping his head low, eyes on his paper, stumbled through three short paragraphs about a camping trip where it rained, the tent leaked, everything got wet, and the pancakes were soggy. Seventeen-year-old Matt Moseby, of whom a more complex effort might have been expected, offered a threadbare effort on a school visit to the Portland Museum of Art in which he apparently saw little and liked less.

Sarah spoke for a few moments about the need for specific details, for action, for words that would make their stories come alive, and then told them that she looked forward to meeting the youngest three boys after school closed for the summer. With Matt Moseby, she would work out a schedule. In the meantime they could start reading a book from the list she would send them.

Sarah collected and packed the boys' essays into her briefcase. And then, ready to leave, she raised her head at the exact moment that Dylan Colley raised his. Their eyes met. And for the briefest time held. And Sarah knew that Dylan, not Brian, was the one. This was the boy who had found the body of Ned Colley. And she understood, in that flash of eye contact, that Dylan recognized Sarah, knew that they met down at the edge of the pines by the seventeenth green, and most important, knew that Sarah now recognized him. And from the convulsive jerk of Dylan's shoulders, from his quickly turned head, Sarah also knew for a certainly that she represented something very frightening to this boy.

She stood up slowly, fixed her eyes on the opposite wall where hung a photograph of black-and-white cows wending their way toward a distant barn—the Colley's former dairy herd perhaps—and then said to no one boy in particular that she looked forward to the next session.

Walking to her car she said to herself over and over, damn, damn, damn. Now what should she do? Drive over to George Fitts office and serve Dylan Colley up to the police grinder? Or do the decent thing and first warn the boy that there was going to be a detective in his future. Oh, damn, damn, damn.

By the time Sarah had turned the corner of Alder Way she had stopped swearing and was looking for a way out of the dilemma. Since she had foresworn meddling in police matters she could simply call George Fitts, hand in Dylan's name, and retreat. Don't taint Dylan's evidence by returning to the Colley house and trying to explain about the responsibilities of a witness and thus make matters worse. So let George and company pounce on him—no, not pounce, perhaps tiptoe into the Colley house and with the kindness of a concerned relative ask him to take a fun ride to the police station. Sarah spent a brief moment as she circled slowly about the perimeter of Ocean Tide picturing George as a friendly uncle, but all her brain could conjure was a wolflike George in a nightgown, a cap on his head, playing the part of Red Riding Hood's grandmother.

By the time Sarah had completed a second tour around the community, she had, after much anxious brain work, found a way. She could wiggle out from between the horns of her dilemma and slither free. Despite the unfortunate analogy to some sort of snake, she felt a huge sense of relief as she pulled over by the entrance to Alder Way and turned off the car's engine. Here's how it would work. First, she would not be the snitch. She had never liked snitches of any sort. But the beauty of her idea was that she could still do the responsible thing. In a roundabout way. She'd find Betty Colley and describe the scene with the frightened Dylan, and ask Betty to call the police. Calling the police in this case was a mother's job, wasn't it? And wouldn't Dylan accept this from his mother a lot faster than from a stranger? A possibly dangerous stranger masquerading as an English teacher.

Sarah, full of righteous purpose, marched up the McKenzies' walk, pulled open the door, and headed for the telephone.

It was all done within the hour. Betty called, agreed to meet Sarah right away at the small park at the end of Alder Way. She sat down on the park bench next to Sarah, her face still flushed from agitation, and listened to the tale. Nodded with understanding. Agreed. One hundred percent. Calling the police about what her son had seen was certainly a parent's job. Not for Sarah to do. After all, the body found was Dylan's very own father. She'd phone them when she got home, and then break the news to Dylan. "The poor kid, he must have been frightened out of whatever wits he has. Not that he's dumb," added his mother, who apparently took a realistic view of her son's potential, "but he's probably not going to go into atomic science or write a best-seller."

"Of course he was frightened," said Sarah. "Anybody would have been. And there I was, about a hundred yards from where the body was found. For all Dylan knows I may have just come from that shed, fresh from murder."

"And," added Betty, her face smoothing as something troubling was suddenly made clear, "that's why he shaved his head. I've been wondering. Other boys weren't cutting their hair off and Dylan usually likes to be in sync. He didn't want you to recognize him. Made Brian do the same to make it seem normal. But God Almighty, when will this thing be over, I ask you that? But thanks for telling me. I've got a prescription for sleeping pills from your husband, so maybe after a good night's sleep I'll pull up my socks and start functioning. It's just that . . ." But here Betty trailed off, gave a shuddering sigh, heaved herself off the bench, waved good-bye, and departed with an uncertain step toward her house.

Sarah left the meeting trying hard to shake the sense that turning the matter of telling the police over to Betty was not entirely the unambiguous action of a responsible citizen. That it was more as if she had washed her hands of the affair like some sort of a female Pontius Pilate in order not to have an unhappy boy on her conscience. And because of these misgivings, Sarah couldn't get rid of that unfortunate image of a snake wiggling free from a trap.

But back at the McKenzies' cottage she found the place abuzz with action. Travel was in the air. Elspeth, wearing an ancient sweatshirt and a pair of faded red trousers, was engaged in sorting out wrinkle-proof travel clothes, things that could be washed in a sink, all-purpose shoes, and jackets and raincoats with multiple inside pockets. Her folding easel, her traveling paintbox lay ready in the hall and John was on the phone asking about the current value of the French franc and the Euro to the American dollar.

"Before Provence, I'll have two days and an overnight in Paris," exclaimed Elspeth. "My old favorite, the Hotel de la Roche. Left Bank, in walking distance to the Musée D'Orsay, the Louvre, and that marvelous shop for pastels and paper practically around the corner."

Sarah could see that Elspeth was on a high; the threat of Uncle Fergus had been pushed to the backburner. "John can deal with him better than I can. It's his uncle, after all," Elspeth remarked as she produced a small wheeled suitcase from the interior of the front hall clothes closet.

John for his part was now acting the helpful mate. Putting down the phone he said that the Euro seemed a little wobbly and that Elspeth had better stick to francs, and that he, John, would devote much of his leisure time to hunting down her stolen bike and anyone else's stolen bike, and playing golf with any age-stricken players the golf pro could produce. And he was not going to buy any new fancy titanium or uranium golf clubs. He would use his old clubs; he was proud to use his old clubs. He was not a man who could be swayed by fashion and fancy-dancy technology. By God, what was good enough for Ben Hogan, Byron Nelson, and Tommy Armour was good enough for John McKenzie.

# 14

MANAGER Joseph Martinelli had been floating on a wave of euphoria after the report of the capture of the bike felon by his sharp-eyed gate guard. The two murders had been bad enough, but the thought that bicycle theft was commonplace at Ocean Tide had been in the nature of a last straw. As Carly had said, murder lent a kind of strange cachet to these events, fear and horror being compounded with a general frisson of excitement. But the lifting of bicycles—and now expensive golf clubs—was everyday stealing and suggested that a full-scale and varied crime wave was well under way.

"You gotta believe, Carly, I'm being driven out of my head," said Joseph to his assistant on the next morning, the first Friday of June. "Everyone is coming in complaining, bellyaching. And the weather, Holy Mother of God, you can't trust anything."

The day was indeed turning grayer and cooler and foggier by the minute, and staff discontent was rife. The head chef, Alberto, was threatening departure if one more ethnic menu was forced on him—last evening's demand by a British guest for a particular Egyptian cucumber and sour milk soup had thrown Alberto into a double helix of anxiety and fury. Alberto finally consoled, Manager Martinelli was assaulted by a demand by the librarian at the Lodge, for an extra sum of money from the budget to purchase a number of books on alternative medicines in order to satisfy the demands of several outspoken residents. She was then followed by the head gardener, announcing with triumph that he had uprooted twelve flourishing plants of cannabis that morning from the plantings at the foot of the terrace.

Carly, who had been standing by during these comings and goings, interrupted Joseph's laments by pointing out that perhaps the stolen rental bikes newly discovered in the pickup truck by the gatehouse guard had nothing to do with two stolen bikes and golf clubs belonging to the Moseby family.

"Like it's a family gang thing. You know, you're Italian. Maybe," suggested Carly, "there's a third family related to the Mosebys and Colleys and they're getting revenge by killing off a couple of Colleys and stealing stuff from the Mosebys. But our rental bikes being taken, hey, that's just usual stuff. Not related. Just like we talked about before, places like Ocean Tide have these things happen. I heard from a friend of mine who works down on some South Carolina resort beach place. Bikes disappear all the time."

Joseph Martinelli looked for a moment as if Carly were kicking him in the stomach. "You've seen too many godfather movies, that's what," he growled.

At which point Naomi Foxglove slipped into the room, a fashion statement in two-piece silver and black with a strand of jet beads around her shapely neck. "The police just called in. They've got a search warrant for the man they caught with the rental bikes. His garage is stuffed with bikes. Mostly rentals from other resorts. Some from around the towns, especially Camden: They took Nick Moseby with them because he's up on our rental inventory, has the purchase records, and he identified four from Ocean Tide. But none matching Mrs. McKenzie's bike. And they didn't find Nick Moseby's own racing bike or his brother Matt's mountain bike. And, for what it's worth, the police didn't find any golf clubs."

"See, you've got two bike scams going here," said Carly. "One's the Moseby-Colley family thing—bikes, murder, and golf clubs. The other's just the everyday bike business as usual that's going on all over the coast. It's really very simple."

For a moment the two assistants watched Joseph flounder, twist in his chair, glower at the gray ocean framed in his window. He wanted a procedure, a plan of attack. A strategy. But even such an optimist as he couldn't conjure away what had happened at Ocean Tide. Nor could he wave a wand and make the Mosebys and the Colleys vanish into the ether—or at the very least order a moving van and send them back where they came from—the distant blueberry barrens and rocks of Union and Appleton. But, as was usual with Joseph, if he couldn't win on the straightaway, he would plan a diversion. Distract, confuse, divert, reward.

"A party," said Joseph, standing suddenly, thumping his desk so hard that a ballpoint pen jumped and rolled to the floor. "A celebration," he shouted. "A gala event."

"What!" Carly and Naomi spoke with one voice. And then Carly, "You just had one, that party at the Fitness Center. We're still recovering. And it's like you're asking for trouble, more bodies."

"Shut up, Carly," said Joseph, almost with a snarl. Then he lifted his shoulders and made a wide gesture taking in the entire room. "We'll show everyone that Ocean Tides is standing tall, is going ahead. To hell with the police. Summer is here. We should celebrate. We'll have a bunch of special-occasion things. Blowouts. Every Saturday. At the Lodge. Start this Saturday. June third."

"That's tomorrow!" squeaked Carly.

Joseph ignored his assistant. "Pirates!" he exclaimed. "We'll have pirate party. Captain Hook. Captain Kidd. Black Beard. Captain Nemo. Captain Ahab."

"Excuse me," said Carly. "Captain Nemo wasn't a pirate. He was kind of a nut case running around in a submarine twenty thousand leagues under the sea."

"And," added Naomi in a reproving voice, "Captain Ahab was a maniac trying to kill a white whale. If you feature him you'll have every naturalist for miles around down your neck. Whaling ships have a very bad reputation these days. Greenpeace will probably dump dead herring on the front steps of the Lodge. People will be sending you CDs with whale songs. Forget Ahab."

"It's the spirit of the thing," said Joseph crossly. "Sailors mean adventure. You know, the high seas." Joseph cocked his head in the direction of Penobscot Bay. "So get on it, Naomi. You, too, Carly. You can do it. Have prizes in a chest. Pieces of eight. A treasure hunt. Access for the handicapped. Our seniors love things like pirates. Maybe get in a singer. A group. What's that musical, *Pirates of Pinafore*?"

"Penzance," said Naomi patiently. "An operetta. Gilbert and Sullivan. Linda Ronstadt was in the movie.

"Whatever," said Joseph. "Just make it happen. Then get to work on other themes. Marooned on a desert island like a *Survivor* tie-in. Something special for the first day of summer. Whadda they call it, Midsummer's Night? You know, magic. Elves. Gnomes. What's that Shakespeare thing? You know, this guy called Bottom."

Naomi nodded. Yes, she knew that Shakespeare thing.

"You could always have mystery night," put in Carly, grinning. "We could give everyone a list of clues and see if they could come up with the murderer of Ned and Jason Colley by midnight."

"Carly, if I didn't need you so bad, like if I wasn't so damned shorthanded, I'd have you outta here so fast you wouldn't know what hit you," said Joseph. "I'm trying to think positive. Think good time. Think how lucky we are to spend the summer on this beautiful coast of Maine. So button your lip, okay?"

"Okay, okay," said Carly, still grinning. She paused. "But talking of mysteries, I forgot to tell you but George Fitts, you know the state police guy, he wants a list of Ocean Tide employees, their addresses, and how long they've worked here."

"Mother of God," said Joseph, "we've only been open since February. It's not like we're some ancient institution. No one's worked here a long time, and that includes me. And you, too, Carly, and you, Naomi, for Chrissake."

"I'll get the list copied," said Naomi.

"And a lot of good it'll do them," grumbled Joseph. "Next it'll be fingerprints and saliva, and a urine sample. Pieces of our hair, DNA, and what our parents died of."

"I'll get to work on your pirate party," said Naomi, ever the soother of the troubled. "I'll print up some fliers and get posters today. It's a good idea and people should think it's fun. We'll have a separate room for the children with prizes and maybe a movie. *Treasure Island* or *Hook* with Robin Williams."

"Naomi, you're what they call a treasure yourself," said Joseph. "And Carly, get it together, girl, and forget murder. Forget bikes and golf clubs."

Joseph watched the two assistants depart, waited a moment, then heaved a sigh and sank his head into his two large hands.

And here Mrs. Eisner, tray in hand, found him, administered a latte heavy on the sugar, and told him that the local chamber of commerce wanted him as their guest speaker at their next meeting. Subject: community living on the coast of Maine.

"They didn't want anything on murder? Or stolen bikes?" asked Joseph.

"Not a word," said Mrs. Eisner untruthfully. The chamber representative had been dying to discuss the whole affair, hoped that Joseph would give them a play-by-play of the finding of unexpected bodies, but had been chopped off by the good secretary before he could get up a head of steam.

The following days that marked the second week of June became in Sarah's remembrance a calm before the storm, where the flow of people's lives—at least those who called Ocean Tide their home or place of employment—ran smoothly. Held in the self-styled ballroom of the Lodge, the pirate party, due to heroic efforts on the part of Carly Thompson and Naomi Foxglove was declared the perfect distraction from recent sad events. The costumed children, sequestered in the indoor tennis court area, had been overfed, given prizes, and dosed with the two movies. Adults of all ages showed up, some arriving in makeshift pirate garb, others wearing the black paper pirate hat complete with skull and crossbones provided by the management, had feasted, had listened to two local talents singing "I am a Pirate King," and "Come, Men Who Plough the Sea" from Gilbert and Sullivan's masterpiece, had been showered with door prizes and left clutching a net bag filled with chocolates masquerading as gold coins. And best of all, in a kind of healing gesture, even Betty Colley and family, together with the Moseby clan, managed a short appearance after dinner.

Adding to a sense (however false it might prove) of normality was the fact that the police seemed to have made an effort to meld into everyday life. No uniforms, only plainclothes detectives moved about keeping their heads down, and since they operated from the VIP Golfer's Cottage, they somehow became part of the scenery. Another happy development occurred during the second week of June when the police, having scoured the area, declared the seventeenth and eighteenth holes and the adjacent stretch of beach now open for use by Ocean Tide residents.

"I mean, why not?" said Mike Laaka, meeting Alex Mc-

Kenzie, who was grabbing a quick lunch at the Rockland Café before his afternoon office hours. "We've sucked the guts out of the beach, seaweed, dead fish, mussel shells, condoms, crap you wouldn't believe. Same with the golf course and those equipment sheds. Vacuumed them clean."

"What about the stolen bikes and the golf clubs?" asked Alex, looking up from the tricky business of containing the strings of sauerkraut from his Reuben sandwich. "That might be the key to the whole affair. Aren't you guys just shoving it under the rug because tracking bikes is a pain in the ass?"

"Listen, you know we've nailed one of the bike smugglers," said Mike defensively. "Picked up a big stash at the guy's house. What more do you want? It's murder that's keeping this thing cooking, not a bunch of stolen bikes."

"And Albert Moseby's golf clubs," Alex reminded him.

"Aaah," said Mike. "Listen, golf clubs are an easy steal. Tuck 'em under your shirt, down your pants, your own golf club bag, and get out. But golf clubs are chicken feed. We're not going to waste much more time scratching around for golf clubs."

Alex nodded. Stealing golf clubs, expensive golf clubs, sets of three or four certainly didn't offer many difficulties. Just a matter of getting into the Pro Shop at the right time and moving fast. An easy operation. He might think of giving up medicine—an increasingly frustrating occupation—and take up golf club heists.

Mike finished his green pepper and onion cheeseburger and drank off his vanilla malt shake, a combination that made Alex's stomach churn. "Relax," said Mike, "we won't shove the bikes and clubs too far under the rug."

"And my mother's bike," Alex began.

"Oh, that," said Mike, dismissing Elspeth's bike with a flip of the hand. "Hell, that's just part of the Midcoast bike racket. What we're working on now is how tough it was for someone to crack Ned Colley's skull and carry the body, dead or almost dead, all the way along the golf course and dump him in that equipment shed. That took timing, maybe some assistance, and the luck of the devil."

"Do you think Ned could have been brought down to the shed in a golf cart?" suggested Alex. "Fixed so he looked alive. Like a golfer?"

"Picture it," said Mike. "This guy checks out a golf cart— I'm calling the murderer a guy. Until a weight-lifting female comes into the picture—after all, Ned Colley was no light-weight."

"Betty Colley might qualify," Alex observed.

"Don't interrupt. Right now I'm saying 'guy.' So this guy then signs up for a starting time, gets loose from any other golfers, goes to where he's hidden Ned's body—maybe off under some brush off the course. Then you're saying he might prop Ned up in the cart so he looks like a golfer, then whizzes away in full sight of God knows how many other golfers who are crawling all over the place like locusts. And all the time he's hoping the body doesn't roll off. Even staying away from the fairway, sticking to the little cart pathways, hell, it'd be impossible. This great sagging body bouncing along, no golfers getting out to hit a shot. Forget it."

"So maybe Ned was tied on to the cart," said Alex.

"Too conspicuous. A tied-up body is worse than a free-bouncing body."

"I meant if Ned was still alive at that point," Alex said.

"You mean if he was stunned or concussed or half-dead? Listen, he'd still be an oddball. To repeat, he'd be slumped or bopping up and down."

Alex shook his head. "I didn't mean stunned or half-dead. I meant alive and well."

"Like alive and kicking? But tied up? Lashed to the cart with a gag in his mouth? Come on, give me a break. You can't have a struggling tied-up golfer as a passenger without anyone noticing."

"How about alive as in alive and ready to play golf? Golf with a friend."

"Huh?"

"Did Ned Colley play golf?"

Mike stared at him. "Jeezus. I never thought of that. But Ned as a golfer? Come off it. Be real."

"You never know," said Alex. He stood up and reached into his pocket for his wallet. "Maybe he'd turned over a new leaf. Was going to be a regular citizen. Sporting type. Met an old buddy, i.e. the murderer, who said, 'Hey, how about a round of golf, Ned.' Stranger things . . ."

"Don't happen," finished Mike. "But okay, I'll give you a couple of points on this one. I'll see if Ned Colley ever played golf."

"It would be interesting if he did," said Alex. "Say Ned goes off in the cart with this mystery friend, they get near the seventeenth tee or green, somewhere in the rough, or off the course in the woods, and his golf buddy bangs him on the head. But now the murderer's stuck with a body. Maybe a bloody one. He's got to do something fast. Looks around, sees the two sheds, and he's in luck. The sheds are open. He chooses the least conspicuous shed, the one with the fertilizer bags. Hauls the body in and hopes by covering up the body with those bags he's buying time, gets into the cart and now he's a golfer again. Makes it back to the Pro Shop, turns in his cart knowing that the carts are cleaned and hosed off before they're given out again. Then he leaves Ocean Tide. Establishes an alibi supporting the idea that he was miles away when Ned was killed."

"You've got it all figured out, haven't you," said Mike. "Of course, your scenario means that the murderer plays golf, may be a member of the Ocean Tide Club, and for good measure might own a house or a condo in the place."

"Narrows it down, doesn't it?" said Alex, shoving a couple of dollar bills under his plate.

"Oh, God. That would mean we'll have to go over every blasted golf cart in the place and how much time has gone by? How many people have used the carts? How often have they been hosed and wiped?"

"A few fibers will have hung on, little dried drops of blood," Alex reminded him.

"Yeah, maybe. But what about the other body? Ned's son? What was Jason Colley doing to get himself killed? Not playing golf, I'll bet. Not looking for lost balls up there in the rough off the practice hole."

But Alex was on his way out the door and Mike followed none too happily. The golfer-as-murderer offered a complication that he didn't want to have any part of. George might regard the idea as foolish, but just in case there was something to it, he'd want to stick Mike with that aspect of the investigation. And Mike loathed golf, thought it a damn waste of time when someone could be out fishing or taking a day off to hit the races at Suffolk Downs. Mike climbed into his "new" car, a five-year-old black Chevy Blazer in need of new shocks, and headed toward Ocean Tide and the den of Sergeant George Fitts. But as he drove, enduring the humps and bumps caused by continual Route 1 construction efforts, he found himself considering Ned Colley, alive or dead, on a golf cart. Dead, he rejected out of hand. No way, Mike told himself, could anyone transport a lolling, flopping body, or a tied-up body along the side of a golf course. And as for Ned, alive, as a golfer! Try as he might, Mike was unable to picture Ned Colley attired in golf clothes, polo shirt, summer weave trousers, both in colors like lime and yellow and royal blue. Wearing white shoes with spikes and tassels or fringes. A golf glove on one hand. A hat with a club logo embroidered on it. No way, Mike told himself. Forget it. He could just as well picture Ned Colley in a ball gown. And besides, the flattened body of Ned under the fertilizer bags had been wearing work boots. Conclusion: Ned did not arrive at the shed disguised as a golfer in a golf cart.

*　　*　　*

Alex arriving home that night found his wife singularly unin-
terested in the possibility that the ancient and honorable game
of golf might have figured as part of Ned Colley's murder scenario. Sarah, fresh from a shower, was stretched out on a sofa,
wrapped in a terry-cloth robe and happily reading the latest
Janet Evanovich mystery.

"I'm keeping clear of the whole business," Sarah told him
virtuously. "I'm doing detective work by reading mystery novels. Easier, cheaper, and perfectly safe. I'll tutor the Colley and
the Moseby boys and keep an eye out for your mother's bike
and that's it. I'm not even faintly interested in sticking my nose
into Mike and George's investigation. Besides, now that I'm
sure that young Dylan Colley is the boy who found the body—"

"Hey, wait up." Alex almost shouted it. "You didn't tell me
that. Have you been nesting on this without saying a word?
Goddamn it, Sarah. Give. How did you find out? Did you tell
George and Mike without letting old faithful dog Alex in on
it?"

"Relax, go get a beer. Cool down and I'll fill you in. I didn't
go squealing to the police. I didn't have to. The boy knows I
know and is in a real twitch about it. So I did the right thing
and told Betty Colley, gave her the whole picture of Dylan
running away from the shed. By now she's told the police and
they're dealing with it. And my hands are clean."

"Why does that sound familiar?"

"I've done the right and proper thing," Sarah said defensively. "And I've fixed dinner. Something for a frazzled physician with an attitude. A cold pasta-and-cucumber thing. We
can eat outside on the porch and swat mosquitoes."

"And the idea that the murderer may be fixing himself,
herself, up for tomorrow's tee time, making up a friendly foursome, doesn't cause a quiver of interest? You are a simple
teacher of literature whose only interests are her students."

"Sarcasm is not becoming," said Sarah. "But I'll tell you what," she added, rising and heading for the kitchen. "We'll brief Uncle Fergus on the possibilities and pack him off to the golf course as a undercover spy. No one will suspect an almost ninety-year-old geezer of sneaking around, and it ought to keep him out of your family's hair."

And as sometimes happens in human affairs, a prediction made in an airy way, in idle conversation, has a strange way of coming to pass.

# 15

NOW that the police had settled into the tedium of routine action: statement taking, the sifting of forensic evidence, the questioning of persons at some remove from the murder victims, the members of the McKenzie clan found their attention focused on the approach of Uncle Fergus who hovered on the horizon like a thunder cloud. Elspeth McKenzie, in particular, felt it only fair to warn the management. Therefore, on bumping into Carly Thompson outside the Fitness Center early Monday morning of that second week in June, she stopped Carly and mentioned that Professor Fergus McKenzie, for whom they had booked a room at the Lodge, could, on rare occasions, be called, well, difficult.

"Maybe that's not quite the word," said Elspeth, searching for a kinder way of saying that John's uncle was a tyrannical old man.

"No problem," said Carly cheerfully. "We've had a few guests who would put Saddam Hussein to shame. A few good meals, Manager Martinelli soft-soaping him, Naomi oozing charm, he'll start purring like a pussycat."

"You think?" said Elspeth doubtfully. Uncle Fergus might have certain animal-like qualities but those would be more in keeping with a wolverine than any domestic article. Uncle Fergus had, she knew for a fact, been the cause of much grief among fellow faculty members, had been personally responsible for denial of tenure in several notable cases, and was blamed, perhaps without cause, for one faculty member defenestrating himself. But who was she to blight the confidence of the Ocean Tide staff.

"Never say I didn't warn you," Elspeth finished. "But you might want to seat him off by himself in the Lodge dining room. He shouts sometimes and it isn't because he's deaf. He hears very well." And Elspeth, having done her duty, let Carly go.

As for Carly, she dismissed the conversation as of minor interest. What was of immediate concern was Joseph Martinelli's next planned community party. And the next. And the next. She didn't see how on earth she and Naomi were going to be able to come up with one gala after another. She was certain that the succession of special costume events would by August have overdosed even the most enthusiastic partygoers. The affair planned for the approaching Saturday, in an oblique reference to the June graduation scenes, was to have a literary flavor. Posters fastened to the walls of Ocean Tide buildings proclaimed in blue and red: Come as Your Favorite Book—Come as Your Favorite Author! Carly had been busy ordering T-shirts featuring the faces of William Faulkner, Charles Dickens, and Emily Dickinson as prizes, plus running around like the White Rabbit shoving invitations under every cottage and condo door. Nobody's Uncle Fergus could undermine this affair. And if it came to a showdown between a sour old professor and Joseph Martinelli, Carly's money was on the manager. He was a man you could no more make a lasting dent in than you could in an inflated basketball. Carly could see Joseph now clapping the man on the shoulder and urging him to come as Scrooge and shout "Bah! Humbug!" all evening.

While Elspeth McKenzie, her conscience clear on the matter of Uncle Fergus, packed and repacked her travel clothes in the wheeled suitcase, John McKenzie scrubbed his old set of Ben Hogan irons in the kitchen sink and announced he was at certain times—these not to coincide with his uncle's—willing to fill in on any foursome of not-too-skilled golfers who might present themselves as in need of a player.

Mike Laaka, too, reluctantly, had golf on his agenda. He had tracked down Sergeant George Fitts in the Jack Nicklaus Library. George, Mike thought, as he viewed the sergeant at the mahogany writing desk, had been marvelously reduced to a faceless robotic presence by the colorful watercolors hanging in the room, each showing glory moments in the career of Jack Nicklaus.

George, if he had had his way, would have hung maps and charts over the paintings, but in deference to the pleadings of Carly Thompson had had to settle for several flip charts on easels packed in against the walls. He, like Mike, considered golf a waste of useful time—about the only area of agreement he had with Mike—but now he was mildly interested in the idea of Ned Colley as a closet golfer and had assigned Mike the job of haunting various local golf courses to see if Ned had ever been spotted with a club in his hand, driving a golf cart, practicing at the driving range, or otherwise engaged in the game. Alone or with other players. "Get on it," ordered George. "Start with the Samoset Resort since it's right next to Ocean Tide. That place is always crawling with golfers."

"Jeezus," complained Mike. "Ned was always broke and he always looked like some kind of tramp down on his luck. No way he'd be playing golf at the Samoset. Big bucks to play there. Forget golf. Bowling maybe, poker, pool, sure. Not golf."

"Check it out," said George. "Start early and work all local golf courses. Talk to the golf pros, look through their books for lessons and tee times. Find out about local tournaments.

If you have time in the evening, get to work on the bike business. The Ocean Tide bike rental operation. This Nicholas Moseby. We've already had his statement about his job there and he claims to have spent any leisure time away training for some bike race in France. I have confirmation of some early morning workouts, some late evening ones, but I want to know more. He and a buddy, a Tom Schmidt, are supposed to be joining a bike team for a race—not a major event—in France. But I gather Manager Martinelli is excited and is giving some money for the trip. Wants them to wear a special Ocean Tide jersey. They'll be riding around some mountain area in the south. Flying from Boston on the fourteenth.

"You're letting Nick Moseby leave the country?" asked Mike, surprised. George usually kept possible witnesses tied down and under scrutiny.

"I admit that we haven't got a perfect fix on the guy," said George, a man who was always loath to admit any gap in his investigation. "But he's in the clear for Ned Colley's death—he was biking in Montville with this same team friend, Tom Schmidt, along with other bike club members from the Lewiston-Auburn area."

"Does the fact that two Moseby bikes were stolen along with Al Moseby's clubs clear the Mosebys?"

"I'm not making any judgments," said George primly. "As far as I'm concerned no one is in the clear. But you might see, before Nick leaves, if he's in serious training. Talk to other cyclists around the area."

"Christ, George, chasing down Ned Colley as a golfer and Nick Moseby riding his bike. I'm not a centipede," Mike complained. "I won't have time to fool around on a hundred golf courses. And I don't know a damn thing about bike racing except watching Lance Armstrong on TV. You get on a million-dollar bike weighing about three ounces, bend yourself double, fasten your feet into these toe clips so you'll break your neck if you fall, pedal until you're ready to vomit, and if you're ahead you wear some sort of special yellow jersey. That's it as far as I'm concerned."

"So read up," said George. "Leave a preliminary report on my desk by five on Wednesday. Before Nicholas and his teammate fly out."

"I hear Alex's mother is," said Mike. "Flying out, I mean. She's going to paint in southern France. Elspeth, Naomi Foxglove, Nicholas, his buddy Schmidt, plus the golf pro are driving to Boston in the Ocean Tide van because there's a pickup scheduled for a golf VIP who's coming in from London. Hotshot player. He's giving a two-week clinic here."

"I don't care about the clinic unless it has to do with Ned Colley," said George.

"If I find Ned Colley's a golfer," said Mike resentfully, "I'll give up my job and go to work bagging groceries. In fact, if you were a betting man—"

"Which I'm not," said George. "Get going, Mike."

And Mike got going. Reluctantly, his dislike for golf growing with every passing moment. Armed with an ancient black-and-white snapshot of Ned on a beach picnic with Betty and her boys in happier days, Mike hit the golf courses. And struck out. No golf person—pro or player, greens maintenance worker, or golf shop clerk owned to seeing, knowing, or hearing of Ned in the guise of a golfer. Even the proprietor of a miniature putting course—a long-shot effort on Mike's part—though he admitted to knowing Ned, swore that his acquaintance with the man began and ended at a local bar.

Equally without results were Mike's afternoon and evening investigations on the matter of the stolen bikes. Nicholas Moseby had paid for his bike with a check drawn on a New Haven checking account. The account had been established when Nicholas first arrived at Yale and had maintained a comfortable balance. Here Mike began to reassess the financial condition of the Moseby wholesale greenhouse business. Even with a scholarship, which Nick claimed he had received—this still to be checked out—costs at a private Ivy League college were unbelievable. Mike recorded that the boy had ridden his now stolen bike and another similar model around Connecticut. Had raced in that state and in Massachusetts. Had ridden both bikes in Maine. Had bought a third backup model three weeks ago. The missing bike, something called a Cobra Super Double X, had not been recovered. Bikes were, as Mike was constantly informed, a cinch to steal, to take apart, to move out of town, out of state, out of the country.

As for Matthew Moseby's Mongoose, nothing there. The sucker cost a fair hunk of money but wasn't in the upper ranges, Mike reported back to George.

"Leaving the bike against the garage was careless," said Mike. "Plain stupid, in fact. But Matthew's seventeen, what'dya expect?"

"So," said George. "Results so far . . ."

"Are zilch," said Mike. "What more do you want?"

"More golf courses," said George. "Try south of Knox County. Bath, Falmouth, Portland. And north, Belfast. Or try Augusta."

"Aw, Christ, George. Ned Colley wasn't traveling around visiting golf clubs all over the state. What he was doing was running out on his family, drinking like a fish, and unzipping his pants. That's what Ned was doing. Forget golf."

"Could it be," said George in a speculative voice, "that maybe Nick and brother Matt staged a fake theft of their bikes? Same with dad's golf clubs."

"I think you're out to lunch on that one," said Mike. "Nick needed the bike for racing, Matt just got his for his birthday. And Dad Albert about blew a gasket when he found his clubs were missing. Quite a scene in the Pro Shop, I'm told. So forget it."

During the pause that followed Mike watched George's pen tapping the desk. Then the pen was quiet. "Okay, go back to the golf scene."

"What you'd better do is check out Nick Moseby's cash

flow. How big a scholarship has this guy got that he can take off from work and go racing all over Europe?"

"Not all over Europe, southern France. And it's only for ten days."

"Even with a mega-scholarship, Daddy must be paying a bundle for Yale," insisted Mike. "The greenhouse business must be pretty hot stuff."

"Actually it is," said George. "Wholesale greenhouses make a lot of money selling things to all the garden suppliers around. Camden, Rockport, the islands. All the summer people do a lot of planting and buying every year. Gardens are a big thing. Tours every summer. But I'll be following out the Nicholas Moseby line. See what sort of a deal Yale gave him, which is touchy, getting hold of someone's academic and financial records. No probable cause that I can think of. But right now I think it's likely that both Jason Colley and father Ned were in the wrong place at the wrong time. Past records on both men show that they made a habit of being where they shouldn't have been. The two of them—maybe working together—may have interrupted some kind of operation. First Jason, then later Ned."

"Operation?" interrupted Mike. "What kind of an operation? Golf? Biking?"

"Not sure. Could be drugs, antiques, could be anything."

"Operation of what? Where? At Ocean Tide?"

"Like something underground going on from the management end. We're going to have a hard look at this whole community. Where does Joseph Martinelli fit into the picture? Why did he drop the Ocean Tide Construction Company, walk away from the business he'd started from scratch to get into this resort-community affair? He's spending money like water and this is just the first year the place has been running."

"Yeah, I know," said Mike, "Martinelli, like he's sort of a kindly czar running a kingdom, acting like he's running for public office. Think of those special menus with food for any group that can't eat beef or eggs or fish or cheese or chocolate or white rice or an animal with a cloven hoof or an animal without a cloven hoof or an animal with horns or one that sheds its skin."

"Cool it, Mike," warned George.

"No, listen. All the vegetables and fruits are one hundred percent organic and probably washed in Ivory Flakes before they're served. As for the eggs, there's something on all the menus that these hens are free and happy and have volunteered to lay eggs. And the cows and goats are hand milked probably by virgin dairy maids and the animals get counseling afterwards to make them feel good about themselves. Tofu omelettes, soy hot dogs. And all those Far Eastern specialties and African menus and Deep South Cajun cooking and south-of-the-border chilies. I mean, sure, some of it probably tastes great, but God Almighty, it sure adds up to big hunks of money. And I'll bet the more he tries to please people, the more he'll make some people mad, even with Carly and Naomi running around like crazy making happy noises and coming up with those pirate parties."

"You've made your point, Mike."

"I haven't even started. This Joseph Martinelli, he's something else. I'll bet he's on something. Sticks a pill under his tongue and blasts off every morning like a rocket. I'd say he's going to blow up someday into a million pieces of DNA and take Ocean Tide with him. Follow the guy around for an hour. I did when you asked me to get a sense of how the place runs. If he's not on drugs, he's got some sort of psychological condition."

"Have you stopped to think that all this activity may be connected with bodies turning up?" said George.

"Hey," Mike objected, "he was manic before the bodies turned up. Finger in every pie, stirring every pot."

"So he has a high energy level," said George. "But now listen to me. You're so busy finding symptoms you don't think about the disease. Have you considered that this Joseph Martinelli is running around trying to please everyone, to distract everyone with a million activities, that it's because he doesn't want any soreheads looking into his operation?"

"You mean a real operation under the pretend Ocean Tide one? Like Ocean Tide is a false front?"

"No, Ocean Tide is real enough. Just like the Ocean Tide Construction Company was real. But that doesn't mean it can't also function as a cover for something else. The construction operation was in hot water a couple of times. Cost overruns, out-of-line estimates, even an indictment once although the charges were dropped for lack of evidence."

"So shall I quit the golf and bike scenes and start in on the front office?" The idea was strangely exciting. Mike briefly pictured himself at the center of an uncovering of a vast multinational scam.

"No," said George firmly. "Stick to golf. Finish what you started. I'll worry about Manager Martinelli." And George bent his head over his notebook.

But Mike Laaka, never one to follow orders to the letter, made a sudden decision. He would stick to golf. And bicycles. But with a difference. With a change in the cast of characters. What, he asked himself, if Manager Martinelli played golf? What if by some strange twist of fate the manager had intercepted Jason Colley on the practice golf course at the exact moment of some crucial interchange of goods, information, drugs? A meeting with persons of sinister purpose? Mike somehow had no trouble picturing the manager felling Jason with a stick, a stone, and his hands twisting a plastic-sheathed chain around Jason's neck. Joseph had the arms of a professional wrestler.

As for Jason's dad, Ned Colley? How about Ned lurking on the golf course for reasons unknown, but certainly not golf. Ned having found out something about the manager's underground activities. After all, Ned moved among lowlifes and he may have picked up some "useful" information. Useful as in blackmailing. So Ned and Joseph Martinelli had a face-off on the subject. Somewhere, somehow. And the end result being that Joseph, in the guise of a player, grabbed a cart, clobbered Ned, loaded him in the cart, and keeping to the paths off the fairway, raced down to the fertilizer shed and dumped the man.

Mike, feeling vastly pleased with himself, headed for the Ocean Tide Pro Shop. Since daylight saving time the golfers were out until twilight. Mike thought that someone probably would be in the Pro Shop and he'd ask if Joseph Martinelli ever played golf. Filled in a foursome. Played nine holes after dinner, after the day's business was done.

By one of those quirks of timing at exactly the same moment that Mike closed the door on George Fitts, Sarah Deane and her dog, Patsy, left the McKenzie cottage, Alex being still trapped at the hospital. Sarah had been at the McKenzie cottage for a small bon voyage cocktail gathering on the little back terrace, had admired Elspeth's new travel raincoat and crushable straw hat, listened to new misgivings Elspeth had on the subject of Naomi Foxglove—and heard for the nth time the fears of John and Elspeth on the subject of that approaching human bomb, Fergus Dugald McKenzie. Realizing that this family thorn was causing more and more anticipatory pain, she decided, as Elsepth had before her, to speak to someone in management. In this project she was pleasantly surprised to find Joseph Martinelli in front of the Lodge standing under a streetlamp inspecting a handsome spread of pink poppies fitted in between a line of blue delphiniums. He appeared relaxed, even producing a dog biscuit for Patsy, and seemed ready to listen as Sarah sketched the apprehensions of the senior McKenzies and their hope that Professor Fergus could be defused and distracted possibly on the golf course.

Joseph took her hand in both his large plump ones. "Not to worry. Not for a single moment. Ocean Tide will be ready for him. I will be ready. I myself will make Uncle Fergus my personal project. For the good of Ocean Tide. Special treatment. Special dining room table. With a view. Early morning coffee by tray. Biscuits and chocolates. Our VIP fruit basket. You name it. I will even play golf with this uncle. I haven't had a chance to play more than a few times and I am turning stale every minute that goes by. And I don't lose my temper with any little thing like someone's uncle who acts like Julius Caesar. I had an uncle just like that. Enrico Martinelli, may he rest in piece. So no problem, Sarah Deane. Put it out of your mind." And Joseph patted Sarah on the shoulder and returned to the frowning scrutiny of the poppies, some of which were almost past their prime.

Mike Laaka emerged in triumph from the Pro Shop—Joseph Martinelli was a golfer. Had played golf apparently off and on for years. Shot in the low nineties. Or at least so he claimed. Mike, finding assistant pro Pete Salieri about to close shop but willing to chat, hadn't wanted to ask his questions in the guise of sheriff's deputy investigator so he had gone the roundabout route as a prospective golfer. He expressed a deep interest in the game, asked about instruction for beginners, and had been shown the mounted set of wooden-shafted clubs that had caught Sarah's attention in her earlier visit to the Pro Shop. There against a framed panel of green felt in a fan configuration were arrayed the baffie, the driver, the brassie, the spoon, the cleek, midiron, a mashie, a mashie-niblick, and a niblick. These Mike admired, then submitted to a short history of golf-in-America, and after redirecting the conversation, learned that Manager Martinelli hadn't played much so far this year, but had a top-of-the-line set of new irons, a new golf bag, and his own golf cart. But Joseph had never been seen, at least not by Pete Salieri, on a bicycle. "Mr. Martinelli likes to walk or use his golf cart," Pete reported. "Likes to cover all bases, go all over the whole property, nose around, see what's up."

Like dead bodies, Mike thought but didn't say. He nodded his thanks, said he'd be thinking about golf lessons, and walked off with the picture in his head of Manager Martinelli teeing off on a late round of golf. The shadows lengthening. Alone. Or with a friendly or unconscious or just plain dead Ned Colley lashed to his golf cart.

And reaching the road, congratulating himself on nailing down a choice piece of information, walked directly into Sarah returning from her chat with the manager. Sarah, who after a cheery greeting, told him, guess what, Joseph Martinelli is a golfer. Has played golf for years and who has just minutes ago offered himself as a human sacrifice to partner Uncle Fergus on the Ocean Tide course.

"Of such things are saints made," said Sarah.

Mike nodded, told Sarah he knew that Joseph was a golfer and what else was new.

"Nothing," said Sarah. "I have not found a body in at least a week. But you'll be happy to know that there's a new amateur detective in the area.

"My mother-in-law, Elspeth, is really furious about her new bike being taken. And she's decided—I heard her on the subject tonight—that maybe it's a management scheme. Run by that gorgeous Naomi Foxglove."

"Naomi Foxglove!" exclaimed Mike. "Listen, the place would fall apart without Naomi. And Carly," he added.

"That's Elspeth's point. I think she's intimidated by Naomi. Perfection gliding around in a size seven sheath. Wonders what she's really up to. Thinks maybe Joseph Martinelli is running a world-class bike-theft business or loading drugs inside golf shafts. And so she's been cycling around looking for trouble. There, that ought to give you and George a high-intensity migraine."

"Except," Mike pointed out, "your mother-in-law will be off to France and Naomi is too damn busy keeping the place from imploding and running parties to work out any kind of operation. She wouldn't even have time to steal desserts from the kitchen."

"And Joseph Martinelli as Mr. Big running an underground business?"

"What an absolutely out-to-lunch idea. Tell Mrs. McKenzie that if she goes on like this she'll be transferred to the assisted-living unit."

With which the two parted: Mike walked off, deflated by having been scooped by Sarah on the subject of Joseph Martinelli-Golfer and depressed by the prospect of having to search at distant golf courses for Ned Colley-Nongolfer. And seriously irked at the McKenzies' idea of Joseph as kingpin for some underground skullduggery since the idea almost exactly matched that of George Fitts. Sarah, however, left the meeting with a lighter step, feeling that she had done a good evening's work.

Wednesday, June 14, arrived. A lovely late spring day, a south-west breeze ruffling the ocean surface, a clear sky with only a hint of a crouching fog waiting for evening. June 14, the day for the departure of Elspeth McKenzie, Nicholas Moseby, et al. for Boston and Logan Airport. The day in which Sarah would finally meet with the Moseby and Colley boys to begin the summer's instruction, the day that Uncle Fergus might possibly turn up at Ocean Tide. A postcard had arrived featuring an Egyptian funerary mask with the message that he might be with the John McKenzies sometime near the middle of the week.

But Fate, who had been hovering over the events of the past few weeks, had now grown weary of the plodding police investigation, the fussing over such trivia as stolen bikes and golf clubs, the efforts of Joseph Martinelli to create the perfect community, the approach of an elderly curmudgeon, and decided to ratchet things up a bit. This effort began in the morning when at 9:00 A.M. Dylan Colley failed to join—again—Sarah's tutoring session. And was not seen afterward.

Then at two-thirty that afternoon Professor Emeritus Fergus Dugald McKenzie, a gnarled, gnomelike man with a wispy white beard and a bald head resembling no one so much as an emaciated version of old John Quincy Adams, arrived by taxi, checked into the Lodge, and announced his intention of visiting his relatives. These, Fergus discovered, were not in their cottage, so he demanded and received a golf cart (management's orders: all courtesy was to be extended to the gentleman), pushed his way in front of an arriving foursome, and teed off with a slice into a planting of birch trees. And subsequently disappeared from view.

At four that same afternoon at Logan Airport, Naomi Foxglove, after waving good-bye to Elspeth McKenzie, Nicholas Moseby, and his teammate, Tom Schmidt, at the doors of American Airlines International Terminal, left the golf pro Wilson Williams to meet the arriving VIP golfer at British Airways. She did not, however, return as expected to the waiting Ocean Tide van. Instead Naomi later appeared in the line of passengers waiting for the departure of Air France flight 321 at the same international terminal, but well concealed by the holiday crowds, and shortly before seven that evening at the sound of the boarding call she vanished from sight.

By the end of the day, as if in response to these removals from the scene of action, the weather, which early had promised sun, now turned sullen and mean, the fog crawled in and hung heavy and threatening at the water's edge, and an east wind rose and blew damply through the trees.

# 16

SARAH was not altogether surprised at the no-show of Dylan Colley. It was what Dylan did: not show up. Except by now Betty and Dylan would have had their meeting with the police so that Dylan's anxiety level must have been lowered. But perhaps Sarah herself still figured in a frightening way for him. In which case his mother had better find another teacher for him.

The tutoring was to be held at nine-thirty in the Moseby kitchen and two Mosebys came into the room under the guidance of Sherry Moseby. Both Mosebys dressed in just-out-of-the-box GAP shorts and T-shirt. And Sherry Moseby again done up to perfection like a "Fun in Summer" magazine ad. But with the same too-bright cheeks, disordered hairdo, and the same anxious hands noted in previous encounters. What in God's name was wrong with the woman? Sarah wondered. Had she been finding bodies on the sly? Or helping produce them? This unacceptable thought Sarah banished, waved cheerily at Sherry as she slipped from the room.

Now she handed Matt Moseby an assignment involving the

opening pages of *The Red Badge of Courage* and told him she would meet him later, after his work as golf course crew member was finished for the day. Say six o'clock. Matt ducked his head in acknowledgment and departed. Sarah settled the younger Moseby, Tim, and Brian Colley, his shaven head now sprouting a growth of yellow stubble, at the kitchen table. Brian, in marvelous contrast to his impeccable cousin, was decked out in ancient jeans, cut below the knee with something like a hacksaw, a T-shirt that mice had apparently used for nesting, and dirty sneakers with no laces. And, thought Sarah as she passed around three paperback copies of *The Adventures of Tom Sawyer*, he smelled like he'd been rolling in dead fish. She moved her chair a few feet to one side of the boy and got to work. But Sarah had no sooner read the first paragraph aloud when Betty Colley stuck her head in the door.

"Just checking," said Betty. Then looking around, seeing only one Colley boy, she frowned. "Dylan. Hasn't he turned up? He started off just after Brian. If he's late after all I've said . . ."

"It's okay," said Sarah. "As long as he gets here soon."

"Wasting my money and your time," said Betty. "Okay, if he's not here in the next fifteen minutes give me a call."

Sarah nodded and returned to Tom Sawyer.

But Dylan remained a truant. Sarah, caught up in the first pages of the book, discussing a written assignment for the next day, let almost the whole hour slide by without calling Betty. When she did, Grandmother Rose answered the phone, she said her hearing aids had disappeared, rolled under the bed, maybe the cat played with them and if she wanted to talk to Betty, well, Betty had gone out.

"Is Dylan there?" Sarah shouted.

"Who?" shouted Rose back into the phone.

Sarah, rubbing her ear, excused herself, returned to the two boys and had them take turns reading aloud. This was a highly unpopular request.

"Like we're in first grade," complained Tim.

"Our teacher never asks us to do that," said Brian. "We're too old."

"Like it's a foreign language," said Tim.

*You said it,* thought Sarah. Aloud, she reminded them that speaking clearly and sounding as if they understood what they were reading was a worthwhile goal.

The session ended with the two boys slurring and grumping their way through three pages apiece and growling at the idea that they were each to write two pages describing what they had just read. In their own words. Complete sentences. Nouns and verbs agreeing. Paragraphs.

Sarah packed up her copy of *The Adventures of Tom Sawyer,* carefully pulled her skin loose from the plastic leatherette cushion of the kitchen chair—she was wearing shorts—and left the house determined to find Betty Colley and settle the matter of Dylan's absence once and for all.

Betty was tracked down at the end of her garden. She was bent over a flat of impatiens, out of sight of the kitchen window. Out of sight of Rose. Sarah, walking through the garden gate, thought this arrangement gave Betty some relief from her strong-minded mother.

Sarah told her story. Betty, straightening up from her kneeling pad, throwing down her trowel, was angry. Would settle Dylan's hash when he came home. With every day going by, she was beginning to think the boy was becoming more and more like father Ned. Which no one needed. One Ned Colley per one life is enough, thank you very much.

"Taking off when he feels like it. And when he turns up he'll have some crazy excuse and think I'll forget about it, which I won't. Bed and no supper. And God knows what else I'll do to him if he doesn't shape up," said Betty.

Was Betty worried? asked Sarah. "I mean," she said, "does he do this a lot? Skip school? Miss appointments? I thought it was connected with finding the body of his father, but has he made a habit of not showing up before?"

Betty thought not. Dylan never was that reliable, but he

usually made it to school and to soccer practice. But he'd been doing it more lately. Sarah was probably right. It was the body business. And getting a little upset last night.

But Sarah was not to hear about last night. The back screen door snapped open and Grandmother Rose stood on the back steps holding a telephone. "Telephone," she shouted. "Someone about your car insurance. I couldn't hear but maybe you didn't sign something." And Betty hustled away, calling over her shoulder that she'd take care of Dylan.

Sarah, unsatisfied, drove away, and because the day was such a promising one, the fog bank barely visible, she turned toward the Ocean Tide beach. She'd park, take a walk, breathe deeply, and then pick up Patsy at the McKenzie cottage, go home and think about getting some work done.

It was low water, the long line of rocks, the broken mussel shells shone with the wet left by the receding tide. Along the steep bank, pulled up out of the tide's reach, their painters tied to mooring posts and blocks, lay a number of odd skiffs, several dinghies, assorted small sailing crafts, "beginner" sailboats, little tubs with a single small sail furled on a short mast. Sarah walked slowly down the wooden steps and was suddenly overcome by a desire to own a boat. A small boat. Nothing fancy. Nothing that would carry her far out to sea. One of those baby sailboats. What were they called? Turnabouts? No, the new tublike things were Optimists. Sarah, no great sailor, could perhaps buy one of these and, using the McKenzie's membership in the Boat Club, keep it right here.

With no purpose in mind beyond a desultory inspection of the boats, she walked along the line of boats and then came to a concrete pylon on which the name Colley ran vertically in black paint. No boat. Only a chain hanging from a metal ring. And along the narrow stretches of dry sand and pebbled shingle, clearly visible, were the marks of a narrow keel having been dragged to the water's edge—or what would have been the water's edge some three hours past. For a few minutes Sarah stared at the gap in the line of little boats and then the numbers began to add up. Dylan Colley a-no show. Dylan not at home. Dylan acting more and more like his irresponsible father. Sarah felt a little twinge of apprehension and then shook her head. Even with a calm sea, a clear sky, Dylan certainly would not have taken a boat. Taking a boat without family permission even on a tranquil ocean was in anyone's book a major act of disobedience.

Were there other Colleys at Ocean Tide? The Colleys Sarah knew had lived on a farm so they might not really be boat people. Betty's boys might not even know how to swim. A remarkable number of Maine children, even those within a few miles of ocean or inland lake, reached adulthood without ever dipping into the water. Few of the schools had pools, the YMCA was located out of reach of many communities, public beaches were small, and instruction not always possible. These thoughts sent another, stronger wave of apprehension down Sarah's back. She turned around, mounted the wooden steps, and took off heading straight for Betty Colley's cottage.

Her questions were answered within the next five minutes. Betty had returned to her gardening. Yes, she had a small fiberglass boat, a leftover from Ned's brief fishing days. Named the *Folly*. A good name, Betty'd always thought, because Ned had paid a sight too much money for the thing. No, Dylan had never had permission to take that boat out.

No, Dylan wasn't a good swimmer. Betty had tried to get the boys lessons, but work schedules and transportation had made it difficult. However, Betty wasn't about to accept that Dylan would take off in a small boat. Not even Dylan. Someone, Betty insisted, one of those older boys around the community, had helped themselves, borrowed it, taken it off for a little fishing. The sort of thing kids would do. Besides, Dylan would much more likely be on his bike. Keeping out of sight. He loved to bike around. And he had never shown any great interest in using the skiff. Betty was thinking of selling it.

"Do you think his reaction to telling his story to the police might be part of this?" Sarah asked. "Maybe he was more upset by this than you thought he'd be. Did they ask him a lot of questions? Interrogate him? Make him uncomfortable? Did he think it was my fault for telling you? That might account for his missing class today."

A long pause. With each of Sarah's questions Betty's face became more flushed. Her hands pushed into the pockets of her cotton trousers. She looked at her leather boots, heavy with garden mud. "As a matter of fact," she said very slowly, words falling as if they had turned sour in her mouth, "I didn't get him to the police. I know I said I would, but I put it off. Put it off again. It just set my teeth on edge, the whole idea. Taking the kid to the police station and having that George Fitts work him over. Worse than taking him to the dentist to have a tooth drilled."

"And last night?" prompted Sarah.

"Last night I knew I had to do it. Told Dylan we'd go after tutoring. I'd take him to lunch at Pizza Hut and then to the police. Where the police are hanging out, that golf guest house. Maybe it would be Mike Lakka who talked to him because Dylan knows Mike. I said no one would hurt him but he had to help the police. After all, it was his own father he'd found dead. But Dylan got all worked up, slammed into his bedroom and didn't speak this morning, but he does that sometimes so I didn't think much of it. And he left for tutoring. Or I thought he did. He had his school backpack filled up, so I supposed he was taking a dictionary and some writing material."

Sarah said very carefully, "So the police don't know yet that it was Dylan who found Ned's body?"

"No," said Betty ruefully. "My fault. It's been a rough few weeks and I'm a coward about some things. What do the kids say? I'm a wuss. About the police, anyway. I'm worse than Sherry and she's always jittering about something."

Sarah sidestepped Sherry Moseby's anxiety problems. Right now, the question was, had Dylan gone to sea to get away from the police? From his mother? From Sarah?

"Do you think," she asked, trying to sound matter-of-fact,

"that we should start looking? Right now. Call the Coast Guard. Some sort of marine patrol. Or let the people at Ocean Tide send out a search boat?"

But Betty hesitated. "Not the Coast Guard. Just about a boy not being where he's supposed to be. Even if our boat is gone. I mean I just don't think Dylan would ever pull something like that."

"Were there oars in it?" asked Sarah, determined to pursue the subject even if it meant that authorities were alerted without Betty's permission. Sarah had a sudden ghastly picture of a small skinny boy adrift in a small skinny boat. Losing an oar, perhaps. Drifting, going out with the tide. Being pulled away into the wider ocean. Sea swells, currents, wind shifts, wind rising. That harmless-looking fog bank sneaking in and covering everything.

"Oars?" said Betty. "Yes. And a paddle. A couple of life jackets in a plastic bag. And when Ned bought the thing a long time ago it came with a little sail and a mast. I think the whole boat was made from a kit."

"You mean it can be rigged for sailing?" demanded Sarah, now more and more anxious. Her mind's eye picturing now a sailing dinghy tipping, heeling in an increasing breeze. With Dylan, who wasn't a good swimmer, clutching the tiller.

"I never did," said Betty. "Rig it up, I mean. I only rowed out a little way a couple of times on St. George Lake where we had a camp once. To see if I could catch some fish. But Ned sailed it a few times on the lake. Maybe he took Dylan, I can't remember. But I think the sail is pretty well shot, full of holes. It has a sort of board you stick down a hole, a daggerboard it's called. And a tiller you can fit on. Or you can just row it."

Sarah had decided. "I know you think I'm jumping to conclusions, but I'm going to call for help. Could you call Carly Thompson and start a real search of the Ocean Tide property, try everyplace Dylan might hide, and I'll see about an ocean search."

"No," said Betty. "I don't want to stir things up. Make scenes about nothing. Wait for a little while. I'll drive around the place and over to the hiking and bike trails by myself and shout for him. And I'll check over by the Lodge. Dylan likes to hang out by the kitchen and get handouts. He's made a friend of one of the chefs."

Sarah gave up—trying to persuade Betty. But not starting her own rescue mission. She went back to her car, dialed Alex at the hospital, found that he was still at lunch somewhere, gave his secretary, a hastily stitched-together message of what she now regarded as a crisis and what she intended to do about it. Drove to the Lodge, found Carly Thompson, told her that Dylan was missing, the Colley dinghy was missing, and to call the Coast Guard or whoever else did search and rescue.

Drove back to the beach. Dug out a hat, a bottle of water from the back of her car. A windbreaker. A Mars bar, a package of cheese and peanut butter crackers, two slightly wrinkled apples—all provisions she kept in case of breakdown or a sudden picnic urge. And now for a private search and rescue. Pushing *Tom Sawyer* and a notebook out of her briefcase, she stuffed in her emergency supplies, threaded her way through a clump of children collecting beach stones, and began an inspection of the boats lining the bank.

Which one? The small white skiff, light and easy to row? The larger more stable green dinghy? Or one that could sail, even if Sarah's strong point was certainly not sailing. Or should she just grab any small boat and row out to the collection of motor boats and see if she could start one up and go off in style? Here good sense intruded since Sarah knew even less about outboard motors than she did about sailing. In the end she chose a little red dinghy complete with furled sail, oars, and thank heavens, a life jacket. A dinghy that was not locked to its concrete mooring post. How trusting of the Ocean Tide residents. Brainwashed no doubt by the management's Dr. Pangloss, aka Joseph Martinelli. The little boat was called *Lady Bug*—its name written in black on its stern—rather an appealing name except it hardly suggested seaworthy qualities.

But now was no time for omens. Sarah turned to the cluster of children who had gathered around full of questions of who, where, and why. Sarah, busy with problems of selection, answered with vague assurances about needing to look for something.

"Like someone who escaped from the Maine State Prison?" suggested a small boy.

"Like drunks?" said a tangled-haired girl.

"Like someone having sex in a stolen boat?" said a red-haired boy, his expression hopeful.

Sarah nodded agreement to all these ideas, and giving fervent silent thanks that the beach was for once clear of adults— and police—recruited the largest of the watching children, a girl of about eleven, for the launching effort. Together with a heave and a ho the two of them shoved the dinghy to the water's edge, and with one final push *Lady Bug* was water borne. Sarah jumped in over the bow, slipped into the bilge, scrambled upright, plunked down on the seat, righted herself, fitted the oars into the oarlocks, and pulled out to sea.

And, busy with her exertions, her search plan still in an inchoate state, Sarah did not see that the distant smudge of fog on the horizon had had a spurt of growth and moved closer so that it now veiled the distant view of the Penobscot Bay islands.


Professor Emeritus Fergus Dugald McKenzie was pleased with himself, a condition he was familiar with. Things fell into place for him since throughout a long career in academe he had successfully shoved, shouldered, carped, and complained his way to the objects, positions, and places of his choice. An only child of elderly parents who lived in dread of his tantrums, he had prevailed since birth. Now a few weeks shy of his ninetieth birthday, unencumbered by children or dependents, he had planned to end his bus tour with a visitation to this Ocean

Tide settlement where lived his nephew and his nephew's wife, John and Elspeth McKenzie. Fergus had no particular love for these two nor for any of their too-numerous progeny, but it suited him to stay by the ocean, be waited upon, perhaps play a few rounds of golf, and then be the center of the party that Elspeth had mentioned: the celebration of his birthday coming up at the end of June. Salt air had always agreed with him and the price was right—John would be paying for his entire stay.

Perhaps, Fergus thought, as the taxi from Rockland bus terminal swung through the Ocean Tide gates at three-thirty that June 14, he would take a serious look at this place and see if a suitable cottage were available. There were, he thought, quite a few advantages attendant on his making a permanent home in such a community. It would be handy having his great-nephew Alex as a physician because Alex surely would not charge him huge sums for office visits. And Alex would be available for telephone consultations, house calls, and best of all, his office would probabably have a supply of free pharmaceutical samples of prescription drugs—Fergus, like so many of the elderly, lived on a large variety of costly medications.

The splendid part of this long-term plan would be that the McKenzie clan would certainly be expecting something from his estate—a favorable mention in his will; a codicil promising lands, goods, securities. This being the case, family members would go out of their way to be helpful. The joke was, of course, that their efforts would be fruitless, their hopes without foundation. Fergus's entire estate would descend intact into the grateful arms of Amherst College.

Fergus McKenzie had once stood a respectable five feet ten, but age and arthritis and general shriveling now had reduced him to something like a hunched-up five seven. He had the face of a dry apricot with a perpetually down-turned mouth. His eyes, somewhat diminished in their ability to see details at a short distance, were pale blue and reminded his associates of a dead haddock. But he was remarkably agile, even with arthritis, and his voice, although losing its bass notes, was clear, grating, and could carry in a crowded room.

Right now this voice filled the reception area of the Lodge. He was expected, was he not? He wished to have the key to his room, he wanted his luggage carried thither. He wished a call made from the desk to his nephew, John McKenzie. Fergus did not use the professorial title with John. In his view there was only room for one professor in the family and the position was already filled.

Carly Thompson, under orders from above, smiled, waved the luggage—three enormous leather suitcases vintage 1930—into the hands of the Lodge worker bees and thence onto the elevator. She produced the key to suite 307 (sitting room and bedroom), welcomed Professor McKenzie in the name of Manager Joseph Martinelli, and dialed the number of the John McKenzies.

And hung up after an interval of waiting. "I'm sorry, but there's no answer," she reported. "Were they expecting you this afternoon?"

"Try again," barked Fergus. "They know I'm coming. Middle of the week, I said."

Carly smiled, dialed again, had no response, and hung up. "Perhaps you'd like to go to your room and rest after your trip," she said. "Then I'm sure Professor John McKenzie will be back. He may be out on the golf course."

"I do not need rest," said Fergus. "I have rested on the bus. I will change and take my golf clubs to the course. Play a few holes."

"Shall I see if I can get you a starting time?" asked the ever-helpful Carly. "I know your nephew has arranged times for the rest of the week. But not for today."

"I don't need a starting time. I will just tee off where it's convenient. Whichever tee is not filled with people. And play from there. I'll want a tuna fish sandwich from your dining room but no pickle or pasta salad. I detest pasta. If you'll order me a car to be ready in half an hour I will drive myself. Not a sports car. A new Ford or Chevrolet will be suitable. Automatic transmission. And air conditioning. Charge the car to my nephew's account. And make sure the gas has been attended to. That's what you people often forget. Cars run on gasoline. See that there's a map of this place on the front seat. I'm thinking of moving to the community. If things work out to my satisfaction."

And Fergus walked with a determined step toward the elevator, his room key hanging from his hand.

"I hope," said Carly fervently to a fellow worker as the professor vanished into the elevator, "he chokes to death on the chocolates Martinelli sent to his room. The usual mints wouldn't do. Oh, no, I had to go out and buy these Godiva babies. A million dollars a bite."

Thirty minutes later Fergus McKenzie emerged dressed in what might have been appropriate golfing attire in the early 1920s. Fergus didn't squander money on clothes, and wore garments until they fell in rags from his body. Patched tweed plus fours, argyle stockings, leather brogues with spikes, oxford cloth shirt, its collars twice turned, and a frayed tie striped in the colors of Amherst college.

The news of Uncle Fergus's arrival had been telephoned in to the Pro Shop by Carly and an Ocean Tide cart was waiting. Assistant pro Pete Salieri, after a short speech of welcome, warned Professor McKenzie that there might be a considerable wait on the first tee—after all, players had prearranged starting times—so perhaps he could tee off from the ninth, which ran parallel to the first. If, and Pete stressed if, no other golfers were in sight. After all, here Pete gave a small chuckle, in the old days a single player had no real rights. Foursomes allowed twosomes to go through—usually—but single players were an anomaly. "In Scotland," Pete said, "golfers have been known to drive right through or even *at* a single player because by the old rules he's a nonperson."

Fergus McKenzie did not smile. "I am not a nonperson,"

he said, "and I always play alone. If I find a green ahead of me crowded I play through. Or if I find a fairway filled with idiots who are spending too much time looking for a ball I tee off on another tee."

"You mean," said Pete, frowning, "you don't play the holes in order?"

"Certainly, if it is convenient. If it is not convenient, I switch. Now if you will get my clubs from my car I will be obliged. They are in the gray Ford Focus I have left at the curb."

Pete Salieri, who didn't know whether to be angry or amused, did as he was ordered and emerged carrying a cloth bag of great antiquity filled with clubs. "These are museum pieces," he exclaimed to Fergus. "Just like the ones on the wall." Pete pointed to the fan-shaped display of wooden shafted irons and woods actually made of wood.

"I know," said Fergus complacently. "I belong to the Antique Golf Club and collect antique clubs. I have a baffie made in Edinburgh around 1909 and a niblick made for Robert Condie of St. Andrews. The clubs are still useful so why squander good money on fancy new clubs because some so-called famous golfer has been given a fortune to have his name written on them. Those clubs up there on the wall are doing no one any good. You should put them in service."

With which statement, Fergus strode to his cart, saw to the safe settlement of his golf bag behind him, refused a pack of complimentary tees on the basis that he saw no reason to switch from a pinch of sand with which to elevate his ball, and took off with a whirr of wheels in the direction of the ninth tee.

To his great annoyance the ninth tee was crowded, a foursome teeing off, the fairway inhabited by three women, and the distant green surrounded by four figures working their way out of surrounding bunkers. Not a problem, Fergus told himself. He pushed his foot down on the accelerator, swept in front of the tee, headed for the rough, and crisscrossing from cart path to fairway to green to tee came to rest at a vacant tee: the fifth hole.

Leaving the golf cart, Fergus took out his wooden-headed brassie, rested a nicked Topflite golf ball on its pinch of sand—the sand kept in a small pouch in his golf bag—took two practice half swings, addressed the ball and drove it straight into a grove of birches. Then, with a scowl at two arriving golfers, sped off for the trees, kicked his ball onto the fairway and pulled out his midiron, sliced the ball into the woods, climbed back in the cart and disappeared from view.

And the growing fog that had watched Sarah row out into Penobscot Bay now advanced to the Ocean Tide beach and began a slow shrouding of the golf course.


Elspeth McKenzie had expected to arrive at Logan Airport the necessary three hours before an international flight but had been surprised that five hours in advance had been determined by Naomi Foxglove, who murmured when Elspeth boarded the van that it was good to be far ahead of time what with all the new extra security rules in place.

Now, as the van pulled in front of the American Airlines entrance, Elspeth discovered that cyclist Nicholas Moseby and his friend, Thomas Schmidt, were to take the same nine o'clock flight to Paris. Elspeth was annoyed by this coincidence and most earnestly hoped that they would not be seated close enough for talk. Energetic youth in the middle of the night she could do without. Elspeth had her routines, herbal tea, a mild sleeping pill, a pillow and her traveling eyeshade; all she needed was a seat partner similarly equipped. The really curious thing was that from the corner of her eye as she entered the terminal, she glimpsed Naomi Foxglove, clutching a large handbag, emerge from the Ocean Tide van and disappear into a group of Japanese visitors who were moving slowly toward the Air France entrance.

How very strange. Naomi was supposed to be joining golf pro Wilson Williams in greeting the golf celebrity. Wasn't she? And he was coming in on a five-thirty flight on British Air. Wasn't he? A super golfer who had come in fourth—something like that—in last year's British Open. He was being presented to the Ocean Tide community as yet another of Joseph Martinelli's "special features." Really, thought Elspeth, there were many too many "special features." Manager Martinelli was like a magician burdened with a surfeit of white rabbits. As for Naomi, whatever she was up to was, of course, none of Elspeth's business, although try as she might Elspeth had difficulty thinking anything positive about the woman. She had been working hard of late to overcome her original impression of Naomi as a slippery character, but now look at her. Why on earth was the woman wearing a long silken raincoat, a carryall handbag, and an umbrella? Honestly, thought Elspeth, the weather in Boston was fair, why did she need a raincoat and an umbrella? Or that bag? Unless . . .

But from these disturbing thoughts, Elspeth's attention was directed to her luggage, her small wheeled suitcase must be checked in, she must see—again—to the safety of her passport hanging around her neck in its black cotton pouch together with a wad of French francs. Also she needed to find a ladies' room at the earliest possible moment. Traveling had a bad effect on the bladder.

But she remained troubled. If, as she told herself, in the very unlikely event that Naomi Foxglove turned up in the General de Gaulle Airport, or was spotted anywhere in Paris, Elspeth would damn well find out why, would shadow her, and find out what this female was up to. Naomi might turn out to be the key to all the untoward goings-on at Ocean Tide. Elspeth remembered worrying over, even reproving, Sarah for her past acts of snooping; now she felt a strong affinity for her daughter-in-law. She smiled to herself; they would make a good team.

# 17

FATE, having created a certain amount of havoc by land and sea as well as effecting the departure of several principal characters from their usual haunts, now decided to make them feel guilty for having done so. She had already done a good job with Betty Colley, who was busy trying to take the blame for the deaths of two of the least reliable characters in Knox County. Now it was the turn for others.

Sarah, rowing out on Penobscot Bay in her attempt to find Dylan Colley, seeing the bank of fog advancing, felt the guilt of one who knows she's done a stupid thing. Foolish. Unthinking. Why hadn't she found someone with a motor boat and recruited him for the search? Why at the very moment she thought Dylan might have taken a boat out, instead of checking with Betty, hadn't first she called the Coast Guard, the state police, the Knox County Sheriff's Department? Valuable time had been lost and now look at that blasted fog sneaking across the bay. So here she was, Sarah the Evil Snoop at her worst. Taking action without a second thought. Mike Laaka was right.

Any time there was a crime, an emergency in the making, she should be locked up.

But at least she had left a message at Alex's office and knew Carly could be trusted to get help. So she'd only been about 90 percent stupid. Now the sensible thing to do was turn around while she could still see the bow of her boat, row back to shore before the fog blanketed her and left her rowing in circles. She didn't have a compass and without the sun or a wind coming from a known direction there was no knowing where she would fetch up.

So okay. Turn around. Go right back where she'd come from while it was still possible. Hard on the starboard oar, steady on the port oar. But somehow both oars, propelled by something stronger than good sense, kept up a steady beat, out, out, out, heading straight into the fog bank.

Sarah squinted. Ahead she could see the murky unformed mass of something. In the fog? Or beyond it. An island? A piece of the mainland, some unfamiliar promontory? Or had she turned around and was now facing the Ocean Tide beach? Slowing her stroke she tried to think. It was too late to go back, particularly since she no longer knew where back was. Dylan might be only fifty feet away rowing in circles. But Betty had said the boat carried life jackets and Sarah hoped the boy had the good sense to put one on. Maybe it was time to call. And then head for the dark smudge. It had to be land of some sort although with the way things were going it might turn out to be a reef bare only at low tide. But a reef was better than nothing. It offered a base, respite even if for only an hour or so.

She rested her oars, cupped her hands and called. "Hello. Hello, there. *Hel-lo.*" She didn't want to call Dylan's name, scare him into trying to get away. She tried it again, louder this time. *"Hello. Hel-lo."*

And then she heard it, the low drone of a small engine. A soft buzz like a distant bee. And then over the buzz a voice calling. An angry sort of call. Or shout. It came closer and

Sarah thought she heard a faraway muffled stream of four-letter words. Dylan? No, not unless his voice had turned baritone since her last encounter with him. Then, somewhere off her starboard bow, "Goddamn it to hell, Sarah. Sarah."

Then, "You, there. Sarah! Call out again. Keep calling."

*"Hello, hello, hello, hello."*

And suddenly the small engine hum stopped and right out of the fog, a dark blue motor boat, came up to her starboard side. An entirely familiar someone yelled, "Sarah, goddamn you, what in hell do you think you're doing?"

Sarah briefly considered lifting an oar and braining her husband. But her aim had never been good, and besides, what in hell did *he* think he was doing motorboating around where he might ram someone, someone like her? You weren't supposed to motor in a fog, were you? Not without a fog horn or radar or something.

"Sarah," said Alex, lowering his voice, sounding as if he were speaking through clenched teeth. "I got that damn message in the office, so what—"

"I heard you the first time," said Sarah. "And I'll argue with you later. When I can scratch your eyes out or sink my teeth into you or push you overboard, which is better than you deserve. Listen, Dylan Colley's missing. He took a boat, the Colleys' little sailing dinghy, and took off. Maybe because he was afraid of the police. Or me. Carly Thompson is calling for help. Betty Colley didn't want to."

"All right," said Alex, his voice steady. "You've managed to scare the beejeezus out of me, but since we're both out in this soup, come aboard and I'll take your boat in tow and we can look together."

"And what if," said Sarah stubbornly, "I don't want to look together. I want to do my own search."

"So do it your way. If you think that's the way to go." Alex's voice was steely. "But I thought it was Dylan you were thinking about, not whether I was trying to give you orders."

Sarah capitulated. They would fight it out later. Even if she detested the man as she did now, he was occasionally right. She shipped her oars, reached for the side of Alex's boat, and hoisted herself in. An aluminum one, she saw now, with blue seats and a steering wheel. A big baby, almost eighteen feet, she guessed, the name *Ouzel* painted in large letters along its bow. A good name, Sarah thought, remembering that an ouzel was a waterbird. Except wasn't an ouzel a bird that walked underwater rather than staying on or above? What kind of an omen was that?

"I do love you," Alex remarked as he stowed her sack. "But you drive me insane."

"I," said Sarah, "for the moment don't love you in the least. In fact, I seriously dislike you. But let's get on with it. What's that dark piece of something over there? To the left. If Dylan was trying to escape somewhere he might have headed for an island. But it couldn't be Islesboro or Vinalhaven or North Haven. They're too far out. And Dylan wouldn't have headed for anything with houses on it. He was avoiding people."

"Secure the dinghy," ordered Alex, "and we'll take off."

"Stop this Captain Bligh stuff or I'll get back in that dinghy right now," snapped Sarah. "To be alone," she added.

"For Christ's sake."

"Oh, all right," said Sarah. She took the painter, did a figure eight around a stern cleat and let the dinghy drift back, and scowling, seated herself well astern of Alex, who sat in central position on a leather-covered seat. He shoved the throttle into forward and the *Ouzel* moved ahead leaving the bouncing *Lady Bug* in its wake.

They motored quietly. "Half throttle," Alex said, "or we won't be able to hear anyone. Is there a foghorn aboard? I should have checked when I took off."

"I can't believe you forgot a detail like that," said Sarah nastily. Then, because after all they didn't want to be hit by a searching Coast Guard boat, she rummaged about in a number of compartments and came up empty.

"I'll keep calling," she said.

"Good idea," said Alex.

So Sarah called out her hellos at intervals, but otherwise they sat without speaking while the *Ouzel* cruised slowly, the engine only a quiet hum, circling from time to time within the wet embrace of the fog. And then suddenly, like an apparition, at the same time they saw a swirl of water, a ruffling tongue of sea against a rock face that rose up before them. Alex cut the motor, backed, and turned the wheel and saw along their starboard side what appeared to be a small fog-blanketed island, a cluster of spruces sticking out of its crown like some kind of crazy hat.

Sarah held her breath as Alex turned and twisted the *Ouzel* between two small claws of rock beyond which there seemed to be the fuzzy outlines of some sort of narrow beach. It was, she thought, in a weird way exactly the sort of island that she might have been looking for if she had been trying to get away from a troubling world.

"I'll try to land," Alex said. "See if anyone's been here lately."

Sarah, who was determined not to indulge in any chat with Captain Bligh, found her mouth open and dripping with sarcasm. "Do you expect to find campfires and laundry hanging up? A note saying 'Find Me'?"

"I might expect to find his boat pulled up," said Alex in a level voice. "Signs of a shelter, a lean-to. After all, the kid's, what'd you say, thirteen years old?"

"If he heard us coming, I think he might be hiding out. Up a tree," said Sarah.

"Who knows," said Alex in the same noncommittal voice.

"The tide is coming in," said Sarah, unnecessarily since already the small waves were reaching farther up the island's shoreline, something that Alex with his sailor's eye would have noticed. She began to say that if the boy had ended up here, his boat might not be properly secured against the high tide. But stopped midsentence. Instead, making an incoherent noise in her throat she pointed behind the large rock where, at this low tide four or five smaller and equally sharp rocks stuck up out of the water. Wedged between one of the larger rocks and a mass of seaweed, an oar. A white-painted oar with a leather cuff.

Alex nodded, nosed the boat close to the object, and Sarah reached into the water and brought it aboard.

"It could be any old oar," she said.

"Yes," Alex agreed. "It could. And now I'll see if there's another oar around and maybe a boat to go with it."

Gently he reversed the boat, pulled the motor halfway up, turned and began a slow progress around the island. Not such a little one, it seemed. At least two or three acres of an island although much of it would be diminished when the tide came in. But it was large enough to support a second growth of spruce trees at its northeast end.

No second oar appeared.

But, stuck between another line of rocks, moving gently in tune with part of a nearby waterlogged tree trunk floated a small white dinghy rigged for sailing. Or, to be accurate, had been rigged for sailing in a non-existent wind. But now the tanbark sail hung in folds over one side of the boat and a tangle of ropes fell in loops into the water. The name on the stern, which faced Sarah, written in faded green paint, proclaimed it the *Folly*.

Ned Colley's boat. Deceased father of Dylan. Former owner of the boat. Boat kept at the Ocean Tide beach. Until this morning.

"Oh, my God," whispered Sarah.


Joining those other community members on a guilt trip was John McKenzie. He finished his round of golf at close to six o'clock and headed into the club house with the trio of duffers who had played with him. John, as a member of a foursome, had several things going for him: he spoke little beyond an occasional oath when he found himself in a bunker, his shots, although sometimes wavering, did not often leave the fairway so he held no one up; and best of all he could be counted on to bet on and to lose almost every hole.

But somewhere between the first and second draughts of dark ale with his fellow golfers, a strong sense of unease took hold of him. What if Uncle Fergus had actually turned up while he was on the golf course? He went to the telephone and called the desk of the Lodge to learn that Professor Fergus McKenzie had indeed arrived, had called the McKenzie house, had had his luggage taken to his room, had changed for golf, and was probably at this moment somewhere out on the Ocean Tide course.

Returned to his table, John McKenzie found drink and companionship no longer desirable. Instead the specter of family responsibility, a sense of how one should welcome an elderly—if difficult—relative to one's home, plus the sharp knowledge that he, with Alex's help, had engineered each golf day so as to avoid his uncle—all these brought John to his feet. Sent him outside. Forced him to commandeer another cart for the purposes of hunting down his guest, and, learning from assistant pro Pete Salieri that Fergus intended to start on the back nine, took off in that direction. "You should know," Pete Salieri called after him, "that your uncle told me that he doesn't follow the holes in order. He goes back and forth."

John waved back at him, thinking grimly how like Fergus that was. Rules, procedure, the etiquette of the game meant nothing to the old buzzard. Nevertheless it was high time to do the honors. If only Elspeth wasn't in Boston about to fly to France. If only Sarah and Alex were around somewhere to dilute the Fergus presence as they had promised they would be. John gunned the cart down the path, turned it toward the ninth tee, noting at the same time that the course was no longer crowded and that the offshore fog had come ashore and was hanging over the land like a gray veil.

\* \* \*

Unlike other members of his family, Professor Fergus Mc-Kenzie had never experienced a sense of guilt. His problems took a physical form. He had a troublesome prostate. Frequent urination was necessary and some of the fairways offered little protection for taking the necessary leak. Therefore, having woven an erratic course from one hole to another, infuriating players by appearing suddenly from a planting of shrubs, spending an inordinate time digging his ball out of a bunker or fishing it with the convenient net from assorted water holes, he found himself again needing to zip open his fly and let go. The seventeenth green offered not much protection even with the heavy fog that was now rolling in, but there beyond the green in a thin grove of pines stood two wooden buildings. Fergus wheeled his golf cart to the edge of the seventeenth green, made his way with an unsure step down a dirt path toward the smaller of the two buildings where he halted, noting without interest a sign on the shed which proclaimed that it contained fertilizers and other hazardous chemicals. Fergus walked a short distance toward the rear of the shed and relieved himself. Turning to begin the return trip to his golf cart, squinting at the indistinct path, he stumbled. And fell. Fell on something sharp. Painfully rising to hands and knees he reached for and found the obstruction. He had accidentally taken several steps off the path and fallen over, actually onto, the middle of a large white bag marked in huge letters: "Green-Gro—Fairway Fertilizer." But since when, Fergus asked himself as he cautiously felt his ribs, had fertilizer bags contained sharp objects?

No one had ever accused Fergus McKenzie of a lack of curiosity. Or of hesitating when he wanted to look into something that was not his business. And in this case, being almost punctured was certainly his business. Fergus got painfully to his feet, climbed the path back to his golf cart and selected his wooden-shafted niblick—a club now known to the golfing world as a nine iron—a wide-faced club used for lofting a golf ball out of difficult terrain. Fergus returned to the offending fertilizer bag, raised his club in a short backswing, then brought the club smartly down on the bag's flank. A ripping noise, a clanking sound, and something silver poked out of the heavy white paper. A second backswing, another downward strike, and the bag obliged with a widening split that allowed Fergus, even in the fast-disappearing light, to see a long metallic object that in no way resembled fertilizer material. Fergus laid down his niblick, and with the painful movements of an elderly arthritic got back down on his knees, reached for the slit in the bag and closed his hand on a tube of smooth metal. And then, in a sudden spasm, he released his grip.

Released because the heavy blow on the back of his head rendered Fergus insensible. A second blow brought him flat to the ground. The third blow split his skull.


Elspeth McKenzie, clutching her boarding pass, kept up hope until the last few minutes that Nicholas Moseby and friend would be seated well away from her. But as Fate—still in her meddlesome mood—would have it, Nicholas and Thomas Schmidt could not have been closer. Thomas in the window seat, Nicholas in the middle, Elspeth on the aisle. For a moment, as carry-on bags were being stowed and seat belts found, Elspeth had wild thoughts about asking a flight attendant if there was an empty seat in business class, or heaven help her, first class. But financial sense intruded. The flight wouldn't last forever; she would put on her eyeshade, insert earplugs, take her pill, and the two young men could get on with what interested them best, which from a few overheard remarks she judged to be cycling. Cycling in the state, in the country, in other countries, cycling in France, the crème de la crème home of bicycle racing.

Settled into her seat, she was served with a light repast— dinner proper presumed to be long over by the nine o'clock takeoff time. She enjoyed a not-too-dreadful Chablis with a small package of cheese biscuits, and topped it off with an almost hot caffeine-free cup of coffee. And as she drained her coffee, Elspeth, like her loved ones before her, felt a sense of guilt creeping over her. Was she so fragile, so needy, so far away from the youth generation that she was unable to have a conversation with two young men? To listen to what they had to say about their plans, their trip? Because both young men seemed to be bursting to talk, to lay before her all the exciting possibilities of bicycle racing in Provence.

There they were, sitting next to her, the picture of athletic health. Nicholas Moseby with his dark cropped hair, his brown eyes, dressed in what Elspeth associated with "Ivy League casual"—navy polo shirt, khakis, low-cut hiking boots, all this plus a beautiful tan as if he'd spent the winter as a lifeguard, not in the winter chills of New Haven. And Thomas Schmidt, blond buzz cut, hazel eyes, snub nose, broad cheeks suggesting a Germanic-Slavic ancestor, seemed equally ready for action in his gray-striped cotton shirt, sleeves rolled up, white canvas trousers, sneakers.

Elspeth, as a conversation gambit, started in on Yale. What courses would Nicholas be taking in his junior year? And did Thomas, too, go to Yale?

Nicholas wasn't sure about his next year's schedule, Thomas denied Yale but after admitting to Pennsylvania, the subject of college was brushed aside. Did Elspeth know, queried Nicholas, anything about cycling? Racing?

No, Elspeth told them, the subject was a mystery although, yes—as Mike Laaka before her had said—she'd certainly heard of Lance Armstrong winning that French race, three times was it, after cancer. And then there was a man about ten years ago that had the same name of a French newspaper. La Monde, something like that.

"Greg Le Mond," said Thomas Schmidt in an awed vice. "I think he won the Tour de France three times, too."

"They even have races for senior citizens," said Nicholas. "But maybe," he added in a kindly tone, "you might be out of shape so you'd be too far behind to start."

Elspeth agreed she was perhaps somewhat out of shape and much too far behind to start and besides her new bicycle had just been stolen.

"Oh," said Thomas, "you wouldn't want a recreational bike, you'd need a safe beginner's racing model. For older riders," he added tactfully.

"Would you like to know something about bike racing?" asked Nicholas.

And Elspeth, even though her guilt was well on the way to being assuaged, said yes. After all, why not go all the way? she thought. Of all things, she told them, she'd certainly like to know about bike racing. And where the team was going to be racing. Although, she warned them, in about an hour or so, she was going to take a pill and go to sleep. "Paris in the morning," she reminded them.

Yes, they told her, it was Paris in the morning, and they were both going to meet friends, team members, plan strategies."

"You have race strategies?" asked Elspeth, feeding the question to them, knowing that for now she could lean back and listen with only an occasional nod or exclamation from her to keep the talk going.

And Nicholas, with Thomas as chorus, kept at it. He kicked off with a brief history of the Tour de France. Apparently the Tour de France would be occurring in July and they, Nick and Thomas, would, in the upcoming week, actually be racing along some of the roads—well, pretty near some of the roads—through some of the same historic towns, that had seen the likes of past Tour riders, including the one and only Lance Armstrong. But of course there were the great and the near great ones, Bernard Hinault, a five-time winner of the Tour, Eddy Merckx, Raymond Poulidor, Charly Gaul, Erik Zabel, Jan Ullrich.

Elspeth leaned back and listened with half an ear as the two young men moved from riders to describe the wonders, the horrors of the routes: Loudun, Nantes, Bannes, Vitre,

Tours, Limoges, and on to Revel, Carpentras, Mont Ventoux, north on the edge of Switzerland to the glory of Paris. Then followed descriptions of strategies, sprints, stages, time trials, while Elspeth thought to herself that details of bike racing, boring as they might seem to the nonracing cyclist, were probably more palatable than, say, a blow-by-blow description of ten rounds of a heavyweight boxing match, or of a mud wrestling event, or even of one of the state of Maine's sport specialties, candlepin bowling.

Then, as Nicholas paused in the middle of a recitation of past drug testing problems that had plagued the Tour, Elspeth said firmly she must now leave them, it had been absolutely fascinating, but good night. She went to the rest room, brushed her teeth with a miniature travel toothbrush, took her pill, returned to her seat, pulled off her shoes and slipped on her new pair of travel slippers—ones that apparently offered great support so that the traveler could if need be make an emergency exit and escape over rough ground. Next, she eased her seat back the few inches allowed by American Airlines coach, shoved her pillow into place, switched off her reading light, settled her mask over her face, and ordered sleep to take over. Which after a certain amount of shoulder twisting and leg twitching it did.

How long she slept she had no idea, but she woke from a confused dream involving painting on an immense canvas a number of bike racers rounding a mountainside, which was unusual since Elspeth was a landscape artist. But now her right leg had gone into such a ferocious cramping that the dream and the heaviness of sleep were banished at the same time. She was about to rear up and deal with her aching limb when she became aware that the two young men were still awake and talking in subdued voices about something that seemed to occupy them intensely, the voices, low and urgent. She pushed her mask up slightly and squinted into the eerie semidark of an airliner at night. Both men had their heads together and someone's hand held a pad of paper. They were speaking, Elspeth decided somewhat groggily, in a foreign language. A language that had an infusion of standard English mixed with rap jargon, German, perhaps Hungarian, and one of the lesser Russian dialects. Esperanto perhaps.

Quietly Elspeth pushed her mask down, but sleep had departed and her ears—where had she put her earplugs?—were full of whatever dialect Nicholas and Thomas were communicating in. Nothing made sense, but finally Elspeth decided they must be talking about bicycles, parts, and prices. There were mumblings about several Diamond Back Responses, Diamondback V-links—were they into snakes?—a titanium hard tail, parts for a Proflex 857, a Giant Iguana, something called a FOES Weasel—more animals. Or were these all bikes? But then the talk became even more incomprehensible with talk of coil spring systems, Shimano Deores 27 speed drive train, Ritchey Logic Comp clipless pedals, easy to accelerate wheelsets, head tubes, fork designs, quick handling geometry.... Elspeth had a last muddled memory of pencils scratching on notepads, then her head sank into her pillow and she slept again.

She woke to the rattle of dishes and creak of the pushcart. Cabin lights had gone on, and breakfast at what was for most travelers a predawn hour was being wheeled down the aisle, pillows were being shoved aside, seats being righted, bleary eyes were trying to focus on orange juice, croissants, and life-saving coffee. Elspeth's mouth was dry, the idea of breakfast was appalling, all she wanted to do was close her eyes again and lose the whole scene. But the flight attendants were relentlessly cheerful, all was bustle and movement, and she gave in. Found her shoes, tottered to the rest room, stood in line, returned to her seat to find her two bike-racing companions stoking up on hard little brown sausages afloat in a dark syrup, the sight of which made her gorge rise, and then breathing deeply through her nose, she spoke the word "tea," accepted a flight tray and reached for the tea bag and began dipping it into what she was sure was now tepid water.

So with a queasy stomach, the onset of jet lag, Elspeth braced herself as the plane flew over land, fields, villages, the distant haze of Paris and began the routine of landing, lost altitude, lost speed, put down its wheels with a thump. And landed at General Charles de Gaulle Airport. Passengers, many of whom looked to be in the last stages of a wasting fever, made their way down the aisle, out the corridor, through a series of doors, stairs, to the luggage claim area. There, having retrieved her wheeled navy blue suitcase, Elspeth found her hand being shaken by Nicholas Moseby and Thomas Schmidt, both fresh eyed and irritatingly upbeat. She listened to their ritual hopes that she have a nice day, a good visit, and maybe think about doing some serious Elder Hostel biking if she thought she was up to it. With that the boys vanished, saying something about a taxi, and Elspeth realized she too needed to nail down a taxi and get herself to the Hotel de la Roche. She must hang on to her passport, her wallet, beware of pick-pockets and rogue taxis, and then collapse on her hotel bed for at least two hours before indulging in the excitement of a museum or two.

Emerging at the line of taxis, ready to take her turn, she was interested to see that Nicholas and Thomas, being quick on their feet, were already shoving their backpacks into a taxi, sliding into the backseat, and taking off. But what was inter-esting, no, that wasn't the word, substitute sinister. What was sinister, was the figure at the head of the waiting passengers, who now climbed into the next waiting taxi, a large handbag hung over one shoulder. A figure who despite a brown-and-black patterned head scarf, very dark glasses, a silken rain-coat, an umbrella in her hand, was perfectly recognizable. Naomi Foxglove.

Naomi Foxglove, who should at this moment be back in the social whirlpool of Ocean Tide. Who, by no wild surmise, could have been planning a secret trip to Paris. I mean, Elspeth asked herself, she couldn't just turn up at Section E, interna-tional departure section of Logan Airport, and jump aboard a flight for Paris, could she? Well, not without foresight. Planning. Reservations. Finding her passport, rounding up any necessary medications. Of course, Naomi was probably in perfect health and didn't take anything more than a multivitamin. But how about a change of underwear? Stockings, socks? France might be the fashion capital of the world, but even instant wardrobe purchases might be awkward, involve stops in shopping districts, especially if Naomi were intent on some dubious trip that involved tailing—I mean, what other word was there for it, Elspeth asked herself—those two young men, one of whose family members had been involved in a double murder.

All right, if Naomi could track Nicholas and Thomas, then she, Elspeth could try to track Naomi. It's what Sarah would have done and, as previously noted, Elspeth admired Sarah's proclivity for dubious action. For a second Elspeth experienced a tiny shiver of excitement. Then reality set in. This was no cinema sequence and Elspeth could not muscle the passengers out of line, seize the next taxi, shout, *"Attention! Allez!* Follow that woman,"* and go careening through the streets of Paris. Instead, with a sigh, she resigned herself to everyday life, waited her turn, allowed the driver to load in her luggage, and in a weary voice, said, *"Bonjour, monsieur, Hotel de la Roche, quartier Saint-Germain, s'il vous plaît."*

Then, leaning her head against the seat cushion, Elspeth, through slitted eyes allowed herself moving views of Paris and its people, only rousing herself as the taxi pushed itself in between two others before the doorway of the Hotel de la Roche. Of Nicholas Moseby and Thomas Schmidt and a following Naomi there had been, as expected, no sign.

Presenting herself at the desk of the hotel, Elspeth found that the desk clerk had received a telephone message for Madame McKenzie of Maine, the United States. The clerk, a small black-haired person with astonishingly long purple fingernails who spoke excellent English, picked up a piece of paper covered with a dense scribble. "I have transcribed it for you," said the clerk.

Elspeth read: "Hope your flight was comfortable. Sarah and Alex have gone off somewhere. Uncle Fergus arrived and went to play golf and hasn't turned up. At least not yet. A dinghy is missing and someone has called the Coast Guard. Maybe Uncle Fergus has taken up boating. Enjoy your trip. Love, John."

This was not a message meant to ease jet lag and bring sleep. Elspeth spent an hour and a half rotating under a silken coverlet in La Chambre *vingt-neuf* picturing shipwreck, lost family members, and Uncle Fergus offending all he met. Then she thought about Naomi Foxglove as a chic member of some underground group whose strings were pulled by Joseph Martinelli. Finally, she rose, splashed water on her face, and headed for the street. An art store, pastels, watercolors, something to distract her. Then perhaps a bench and watching the boats go by on the Seine. Really men, or at least John McKenzie, had not the least notion of what to say to a tired wife who needed her rest. As for Naomi Foxglove, the woman had probably simply had it with the whole Ocean Tide scene and had taken off for pastures new.

# 18

A small sailing dinghy named *Folly*, wedged between two rocks, minus an oar, its sail half-hoisted, its tiller propped high in the air, suggested a variety of disturbing events.

"Don't jump to conclusions. Wait and see," said Alex, who knew his wife's propensity for thinking of catastrophe.

"I wasn't," said Sarah shortly. But she had been. That whole afternoon on the fog-blanketed water she had been seeing catastrophe. Had scenes involving drowned bodies forcing their way into her head. David Copperfield gazing sadly at Steerforth's body, Shelley washing up on the beach, Ophelia weighed down by her wet dress, all those garlands, that poem by James Dickey, "The Life guard," Winslow Homer's *Undertow*. None of which she was going to admit to Alex.

"Dylan might not have hauled the boat far enough up on the shore," she said. "Forgot about the tide or didn't tie it up. Remember, he was running away."

"From what?" asked Alex reasonably.

Sarah frowned. And then remembered. Alex didn't know

that Betty Colley had put off telling the police about Dylan's role in finding his father's body.

Quickly Sarah brought Alex up to speed, and to bolster her not very certain idea that the boy might be alive and well and on the island, up a tree, in a cave, ended by suggesting that he might be hiding from anyone looking for him.

"I remember," she added, "that Betty said he'd gone off this morning with his backpack on. She thought it was filled with books for the tutoring session. But if Dylan had been planning to take off, he might have put in camping equipment, some survival food."

"So we'd better start looking," said Alex. "I'll make his dinghy fast to a rock and fix the anchor into the ground for our boat. The tide will have them floating within the hour."

But as Alex went about this business Sarah found herself again staring uneasily at the *Folly*. "Why," she asked, "is it such a mess? He's left the sail half up. Lines all over the place. And the tiller hasn't been secured. Does that make it all look more like . . . well, an accident? And there's no life jacket in the boat. Betty said she'd left two life jackets in it."

"Did she say Dylan knew anything about sailing? Anything about boats?"

"The boy didn't know much. And he can hardly swim."

"So, if he fell into the water, he was probably wearing a life jacket, and we hope will be picked up. He may be using the second life jacket for a raft. Something to hang on to. And if he beached the boat here, he'd simply get out. Wearing a life jacket. Leaving the boat in a mess and not tied because he doesn't know any better. And since he'd left the daggerboard down the boat probably hit bottom, got loose, drifted in and became wedged."

"You have an answer for everything," said Sarah. "And," she added more charitably, "I suppose it makes sense. And that explanation makes me feel better."

"So let's move it," said Alex.

Sarah nodded and started to clamber up the rocks that led

to a small overhang of prickly bushes and high grasses. The island seemed larger than it looked from the water and now she could see that the nearby grove of spruce gave way to rising slabs of rock and beyond that more spruce and scrub. "I'll start calling," she said.

"But," said Alex, "if Dylan's afraid of you? Or of being found, wouldn't that alert him? Keep him quiet?"

Sarah was spared the necessity of agreeing. Instead she stared at something bright orange at her feet. Leaning down she picked it up, grinned and waved it under Alex's nose.

"Look. A Reese's Peanut Butter Cup."

"So?" said Alex. "People come to the island, picnics, fishing."

"This is a fresh wrapper. So why not check the trees and I'll try the ground. Look for hiding places. Making no noise."

Sarah found him. Under an overhanging rock. Nicely camouflaged with fresh-cut spruce boughs. Very neat. Almost comfortable. One yellow life jacket and his backpack sat open in front of him, and on both sides Sarah saw a root beer can, a package of doughnuts, and paperback titled *Wilderness Camping*. Dylan sat hunched on his boat's second life jacket, his arms around his knees, making himself as small as possible. But thirteen-year-old boys and yellow life jackets are hard to conceal in a space of about eight feet by six.

He started to scramble up, but Sarah, fearing a reprise of the scene at the seventeenth tee when Dylan had taken off, made a dive for the boy, fastened her hand around his wrist, bent his arm back behind him, and yelled for Alex.

Sarah tried to say some words of reassurance to the boy. But she kept her grip tight as the boy was twisting around trying to sink his teeth into her hand like some sort of suddenly captured wild animal, a fox, a weasel. Then all at once he gave up the struggle. Seemed to shrink inside himself, and without moving or speaking, glared at her. Mouth snapped shut, jaw extended.

Then Alex arrived and the return journey was put into motion. Dylan gently but firmly was fastened into his life jacket, placed next to Sarah on the *Ouzel*'s seat, the *Folly* strung behind the *Lady Bug*, and, using an oar as a pole, Alex pushed off into the oncoming tide. And into the thickening fog.

"Do you know which way to go?" asked Sarah. On this score she had to be humble. As far as she was concerned any direction she would choose would probably take their three-boat convoy straight to Newfoundland. Or Dieppe. Or, God help them, to Miami.

"Listen for other boats," instructed Alex, now back in his command mode. Alex was one of those individuals born with a compass fixed in his head. It was irritating but also comforting, and Sarah did not care to renew hostilities. Later, much later, he and she would have a chat about male dominance.

Meanwhile there was Dylan. Sitting rigid on his seat, lips pressed together, staring straight ahead into the fog. Dylan the Silent. Well, Mother Betty Colley could probably make him say something. And George Fitts was a past master at it. Poor Dylan, Sarah thought with a sigh. But, to look on the bright side—if there was one—surely this whole grim affair should be grist for a number of essays to be produced for the summer tutoring session and even get the boy through the first half of eighth grade English.

John McKenzie, tramping from one hole to another on the back nine all in the increasing fog, found himself by six o'clock that evening almost the sole inhabitant of the course. Golfers, no matter how fanatic, must be able to follow the flight of their ball, and a gray blanket of fog had by the end of the afternoon sent most of the diehards back to the clubhouse and the comfort of a stiff drink.

Several times, John himself became disoriented and only the markers on the tees and the flags on the green enabled him to find his way from hole to hole. But with no sign of

Fergus, no answering voice to his calls, John grew increasingly uneasy. And annoyed. The dampness of the evening made his shirt cling to his skin, his feet squelched in their sodden socks and wet shoes, so that at last he gave it up and began a fumbling return to the Pro Shop. After all, he reasoned, Uncle Fergus was not one to suffer discomfort gladly; he most certainly would have gone back to the Lodge for a drink and a hot bath. And he would have called his nephew at home so now it was high time for John to get back to receive and welcome, to wine and dine his ancient relative.

But no Fergus McKenzie. Not in the Pro Shop, not in the golf bar. Then after repeated telephone calls from the desk at the Lodge, John had asked for a key to his uncle's room expecting that he would perhaps find Fergus senseless on the floor—a likely event perhaps for a very old man, John told himself. But instead of a medical crisis he found the room empty. Two of his uncle's suitcase, ancient models covered with what might once have been crocodile hide, stood on the floor. The third sat open on the luggage stand, the toilet article kit was tucked under a pair of purple silk pajamas, this last suggesting possibly that no sudden attack had necessitated medication. Returning to the first floor, John began to search in earnest. But Fergus was not in the lounge, the dining room. Nor yet in the sauna, having a massage, nor working out in the Fitness Center—surely a stretch, that one. John drove to his own cottage to see if his uncle had been sitting there the entire time, enjoying a glass of John's favorite scotch. There he drew a blank, admitted defeat and, after a call to the local hospital to check on recent visitors to the emergency room, he decided to call in the troops.

He ran down the steps of his house and discovered what he in his preoccupation had missed. Something was going on. The place was alive with people with flashlights. Several cars were slowly circling the lanes and drives of the community. And down at the beach, John could just see the blurred beam of a searchlight rotating in the fog. Grabbing at a passing man he demanded information because these widespread efforts could hardly be directed at finding Fergus McKenzie.

"No," said the man. "It's a boy. Missing since late this morning. They think he might have taken a boat out in this fog, so the Coast Guard's been called. But just to make sure, we're doing a search. They've called in the sheriff's department."

John thanked him and drove back to the Lodge. The search for an irascible senior citizen could hardly compete with the hunt for a missing boy. But it did no harm to inform as many people as possible that if they came across a disoriented elderly man with or without golf clubs, a man who might have had a sudden attack of amnesia or lost his way in the fog, well, please point him in the direction of the Lodge.

This being done, John decided that looking for the boy might be as good a way of finding Uncle Fergus as anything else he might do, and offered his services to Carly Thompson, who, along with Mike Laaka and several men from Ocean Tide Security, was directing the search. John pointed out that he had just come from the last nine holes of the golf course and they appeared to be uninhabited. His information was taken and Carly suggested that he stay at the Lodge and keep his eye out. Old men tend to fall asleep in odd places; perhaps Mr. Fergus McKenzie had gone off to one of the libraries, one of the smaller lounges, and fallen asleep.

John took Carly's remarks to suggest that he, like his uncle, was too enfeebled by age to search actively, made an ambiguous noise in this throat, and headed back to his cottage. Not because he'd been dissuaded from searching but a minor brainstorm had taken over his plans. Sarah had left Patsy in the house for her tutorial period but then she had not come back. Was off somewhere in an irresponsible manner, perhaps with Alex, who was also off somewhere, and she must have forgotten she owned a dog the size of a large pony. But John, who was genuinely fond of dogs, decided that a wolfhound through centuries of breeding must be a tracker. Didn't the word *hound* express this virtue? John broke into a slow jog, arrived puffing at his doorstep. In minutes he had leashed Patsy, put on a rain jacket, and headed for the scene of the recent body discovery—the rough around the third practice hole green. He, of course, should have dragged Patsy up to his uncle's room for a good sniff at Fergus's clothing, but time was a-wasting and perhaps with Irish wolfhounds this wouldn't be necessary.

But at the entrance to the trail John stopped. Two parked police cars, searchlight beams, and muffled calls suggested that this prime search area was being attended to. He reversed, dragging a reluctant Patsy who remembered good smells and canine encounters in the area, and considered. The beach? No, that was being searched. The houses and buildings of Ocean Tide? No, they were already covered by those circling cars, those men going in and out with flashlights. What was left? The golf course. John had not yet seen any great activity on the golf course. As he himself had earlier testified. Apparently the searchers thought it was unlikely that a young boy could choose a golf course as a sanctuary. Too open, too civilized. But this time John would do a search in reverse. From the eighteenth hole back to the first. This would cover the possibility of Fergus still lurking, wandering—or fallen insensible—and also do service as a lost boy search.

But now the fog was thicker and the evening more advanced. And John's small flashlight shed only a narrow yellow light for a distance of about seven feet. The eighteenth green and its approach with three surrounding bunkers was fairly well lit by the illuminated buildings of the Ocean Tide clubhouse and bar, the Pro Shop, but as John felt his way backward down the fairway toward the seventeenth green, repeatedly stumbling in the dark, he had all he could do to prevent an enthusiastic Patsy from dragging him into a bunker, against a tree, into a water hole.

Finally, picking himself off the edge of the sixteenth green after a misstep, swearing at himself for undertaking an impossible task, swearing at Patsy who had wound the leash around a bush, cursing young boys and elderly uncles, unhappily thinking of his wife enjoying the sun of Provence, John brought himself to a halt. Waved his flashlight and saw nothing but misty dark. No sign of the fifteenth tee. "Goddamn it," he said aloud. And Patsy, as if suddenly alerted by the unexpected voice, lunged, wrenched the leash away from John's hand and disappeared.

And John, after a more explicit oath, one he kept for private occasions of frustration, called, reached out in the dark, called again, and then fumbling his way across what might have been the looked-for tee, encountered a bench, grabbed its back and sank down.

For a few minutes John simply sat, breathing hard, grateful only to be on a strong piece of furniture set on firm ground. And then he became aware of heavy breathings, the sound of digging. Scrabbling paws, canine whining. Somewhere over to the left. He circled his flashlight and was rewarded with a glimpse of an elevated flag with the number sixteen in black against a light background. It was an area he had already searched. But the location of the flag coincided almost perfectly with the dog yips and glottal noises. Patsy must have backtracked and was somewhere around the sixteenth green. And was digging. Digging with great energy and enthusiasm.

John called without result. Then, "Goddamn that dog," and John pushed himself off the bench, groped unsteadily down a grassy slope, back toward the sixteenth green, visions rising before him of smooth turf destroyed by large dog paws.

But Patsy was behind the hole. In a sand trap, digging for treasure. So absorbed was the dog in his work that he paid no attention to the end of the leash being grabbed by his human companion. But he wasn't going to give in to the man when such an interesting odor was rising from the torn-up sand.

Then John, holding his flashlight low, saw it. A golf shoe. Complete with spikes. An old-fashioned dark shoe with fringed tongue. Attached in the usual manner to a leg. A leg with a dark patterned sock. A leg if followed upward for about ten inches dressed—in a loosened plus fours.


Carly Thompson's opinion was that Manager Joseph Martinelli was fast approaching multiple mental breakdown—rather in the way an amoeba divides itself into separate entities. Up to his bushy eyebrows in the Senior Citizen Social Barbecue and Raffle, the arrival of an instrumental trio for a Sunshine House concert, Joseph, since the report of the missing Dylan Colley, had put a large part of himself into an Action Red Alert mode. Already unnerved by the persistent presence of the police, the echoes from the double murder, the irritations from the bike and golf thefts, now he had to face the possibility that a boy closely related to the murder victims had run away, gone out to sea and drowned himself. Both energized and at the same time in a nervous twitch by this new development, Joseph tried to be at the center of the Dylan Colley search, turned up at the beach to wave his hands and bark orders and then to repeat the performance at the mountain bike trail, the Senior Citizen Center, the Lodge foyer, the Pro Shop, the Fitness Center, and there to find that Professor Fergus McKenzie was missing from his round of golf.

Joseph flung up his hands at this information and called on God and Mary the Holy Mother above and the devil beneath to testify to the fact that he, an honest man who only wanted to make the citizens of Ocean Tide happy, was now being faced with trials that made those of Job look like a visit to Disney World. And, if he hadn't been burdened enough, where had Naomi Foxglove got to? A sudden vacation without telling anyone? When he needed her so badly. His trusted social assistant to take off like that.

"Why don't you go back to your office?" said Carly. "You can take messages. All the searching parties, the police, the Coast Guard, they need someone to report to. . . ."

"You mean I should be there to—"

"You need to be Mission Control," said Carly. "To stand by the telephone. You can let us all know on our cell phones if messages have come in. We need you, Mr. Martinelli."

And Joseph Martinelli, somewhat mollified by the idea of a command post, started down the drive toward his personal golf cart, which he had been using as a reconnaissance vehicle. And as he swirled the cart around Lavender Lane and pointed it toward Beach Road and the Lodge he became aware that out of the fog a small procession burdened with a longitudinal bundle, their progress lighted by a number of heavy-duty flashlights, was moving on the path that led from the sixteenth and seventeenth holes of the golf course. And they were heading toward the outer rim of Beach Road. Where, Joseph noticed for the first time, a police car and an ominous dark van waited, both vehicles with headlights full on.

Openmouthed, Joseph waited and then he put the scene together. "It's the Colley boy," he said aloud in a kind of despairing groan. "He's dead, he's drowned, they're bringing him back." He waggled his head back and forth, shaking like jelly. Where he was found by Carly, who had just heard from the police.

"Now, Mr. Martinelli," said Carly in the voice of a grandmother to an out-of-control eight-year-old, "it's going to be okay. It's a terrible thing and we're very sad about it and the police are looking into it, but at least he was almost ninety years old. He'd had a good life."

Joseph reared up. "Ninety!" He exploded. "Ninety! Who's ninety? Dylan Colley isn't—"

"No," said Carly. "Dylan Colley isn't ninety and he's been found. That's the good news. Sarah Deane and Alex McKenzie found him on Shag Island out on the bay. He was hiding and now he's back. Safe. No, it's Professor Fergus McKenzie. The one we were supposed to be extra careful about."

"He's dead," said Joseph in a quavering voice. Then, "But why is he dead? Was it an attack? A heart attack? A stroke? Did he hit his head?"

"Yes," said Carly carefully. She meant to leave all the unsavory details for later. "He sort of hit his head. Or something hit it. A head injury. It's very sad but he was," she repeated in her most consoling voice, "very, very old."

"But we don't want any more dead people, young or old," said Joseph plaintively. "I mean even if it wasn't Dylan Colley, it's driving me crazy and we're getting the reputation of some kind of morgue. But you're right, this Fergus, he could have dropped dead anytime. No surprise. But I'm sorry he chose the Ocean Tide golf course instead of the taxi he came in. Or even his own room. That we could handle. Body down the service elevator, out the back door to the business parking lot, off to the undertaker. So why did it have to be out on our golf course? You can't be much more public than that."

"Too bad Fergus McKenzie didn't control himself until he was off the property," said Carly, her voice taking on an edge. Really, Joseph Martinelli was something else. And wait until he heard that the death was anything but accidental and that there might be a homicidal golfer at large.

"At least there was the fog," Joseph went on, reaching for the bright side. "I don't suppose there were many people on the golf course that late in the afternoon."

"So count your blessings," said Carly. "At least Mr. McKenzie had the good sense to die out of sight of the clubhouse."

"You're being sarcastic again, Carly, and it's not helpful. Keep your mind on our positive image. Rescuing Dylan Colley gives a positive image. Fergus McKenzie alive or dead, he doesn't."

"I won't say that I'm sorry this Fergus won't be around this week," said Carly, who didn't hold with useless sentimentality.

"Everyone said he was a pain in the butt," agreed Joseph, spirits reviving and forgetting in his relief over Dylan Colley's return, the sympathetic respect due to a deceased guest, no matter how undesirable he might be.

"From what I hear," said Mike Laaka, back at the VIP Golfer's Cottage House in the Arnold Palmer sitting room later that evening, "this Fergus was a guy you wanted to strangle as soon as you met him. But," he added, "this wasn't a strangulation job, was it?" He turned to Johnny Cuszak, fresh from supervising the crime scene and giving the corpse a once-over before it was driven away to the morgue. "So any bright ideas, Johnny? That crack on the head? Do you think he fell, hit a stone?"

"And then buried himself in the sand trap?" asked Johnny.

"He might have fallen. A couple of golfers come along, freak out when they find the body. Nervous types. So they bury the guy. They don't want to be finders."

"As far-fetched as anything I've ever heard," said George Fitts, walking in and shrugging out of his waterproof jacket. "The man was slammed on the head. Right, Johnny?"

"Yeah," said Johnny. "I'll go along with that. One big question, though."

"Which is," said Mike, surprised because Johnny usually had a million questions, all of which he kept to himself until the lab tests were in and he'd done the autopsy.

"Choice of weapon," said Johnny, grinning.

"Well, sure," said Mike. "We'll be combing the place. You know that."

"What I mean," said Johnny, still grinning, "is which club? What would you say? A sand wedge? Pitching wedge? Nine iron? Even an eight? Or hey, how about a putter? Some of those babies have real heavy heads. Short shafts. Make a nice tool."

"Aaaah," said Mike. "You're making jokes in front of George Fitts, who ain't that crazy about homicide humor. And me, I'm hungry, wet, tired and mean. All day tramping around in that fog. Hunting for that Colley kid."

"Actually," said Johnny, "I'm making a point. The wound was fairly deep, wide at the place of entry, narrow where the injury terminated. I'll get a better sense of it when I've got him on the table. A golf club makes a hell of a good weapon. Easy to handle, easy to swing, made for the job. Murder mysteries are probably filled with golf club victims."

"You think the murderer was a golfer?" asked Mike. "Someone playing with Fergus McKenzie?"

"That's George's business," said Johnny. "All I'm saying is that golf clubs can be found on golf courses. And that the wound—from a quick once-over—is suggestive."

"So it's worth mentioning," said George, flipping open a small brown notebook.

"You mean golf clubs as in weapons," said Mike.

"Correct. Golf clubs plural," said George. "They're missing. Fergus McKenzie was playing golf. With golf clubs in a golf bag. Both noticed at the Pro Shop because they were ancient, wooden-shafted things. Collector's items. The golf bag was tan canvas. His cart was back on the edge of the seventeenth green. His clubs weren't anywhere around."

"You're saying," put in Mike, "that old Fergus was killed with his own club?"

"To repeat," said Johnny, standing up and pulling on his slicker. "Which club would you choose?"


Paris. The middle of June, the wind soft, the sky blue, the sun benign. What more could a visitor desire? However, one visitor remained untouched. Elspeth McKenzie found that her attention could not be fixed for more than a few minutes on the shops, the *patisseries*, the offerings of stalls along the Left Bank. Nor by the wonderful art shop that sold all manner of special papers and pastels, not by the cafés, the gardens, or museums that ranged along the banks of the Seine. Elspeth McKenzie was bedeviled by the thought of Naomi Foxglove as some sort of serpent weaving her way in pursuit of Nicholas

Moseby and Thomas Schmidt. Perhaps in Paris. Perhaps, later, in Provence.

This pursuit by Naomi could mean two things, both ominous. Naomi, as the brain behind some criminal organization that specialized in bike thefts and homicide, was, for reasons not yet revealed, pursuing these two young men with an eye to perhaps expanding her bike-theft ring, adding Nicholas and Thomas to her workforce. Or perhaps eliminating them. Bike races must be prime places for latching on to outrageously expensive bikes and bike parts. And making deals. Making a killing in more than one sense of the word. Although the idea sounded far-fetched to the point of being ludicrous, even to Elspeth's jet-lagged brain, it had to be thought of. The other, more likely scenario had to do with Naomi as the prime mover of a bike-scam team of which both Nick Moseby and Thomas Schmidt were already in place as secondary cogs. Or agents. Middlemen.

Elspeth, oblivious of the art lovers crowding around her, found herself at noon the day after her arrival standing stock-still in the darkened room of framed pastels in the Musée D'Orsay while she fumbled to put these muddled ideas into some sort of acceptable shape. But the more she worried the matter, like one of her terriers with an old shoe, the more she found that the joys of viewing one of the world's great collections of impressionists had been completely blunted. What were Monet and Degas and Cezanne to homegrown double murder compounded with bicycle theft?

Finally, turning her back on Art, banishing the idea of lunch at the museum restaurant, walking fast, she worked her way back to her hotel, summoned a taxi, called her friend in Venasque that she would be arriving a day and a half early, would be happy to sleep on the floor if another guest was present, and in a matter of an hour found herself at the Gare de Lyons cramming a sketchily wrapped croque monsieur into her handbag, and climbing aboard a train for Avignon.

Luck all the way. A seat on the train. Tea available (to

wash down the croque monsieur). And in Avignon, an auto-mobile available for rental (a minor miracle) due to the dis-satisfaction of a noisy Belgium couple with the offered Ford. Then, another minor miracle, Elspeth without the aid of a map managed to take the correct route out of Avignon, weave her way to Venasque with only twice ending up in Pernes, drive up the winding road to her friend's house by evening. To be welcomed by Penelope Sachs, find an empty bed in a delightful nook of a room overlooking a charming landscape, and then fall asleep in minutes. And awake the next morning to inform her friend that she had decided that her art had taken a new turn.

Not landscapes, she informed a startled Penelope. And not still life, not seascapes, not any form of abstract expression-ism, the new realism, nor a venture into the surreal. Action was what Elspeth wanted. People doing things. The sense of motion in light. Or was it light in motion? The human challenge to the intractable forces of nature, Elspeth told her friend with an almost straight face. Bicycle races for instance. One that she'd heard about. People she'd met on the plane. Carpentras to Mont Ventoux. Or the other way round. No, her friend, Pe-nelope needn't think she had to come with her. Penelope was a landscape person. A wonderful landscape artist, Elspeth as-sured her. It was hard to explain but each must paint alone. Find her own truth. In Elspeth's case, a new truth. The muse would arrive in a different form to a different artist. At a dif-ferent place.

"Hold it," said Penelope, staring at her friend. She subsided on a stool at her small tiled kitchen table. Penelope was a long-legged thin woman with gray clipped hair, an open freckled face that usually reminded those meeting her of their high school field hockey or soccer coach. "That sounds like you've been to a bad lecture. I thought we were going to float about for a day or so. Go to the Abbaye de Sénanque, stay for ves-pers, see the lavender fields, visit around. Choose sights to paint. The light is wonderful at this time of year. And marvelous restaurants in every direction. Maybe we could drive down to Aix. Check out the exhibits."

Elspeth ran her hand distractedly through her already disordered white hair. "It's just that I'd like to try out this action idea. It might be a whole new turn in my work. I can't just stick in the same rut, landscapes, ocean scenes for the rest of my life. It's time to go on."

"What kind of action? Like running? Or pole vaulting or boxing. Wind surfing?"

"I'd thought I'd start with bike racing. It's so, well, action loaded. And wonderful colors, all those different jerseys and logos on helmets and shirts. And flags. And we're so close to the scene with the Tour de France next month. And Peter Mayle wrote that book about bicycles, *Hotel Pastiche*. And there was that movie in Indiana, *Breaking In* or *Breaking Away*. So I thought I'd start with Mont Ventoux and the roads around it."

"Say no more," said Penelope. "I can see you've gone completely off your rocker. Get on with it. Get it out of your system and when you get your sanity back, which I'd say would take about forty-eight hours, then we'll drive around and enjoy Provence and do some real sketching. I've got some wonderful new Italian paper and I'll share."

Elspeth's plan to hunt down the bicycle racers suffered only a small setback. While she was out buying picnic supplies at the little *boulangerie* Penelope took a call from John McKenzie.

"He said," reported Penelope, "for you not to worry but that Uncle Fergus has had an accident. That he'd call you when he knew more. And he also wanted you to know that Alex and Sarah got back all right and that the Colley boy is fine."

"I didn't know they'd gone anywhere and I didn't know that the Colley boy wasn't safe at home," said Elspeth. "Honestly, men. He hasn't told me a thing. And what's this about Uncle Fergus having an accident? His last message was that

Uncle Fergus had gone off somewhere and they were looking for him. He's almost ninety, so I thought maybe he'd gotten lost somehow. Now perhaps he's fallen down. Hurt himself."

"He didn't say. Just said again not to worry. There was nothing you could do and he'll call again later. So you might just as well go off and paint people on bicycles if that's what you want but I loved that series you did two years ago. When we were in Tuscany. You have a real touch with landscape. Your sense of light fading. North of Siena or was it Arrezzo? When it was almost evening."

"Maybe I'll go back to them," said Elspeth, beginning to put her picnic supplies into a canvas bag. "We'll see how action painting goes. Maybe I'll only do some sketches."

"Well," said Penelope with disapproval, "if you're going to do something new you might as well go whole hog. Find out if action really grabs you."

"See you later," said Elspeth brightly, turning, heading for the door. Into the car. Down the road from Venasque and . . . And to where? Where did the bicycle races start? At Mont Ventoux? Or end there? Or start *and* end there? She needed help. A proper map of the area. Elspeth stopped at the local *patisserie* for help, and after a tangled French and English explanation the shop proprietor made a rough pencil map. The race—a time trial—was scheduled for today. Eleven o'clock. Starting at Carpentras. A route similar to a leg of the Tour of the previous year. Then in three stages to end on Mont Ventoux. A difficult last leg. Not the best cyclists. But good enough. About fourth rank. Maybe fifth. "*Pas les champions, pas les novices,*" the man explained.

And Elspeth, clutching her homemade map, returned to her car and considered. Well, why not start at Carpentras. As the cyclists did, so would she. And if Naomi Foxglove were indeed fooling around with a group of bicycle thieves, she, Elspeth would have a chance to see the woman in action. See if she was spying, taking notes, preparing some sort of trap? Or perhaps simply joining her confederates? For a fleeting moment, Elspeth considered the lure of sex. Some bike racer, certainly not the callow Nicholas and Thomas duo, might have caught Naomi's attention. Somewhere and sometime. Some irresistible French racer met somewhere or other who had urged the usually levelheaded Naomi to leave her job and rush to his side, his bed? Unlikely. Elspeth did not wish to consider that the woman might be engaged on an innocent and/or amorous visit to Provence. And that name! Foxglove! Foxglove as in digitalis. A nom de guerre if there ever was one.

Satisfied with these contradictory lines of reasoning, Elspeth hit the road and made it to Carpentras to find that market day was in progress. Stand after stand, food, tools, fabrics, toys, pottery. And bicycles standing, moving, stacked. And there, by heaven, over there, she could hardly believe her eyes, a quick silver view of Naomi like some sort of daylight wraith slipping behind a building set away from the market scene. A building with a corrugated roof and a large sign showing a racing bicycle surrounded by the silhouettes of disassembled bikes: pedals, handlebars, wheels, tires, frames, the works. Before Elspeth could decide if this was a place to be visited, she heard a shout from the lines of spectators and over beyond the building at the head of the curving road came a stream of bicyclists, bent over their handlebars, peddling for all they were worth. Well, Naomi would have to wait. Now she had the two boys to find.

Wishing she had a telescopic neck or was built on the lines of a giraffe, Elspeth pushed to the edge of the gathered crowd to see if she could possibly catch a glimpse of young Nicholas Moseby and pal Thomas Schmidt whizzing by on their bikes.

Some ten minutes later two things seemed fairly sure: with that crowd of bicyclists, no one could possibly identify more than the leaders, the ones on the outside, the ones ricocheting off a plane tree, bouncing against a curb. Nicholas and Thomas could have been quintuplets and she wouldn't have seen them.

Elspeth, backing away from the crowd, could only reach two not very satisfying conclusions. One: Neither Nick or Thomas seemed to be among the race leaders or the stragglers. Nor for the part of the race she had glimpsed had they come to grief in a collision. Two: When Elspeth had turned her attention back to Naomi, the lady, after a five- or six-minute period of invisibility, suddenly emerged from behind the bike parts building and disappeared through the crowd and into a mass of parked cars. And vanished.

Elspeth had never felt so useless. Futile. What in God's name did she think she was doing? If tracking those three persons was her object, she had failed. All right. Regroup. One more try tomorrow. Mont Ventoux. She would cover the place like a mother whose entire family were competing. And if nothing came of that adventure, then she would do what she was supposed to be doing in Provence. She would sketch. Paint. Visit. Admire. And be a painting companion to Penelope, her kind hostess. Tell her that sketching bodies in action wasn't what it was cracked up to be.

But these good intentions came to naught. Penelope met her at the door with a creased brow and a tight smile.

"John called," she said. "It's his uncle. Fergus. He was murdered. John found the body out on the golf course somewhere. The police are acting as if John himself was a possible suspect. He didn't say in so many words, but I think he'd like you to come home."

# 19

THE Sunday morning following the telephone call to his wife, John McKenzie headed reluctantly toward George Fitts's inner sanctum in the VIP Golfer's Cottage. The fog had burned off, the sun was already drying up some of the damp patches on the path, and a salty breeze was beginning to rustle through the trees and bushes of Ocean Tide. In fact, John thought with irritation, a perfect day was in the making. A day for sailing, swimming, walking the beach, even playing golf if the course had not once again been placed off limits.

But the day as far as John was concerned was already befouled by the coming interview. He knew, from the very moment of the dog's uncovering Fergus McKenzie's leg in the sand trap, that at some point soon he would be having serious moments with the police. He had made a preliminary statement but that was only the beginning. As the body finder and close relative of the deceased, as well as someone who had broadcast far and wide his negative feelings about his uncle, he would now be on the hot seat. As he had said to Elspeth's hostess, Penelope, he was probably a suspect. And knowing the suspicious minds of the police, he might now have been promoted to being considered as possible agent in the deaths of Jason and Ned Colley. Completely crazy, of course, but John had the disturbing idea that the investigation might be stalled for lack of candidates, so why not add another one? "Damnation," said John as he fastened his necktie in a gesture toward the formality of the occasion, and then headed for the VIP Golfer's Cottage.

But at least Alex would be coming. John had requested his son's presence and George had allowed it. Alex, after all, had been summoned as the closest medical examiner around and had in this capacity pronounced Fergus dead.

George sat, elbows on his desk, chin on his hands, reminding John of a predatory bird who'd had a tough time with a recalcitrant prey. The slatted blinds had been pulled against the sunlight and the dulled light didn't hide the fact that the sergeant looked tired, his eyes shadowed—unusual for George, whose appearance rarely seemed touched by untoward events and late hours.

"Alex?" said John, looking about the Jack Nicklaus Library as if his son might be concealing himself behind a golf trophy.

"Coming right along," said George. He closed a notebook and indicated the green leather chair with bright brass studs marching up and down its arm. "Please sit down, Dr. McKenzie. Or should I say Professor?"

John squinted at the sergeant. After the daylight, the room seemed all gloom and shadow. "Mr. McKenzie will be fine. I'm retired and I don't hang on to titles. Or John. I'm generally known here as just John."

"Just plain John, an ordinary man," said Alex, looming in the doorway, and looking to John's eye, as he swiveled around to inspect his son, almost as used up as George Fitts.

"Alex, you look awful," said John as a way of greeting.

"We all do," said Alex. "George here has been up every

night since Wednesday. I used up whatever energy I had with that boat trip to rescue young Dylan, hauling all the boats back, reporting to Security what Sarah and I were doing stealing boats, and then examining poor Fergus. And you, Dad, are also looking the worse for wear. What did you think you were doing out in that blessed fog looking for Uncle Fergus? . . ."

"What I was doing," said John testily, "was being a god-damn useful citizen."

George looked up from his notebook. "It's a good question. Given the weather conditions last Wednesday, the time of day, did you honestly think that your uncle would still be out playing golf?"

"I'd looked all over the place, his room, checked back at my cottage, the Pro Shop. I've told you all this. Fergus is—or he was—a stubborn old . . ." John stopped, rejected the expression "bastard" and finished lamely with ". . . a stubborn old man. He might have just gone on playing even if he could hardly see a golf ball next to his feet."

"Were you fond of your uncle?" said George in a low voice.

John hesitated, looked over at Alex, who gave a noncommittal shrug. "Not exactly," said John. "Fergus didn't make it easy to like him."

"So you invited him to visit but you weren't looking forward to his arrival."

"Fergus," said John, now sounding defensive, "didn't wait for invitations. He had said that he was coming for his birthday but didn't tell us exactly when. If he had, I wouldn't have gone off to play golf. I would have waited for him."

"The golf shop people," said George, "said you made an effort to give him golf tee times that didn't coincide with yours. That your wife and your daughter-in-law warned Mr. Martinelli and some of his staff about the man. That he was difficult. Could be impossible."

"We thought we should let the people know that Uncle Fergus needed kid gloves," said John, his face reddening, one foot tapping, a sure sign, Alex knew, of a temper rising.

"Are you and your family the professor's only living relatives?" said George in his mildest voice.

"As far as I know," said John. "He might of course have progeny, ex-wives, ex-mistresses somewhere around, but I've never heard of them. And tell me, Sergeant, where is all this going? I suppose next you're going to ask if I'm his heir. Heir to the great Fergus McKenzie fortune."

"Are you?" asked George.

"I haven't the faintest idea. It's not a thing Fergus discussed with us. He kept his business to himself. Knowing him, he may have left his entire estate to the American Nazi party or a home for lost groundhogs."

"Or even to you," said George.

"Yes, even to me. But that's hardly a reason to kill him, which is where this conversation is going. And for your information," John went on, warming to the attack, "I bloody well didn't kill my uncle. I was wandering around in the fog on that damn golf course trying to find the old goat. I'd reported him missing to the Ocean Tide staff people. I told them I was going to search. And that I'd look for the missing boy while I was at it."

"Your search might have been a smoke screen. You'd been out on the course earlier by your own admission. You could have found your uncle then, killed him, buried him, and returned to the clubhouse and offered your assistance in the search."

"Oh, for Christ's sake!"

"It's a possible scenario. I didn't say likely. You're not being accused of anything. We just want any information you might have forgotten to give us. For instance, did you notice his golf bag anywhere near his golf cart? Or in the area where the dog dug up his body?"

"I didn't see his golf cart," said John. "Nor his golf bag. Are you trying to say that having clubbed the man to death with one of his clubs, I took his golf bag and buried it in another sandtrap? Then took a joyride in his golf cart?"

"How do you know if Fergus McKenzie was clubbed to death with a golf club? If he was. The police don't know yet what he was killed with."

"I'm guessing. No one seems to be asking around about guns. Or whether Fergus carried one. He might have been strangled for all I know. But a golf club, an iron, makes a hell of a weapon."

At which point, Alex, silent until now, leaned forward in his chair. "Dad, I don't think George is accusing you. He's just trying to clear up a few points. Fergus was difficult. George is trying to get a handle on the situation."

"So your uncle had enemies?" pursued George, after a reproachful glance at Alex, who had agreed to remain silent.

"My uncle probably had enemies like a dog has fleas," said John. "But I didn't kill him. I wasn't an enemy. Just a sometimes exasperated relative. So may I go?"

"Yes," said George. "But if you know it, I'd like the name of his attorney. We should check up on the disposition of his estate. Clear that matter off our plate."

"You mean your plate," said John, now quite red in the face. "I don't give a damn about his estate. Alex, are you coming?"

Alex shook his head. "I just want a quick word with George. I'll see you back at your cottage." Then, as his father stamped out of the room, Alex turned to George. "You've probably sent his blood pressure up twenty points. And upset his pacemaker."

"I don't think your father killed his uncle," said George. "But I have to go that route. He's the relative, he found the body. His actions before that day, hunting around the golf course, aren't substantiated. And he may inherit a sizable estate. And your father obviously couldn't stand the man."

"That goes for the whole family," said Alex. "But thank heaven he's let my mother know. She'll cool him down. And explain to the police that killing the old boy wasn't a family project. In fact my parents have been planning a party for his birthday in a few weeks. Suitable presents being looked for. Balloons and lanterns ordered. None of which would have been done if murder was on the planning table. And now I'm off to see if my father's stamping around the cottage throwing china." And Alex headed for the door.

And met Mike Laaka at the point of entrance. "Hi, Alex. You going?" said Mike. "Listen, get in touch with Betty Colley. She just cornered me about young Dylan, who is keeping his mouth shut. Won't give us a word about finding his father. Or what he saw."

Alex grimaced, nodded, and departed, and Mike advanced on Sergeant Fitts.

"George, I'm getting a hell of a lot of flack from the Ocean Tide people. Do you want to keep the entire golf course taped off? The golfers are howling about their rights. The visitors at the Lodge want their money back. How about just working on the back nine?"

"The whole course," said George firmly. "After all, the murderer may have transported Fergus from whatever hole he was playing to the sand trap. His cart was on the edge of the seventeenth green. No clubs. His body buried just off the sixteenth green. Whoever did it couldn't have carried the body, lightweight though he was. Too risky on foot. The murderer must have driven Fergus in a golf cart to the burial place."

"Whose cart?" demanded Mike. "The murderer's? Fergus McKenzie's?"

"We won't know until forensics finish going over the golf cart collection."

"But why drag the body all the way from where the old boy's cart was—the seventeenth green—to a sand trap by the sixteenth green?"

George tapped his pencil impatiently on the desk. "Mike, did you ever consider that Fergus was killed out of his cart? Away from his cart. Looking for a lost golf ball maybe. And that the murderer found Fergus an inconvenient presence. Or, if it was a personal thing, and he thought—"

"Thought, Golly-gee, holy Moses, here's the old bastard all alone and unprotected, hanging around where he shouldn't be. Let's see if a nine iron will do the job. And here's a handy bunker, just the place for a body."

"The sand trap on the sixteenth green," said George, "may have been chosen because the fog was thickest there. The sand trap was a deep one. Or a shovel was available."

"Who plays golf with a shovel in his golf cart?"

"That's something we'll have to find out. The marks around the burial sight suggest a shovel was used."

"And there are shovels in the big maintenance building off the seventeenth green. Next to the shed where we found Ned Colley."

"Correct, and we've put that building off limits. So far the prints seem to be matching those of the green's crew."

"How many of those guys are there?"

"Over forty, counting part-timers. And high school summer helpers."

"Oh, brother," said Mike. He sighed, walked over to the green leather wing chair, threw himself down, and clasped his hands behind his head. "The real problem right now is where did the murderer dump Fergus McKenzie's clubs? Did he take the old guy's clubs and stuff them in with his own clubs? Bring 'em home. Throw 'em away. Into one of the quarries or off some dock where the water's deep."

"Yes, the murderer could have driven his golf cart to the parking lot and driven off with both sets of clubs," conceded George. "But we're still going to keep the whole course off limits. The guy may have buried the clubs as well as the body. We'll need a metal detector. The golf course is very extensive. And there's the three practice holes and the driving range to consider. Then we have to start dragging the water holes. Dig up the other bunkers. Comb the woods. We need more time. The golfers will have to suffer."

"How about the ocean? Down on the beach?"

"Pretty risky. Fog was very thick near the water late afternoon. Let's stick with the golf course for now," said George closing his notebook. A sign of dismissal Mike knew well.

But Mike lingered briefly by the door. "What are you going to do about the Colley kid? Dylan. He must know something or why would he clam up like he's doing?"

"He might hate the police," observed George. "People do. Or is afraid of them. His mother is working on him but he's dug into position. I sent Katie Waters to talk with him but she couldn't find out anything. We may have to wait him out. I'm not much for junior psychology but maybe the fright of finding his father is still working on him."

"More like the fright of coming here and facing Sergeant George Fitts," said Mike, and made his escape.


Sarah decided to try one last time to make peace with Dylan Colley that morning and turned her steps toward Betty Colley's house. Dylan, on his boat ride home Wednesday evening had remained sullen, uncooperative, and never once answering Sarah's sympathic overtures. He had been swept up by his mother, Betty—she in a state of mixed fury and grateful tears—and taken home. Sarah had since heard that he had been visited by Deputy Katie Waters but had not heard if the meeting had borne useful fruit. But now, Sarah, on the completely legitimate errand of finding out if Dylan had any intention of joining the summer tutoring program—he had of course missed the Friday morning meeting—hoped to meet the boy face-to-face.

But on Betty's opening the door, Sarah saw the back of Dylan vanishing into a hall and heard the bang of a closing door. Betty made a face indicating exasperation and followed the boy. She returned some five minutes later indicated by her shaking head that Dylan was not available. "He's gone impossible," said Betty waving Sarah to the sofa. "From difficult to impossible. I told him he should come out and say thank you for helping rescue him. But he claims you and Dr. McKenzie kidnapped him. Well, there's no arguing with him when he's in that state, though the palm of my hand is itching to give him a whack. Anyway, I hope he's going to start the tutoring sessions but who knows? Now it's one day at a time and right now I'd say Dylan is a match even for that Fitts man."

Sarah looked at Betty with concern. When she had first met her, she was the picture of hearty health with color in her face and vigor in her movements. Then followed the puffy-eyed Betty shocked by the two deaths. Now with her face turned sunken and pale, her eyes shadowed, she looked like one of those old-fashioned rag dolls whose stuffing had started to leak. Sarah, trying to move the conversation away from Dylan—a non starter if there ever was one—cast about for a new subject and ended asking how Betty's mother, Rose, was doing with all the tension.

"It's not just Dylan," said Sarah. "After all, he's alive and well. Well, pretty well," she corrected. "But finding that last body, my father-in-law's uncle Fergus. That must be a last straw for quite a few people. Particularly your family."

But Betty shook her head. "We were both so relieved it wasn't another Colley. Or one of the Mosebys. Mumma didn't blink an eye. Said she'd heard he was a mean old nuisance and so good riddance. And me, I'm inclined to think the same."

With these cheerful words ringing in her ears, Sarah took her leave saying that by the end of next week she hoped Dylan would feel he could join his cousin in the tutorial session. This said, she decided on a walk. She and Patsy. A quiet walk away from the distractions of police and the ongoing golf course search. Away from yellow tape. From an agitated John McKenzie. She and Alex would take John out for lunch later, distract him. Some little restaurant at a good distance from Ocean Tide. Thank God Elspeth was coming home. Sarah extracted Patsy from her car and snapped on the leash. Perhaps fresh air would clear her head. A head much troubled because the more she had tried to back away from this whole murder scene the more snarled in it she had become. And now there was Uncle Fergus dug up by her dog, Patsy. Sarah, heading toward the beach stairs, considered the problem of burying a body in a sand trap. Most sand traps, if she remembered correctly, had a rake on their rim. A rake for smoothing footsteps of the unlucky golfer who had to play out of the sand. But as a tool for burying a body? It wouldn't work. Nor could Sarah remember seeing a shovel, an entrenching tool, nor even a hoe on the lip of a bunker.

But she was familiar with the two sheds near the seventeenth green and remembered clearly that the larger building had been filled with a fine collection of rakes, scythes, weed whackers, and an array of long-handled shovels. Perfect tools for digging a quick grave in sand.

Surely, Sarah thought, as she tugged Patsy away from a very dead crab that had rolled in with the tide, the police hardly needed Sarah the Nosey to tell them this. Except. Except did they realize that not only maintenance workers would know about the shed but also that finger-in-every-pie manager, Joseph Martinelli—Joseph, who was an occasional golfer—would probably know where to find a shovel in a hurry? But again, the police, George Fitts with his brain like a honed razor, wouldn't he be on top of that? Grilling every staff member? Unless George was so obsessed with covering every inch of the eighteen-hole golf course with the equivalent of a pair of tweezers, as well as vacuuming every golf cart on the place, that he hadn't gotten around to considering whether Manager Martinelli with or without a member of his staff had gone homicidal.

Sarah increased her stride. Now she was approaching the end of the beach and the rising face of rocks that marked the border of Joseph Martinelli's kingdom. She turned and banished the thought of shovels from her head. If a shovel had been used to dig Uncle Fergus's temporary grave, it would only show sand residue. Not blood and flesh and bits of clothing.

And so useless as evidence. Forget the shovel. Except of course, there were the fingerprints on the shovel handle. *Oh, stop it,* Sarah ordered her brain. *Get on with some exercise. Clear your mind. Get moving.*

"To hell with it," Sarah said aloud to a swooping seagull. She broke into a jog, hauling at a reluctant Patsy, who always enjoyed the smells and dead fish fragments found on the beach. A satisfying thirty minutes of energetic running followed, and then Sarah with a gasp of relief settled herself on a large driftwood log that had been rolled up by some long-ago storm.

But Patsy wasn't ready to settle. He pulled at his leash and began taking a strong interest in the log. The end of the log, to be exact. Whining and sniffing and scrabbling at its end, which appeared from the detritus, branches, and leaves Patsy was digging out to be partly hollow. Sarah, exasperated, shouted at Patsy to lie down. All she wanted right now was to get her breath and to contemplate in peace the clouds, the sky, all the good things of the earth. Not to deal with a noisy scratching Irish wolfhound.

But Patsy wouldn't sit down. Snuffling, digging, pulling at broken branches with his teeth, he worked like an animal possessed. And Sarah, focusing, looked down at these branches with sudden interest. They looked new. Not bits of washed-up wood. In fact some of the branches still had leaves, albeit dry leaves, clinging to them. Trying to fix on the implications of a hollow log stuffed with fresh branches and twigs, Sarah saw Patsy's gray head disappear entirely and then, backing up, he emerged with the strap of a tan canvas object in his teeth. Which he pulled out foot by foot, and then putting both paws atop what was undeniably a golf bag, began attacking the small zippered pouch on the bag's side.

Golf bag. The two syllables clanged in Sarah's head like a gong. What had she heard about a missing golf bag? A golf bag belonging to Uncle Fergus. She jumped to her feet about to wrest the bag away from her dog. But stopped. Fingerprints.

She fumbled about in her jeans pocket, found a bandanna, wrapped her hand in it and attempted to detach the bag from Patsy's tooth hold.

Easier said than done. Patsy had his mouth clamped around the now torn pocket. And now Sarah saw the tip of a plastic baggie. A baggie holding what might have once been a sandwich. This confirmed by a foul odor rising from the thing. Rotten meat. No wonder that Patsy wouldn't let go. Nothing he liked better than rotten meat. To eat, to roll in, to enjoy.

Sarah, with every bit of arm muscle in play, her feet dug into the shifting sand and stones of the beach, heaved the dog upright, pried his mouth open, and the golfbag dropped to the sand. Then, with Patsy dragged into a heel position on her left side, her bandanna-wrapped hand grasping the golf bag's strap and held against on her right side, she began to work her way in the direction of the nearest beach stairs, all the while shouting "Police" at the top of her voice because surely one of those state police searchers would turn up before she had to drag dog and golf bag all the way to George Fitts's chamber.

Her shouting did the trick. Two members of the state police evidence team, pawing around the edges of the seventeenth hole, heard her shouts, clambered down the bank to the beach and relieved Sarah of the golf bag. Ordered her to report to Sergeant Fitts. Ordered her not to discuss what she'd found with anyone. And then, the older of the two men sniffed the air and asked what in God's name was that smell.

"I think," said Sarah, pulling Patsy away from the bag, "it's Uncle Felix's lunch. Or an afternoon snack. Be careful of it. It's probably important evidence."

And with that, Sarah and Patsy walked briskly away down the beach and climbed the beach stairs and made their way to the parked Subaru. Patsy, deprived of his treasure, collapsed on the backseat of the car, Sarah turned on the ignition, and in minutes was parked by what she now thought of as the George Fitts Cottage. Slowly she walked up the flagstones leading to the door, slowly she rearranged her brain to admit that rather than distancing herself from the investigation, she had moved herself directly onto the front burner. Or at least one of the burners. George she knew probably kept a variety of these ready for all occasions and persons.

But as Sarah reached the top step of the cottage, George himself appeared and took her by the arm. "Come on. We're going to our evidence building. Behind us. They're bringing the golf bag there. I've asked for one of the golf pros to meet us there. And Alex. We need to see if all of Fergus McKenzie's clubs are in the bag. You can tell me how you found the bag as we walk. Where exactly you found it. And what you were doing when you found it."

Sarah, hustling along beside George, gave a short version of her discovery. The hollow log. The fresh twigs and leaves— meant, she supposed—to hide the golf bag.

"It was that awful sandwich. It was inside the pouch of the golf bag. Patsy smelled it even inside the log. He went right after it, and if he hadn't tried to dig it out, I suppose that the golf bag could have stayed inside the log forever. Or until the next hurricane."

"Honestly, Sarah," said George in a voice of exasperation. "I thought you'd turned over a new leaf. No more investigations. That's what Mike said."

"George Fitts," snapped Sarah. "I was taking a beach walk. I sat down on a log. If Patsy hadn't sniffed out the sandwich, I never would have looked inside the log. I'd like a little gratitude from you. Or gratitude to Patsy. Weren't you looking for that golf bag? Well, now you've found it. So be quiet."

George smiled—it was a rusty smile at best—and said mildly, "Thank you, Sarah. Now let's see if we can manage to identify ancient golf clubs. See if the whole set is there."

But Pete Salieri, the assistant golf pro, objected to this idea. "Not many elderly players carry a full set of clubs. Not antique ones, anyway."

"You don't know Uncle Fergus," said Alex, who had just arrived. "To be perverse he might have carried double the usual number."

"Just look over the collection, both of you," said George, pointing to the golf bag now lying on a sheet in the middle of what had once been a utility shed. The clubs had been removed and were now spread out by size and shape alongside the bag.

They were, Sarah thought, twins to the ones featured on the wall of the Pro Shop. Wooden shafts, black leather tape around the club grips. And a variety of heads of different lofts. Irons and woods. Not too different in basics from their contemporary counterparts.

"Identify them one by one," commanded George. "Explain how they're used and give me the names if you can. I only know the modern ones."

"Well, there's the driver," said Alex, pointing to a wooden-headed club.

"Use the driver off the tee," said Pete. "Straight head. Then there's the brassie. More loft."

"Followed by the spoon, and the baffie," added Alex. "Each one more laid back."

"How do you know all this?" demanded Sarah. It was annoying. Alex had never previously indicated a knowledge of ancient golf clubs.

"You could use some of these woods on the fairway," said Pete. "The baffie could even be used in the rough if the lie was good enough."

"Okay," said George making a note. "So there's a full set of woods here, you'd say? Nothing missing?"

Alex and Pete nodded agreement. Nothing was missing.

The irons were a different matter. Pete went from the cleek, midiron—little loft—to the mashie, the mashie-niblick. And stopped. "No niblick," he said.

And George, remembering the discussion of what club one would choose to commit homicide, lifted his eyebrows. "I suppose," he said, "you could get around the course without a niblick."

"Doubtful," said Pete. "Lots of places you need to get the ball right up in the air. Over a hazard. You need a niblick. Now we use a pitching wedge. Or a sand wedge."

"And there's the putter," said Alex, pointing at a stubby flat-headed club.

But George was on the phone. He listened, nodded. And then said briskly, "Bring it right over. On the double."

He turned to the group. "One of our team working the water holes, has just come up with a wooden-shafted club. Middle of the pond on the tenth hole. Fished it up with a net."

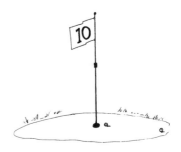

# 20

SARAH lingered in the evidence building long enough to witness the arrival of the newly dredged-up golf club and to see that it closely resembled the niblick she'd seen on the Pro Shop wall display. This one, not surprisingly, looked a little the worse for wear; the wrapping around the grip had come loose and a wet black leather strip dangled down. But the club was, by agreement, a genuine antique niblick, a close cousin to Fergus McKenzie's other clubs.

"As I told you," said Pete Salieri. "Old-timers didn't go in for matched sets the way people do now. Not all Fergus's clubs matched. His brassie is a Walter Hagen and his spoon is a special from North Berwick. And his midiron is from the old sporting goods outfit, Wright and Ditson."

"Okay," said George taking charge. "Get the club over to Forensics. I want it gone over, the handle wraps used for the grip analyzed, and the contours of the club head compared to the wounds on Fergus McKenzie's head." George turned around and fixed Sarah with a look. "Anything more, Sarah?

No? Then, we'll call you as soon as we can to give a statement on finding the golf bag."

Sarah departed and headed for her car. It was still Sunday, only eleven-fifty, although she felt that several days had gone by since she had sat down on that hollow log. She mentally ticked off "things to do." First she and Alex would take John McKenzie out for lunch. Cheer him up. Then, since Elspeth would be flying sometime tomorrow she might really appreciate a full refrigerator. The poor woman would have made two six-hour time switches in less than a week and would be jet-lagged. Okay, after lunch Sarah could drop Patsy off at home and go out to buy a few supplies for the senior McKenzie larder. Perhaps a cooked turkey, a couple of baguettes from one of the local bakeshops. Fresh fruit, vegetables, a flowering plant.

These plans in place, Sarah drove to the McKenzie cottage where she and Alex dragged John away from a can of vegetable soup and took him to the waterfront in Belfast for lobster bisque and stuffed haddock, returning him somewhat restored in cheerfulness to Ocean Tide.

"The course is still closed, I can't even play golf," complained John.

"Look, Dad," said Alex. "Up until a few weeks ago you hadn't touched a golf club in years. Go and write a heavy-duty article on something. That new free-verse translation of *Beowulf* you were criticizing. Or buy yourself an up-to-date set of irons. State-of-the-art. Yours are almost as old as Uncle Fergus's. They have great clubs now for . . ."

"Don't say what you're about to say," said John. "Go away, both of you. Have a nice day. Or a lousy day. Whatever turns up."

"Concentrate," said Alex, "on the fact that Mother is coming home. She won't let you get away with being such a grouch."

They parted. John, walking in the direction of the Pro Shop, the idea of new clubs having lit a small fire in his head;

Alex to the hospital to check on some just-admitted patients; Sarah to give Patsy a quick run before depositing him in their old farmhouse on Sawmill Road.

Patsy's "quick run" almost turned into his last. Sarah had taken him behind the Pro Shop onto a sort of grassy no-man's-land that led to the driving range and to the three-hole practice course—both of course put now off limits by the police. A red squirrel was the mischief maker. Sarah, who held the leash loosely in her left hand, was still mulling over her itinerary when the squirrel shot past Patsy and paused chattering two feet up an oak tree. Patsy reared, woofed, and lunged, the leash flew from Sarah's hand, and Patsy launched himself into space. At exactly the same time, around the corner from the Pro Shop shot one of the ubiquitous small utility tractor-carts used by the greens crew. There was a screeching of brakes and squealing of tires on torn turf and the vehicle stopped some two inches shy of Patsy's rump. Cries and apologies were exchanged and the driver departed, accelerating in the direction of the clubhouse shed while Sarah, scolding, dragged Patsy back to the car.

It wasn't until Sarah was turning off Route 17 and heading for the Bowmouth town line and Sawmill Road that she began to consider the encounter in a new light. From Alex directly, and from Mike Laaka indirectly, she had the impression that one of the targets of the homicide investigations had been and continued to be the golf carts. A golf cart, the argument went, must have been used by the murderer to pursue Uncle Felix across the golf course to the seventeenth hole where Felix's own cart was found, and then possibly used to transport the body for burial to the sand trap next to the sixteenth hole. Then after the golf bag minus the niblick, i.e., the putative murder weapon, had been stashed in the hollow log, the murderer would have used his cart to flee, to circle around to the pond on the tenth hole, throw in the niblick and return the cart. Here Sarah tried to banish a sudden Arthurian vision of a hand rising out of the water, seizing the club, brandishing it, and disappearing.

Back on track she commanded her disorderedly mind. Okay, a golf cart was almost a necessity for the Fergus scenario. Ditto for the Ned Colley operation. That was another body transportation scene. And, although this was a stretch, a golf cart might have been used to transport the body of young Jason Colley from wherever he had been killed to its resting place in the rough around the third practice hole.

This line of thought was fine as far as it went. But what about that minitractor-cart combo that had almost finished Patsy? Now that Sarah thought about it, those little tractor-carts were all over the place. She had seen them on the beach, the maintenance team raking up debris, smoothing the small strips of sand; seen them driving around the roads and lanes dealing with leaves, seen them standing by for gardening projects, planting flowers, moving shrubs, trimming trees. And most especially Sarah had seen them at a distance buzzing about the golf course, disappearing here, reappearing there. They were apparently all-terrain, maneuverable, and could do anything, or even more, that a golf cart could do. In fact when it came to hauling bodies they were much more suited to the job. No need to prop up a corpse on the seat. Just roll the body into the back of the little boxlike trailer, and pull a cover over it, or more to the point, a few fertilizer bags you were planning to deliver to that little shed by the seventeenth hole. And to make that one sand-trap operation easier, most of the carts Sarah had noticed carried a supply of tools—especially shovels!

So the real question was, Sarah asked as she swung up Sawmill Road and turned into the rising lane that led to the house, were the police so fixated on golf carts—and golfers—as the sine qua non of murder and body disposal that they were ignoring the grounds crew who chugged around the entire Ocean Tide community in a fleet of small tractors.

Escorting Patsy into the old farmhouse, a work in progress that never seemed any closer to completion, Sarah chided herself. Of course George and his slaves would have thought of the maintenance vehicle angle. They just weren't talking. Or was it just possible that because these vehicles were so constantly in the faces of the police they were no longer seen and so not reckoned with. Well, she didn't want to make a fool of herself. She would leak the idea—in a casual offhand way as if it didn't really matter—to Alex—or Mike if she bumped into him. If the thought was shot down or she was told that of course these vehicles had been completely checked, well, so be it.

After releasing Patsy into the kitchen, checking his water bowl, cleaning up his run, Sarah was about to leave when the telephone rang. A reminder of a town meeting that night. The recycling committee. "Damn," said Sarah putting down the phone. And then, with another ring, picking it up again. Alex. He had a hospital meeting that night, would be home around eleven. "And," he added, "have you heard?"

"No," said Sarah. "What?"

"Young Dylan Colley. The footloose kid. Took off this A.M. on his bike—at least his bike is missing—and didn't turn up for lunch. Betty won't go to the police, so I will. Probably just in hiding but this time we hope on the mainland. If you see him along the highway, try and tie him up and bring him back."

"If I see him," said Sarah crisply, "I'll call the police, the National Guard, and the Boy Scouts. But I won't touch him. I think he'd bite a piece out of me. Now I'm going to get some welcome-home food for your mother."

"Good," said Alex, and the phone went dead.


When Alex had returned his father from their lunch excursion and after he had bumped into Betty Colley, he hunted down Mike Laaka and found him back in the Jack Nicklaus Library seated by a small table lit by a student lamp. Behind him stood row on row, as far as Alex could tell at a quick glance, of every book published in English that featured golf. Mike gave a quick jump of surprise and closed the book that was open in front of him.

"Dirty golf stories?" suggested Alex. "Obscene things done with a putter?"

"Nah," said Mike. "But I don't want George to find me reading fiction. This is P. G. Wodehouse, *Golf without Tears*. Kind of funny. Woman in here is driven crazy because her lover talks a blue streak when she's trying to hit the golf ball. So she nails him with her niblick. Sound familiar?"

"I once said that I thought gardening tools were the most lethal handtools around," said Alex, settling himself in a chair. "Now I'm revising. Sporting goods are almost as bad. I know of a field hockey stick murder last winter in Massachusetts, and there have probably been hundreds of baseball bat homicides. And think of bowling balls. Even tennis rackets could do a job on a skull. And now we have golf clubs."

"Well, that niblick found in the pond is off to the lab for a good going over. See if Uncle Fergus left a blood cell or two. So what brings you to our den?"

Alex told him about the missing Dylan. "Betty Colley doesn't want to make a big deal out it although she's mad as hell. She'd forbidden him to leave Ocean Tide."

"Maybe he's hiding out. One of those popular sheds. Maybe Dylan is behind all these events. And okay, I'll get on the horn right now and alert George." Which Mike did in a few short words. Then he turned back to Alex. "That's that. So back to work. Right now I'm trying to work out for George a timetable for each homicide and see which of the good citizens of Ocean Tide was in the area when the victim was done in. Then I have to get back to the business of seeing if Ned Colley was a closet golfer."

"It would be easier to check off the people *not* around at the time of death. Though you know that a week went by before Jason Colley's body was found."

"Johnny Cuszak, after a long song and dance about not wanting to be pinned down, said that off the record, Sunday, May twelfth, was a possible.

"So who does that eliminate?"

Mike shuffled a pile of papers and selected one. "Of our Ocean Tide suspects including Manager Martinelli and his cohorts, only Nick Moseby is let off. He is confirmed for biking north of here. Otherwise it's a crap shoot."

"Okay, so how about Ned Colley?"

"Time of death, fairly early that morning. The morning of the big Fitness Center fiesta."

"My mother has a favorite suspect," said Alex. "Naomi Foxglove. I think she thinks Naomi is head of a bike-stealing syndicate. Or is a double agent working for some Slavic republic."

"Let's be realistic. Ned really had to be killed by someone who knew the golf course—"

"Like a golfer," put in Alex. "But maybe Naomi's a secret golfer. Like Ned."

"Any of the Ocean Tide staff could have done it," said Mike. "Someone with access to a golf cart for body transport. Of course, they're locked up at night but anyone with a little ingenuity could cut one loose. And quite a few residents have their own private cart—including Martinelli. He's not accounted for until about seven A.M. that day."

"Why on earth would he want to besmirch the good name of Ocean Tide by killing anyone? He had fits over each new body found."

"Yeah, I know," said Mike. "It could be an act, but I sort of doubt it."

"Move on to Uncle Fergus. How does killing him make sense?"

Mike again flipped over the sheets of paper and gave a sort of groan. "That's where it gets really weird. Up to then we were certain that the first two homicides were connected with the Colley—and the Moseby—families. But your uncle Fergus.

Come on. He has zip to do with the Colleys. Or this place. He'd only just checked in."

"I'd say that Uncle Fergus is a classic case of being an accidental arrival on the scene."

"He turned up where he didn't oughta be. Just when secret goings-on were taking place somewhere near the seventeenth and sixteenth holes. In that fog?"

"If I was up to no good I'd choose a fog. What about those two sheds?"

Mike snorted. "Those two sheds—which we have been keeping an eye on almost daily—are not the headquarters for evildoers. We've watched the greens crew taking tools out, putting tools back. Ditto with lugging fertilizer bags in and out."

Alex stood up. "Got to be off. But I'd say you have a hundred suspects for each murder."

Mike grinned at him. "At least your mother's in the clear for Fergus. Wednesday, she was driving down to Boston and flying out of Logan that night."

"And Naomi Foxglove is out of it, too. Left for Boston at the same time and hasn't been heard of since. And you'll have to cross off Nick Moseby and his biking buddy from the Fergus hit list. They flew to France that same evening."

"Naomi will be back. I've a report that she called in citing a personal emergency. As for young Moseby, George has put in a call to the Registrar's Office at Yale to see if he's a genuine student. But since he's off the Fergus suspect list, as you say, it's not quite as urgent. We'll have to make do with your father. We only have Sarah's word that he was snoozing on a bench the afternoon she found Ned Colley."

"Go to hell," said Alex cheerfully, and he vanished through the door.


Sarah decided to look for Elspeth's welcome-home flowers first, then do the food. After all, it was a beautiful day. Didn't she deserve a few fine June moments not connected with Ocean Tide, she asked herself as she turned off Sawmill Road. She would drive about the hills of Camden, Appleton, and Union and see what greenhouses turned up. She would also, to give herself a sense of worthwhile time spent, keep an eye out for young Dylan Colley. After all, Dylan was on a bike and he was a determined young man. A boy who thought ahead. Witness his preparations when he went out to sea. Wouldn't a boy taking off, leaving Ocean Tide, head for familiar territory? He'd grown up on a farm in Appleton, must know the area fairly well. Of course, it was quite a bike trip but he'd been gone since morning. A boy in good physical condition, taking time out for food and water, could make the fifteen-plus miles to the Appleton hills without undue stress.

Here Sarah experienced a mild shiver of familiar excitement. Why wouldn't the boy head for the old homestead? Where he'd spent the first twelve years of his life. A place where he felt safe. Yes, the farm had been sold, was being renovated, but hadn't Betty mentioned that the owners weren't natives, were from "away" and didn't plan to live in the house until next summer? So Dylan might have the place to himself because it was Sunday. Probably no workmen around.

Putting the plan to buy flowers on a back burner—it was only midafternoon—Sarah headed for the town of Appleton. A stop at a local gas station gave her the location of the old Colley farm. Take a right past Grover Road, left at Kimball Road. Then about half a mile and turn left down a long tree-shaded road; that would be Brinker Falls Road. And there it was, a battered silver mailbox still bearing the name Colley in faded blue paint. Sarah slowed and stopped. And saw it. A bicycle, its dark blue paint shiny in the afternoon light, leaned against the white porch by the front of the house. Sarah accelerated to some hundred yards past the house to where a dirt lane leading to a pasture allowed a single car to pull in and be well hidden by a thick tangle of locust and alders.

Dylan. Just as, by a wild stretch of her imagination, she

had seen it in her mind, the boy had come "home." But, Sarah told herself, the boy was probably on the alert for any sign of pursuit. Would be hiding out. Hunkering down with his knapsack. Camping out in the pasture. Sarah squinted into the distance where a rising field of tall grass rolled toward a distant line of trees.

Well, she couldn't just sit in the car. She would walk quietly up to the farmhouse. A woman on foot, alone, even the infamous Sarah Deane, couldn't be that threatening. And, even if there were no immediate sign of Dylan, she might as well make a good job of it. Search the place, check out the pasture. Trying to keep the lowest of profiles. But to keep her conscience clear, Sarah put in a call on her car phone to Alex's father's house hoping to pass the news along. John answered, sounded groggy, he'd been having a nap but took the message after hunting about for a pencil and three times asking the name of the boy in question. Sarah hung up and called Betty Colley. Got Rose whose deafness was nearly impenetrable. Hung up again, called the Ocean Tide Lodge desk and asked the clerk to tell Sergeant Fitts that the Colley boy's bike, or one like it, was at the old Colley farm.

Then, duty done, Sarah began a slow walk up the short drive to the house. The bike was unlocked and an almost empty bottle of Gatorade was clamped on the frame. Not wanting to shout or call attention to her presence, Sarah cautiously tried the front door. Locked. Then she peered in a window and saw a pile of construction material, drywall panels, insulation packages, but no sign of present human habitation. The back door—also locked. Next a large barn, its door open. Empty except for a collection of rusty farm tools, a couple of snow shovels, and two overflowing trash bins. A former hay loft reached by a ladder yielded nothing more than a broken sled, a baby stroller, and an empty army issue trunk. But no Dylan.

Descending the ladder with care—two rungs were cracked—Sarah proceeded to an inspection of what were obviously three former horse stalls. These also empty except for old feed buckets fastened to the wall and the remnants of salt block holders. Next to the far side of the barn, down two steps to a kind of annex, she saw a concrete strip with troughs running through and ten cow stanchions in place. Nothing else. Certainly not a thirteen-year-old boy crouched in a corner. Nothing left now except a small door at the far end of the cow section. A wooden door with a metal latch. Unlocked. Quietly Sarah pushed her way into the dark. Stood still for a minute letting her eyes adjust. In the shadows she made out the shape of wheelbarrow. Two oil drums. A sawhorse. And against the wall, two hanging pitchforks. On the floor at the far side of the little space what looked like an awkward piece of machinery or furniture wrapped in burlap.

Machinery, furniture? Sarah stared trying to get some sense of the dark bundle. But then, unless her senses had completely departed, she thought the machine moved. And made a noise. A sort of strangled gurgle.

A cold finger of ice moved down her spine. She swallowed hard and took two tentative steps forward, frowning into the dark. "Dylan?" she said in a hoarse whisper and was rewarded by a second gurgle.

She needed more light. Not wanting to take her eyes off the burlap lump, she backed up, reached behind for the wooden door to push it open and let in the light from the cow barn.

The door creaked back, the black shadows turned to a light gray. And then the dark. Complete dark. A metallic smack on the head from a flat object and Sarah was down. Not out but dizzy. Hurt. And blind. Blind because over her head someone pulled a bag, fastened the end around her neck. Snapped her hands behind her back, wrapped her wrists together. Grabbed her ankles and tied them, and then for good measure a hand pulled off her sneakers. A moment's pause in the work, someone breathing hard from exertion. Then Sarah was tugged and rolled backward, bumping her head into something hard— the wheelbarrow?—and pushed against a wall.

Disoriented, her head throbbing, her nose dripping blood, Sarah lay. With an enormous effort she stifled the cry that was rising in her throat. The rough-handed person was probably just waiting for her to call out for help.

For a long while, not a sound. Not even the throttled noise from the burlap bundle. Then at last she heard the sort of shuffling that suggested someone's retreat. A door banged far away. The silence. Sarah waited. And waited. Then lifting her head, softly whispered "Dylan." But the bag over her head—it was of a rough but happily porous material—must have muffled her voice. She tried again, a few decibels louder, and now was rewarded by the same gurgling noise she'd heard when she first walked into the little room. But this time the gurgle turned into a snuffling as if someone was desperately trying not to cry.

"Dylan," Sarah said, even louder. "I won't hurt you. I'm tied up, too. But I'm going to try and get free. Let me know if you understand. And," she added as an afterthought, "if you are Dylan."

And then, in a much clearer voice so that actual words emerged: "I'm Dylan. Someone got hold of me. Put me in a bag." More snuffling and a sort of choking followed this admission.

"Okay," said Sarah. "Keep as quiet as you can and I'll start to work on my hands. If I can get one hand free, then the rest should be easy. Okay?"

Most faintly came the answer. "Okay."

# 21

SARAH, lying on her side, holding out her arms, worked on her bound wrists rubbing what felt like twine against the rough board floor. Against the metal rim of the wheelbarrow wheel. Against the edge of what might or might not be a scythe. This last object produced a result both painful and satisfactory. Her right wrist was bleeding, smarting, but the binding had lost one of its wraps and had come loose.

With an uprush of hope Sarah was about to extract her hand from its fastening when purposeful steps sounded, the door creaked open and rough hands hauled her to her feet, jammed the bag—it had an earthy, moldy smell—more firmly over her head, and hoisted her to someone's back, where she hung head down, bobbing like a wounded animal. In this posture she found herself traveling down what must have been the length of the barn. Then outdoors where a small measure of daylight filtered into the interior of her bag. She couldn't really see, not even shapes, but there was a small increase in her sense of place.

It didn't last. She felt herself lifted up, twisted around, and dumped onto a hard surface, and then given a heavy shove into whatever it was. A pickup truck? An old coal chute, except she was on the level? Now the most important thing she told herself was to keep her wrists tight together as if the twine were still doing its job. But where was she going? Or being taken? And Dylan? What was happening to him?

But before Sarah could work herself into a panic on the boy's behalf, she felt the thump of a small body landing beside her, a protesting cry coming from inside its wrapping. Next a scraping sound and a sharp metallic object landed beside her and was crammed painfully against her feet, unprotected in their cotton socks. Awkward exploration by her bound arms told her that the object involved a chain and something with spokes. A bicycle. Very likely Dylan's bicycle last seen leaning against the farmhouse front porch. It made sense. Whoever was in charge of this operation—or kidnapping—didn't want any trace of the boy left for a curious policeman to find. But perhaps, if a policeman arrived to look around he'd see Sarah's car parked down the road. A slim hope; her car had been very well concealed. But as this depressing conclusion forced itself on her, a heavy cover of some sort—a tarp, a canvas—was pulled over her body, and presumably over Dylan's, and Dylan's bicycle.

They were on the flatbed of a truck. That was proved by the slamming of the truck's doors, the rumble of the engine, the brief spinning of the tires on the loose gravel. Then the truck bumped down the short driveway, along the dirt road, and swung onto a smoother surface. Turning right, Sarah thought, trying desperately to keep her sense of direction, have some dim idea of where they were going. And the truck? Where had it been when she had first walked down the driveway? Probably right behind the barn and she'd been too damn careless to check there. Not Sarah the Nosey or Sarah the Good. Just Sarah the Stupid on one more misadventure. Only this time a boy called Dylan Colley was involved. More than involved. Might even be next on the list of Colley victims. Serial killings for some unknown reason focusing on Colleys. Sarah, like Alex and Mike, had long since decided that Uncle Fergus's death was an unplanned event.

Sarah, searching for something positive in the situation, told herself that at least no one had noticed her loose wrist ties. Now it was important to communicate with Dylan. Tell him not to struggle. Or try to shout. Nothing good could come from trying to annoy the powers in charge. But as long as the truck ride lasted they had the luxury of being able to speak in a normal voice. Sarah could speak out and make sure Dylan heard her, maybe get from him some idea of how he came to be tied up. Who had done it—if he knew? And most important, why? Did his predicament have anything to do with his refusal to come to the tutorial sessions, his escape to the island, his long bicycle ride to the Colley farm?

She first tried to get her hand completely free and begin work on the bag pulled over her head. But the one remaining knot proved stubborn, and with a sense of panic that time was passing, the truck might be reaching its mystery destination, she squirmed over to the shape that was Dylan, and with her head and bound arms determined which end of the bundle held Dylan's head.

"Dylan," she said as loudly as she dared. "Can you hear me?"

"Yeah." A muffled but understandable answer.

"Do you know what these guys want?"

Louder this time. "Me. They want me."

"Why? Do you know why?"

"They think I know something. That I told the police something. But I didn't."

"What do you think they know?"

Silence.

"Dylan? Dylan, what do you think they know?"

"Nothing."

Sarah could almost hear Dylan's mouth snap closed with his last response. Dylan still claming up.

Sarah tried again. "Dylan, it's me. Sarah Deane. I know you've been avoiding me but now I'm caught. Tied up just like you. We've got to work together. Can you tell me anything that will help?"

Long pause. Then, "You got tied up because you followed me. You were hunting for me. It's your fault. If you'd let me alone you wouldn't be tied up. And I wouldn't be tied up. If you hadn't come to the farm they'd let me go."

Sarah felt a surge of exasperation. "Forget I asked. Now let's work out a way to get out of this mess."

"We can't," said the voice, and Sarah almost thought she heard a sob of desperation. "I'm tied up and I can't see and maybe they're going to dump us somewhere or maybe they're going to kill us. And," the voice went on thickly, "you started all of this chasing me around the way you did."

"Okay, it's my fault," said Sarah. "That's settled. So let's think about what to do. First, if they take us somewhere let's try and figure out where the place is. Does it smell like a farm? Or a gas station? A wharf with fish smells? And listen for sounds. For traffic. Animals. Kids yelling. Okay, will you help me?"

Another long pause. Then, "Yeah. I'll try. But it won't do any good."

"Damn it, Dylan, you're a smart kid. You have guts. It took guts to take that boat of yours all the way to that island and it took guts to bike all the way here. So don't say things like that."

But any response was drowned in the sound of heavy braking, the turn onto a long road, another turn onto a crushed-gravel surface, a quick swing, and a grinding stop. They were there, wherever there was.

The back of the truck opened. Sarah felt two hands grab at her ankles and felt herself pulled along to an edge. Then hoisted for a second time onto someone's shoulders and borne away.

Mike Laaka met Alex for dinner at Café Milano in Rockland. Alex, coming from trying to nudge his father into a positive frame of mind, felt like a nonhospital cafeteria dinner before his medical committee meeting, and had talked Mike into breaking free at least for an hour before he had to get back to the murder investigation.

"George doesn't approve of dinner," said Mike. "He has a bagel and a soup cube sent in. And so where's Sarah?"

"Recycling Committee," Alex told him. "But she was going to pick up some food for mother's homecoming. I did tell her to keep an eye out for young Dylan biking along the road."

"George has sent a deputy sheriff out to the old Colley farm. His mother thought he might want to go there to hide out. A familiar place."

"Good," said Alex, picking up his menu. "I think I'll go for the shrimp with fettuccini. So any news from the forensic front? Or any front?"

"Nothing new. We're waiting for a lab report to verify that Fergus was killed with his own golf club, the one from the tenth hole pond. Meantime George rather takes to the idea of Manager Martinelli managing some smuggling scheme. Stolen bikes. Maybe with drugs hidden inside the frame. And Naomi Foxglove as his international liaison. Or representative. Whatever. And maybe some of the Colleys are—or were—part of the distribution machinery."

"My mother will enjoy anything that sheds a dim light on Naomi Foxglove."

"I'm settling for the sausage lasagna," said Mike. "And speaking of your mother, how's your father making out? He seems pretty irritable."

"As the expression has it, you said a mouthful. My mother can keep him calmed down, but take her away, add the body of Uncle Fergus, and Dad is one unhappy camper. I wouldn't be surprised if he announced that he was packing up ready to go back to Cambridge."

"And your mother?"

"Will put a spoke in that wheel. Mother's making a determined effort to be part of the community, be a good citizen. And speaking of Mother, any sign of her bike? Or anyone else's stolen bike?"

But Mike wasn't listening. Reaching into his back trouser pocket he extracted his cell phone, flipped it open, and said "Laaka here." Then listened, made a face and snapped the phone closed. "Wouldn't you know," he said.

"Know what?" asked Alex, watching hungrily as a mounded plate of pasta decorated with a collection of shrimp was placed in front of him on the red-and-white checkered tablecloth.

"That was George. Report from the lab," said Mike picking up his fork. "Only a prelim. As follows: Every club in your uncle's golf bag gets a clean bill of health. Not used to kill him. But our number-one suspect, that niblick from the tenth hole pond. Lab says not the least sign of blood or hair or tissue. Or imbedded bone fragments. Signs that the shaft has been treated with wood oil and the face of the niblick rubbed with metal polish. But as far as being a weapon, it's as clean as a whistle, though why in God's name a whistle is clean, when its probably all glopped up with saliva, I don't know."

Alex paused, his hand in midair, a shrimp impaled on his fork. "Wonderful dinner chat. But what's so odd about a cleaned club? Any conscientious murderer would have done that."

Mike shook his head. "It takes a hell of a lot of work to eliminate every blood cell, those microscopic fragments of tissue. The guy could scrub it and the club would look clean enough, but something would stick."

"You said the report was only a preliminary one."

"George said the lab sounded pretty sure. And consider

this," said Mike waving a thick piece of bread at Alex. "The murderer had a lot of zipping around to do. Kill Fergus, stick the golf bag in that hollow log, lug the body to the sand trap. Or do it in reverse order. Bury the body with whatever implement he could find, maybe breaking into the maintenance shed for a shovel. Except where is the shovel now? Back in the shed I suppose, but that's another trip back and forth. And then, there's the golf cart, because you can't tell me the whole operation takes place on foot. Anyway, after the body is dug in, the murderer drives to the third hole. Stopping somewhere to scrub the club? Where? A lavatory in the Lodge? In some other water hole? In the ocean? No, I'll bet if he had really used Fergus's niblick, he'd have done a quick wipe down by the tenth hole pond and tossed the thing into the drink with plenty of physical evidence still stuck to it. Trouble is the damn thing is clean. So maybe this niblick is an accidental find." And Mike bent his head over his plate and began the work of finishing his meal in an unseemly haste.

"Maybe," said Alex, "a lot of golfers had fits of temper and threw their clubs into the water. If the one they found didn't do the job, I suppose you have to start making a golf club inventory. Drag the water holes and impound golf bags."

Mike closed his eyes. Opened them, his expression one of a man in serious pain. "When all hell will break out. The golfers are mad enough over the closing of the course. Think of the noise they'll make if we start collecting their toys. Well, let George worry about the weapon. He can handle the flack. Me, I'm supposed to be overseeing the examination of God knows how many golf carts. And I've still a few golf courses to visit to see if Ned Colley ever turned up to play. Or to drink. Listen, Alex, dinner was a good idea, but I've got to get a move on. We'll try it again when the case is over. Sometime when Sarah's free."

\* \* \*

The question of being free was certainly foremost in Sarah's mind. She and Dylan, from some outside entrance, had been hauled downstairs—one long flight, two flights, she wasn't sure—and now they lay bunched like discarded objects on what felt to her elbows like a concrete floor. Cold, hard, and rough.

And it was dark. Only the dimmest blur of light showed through the bag that covered her head and what air there was held a smell of oil and solvents. And worst of all, the bindings around her wrists had been retied so she must try again to loosen a hand. And keep Dylan from making a sound. When they had first been deposited on the ground, Dylan had begun struggling and shouting and for his trouble been given what sounded to Sarah's ears as a heavy kick into some vulnerable part of his body. He gave a scream, then began to sob. But the crying at last had subsided to a whimper, and Sarah, listening, waiting, finally heard retreating steps, the creak of wooden stairs, and thought that now she might be able to speak to the boy. She wiggled her body over until her bound wrists touched what must have been the top of his bristled head. "Dylan," she whispered. "Where did he get you? Are you hurt? Are you okay?"

No answer. Sarah tried again with words of consolation and comfort. Questions relating to his injury. If he was indeed injured. Persistence on this subject finally elicited a hoarse, "I'm fine, and you get away from me." Sarah, patiently, repeated the information that they were in the same boat. Or on the same floor. Both tied up. They had to work together.

At which the Dylan bundle jerked itself apart from Sarah, and judging from the subsequent sounds seemed to be rolling as far away from her as possible. In fact, only the sudden crash of what sounded like a falling metal garbage can put a stop to his progress.

Sarah, now desperate, knowing that cooperation, however reluctant, was vital, said with as much edge to her voice as she could muster that she hadn't thought he was such a coward. She'd thought he was pretty brave, but now she could tell that he was pretty useless in a crunch. He couldn't handle a crisis. A complete wuss. "I thought we could help each other. I was going to try to get one hand loose. Or use my fingers to get you untied. But now there's no point. You just haven't got any backbone."

This approach, although not calculated to make friends, worked. There was sputtering noise. A sharp sound as if something was being kicked by Dylan's two bound feet, that garbage can perhaps. Then, in a growl, "I'm not a coward. I've never been a coward. Go on, ask anybody. And I'm not afraid of these guys. Or you," he added with what could be called a high-pitched snarl.

"Then get back over here next to me and let's see if I can get your wrists loose. If I do, then you can untie me. But no noise."

"You already said that," said Dylan in the same voice. But he began to roll himself back toward Sarah until his back rested against her back and she began, with the limited motion left to her fingers, to pick at his ties.

The twine used was not, thank God heavy duty, and after much twisting and turning of Dylan's wrist Sarah was at last able to pull his thumb free. Then the forefinger. Then one hand, and with the twine no longer holding, Dylan had both hands free.

"Great," said Sarah. "Now take that bag off your head so you can see what you're doing. And get my hands loose."

"You like ordering people around, don't you?" said Dylan. But before Sarah could answer, she heard a tearing sound— the head bag being torn off—and then an exhalation of breath. "Oh, wow!" he breathed. "Oh, man, look at the stuff."

"Dylan," said Sarah. "My hands."

A long pause, scratching sounds, and then Dylan again. "I got my legs free. I can stand up."

For a moment Sarah had a sudden awful picture of Dylan,

now a free man and the confirmed hater of Sarah Deane, racing up the stairs and beating it. Out and away. Leaving Sarah to get out of her own mess.

Or worse, racing up the stairs and being recaptured. And probably then having the tar—or the life—beaten out of him. And her. Because nothing in their treatment so far had suggested a future of tender mercies.

But Dylan proved staunch. Reluctant, no doubt, but staunch. He bent to undo Sarah's head covering, and then while she was blinking, taking in her surroundings, he went to work and in minutes they both were on their feet. Taking stock.

And Sarah could almost echo Dylan's gasp of "wow." They stood in a cavernous underground space, the only light coming from a distant bulb over a workbench and the slits from low cellar windows. And on every side, bicycles. Bicycle parts, wheels, chains, gears, bicycle seats, tires, pumps, tins of spray paint, tubes of lubricants, cans of oil. Bikes on racks. Suspended on hooks. Bike wheels upside down in vise grips. Bike parts on workbenches, in open packing boxes. In short, Dylan and Sarah stood in the middle of Bike City.

For the count of five they stared. And then, Dylan with a convulsive jerk of his shoulders took off for the stairs. And almost got away, Sarah grabbing the back of his T-shirt as he started up the first step.

"Dylan, for God's sake. Hold it. You don't want to walk right into their arms. Get tied up again."

"Whaddya want to do?" Dylan, the belligerent, had returned. "Those stairs go outside. We came in from outside."

"We want to get out safely. And not up those stairs. Every now and then I hear footsteps. We've got to move fast. They'll probably be checking on us any minute."

"So," said Dylan. "We can't just blast out of here."

"Windows," said Sarah. "The cellar windows."

"How about we grab a bike, drag it upstairs, and take off."

"Think," said Sarah. "The noise. They'd wrap a bike around

your neck. And mine. Come on. Let's see if those windows open."

They tried one at the far end of the vast room. It was an area that seemed devoted to the sorting of bikes by make and by size. Dylan climbed atop a workbench, pushed the window. Which opened just like that, the single-framed piece of dirty glass moved up and out of sight. The open space left would accommodate, Sarah thought, a fair sized woodchuck. But a human? A close call.

But Dylan was in motion. Head through the opening, then shoulders wiggling, then torso, legs, and out. And then his hand reached back in.

Sarah, scraping most of the flesh from large sections of her shoulders, back, butt, and thighs, emerged into a tangle of prickle bushes and brush. Dylan lay prone under what looked like a some kind of overgrown syringa and Sarah joined him. The light was fading, the sun was disappearing behind a grove of trees in the distance. And over their shoulders to the right they could see the cabs of several parked pickups. To their left rose a two-and-a-half-story building with vast insets of glass along its top two floors. In short, a greenhouse. From the far end a man emerged carrying a trash bin. But otherwise the surroundings seemed uninhabited.

Sarah peered ahead, making sense of what appeared to be an army of small pine trees. Sheered spruce. Feathery hemlocks. Burlap-wrapped rhododendrons, azaleas, mountain laurel, holly. A nursery.

"If we get to those trees," said Dylan. "No one can see us. We can make a run for it."

"Wait," said Sarah, relieved that Dylan and she had suddenly become a "we." "That man. The one with the trash bin."

"He's outta sight," said Dylan. "Let's go." With which, crouching low, Dylan, like Sarah, in his sock feet, sprinted to the first row of pine trees, twisted his body around into the next row. And Sarah, cursing her companion for headstrong action, followed. Safe behind the second row, she turned to the boy, who squatted behind a thickly branched spruce.

"Look, Dylan. I don't think you're a coward. I said that to get you moving. So don't try to prove you're brave. I know you are. Let's make our moves together. This isn't no-man's-land with the enemy shooting at us. Let's make a very quiet, sneaky escape. We can run one after the other and try to get to the end of the trees and see if we can find a field with some cover. Okay?"

"Okay," said Dylan. With which he was off, twisting, turning, keeping low, reminding Sarah of nothing so much as a quarterback, ball clutched to his chest, making for the goalpost.

So much, she told herself, for cooperation. Now she would have to keep up with Dylan even if it killed her. And it might do just that. She was out of condition. She'd meant to work out, but summer had come and so had sloth and lassitude. Bending low, mimicking Dylan's running posture, Sarah followed his twisting route through the evergreens until suddenly the ground dipped and she found herself sliding, then tumbling, rolling into a deep and very muddy ravine. A ravine through which ran a small stream of foul-smelling water. At the bottom she found Dylan, on his feet standing on a rock, entirely clean, grinning broadly at her.

And then his grin faded.

From somewhere behind them they heard a shout. Not too far away. And another shout. A dog barking excitedly.

"Down," ordered Sarah. "Flat. Get down in the mud. Pull something over you."

And this time Dylan didn't argue. He flattened himself into the ooze, reached one hand up and pulled a rotting branch over his head.

Sarah did likewise.

# 22

ALEX'S hospital committee meeting finished early. The chairman had failed to arrive, pleading a family problem, and the rest of the members, pointing out to each other that Sunday evening was a bad time for a meeting anyhow, were glad to shuffle quickly through a few items on the agenda and then call it quits.

Alex had intended to drive directly home, enjoy a cold beer and a warm shower, and welcome Sarah home from the excitements of her recycling meeting. Instead, with an extra hour and a half on his hands, he decided to go back to his father's and see if he could bring some light into his father's increasingly dark view of the world. A very bad sign was that John hadn't finished putting his books away, hadn't yet set up his office. He had even stopped reading academic journals, the bulletins from his former university department.

Of course, when his mother and father departed for the summer to their beloved Weymouth Island, Alex was sure the troubled waters, at least for July through September, would smooth. But in the meantime . . . Alex shook his head and pulled into the driveway of number 7 Alder Way.

And found his father in the act of walking toward the garage. His father looked up and walked hurriedly over, an expression of relief on his face. Elspeth had called. Had caught an earlier flight. Made it to Boston, caught a late-afternoon flight to Portland, and taken a taxi to a friend's house in Yarmouth. Could he? Yes, John could and would.

"Except," said John, "I hate driving so late. My night vision is not too good, but I know you want to get home, catch up with Sarah. Put your feet up."

Alex smiled, climbed out of his car, steered his father into the passenger seat, passed him the end of the seat belt, and took his place behind the wheel. And then, telling his father not to be ridiculous, of course he would drive, they could catch up on the news of the world. Privately Alex thought his father was looking distinctly seedy. He needed a haircut, and in an old moth-eaten gray cardigan he looked like someone's great-grandfather.

"It's no bother," Alex told his father. "Sarah will be fast asleep anyway by the time I would have made it home. A few more hours won't make any difference. And I'd like to hear all about Mother's trip while she's still got a good grip on the details. If we wait too long she'll be all caught up in the Uncle Fergus affair and won't even remember she's been away."

"Your mother did mention something odd," said John, settling back in his seat as Alex swung the car past the gatehouse. "She said that she had an idea about what she called the Ocean Tide mystery. Not the murders but some sort of a conspiracy that might be connected with them. That she saw two people from this place doing something suspicious. One of them was that gorgeous hostess, what's her name? Naomi something."

Alex groaned. "My God, now it's Mother. Listen, Dad, cross every finger, pray to the gods, say your beads, recite a couple of psalms that your wife and my mother saw absolutely nothing out of the ordinary. That it's simply a matter of severe jet lag."

"Amen," said John. "And now I'd like to get the police off my back."

"No one suspects you of anything," Alex reassured him. "They just want details. What you might have seen. Heard."

"Which was nothing," said his father, sighing. "I was alone out there in the fog with Patsy."

Alex nodded, and they drove in silence down Route 1, Alex reflecting that the police could probably put together a good argument for continuing to question his father, and John McKenzie thinking what a pleasant thing it was to be driven by his son and how glad he would be to have Elspeth back in residence. *Maybe,* he thought to himself, *we don't have to stay at Ocean Tide for the rest of our lives. Maybe there's someplace else.*


Mike Laaka had been only too glad to be detached from the fruitless job of trying to find out whether or not Ned Colley had ever played a game of golf in his life. George Fitts had received a garbled message from the desk clerk at the Lodge to the effect that Dylan Colley's bike—or one like it—had been spotted at the Colley farm. "Who," demanded George, "told you?" But the clerk, new to the job, hadn't recognized the voice, hadn't asked for a name.

Now, with Deputy Katie Waters at his side, Mike, under orders from George, drove his Blazer fifteen miles over the speed limit heading for the old Colley farm. Betty, by phone, had briefed him on its location and pleaded with him not to come charging into the drive as if he were about to make a drug bust.

"Sure as hell you'll scare the pants off him and he'll take off. Leave the car out on the road. Go in on foot. Let Katie go first, she's not scary."

Mike had stifled the impulse to salute Betty, and they had taken off. Now with the white farmhouse and the faded red barn in view he slowed down, pulled over on a grassy slope some distance before the mailbox, and he and Katie moved quietly toward the driveway, both trying to look, as Sarah had before them, as if they were out for a casual walk in the country.

By the time that the two had sauntered around the farmhouse, poked their noses into the barn and the outbuildings, had climbed the stairs to the porch, peered in the window, both had come to an agreement about three possibilities. First, Dylan was hiding somewhere along with his bicycle and so a major search effort should be undertaken, locks broken, doors forced open, the farmhouse entered, and for good measure a call made to the canine unit. Second, the boy wasn't here, hadn't been, and the bike reported wasn't his. Third, Dylan had come on his bike. And left on his bike.

Of these three possibilities only number one seemed to offer useful action, so Mike had called George for a couple of backups and a dog, then he and Katie began another slow circuit of the interior of the barn, coming only to the conclusion that there had been recently a number of persons tramping about on the lower barn floor. Just as there had been many tracks of various tire sizes outside, not surprising in view of the fact that the whole property was being renovated by its new owners and was probably overrun by workmen.

An hour later, however, with the arrival of two deputies and a state trooper with a German shepherd called Bear, hope rekindled. The trooper had requested and been given a pair of Dylan's well-worn and not-yet-washed jeans by Betty, and Bear had shown great excitement on being taken into the barn. In a matter of minutes he had zeroed in on the little room off the cow section.

"So," said Mike to Katie. "The kid's been here."

"He used to live here," Katie pointed out. "His scent is probably all over the place."

"That was over six months ago so let's not complicate things," said Mike wearily. "Let's get going with a real search of the whole area. We should be able to screw George out of a few more men. Make a proper job of it. God," he added. "Dogs are wonderful."

Sarah and Dylan, plastered facedown in the bottom of the ravine, their bodies squashed into a soup of mud and water, would not have agreed with Mike. The barking dog had come nearer, he could be heard snuffling around at the top of the ravine. And then with a sort of joyful yip, he crashed down the slope, ran over to Dylan and began to lick his mud-streaked face.

"Hey, it's Ranger," said Dylan, grabbing hold of the dog's collar. "Good boy. Down, Ranger. Lie down."

Sarah raised her head in time to see a golden retriever flop down beside Dylan and resume the face washing.

"I know Ranger," said Dylan. "He's okay. He's my buddy. I can make him do anything. He was mine but Mom made me give him up when we moved because we had two other dogs and he was the youngest."

"Then," said Sarah tersely, "make him stay down and not make a sound."

Dylan, still holding the dog's collar, whispered, "Ranger, play dead. Good boy. Play dead. You'd better play dead, too," he told Sarah. "Both of us."

Dog, boy, and woman played dead, the boy for good measure keeping his hand over Ranger's muzzle. Rivulets of brackish water crept into every crevice of their clothing, covered the lower part of the retriever's body. And the steps, the shouts came closer. Stopped. Waited. Called. And retreated.

"Now," said Sarah. "Keep low, climb up the opposite bank, and beat it."

"With Ranger," said Dylan.

"No," said Sarah. "Let the dog go. He'll hold us back. And he might start barking again."

"Ranger," said Dylan, and Sarah could hear the stubborn emphasis of the word, "he comes with us. No way I'm going to leave him with those guys."

"Those guys, who are?..." Sarah began. But stopped. It was no time for questions. No time for fighting over a dog. "Okay," she said. "Here's my belt. Use it as a leash. Please try and keep him quiet."

And, as if they had practiced it, Sarah and Dylan rose as one, bent over, and scrambled up the bank, over the top and into the high grass of a field. And ran. And stumbled. And ran. Until, both breathless, the dog Ranger panting, they flung themselves under a clump of midfield alders.

The shadows had lengthened along the length of the pasture, the woods beyond had turned into a dark smudge, and the small breeze had subsided. Along a distant ridge beyond the pasture, Sarah saw the lights of a small farm come on, saw distant white-and-black shapes, Holsteins probably, moving in a slow line toward some distant gate. But, twisting her head this way and that, she could not see any approaching figures coming up from behind them.

"Maybe we're safe," she whispered.

"Nah," said Dylan. "These are smart guys."

"Dylan, for God's sake, who are they? You know them? Come on, tell me if you do know." It was a command said with great urgency. Sarah felt that to know the enemy was halfway to beating them. Or getting away from them.

But Dylan shrank away from her, shaking his head. "I'm not saying," he told her in that same hoarse defiant voice. "If you try and make me tell I'll . . . I'll split. Beat it."

"Take it easy," Sarah soothed. "It would really help if I knew, too. I could get to the police—"

But with the word "police," Dylan rose on his knees and shortened the belt-leash on Ranger.

"Okay," said Sarah. "Forget it. But if you know where we are it would be great if you'd let me in on it. We've got to get back to Ocean Tide. Is there a main road somewhere around? Or should we try and get to that farmhouse across the way? Make a few phone calls."

But again Dylan shook his head. "No, let's get back on our own. I've lived around here. There's a road over there, past the woods." The boy waved at the line of trees. "The road goes into another road and there's a big road that comes into it."

"It's too far," Sarah protested. "We can't possibly walk. I don't know how far it was from your farm to that basement with all the bikes."

"Our old farm isn't safe anymore," said Dylan. "Nothing's safe. Except Ocean Tide as long as I keep away from the golf course."

"Dylan," said Sarah in an explosion of exasperation. "What do you know about the golf course? What happened there? Who did you see? Is it connected with what happened today, being tied up? Taken to the greenhouse?" She paused, suddenly remembering. "Doesn't your uncle Albert Moseby, own a greenhouse?"

"No!" Dylan almost yelled it. Then, more quietly, "Not a real greenhouse. It's sort of a wholesale business. People don't buy flowers there. He sells to other landscape places."

"Have you ever been there?"

"Yeah. Three or four times. Maybe more. But we weren't there today. Uncle Al's greenhouse doesn't have a basement."

"You mean not a basement with bikes in it?"

"Not a basement period. Tim and I used to go there and chase around the whole place. There wasn't any basement. Just a big greenhouse and outside he had trees and bushes with their roots tied up in bags. But no basement," he repeated.

Sarah now spoke softly, trying for a nonthreatening way to put it. "I suppose that there might be several greenhouses in the area. But," she added, "it wouldn't hurt to tell the police about it, would it? What happened to us. Find a phone as soon as we can." Sarah paused, knowing that the word "police" might be enough set the boy off again.

It did. Literally. "Listen," Dylan yelled. "You're just trying to cause trouble with my family. And me. That's what you've been doing all summer, like you're some sort of spy. A police spy. So I don't want to have anything more to do with you. So there." And before Sarah could get hold of his shirt or grab the dog, they were off at top speed. The boy galloping over through the long grass, the dog bounding beside him, and by the time Sarah was on her feet after them, they had made it across the pasture, had disappeared into the left side of the woods and vanished into the shadows.

Sarah stifled a shout. Who knew who—or what—was lurking behind the boy and the dog. Or ahead of them. She increased her speed, a painful exercise in her sock feet, and as she ran she knew perfectly that once Dylan hit the woods she had little chance of finding him. He knew the territory, had grown up in the Appleton-Union area, and so might have a good sense of where he was going. But she thought, even if almost out of breath, she would keep up the chase, give it an honest try.

No use. The woods were dark, fallen branches, moldering logs hindered progress. After what seemed like hours of blind running this way and that she stopped and listened. No running feet. No barking dog. But in the distance, somewhere over to the left, the noisy sound of a vehicle with an imperfect muffler. A vehicle meant a road. For the moment Sarah gave up on Dylan—unless she literally stumbled over him—and began to edge her way through the trees, down a small declivity. More mud, another stagnant stream. Her feet were now not only soaked but bruised and cut from running over rough ground. What a holy mess. Why hadn't she kept her mouth shut? Why did she have to keep trying to screw something out of the boy, scaring him by suggesting the police? Of course, it was his mention of the golf course as an unsafe place that had set her teeth on edge, kept her asking questions. And by now even if Sarah was convinced that Dylan probably knew more about at least one of the murders than George Fitts and Company, well, she should have buttoned her lip. Sarah the Stupid strikes again.

These depressing reflections brought her across a small plowed field and, yes, to a road. A road with a smaller road branching off. With a single light from a pole illuminating a sign. Brinker Falls Road. And the old Colley farm stood on that road. Not too far along, she remembered. And just past the Colley farmhouse, tucked out of sight, sat Sarah's Subaru, the ignition keys under the front seat. With any kind of luck, she told herself, it would be sitting there waiting. And all the way home she would drive with an eye out for a boy and a golden retriever.

Twenty minutes later, Sarah heaved her mud-soaked, shivering person into the Subaru and without switching on the headlights, backed out onto the road, turned, and drove away at a crawl. Not until she was safely on a main road did she turn on her lights, pull over to the side, activate her car phone and leave a message with the state police dispatcher that a thirteen-year-old named Dylan Colley was on the run in the Appleton area along with a golden retriever named Ranger. And her name was Sarah Deane, town of Bowmouth. Good night.

It was not much after eleven when Sarah, showered and clean, crawled into bed, noting only briefly that Alex must be at an especially long hospital meeting—hadn't it begun at 7:30?—and then fell asleep so soundly that even Patsy jumping up next to her, his head on Alex's pillow, didn't rouse her.

Arriving in Yarmouth at something after eleven-thirty that night, John kissed Elspeth, settled her in the front seat, climbed into the back, pulled his wife's travel bag under his head and slept. This left Elspeth free to give Alex, during the two-hour drive back, a garbled account of the nefarious doings of Naomi Foxglove, Nick Moseby, and his friend, Tom Schmidt. Alex, trying to concentrate on driving, heard bits and snatches. Naomi was up to no good, he gathered, sneaking around after the boys. Or conniving with them. It might be a consortium. Bike part stealing and selling. Or maybe drugs in the handlebars. She didn't think the boys had raced. At least she didn't see them. If this was true, why hadn't they? Bicycling was all they talked about on the plane. Details you wouldn't believe. But something was fishy. And Naomi was something else. All smiles and graciousness and a dagger down her bra.

To all this Alex murmured, Yes, mother, how interesting, did you, yes, I am listening, and at last his mother fell silent and the miles fell away, through darkened Maine villages, down Route 1, and finally to Alder Way. The two McKenzies senior were decanted from the car, luggage was carried in, farewells were said, and Alex most thankfully turned toward home. Where he found a heap of mud-fouled clothes topped with a pair of filthy socks in the bathroom. And in the bedroom, Sarah dead to the world, her pillow over her head. Too tired to puzzle over the dirty clothes—Sarah must have fallen into something—Alex pushed Patsy off his side of the bed and dropped immediately into a confused set of dreams featuring a particularly chaotic emergency room set on a uninhabited offshore island.

At about this same time, a footsore Dylan Colley and his buddy, Ranger, found themselves at a familiar barn in Union township belonging to Betty Colley's cousin David. After a brief and noiseless reconnoiter, boy and dog found an empty storage stall, settled themselves on a pile of loose hay, and tumbled into an exhausted sleep.


The next morning, Monday, June 19, brought muddled tales (Sarah), incoherent suspicions and accusations (Elspeth), and stonewalling (Dylan). For the likes of John McKenzie, Alex,

Betty Colley, and the upper investigative echelons (George Fitts and Mike Laaka) the day brought extreme irritation and very little in the way of resolution. The search of the old Colley farm was ongoing but identifying recent visitors would take time, too much time for the impatient police.

As far as the boy Dylan was concerned—he had been returned by Betty's cousin in the early hours of the morning together with Ranger—the police were stymied. All they knew from Mike Laaka and Katie Waters was Bear's confirmation that Dylan had spent time in a small room in the cow barn. Of this or anything else the boy wouldn't talk. Period. His mother couldn't make him despite dire threats of grounding him for an entire summer. Mike and George, each in turn spent a fruitless hour talking to the walls and furniture of the VIP Golfer's Cottage. Even when the subject of the abduction of himself and Sarah, the tying up, the transportation to the greenhouse came up, Dylan would not confirm or deny by even the slightest nod of the head.

"I'm thinking fondly of rubber hoses and lighted matches," said Mike after Dylan the Silent had departed—on sore feet—back toward his house.

As for Sarah, also with damaged feet, she hadn't had a clear view of the exterior of the greenhouse and could tell little about it. She and Dylan had arrived with bags over their heads and had departed by scrambling out of a cellar window, dodged through rows of specimen trees and shrubs, and taken off like frightened rabbits down a ravine, across a pasture, pursued by a golden retriever. At no point did Sarah have a clear idea of the location of the greenhouse. After running and wandering about finding Brinker Falls Road was dumb luck. The only useful information Sarah could give them was that Dylan Colley claimed his uncle Albert Moseby's greenhouse did not have a cellar or anything underground. Two floors only. And that Dylan was afraid of the golf course and that the dog Ranger had once been owned by the boy.

Betty, when called, said that she'd given the dog to Al

Moseby. But Al had told her the dog chewed everything in sight and was subsequently given to another farmer who had goldens. Name of farmer lost in the mists of time. Yes, it was possible that this farmer had a greenhouse for all Al Moseby knew. No, he had not seen the dog again. But anything he could do to help, etc. etc.

"Can we get a search warrant for Moseby's place?" Mike asked plaintively.

George whose specialty was quick decisions, waited. Clicked his pen up and down, made indeterminate noises in his throat. Wiped his glasses, polished each lens with his handkerchief. Then shook his head. "I don't think we've got sufficient reason. Let's make an informal visit to the Moseby outfit today and tomorrow hit all the greenhouses in the area. Send someone to Moseby's who hasn't been around the Ocean Tide scene, isn't known by sight, to look at trees and bushes. Wander around inside, see if they can find a basement entry. Evidence of underground storage. Remember it's a wholesale operation so our investigator needs to make up a landscaping outfit name.

"Deputy Katie Waters," suggested Mike. "She's been mostly out of sight. But give her a backup. So bring me up to speed. I've been spending most of my time visiting golf courses. Who are the favorites?"

"This isn't a horse race," said George, "but if we eliminate Betty Colley and her mother, Alex and Sarah, and the senior McKenzies, we have the following: For Jason Colley count out Nick Moseby, who spent the weekend bike training. Count out Matt Moseby who was away for a weekend of baseball. For the Ned Colley murder, father Al Moseby seems in the clear. He was at work the day of the Fitness Center party. Confirmed. Manager Martinelli doubtful but he would have had to do it before daylight as he was front and center all day with that party. With Fergus McKenzie, count out Nick Moseby, Elspeth McKenzie, and Naomi Foxglove because they were heading to Logan en route to France."

"So no one person could have done all three. Except Dylan and Brian Colley, young Tim Moseby, or maybe Martinelli or one of his henchmen—is there really such a word?"

George scowled at Mike. "Move along. I've got Elspeth McKenzie coming in. Full of ideas about Naomi Foxglove and the oldest Moseby boy. Or man. Yale man, that is. I've been in touch with the substitute registrar in New Haven and I hope to hear something about Nick's student status by the end of the week. Seems the regular staff is off on holiday."

"Hey, wait up," said Mike. "Didn't I see Naomi coming out of your office at dawn this morning? Or before breakfast anyway."

George nodded. "Yes. I got an earful. But whether it's legit or whether it's a preemptive strike—she knows Elspeth was sneaking around Provence—that remains to be seen."

"What will break this case," said Mike, "is giving Dylan Colley a dose of truth serum." And Mike departed, meeting Elspeth McKenzie with her support team coming up the steps, Elspeth looking worn, John haggard, and Alex grim.

"Don't you ever work?" said Mike to Alex after greeting the others. "No sick people left in Knox County? Or have you been disbarred?"

Alex looked at him with irritation. "I made early rounds and have taken forty minutes away from morning office hours. But if you're not feeling up to par, Mike, I can send you for a colonoscopy exam this afternoon."

The meeting with George Fitts was not, from Elspeth's point of view, a positive experience. George Fitts was about as responsive as the chair he was sitting in. Actually, she thought there was more life in the photograph of Jack Nicklaus striding down the tenth hole in the 1975 Masters than in George Fitts. However, Elspeth, trying to avoid the subject of why she had appointed herself an international investigator, described her flight, her visit to Venasque and other points in Provence. She told George of the eagerness with which on the flight over Nick Moseby and pal Thomas Schmidt had talked about the bike race, how when she was half-asleep she heard both young men going on and on ad tedium about bike parts and pieces. Not about race strategy. "Doesn't that seem sinister, Sergeant?" she asked.

"Not particularly," said George. "Bike racers are focused on their bikes. Parts are important."

"But," expostulated Elspeth, "if they really *didn't* race?"

"You may have missed them," said George.

"But," said Elspeth again, now on the defensive, "how about that Naomi Foxglove slithering around, following them? Or at least I suppose she was following them. I did mean to go the next day to Mont Ventoux where the race was supposed to be ending and try and see if Nick and Thomas *were* racing and see if Naomi was still hanging around. But then I got John's telephone message about Uncle Felix being murdered. So I came home," she ended, feeling as if nothing she had said had made a dent in George Fitts's head.

"Has it occurred to you, Mrs. McKenzie," asked George softly, "that the reason that the two young men did not race was because they had failed to qualify?"

"No," said Elspeth. "They seemed so sure they'd be racing."

"Perhaps there was a time trial during the period you were in Paris," suggested George. "And they failed the cut. Or they failed a time trial in the States. Who knows? But they had to save face. After all, Manager Martinelli was giving them cash for the trip. Paid for Nick's air ticket. Gave Nick time off from his job in the bike rental shop. They had to go. Do you see my point?"

"Yes," said Elspeth in a subdued voice. "Yes, I do. I'm sorry."

John McKenzie, who with Alex had been sitting in the background, could stand it no longer.

"Elspeth," he thundered. "For God's sake, fight back. He's doing a snow job on you. Stick to your guns. If you thought the boys were up to no good, well, say so, damn it. Why were they going on about bike parts and not race strategy? That's what you thought wasn't it?"

"Dad," said Alex. "Keep it down. This is Mother's show."

"Well, tell her to make it a show," said John. "She's tough enough at home. Don't let this Fitts fellow bully her."

"He's not bullying me," said Elspeth. "He's being logical. And I'm not."

"Humble isn't your dish," said John.

"John," said Elspeth, her voice rising, "just shut up."

At which George rose, thanked everyone for coming. "Mrs. McKenzie, I'm not throwing out what you've told me. I'm just suggesting alternatives. And every little bit adds up to the whole picture, so I hope we can reach a conclusion soon and you can all get on with your summer."

Elspeth, feeling like a college freshman who had failed an exam, stumbled out of the room. "Damn that man," she said as Alex steadied her elbow. And then, "He belongs in the State Department. Working in the Middle East. Those guys would have him for lunch."

George Fitts felt with a despondency unusual for him that he was very far from any conclusion. Meeting with Elspeth McKenzie had produced nothing but clouds. Without any particular hope in the result he reached for the telephone and punched in the registrar's office number at Yale University.

However, George's pessimism was unfounded. Fate, tired of contradictions, multiple suspects, fumbling amateur investigators, confused police, had settled it in her mind to wind up events on that very Monday. Enough was enough, she told herself. There were other parts of the country in which to make trouble.

# 23

SARAH, having in the early hours of Monday met George Fitts and delivered herself of an account of the events at first the Colley farm and then in the basement of the mystery greenhouse, now found herself caught in the daily routine. It was tutoring time. The Colley kitchen and *The Adventures of Tom Sawyer* awaited, but she doubted her students would include Dylan.

Wrong. Dylan, pale of face, spiked of hair—the scissor job was growing in—sat stiffly, a reluctant captive, between Betty and his aunt Sherry, both hands shaped into a fist. Sarah saw that he was wearing bedroom slippers; his feet, like hers, must still be suffering.

"We thought we'd sit in," explained Betty. "I told Dylan that if he got his act together and stayed with the tutoring, maybe he could keep Ranger. And besides, it'll help if Sherry and I know what you're up to. Then we can keep an eye on the boys' homework. Sherry agrees with me, don't you Sherry?"

Sherry, who appeared to be sitting with almost the same rigidity as Dylan, gave a slight jerk, and then nodded. "Yes," she said. "It's a good idea."

"Of course," said Sarah, "I meet with Matt separately. He has an essay this afternoon on *The Red Badge of Courage.* After he finishes work."

The tutorial session was low key and in Dylan's case, not productive. When asked if he could offer anything, written or spoken, on the subject of Tom Sawyer, he kept his head down and brought up from a subterranean part of his anatomy the gruff message that he hadn't started the book yet.

The two other boys, Tim Moseby and Brian Colley, read from their two-page essays on Chapters Five and Six, but Sarah's gaze kept moving over to Sherry Moseby. The living Orvis catalogue model was on a real skid. Now dark roots marked the end of the blond dye job, her hair was tangled, her complexion muddy, no eye treatment, no lipstick, her linen slacks creased, her raspberry T-shirt rumpled. For the second time, Sarah began thinking of Sherry as up to her knees in the family muck. Was she strong enough to wield a golf club, lug a body into a fertilizer shed? Strangle a man with a bicycle chain?

But this was wild speculation, and Sarah with an effort returned to her students and told the two participating boys that they were beginning to get a feel for life on the Mississippi. Putting an end to the session, she assigned the next three chapters and asked for a two-page description and analysis of one of the notable characters met so far.

Released from the schoolroom, knowing that in the afternoon ahead she had another serious date with Sergeant Fitts, Sarah decided on refreshment. Pick up a sandwich out on Route 1, then take a vigorous walk on the beach. Then call on Elspeth, who should be recovering from her trip exhaustion and find out how her session with George went.

The part of the beach featuring the dock, the floats, the

moored boats, and the beached rowboats, skiffs, punts, and small sailboats, was abuzz with activity. Sarah, wanting nothing to do with happy crowds sporting in and around the water, took herself off in search of peace toward the far end of the Ocean Tide property. For a while she walked with determination. Then sat down and finished her killer egg salad sandwich and her bottle of pink lemonade. Then, at a slower pace she wandered toward the high rocks that marked the boundary of the community, turned and sat down on a rock facing the sea. It was a chance to ask herself questions. Did either Jason Colley or Ned Colley have anything to do with either bicycles or golf? Yes. Jason had a new mountain bike. Was that why he was killed? Had he muscled in on one of the multiple bike scams that flourished on the coast? How about Ned? Nothing to do with bikes—as far as she knew. Nor golf, judging from what she'd heard. So why was *he* killed? No answer. As yet. Who knew a lot about bicycles? Easy. Nick Moseby. But two bikes had been stolen from his family. As well as expensive golf clubs. Smoke screens? How can a body be conveyed to a bike or hiking trail or to the seventeenth hole maintenance shed? Answer: golf cart. ATV. Small utility tractor as used by the greens keepers. Who worked on the golf course? Matt Moseby. Who owned a greenhouse? Albert Moseby. Three Mosebys. Working together or accidentally linked? Why? Bike scam? Golf scam? Family revenge plan being worked out? But why? Sherry looked like she teetered on the edge of a breakdown. Because she was the nervous type? Or her family was making her nervous. Or was Sherry in charge? Along with her husband. But Sherry was Betty's sister. The Moseby boys were her nephews. Betty was the salt of the earth. Were some—or all—of the Mosebys the scum of the earth, only Betty hadn't figured that out?

And what was eating Dylan Colley? What had he done? Killed someone by accident? By plan? Been used by . . . a cousin called Moseby? Seen something? Was being blackmailed? Terrorized? Frightened out of his skin? Or did he really believe that she, Sarah, was an ill-omened creature tied in with the murder of his father and his cousin?

For answer a large round stone hit something hard on the bank behind her, bounced against a log, and came to rest close to Sarah's ankle. Then a branch creaked, cracked, and another loose stone rolled down onto the beach. Sarah swiveled around in time to see a pair of bare legs, feet in bedroom slippers, pushing up the slope and then disappearing past a bordering line of beach grass and bayberry into a grove of white spruce and pine.

Dylan Colley! What in God's name was the boy up to? She remembered with a shudder that the golf course was the unsafe place to be—at least for Dylan. He wouldn't, surely he wouldn't, decide to case the golf course. Looking for something? Meeting someone?

As quietly as possible Sarah walked to the bank and grabbing hold of a branch here, a root there, managed to climb up and forward, working slowly to avoid making noise. All Dylan needed was to find her on his tail again. He'd probably help himself to one of those shovels in the big shed and finish her off for good, for which she could hardly blame him. She made the top of the bank in a crouch, got behind a thick oak tree and tried to orient herself. She'd been here before. It was the area just past the two maintenance sheds beyond which lay the rise of ground that led to the seventeenth hole. The infamous seventeenth hole.

And Dylan? Sarah moved ahead two trees and saw him. A silhouette standing on the rim of the seventeenth green. And he was waving, one hand in the air. Sarah hoisted herself halfway up the rough grass on the side of the green wondering who the boy could be signaling to. The course was closed. No golfers allowed. Besides the police and the forensic team, only the greens-keepers and the two golf pros had the privilege of being on the course, seeing that the grass was cut, the bunkers were raked, and checking on the watering of the fairways, the tees, and the greens. Sarah, letting herself down on her stomach, crawled farther up the rise and now saw that a greenskeeper's tractor-cart was approaching at a slow speed. Dylan waved again. The driver halted a moment, waved back, and then the vehicle gathered speed, zipped past the lip of the sand trap, and headed uphill for the green. Dylan was now waving both hands over his head. First in greeting. Then the boy took a step backward, both palms forward like a traffic cop.

The tractor motor roared, the tractor shot toward the boy. Dylan, suddenly frozen, dropped his hands and stood still.

And Sarah yelled. Shouted. Screamed. Scrambled up to the edge of the green. Dylan roused himself and leaped aside. The driver, distracted for a moment by sight of Sarah, slowed, then at full throttle turned his machine toward the boy. But on the turn a wheel caught on the heavier grass on the green's edge, the whole tractor tilted briefly, came upright and yawed to the left. At the same time Dylan flung himself facedown on the ground. But now the driver, trying for control, his eyes on Dylan, twisted the wheel, but the tractor, as if it had a stubborn life of its own, swung past the boy, nicking part of the boy's outflung arm, and then plunged down the hill and with a heavy smack, a metallic crack, smashed into three birch trees at the foot of the green.

And the driver, briefly airborne, slammed headfirst into the trunk of nearest birch tree. And lay quite still.

"It's hard to say, with head injuries, which way they'll go," Alex told a tearful Sherry Moseby. "We've got a neurosurgeon coming right in. And the police, as you know, will want to be around when he regains consciousness."

"Or if?" said Sherry in a choked voice.

"Let's wait and see," said Alex. "Just take it easy. We'll hope for the best."

"But," said Sherry, "I don't know anything. I don't know what Matt's been doing. He's a good boy. He works hard. A responsible job all summer."

"Responsible job or not, you should know he may be booked for attempted assault," said Mike Laaka, turning up behind Alex. "And Mrs. Moseby, the police will want to talk to you. As well as young Matthew when he comes to."

Alex frowned at him. "Not now, Mike." He turned to Sherry. "You can go into the intensive care unit and sit by Matt if you want.

"And Mike," he added as Sherry scuttled away, "stop scaring people and come on out to the cafeteria. I haven't had lunch."

"You, Mike," said Alex as they went down the cafeteria line, "have the sensitivity of a hyena. That's the mother you're dealing with. Ease up. She's going to be in for enough hell as it is."

"Oh, relax," said Mike, as the two settled at a table and Mike pulled a plate of the mushroom hash special in front of him. "I'm just letting her know that she's going to be answering some questions. Sort of preparing her before George comes knocking."

"Knocking, knocking at her chamber door," said Alex.

"Huh?"

"That's from a poet, who might have enjoyed what's been going on here."

Their window table overlooked the rounded tops of the Camden Hills. The Mary Starbox Memorial Hospital at the north end of the Bowmouth College campus had been sited so as to offer, if not big-city medical advantages, at least the best views of any health care facility (as they were now termed) for miles around. Alex looked longingly at the scene and thought that this was the sort of day not to be within miles of a building, especially a hospital.

"Wake up," said Mike. "Give me the medical news. Matt Moseby. And Dylan. That arm of his the wheel went over."

"Badly bruised and a not-too-serious fracture. He'll be in a cast and a sling for a bit and do some time in orthopedic rehab. Mostly with Dylan it's shock. Psychological trauma. According to his mother, young Tim Moseby is his best pal. But older brother, Matt, was something special. Dylan looked up to Matt Moseby in a sort of hero-worship way. You know, the older boy, soccer hero, baseball pitcher. Dylan can't believe Matt wanted to hurt him."

"Yeah," agreed Mike. "He's trying to say that the greens cart went out of control by itself. He'd made a date to talk to Matt. To be reassured, even though he knew better, that the Moseby family had nothing to do with his, and Sarah's, abduction. He says it must have been a big practical joke. And for once, Sarah's snooping paid off. I gather she jumped up, shouted, and threw Matt's attack off course." Here Mike took a bite out of his stuffed green pepper, and added, "So is Dylan speaking to Sarah? Even thanking her?"

"Dylan doesn't think she saved his life. She simply interfered with his meeting with his cousin and caused the accident by running up to the green and yelling like a banshee. Which makes Sarah the villain."

"Wonderful!" said Mike. "And Matt? What's the prognosis there?"

"Severe head traumas are tough to call. The longer he stays unconscious, the more trouble he may be in."

"Well, if he makes it okay, he'll be charged. But as adult or juvenile I don't know. He's seventeen. So you want to hear the rest of the news?"

"All ears."

"George got a search warrant for the Moseby greenhouse operation right after he heard of Matt's attack on Dylan. And Dylan was right. Inside the greenhouse, really three connecting greenhouses, there's no entrance to a basement."

"You mean . . ."

"But," said Mike grinning, "there's a back cellar door—a bulkhead—that leads by way of stairs down to a basement.

It's well hidden behind a mass of bushes and two spruce trees. Dylan had probably never seen it. But that's how Sarah and Dylan were carried into the basement, their heads in bags. Some basement. It's a bike factory. Bicycle shipping facility. The works."

"And what else?" prompted Alex, pushing aside his half-eaten salad plate and reaching for the apple crumb pie. "Don't tell me you found bloody rags and a niblick with Uncle Fergus's hair stuck to it."

"You're batting five hundred. Bloody rags that had been part of a T-shirt sitting in a big pile of oily rags. Stupid fools. They must have rinsed the shirt off, cut it in pieces, and used them. Waste not, want not. Good old New England custom. George practically had the pieces flown to the lab and they show Jason Colley's blood type. B positive. DNA report to follow."

"But no niblick?"

"Don't be greedy. The police have taken Albert Moseby in. Charged, for the moment, with possession of stolen goods. Later, when forensics and the labs finish, George will crank up and add homicide."

"And Ned Colley's murder?"

"Right now we're figuring that Nick Moseby and Matt did it. A joint venture. Very, very early in the morning. Those two had the opportunity, not Albert, who was around all day and pretty much accounted for. But we think early in the morning Nick and/or Matt found Ned snooping around. Maybe. Who knows? Knocked him dead. Maybe with a spade handle—we're still looking. And then Matt drove the body away in his mini-tractor outfit and stashed Ned under the fertilizer bags. That tractor-cart is perfectly designed for the job. Just put some branches, clippings, or fertilizer bags you're delivering over the corpse and off you go. So much for inspecting golf carts."

"That's what Sarah said. Thought it might be one of those greens carts."

"She's right. Sometimes she is. But don't let it go to her

head. George did think about those vehicles, but decided that the grounds crew people were so out in the open that they wouldn't dare tote bodies around. Besides, in Manager Martinelli's words, all the grounds people were clean, bonded, bred from saintly parents, just like family, one hundred percent reliable, so George put the idea on the back burner. He really liked the idea of a golfer running around in a golf cart doing the murders. I think he was hoping to book Maestro Martinelli, but no such luck."

"And because," Alex asked, "the Mosebys reported they'd been robbed of bikes and golf clubs, George didn't keep them on the top of his suspect list?"

"Oh, yeah, they were suspects all right—George makes everyone in a case a suspect. But they weren't top dogs. And George never bought in to the bike business a hundred percent."

"Which brings us to my great-uncle Fergus, who certainly wasn't connected with anything going on at Ocean Tide."

"A homicide waiting to happen. We're still scratching around for whatever club nailed him, but since his golf bag hasn't the equivalent of a nine iron, we're betting on a niblick. Right now we have a body without a weapon. Nick Moseby flying to France is out of that picture. We figure Al Moseby and son Matt did the deed. Moved Fergus from the seventeenth hole area and buried the body in the deepest sand trap around, the one by the sixteenth hole. Matt has keys, has access to shovels in the maintenance shed. Like with Fergus, by a sort of coincidence maybe Jason and Ned Colley interrupted some bike-stealing operation and had to be eliminated. If Matt comes to, maybe we'll find out."

"As you said, a Moseby family affair," said Alex with a grimace. "Except for young Tim, who's only twelve, and Sherry, who must have been pretty dense not to see that something out of the ordinary was going on."

"I'd say that Sherry likes money and the things money can buy, didn't want to know what hubby was up to in his spare time, closed her eyes, and put her head in the sand. But look at the woman, she reminds me of one of those paintings of women in the French Revolution sitting in wagons going to the guillotine. I'll bet she had more than an inkling."

Alex pushed himself away from the table. "Having three members of your family involved in killing other members of your family as well as a perfect stranger, all that is bound to push someone to the edge. And speaking of edge, I've got Betty Colley coming in for a consult about Dylan. I told her I wasn't a psychiatrist, but she said she's gotten used to me. Can talk back to me, give me a piece of her mind, and that makes her comfortable. Of such stuff are doctor-and-patient relations made."

Sarah, after giving a hasty deposition in the early morning to George Fitts about events on the seventeenth green, found herself floating about without a sense of what to do next. She had left Patsy with John and Elspeth, so she could collect the dog and see if the McKenzie scene had settled into some kind of tranquility. Arriving she found the subject of the Moseby operation was taking a backseat to a rehash of questions about Uncle Fergus.

"Didn't you tell me," said Sarah as she collared Patsy, "he was always sticking his nose into things? Maybe he did it once too often."

"If Fergus," said Elspeth with feeling, "caught the Mosebys doing something funny, I wouldn't have put it past him to have given them a lecture and then tried a citizen's arrest."

"We may never know," said Sarah, turning the subject off. "But look. It's a gorgeous day and it's going to stay in the seventies. Not a cloud in the sky. Why don't you and John come for a nice walk around the place. We could try the bike trail by the gate. Or go along the beach walk."

"No, thank you, dear," said Elspeth. "I haven't quite recovered from my trip. Besides, John and I have some serious talk ahead of us."

John lifted his head. "We do?"

Elspeth, looking hard at her husband, nodded. "Yes," she said. "We certainly do."

Sarah set out. Patsy, a dog to whom the word heel might as well have been spoken in Swahili pulled hard on his leash. But Sarah's mind was occupied with matters other than dog obedience. She was thinking it was high time Elspeth and John had a talk. John was fast morphing into an Uncle Fergus and the many attractions of Ocean Tide seemed to be acting on him like a case of smallpox. Elspeth had her work cut out for her.

Sarah and Patsy hiked along the edge of the eighteenth and seventeenth fairways of the still-sealed-off golf course, jogged along a section of the beach until Patsy stopped heaving at his leash and then stopped at the outside refreshment stand by the playground for a BLT and an iced tea. Ten minutes later at a slower pace they started back along East Ocean Drive, pausing briefly at the Fitness Center where disgruntled golfers were being bused to get in their rounds to either the Samoset Resort (scenic, tough, and very pricey) or the Rockland Golf Club (not so scenic but user friendly and less pricey). From the Fitness Center Sarah circled around the tennis courts and found herself near the Pro Shop. Remembering that even though Fergus McKenzie's birthday party had been canceled, John McKenzie's was coming up, June 28, as well as the senior McKenzies' anniversary, so she should be thinking of appropriate gifts.

Start with John, she told herself. His entry into the world of golf had certainly had its downside, but the ghastly business of finding Uncle Fergus would in time fade and the game of golf could hardly be blamed. How about some really hot golf club? A super driver. One of those sand wedges that makes a ball fly out of a sand trap. Or a never-fail putter.

Sarah suddenly felt happy. Forget homicide. Find a state-of-the-art golf club. She tied Patsy's leash around a small birch tree, walked into the shop and put herself into the hands of Pete Salieri. With the golf course closed, the Pro Shop was empty, and Pete in his V-necked navy golf sweater with crossed clubs on the pocket, had a lonely aspect. He brightened at the sight of Sarah and was pleased to present her with every up-to-date piece of golfing equipment he had in the shop.

Twenty minutes later, her head reeling with expressions like "high-rebound zirconium-titanium heads," "computer engraved U-groove score lines," "tungsten sole weight," which promised everything from "added forgiveness on the fairway" to "self-correcting easy ball flight," Sarah asked for a few minutes to think it over. She had rejected the "new La Jolla Senior Utility Woods" knowing John's feelings about senior products, had toyed with the Hog Driver with its "springlike effect," but the price at over $600 plus tax took her breath away.

Now thinking that perhaps a golf glove, an umbrella, and perhaps a waterproof rain suit, would be just as acceptable, Sarah leaned back in her chair and idly scanned the handsomely framed prints on the wall, the ancient and famous golf courses: St Andrews, Prestwick, Pebble Beach, Augusta, Carnoustie, Pinehurst. Next her eye roved around to a glass shelf showing golf balls, featherie balls, gutta-percha, brambles, dimple balls, and other oddities. Then, forcing her mind back to golf clubs, she found herself reexamining the Pro Shop fan-shaped display of ancient clubs mounted on green felt in the glass-fronted cabinet that hung over the service desk. She remembered Pete's lecture on them. What were the names? It was a good test for memory. Let's see. The driver, the brassie, the spoon, the baffie—those were the woods. And then the metal ones, the cleek, and the midiron. But what were the rest of the irons?

"Pete," called Sarah. "What are the names of the clubs after the midiron?"

"You're not going to be giving John McKenzie one of those, are you?" asked Pete. "They cost an arm and a leg and you can't stop with one. You'll get him hooked, he'll start collecting and be ruined. I've seen really old drivers, ones from around 1880, sell for five, even six thousand dollars. Even cheap ones made after 1900 aren't so cheap. If everything on the club is original like the suede grip, you're looking at four or five hundred dollars."

"I wouldn't do that to John. He'd probably like a new club. Or some gadgets. I'm just curious," said Sarah.

"Well, there's the jigger and then you've got the mashie-niblick and the niblick."

"How could I forget the niblick," said Sarah with a slight shudder.

"And the putter," said Pete. "We've got a Gem-style putter stamped Glasgow Golf Company, Glasgow. That satisfy your curiosity?"

Sarah held her breath. Then, cautiously, "You've got a niblick?"

"Yeah, sure. A nice old niblick. Made by Wright and Ditson, the sporting goods outfit."

"What about the old niblick the police found in the pond on the third hole?"

"What about it?"

"Did that one come from here? From your display?"

"Our niblick's never moved an inch. I would've noticed."

"May I use your phone?" said Sarah. "I've just remembered something."

"Sure. Take your time. I'm not being run off my feet. Only three lessons for this afternoon and William's taken them. And our U.K. champ is over at the Samoset giving a clinic and going on the practice rounds we were supposed to be having here. Until the police fouled things up," he added bitterly.

Sarah, biting her lip to prevent her saying that the police

weren't exactly the ones who started the fouling up, went to the desk and picked up the phone. After three calls involving a dispatcher and the state police station, she was connected with George Fitts at his Ocean Tide retreat. It would have been easier, Sarah thought, to have walked. But she got to the point. "George, it's Sarah, and don't hang up. That niblick, the club you pulled out of the pond on the tenth hole. What make was it?"

Silence. Then, "Let me look it up." The receiver put down. A rustle of paper. The phone picked up. "I have a note that it was made by Wright and Ditson. It's still at the lab. They want to go over it again."

"George," said Sarah carefully. "Would you be surprised if I told you that Pete Salieri, the assistant pro here, says that the niblick on the wall of the Pro Shop is also made by Wright and Ditson."

Pause. Then, "I suppose there are a lot of those around. Wright and Ditson was a well-known outfit."

"Shall I or Pete Salieri take this one down and see if it's really by Wright and Ditson. Or maybe it's an imposter. That it's another make and might have belonged to Fergus Mc-Kenzie."

A longer pause. The scraping of a chair. George, sounding as if he were grinding something in his mouth. "Do not, repeat, do not touch that golf club. I'll be right over. And don't let anyone in the Pro Shop."


George, wearing surgical gloves, climbed a stepladder fixed against the wall. Took the key from Pete Salieri's hand, turned it in the cabinet lock, then with infinite care lifted the niblick from its holding bracket, descended, walked over to the desk light, held the club up to the light, and examined the name engraved. Then he turned the club face over, held it close to the lamp. Even to the naked eye, Sarah could see that there was a faint smudging.

"He didn't have time to clean it," she said, as her stomach rolled in protest.

George nodded. "This is by Louis Berrian, not Wright and Ditson" he said slowly.

Pete looked stunned. "That's not ours. Berrian worked in the twenties. From Los Angeles. I just wish we had one of his."

"I suppose," said George, "the murderer had to make the substitution fast, give the Fergus McKenzie niblick a quick wipe, stick it up on the wall, and then get rid of the display niblick. Toss it in the first pond that he came to. The one on the tenth hole."

"You mean," said Pete Salieri in a bemused voice, "that all the time since Fergus McKenzie got killed I've had the wrong club up there? And I didn't even notice the difference?"

"Both had wooden shafts, black leather grips, and were in similar condition," said George, unexpectedly generous. "And you saw what you expected to see."

"People do that a lot," said Sarah in a consoling voice. Pete looked like someone had kicked him hard in the ribs.

George turned to Sarah. "I hate to say it because it might encourage you, but thanks for the call. This may take care of a missing piece. I think we'll get a blood type and maybe prints. The guy must have been in one hell of a hurry."

Sarah, even with nausea rising, managed a weak smile. "Anytime, George," she said.

# 24

THOSE last few days of June brought a bright sun and cloudless sky and a rise in the temperature that reminded the perspiring residents of Ocean Tide that summer had finally settled in.

Sarah had been invited to a senior McKenzie Sunday afternoon meeting-cum-iced drinks to go over the confused events of the past few weeks. In preparation she had left Patsy in the cool of the McKenzies' cottage and taken herself to the beach for a plunge into the icy ocean waters of Penobscot Bay. Striding out of the water, her limbs pleasantly chilled to numbness, she saw that Betty Colley in yellow shorts and black T-shirt had planted herself down on a small sandy patch of the beach, a striped umbrella stuck in beside her. In the shallows, clutching kickboards, their feet flailing the water, Dylan and his brother, Brian, were having a workout. Betty waved at Sarah and indicated the boys.

"They're going to learn to swim or I'll know the reason

why. When Camp Ocean Tide opens at least they'll be able to get across the pool."

Sarah, drying herself off with one of Elspeth's threadbare towels, monogrammed no doubt as part of her 1957 wedding trousseau, decided that this was a fine time to ask about Dylan. His mental health, his fear of the police, his fear of questions about his family, his cousins. And his fear of Sarah Deane. She sat down on the sand next to Betty,

Betty nodded, shouted for the boys to keep up, sixty kicks, turn, sixty kicks back. Then practice floating.

"There," she said with satisfaction. "That ought to take the starch out of them."

"About Dylan," Sarah began.

"Hell of a problem," said Betty. "You see, it's what they call a two-edged sword thing. I mean, there were sort of opposite reasons for all he was doing. You've got to understand that Matt was sort of hero to Dylan. From the word go."

"But Dylan found out something about Matt that scared him?" prompted Sarah.

"Dylan *saw* something that scared the bejeezus out of him. Not just two legs sticking out from bags of fertilizer He finally broke down last week and told me and the police. He was fooling around on the beach the day of the Fitness Center party in the area of the seventeenth green and heard the noise of a cart. Thought it might be Matt and it was a chance to say hi. Sometimes Matt gives him a ride in the back wagon of his greens tractor. Well, Dylan climbs up the bank and was about to give a yell when he saw Matt dragging what was obviously a dead body—wrapped up in garbage bags but an arm and a hand were sticking out. Saw Matt haul the body into the small shed, come out and begin unloading fertilizer bags and take them into the shed. About twenty bags, or more, he thought. And then Matt drove away, leaving the door unlocked because I suppose he was in a rush. Anyway, Dylan went into the shed. Saw the legs and—"

"Freaked out," finished Sarah.

"Totally," agreed Betty. "He didn't know of course that the body was his father's, but even when he found out he was caught between a rock and a hard place. His father had been a nonperson in the family for quite a while. But losing your dad is still a shock. But Dylan wanted, crazy as it was, to protect Matt. And there you were, almost on the spot. And then you chased him. Either you knew something, or you wanted to drag him to the police."

"Which I did," said Sarah. "Or at least drag him to someone. The Security people, maybe, because I didn't know he belonged to you."

"Well, after that scene in the shed," said Betty, heaving a sigh, "Dylan wanted out. Of everything. Cut his hair off, talked Brian into doing the same in case you hadn't really gotten a good look at him, might not be able to tell which was which. But when he figured out you knew who he was, he certainly didn't want to be tutored by you, the enemy, the person who might have seen what he'd seen and would spill the beans. He wanted to protect Matt, and he didn't want to be grilled by me or the police. So off he goes in the boat, is brought back by you and Alex, of all people. So when he has a chance, takes off on his bike. Looking for peace and quiet and a place to hunker down in. Our old farm. Of course, you'd called in the information, the police were onto it."

Sarah interrupted. "But you told other people about your idea."

"Sure. I told everyone I saw, including Sherry and Tim, that the farm was a likely hideout. So Matt and Al Moseby got into the act, maybe with a hired helper or two, found Dylan and tied him up."

"Did Dylan say he recognized either of the voices back at the farm?"

Betty stared at the sand, let a trickle through her fingers and then said in a troubled voice, "Says no. Either he's lying, or into denial—isn't that the term? Or, two of Al's helpers did the kidnapping job. But I just hope they weren't going to kill him. His own uncle and cousin. Though God knows they already had plenty of Colley blood on their hands. Perhaps they were just going to scare him. Dylan said he had a bag over his head so he couldn't identify them by sight."

Here Sarah nodded, remembering the bag, the smell of mold.

"But then you came along and they had to tie you up. Who knows what the final plan was going to be."

"I'm glad we didn't wait to find out." Sarah paused and then asked the question that was really bothering her. "But that last scene. When Matt tried to run him down on the seventeenth green. How does Dylan feel about that?"

"For now he's saying it didn't really happen. Said that Matt's tractor went out of control. That by shouting you distracted Matt and so you caused the accident. Sorry, Sarah, but Dylan, if he gets an idea in his head, it takes TNT to dislodge it. Particularly where Matt is concerned. Poor Dylan, he had a major fit when Matt was knocked unconscious and it seemed he might die. Matt's lucky that he's alive and getting out of the hospital but he'll be facing a tough time. I don't think Dylan will testify against him. You may be stuck with the job."

"Oh, God," Sarah groaned. "There's no end to this thing."

"I guess they've got other evidence against Matt. For that old man's death. Alex's uncle. Something about the substitute golf club and fingerprints."

Sarah gave a long sigh. "Well, I'd better get back to doing my own job. So what about the tutoring? You think I should try to go on with Brian and forget about Dylan? He didn't seem very happy today."

"Take it one day at a time. He wants to keep Ranger, which is one dog too many. We'll be tripping over them, but it might be worth it if Dylan sticks with the tutoring and manages to pass English next year. He's reading *Tom Sawyer*, which is a good sign. And I'm looking for some sort of psychologist to see if having your favorite cousin and uncle kill your stepbrother and your father and maybe somebody's old uncle is too big a lump for any kid to swallow."

"Some kids are pretty resilient," Sarah offered without too much conviction. She pushed herself off the sand and stood up and smiled at Betty. "Having a great mother and getting his dog back should help."

"Let's hope," said Betty. "Besides, I have a plan. One that might just fix things. It's a secret but you'll find out sooner or later."

Sarah grinned. "I can't wait. And tell the boys they look like pretty sharp out there in the water." She turned and walked away, wondering how Betty was going to get around the Ocean Tide two-dogs-per-family rule, the notice of which was posted on the Lodge bulletin board. But if it came to showdown between Joseph Martinelli and Betty, Sarah's money would be on Betty.


On the McKenzie cottage deck, by special invitation, wearing an open polo shirt and navy shorts, sat Deputy investigator Mike Laaka. He was surrounded by Elspeth, afloat in a light-weight blue caftan, Alex, in khaki shorts, and Sarah Deane in her still-damp yellow bathing suit. John McKenzie, at the urging of his son, was having a nine-hole lesson with Pete Salieri in the hope that the game of golf with the notable absence of buried bodies on the course might finally grab him. Alex had purchased for his father one Great Big Bertha Hawk Eye Driver made of super-light, super-strong titanium with super-heavy, super-dense tungsten. This object, Alex assured his father, could with a flick of the wrist be guaranteed to send the ball flying down the fairway.

A much welcome afternoon breeze off the ocean had risen and was rustling the bushes around the deck. Elspeth, after passing around cold Heineken to Alex, a frosty glass of Moxie to Mike (who was due to go on duty in an hour) and iced tea for Sarah and herself, placed on a wicker table an artichoke dip, chips, carrot strips, a wedge of Brie and a plate of water biscuits.

"You're softening us up," observed Mike. "Trying to get me fired."

"Just a friendly gathering," said Elspeth. "But we should start."

"Start with Matt Moseby," suggested Sarah. "He's the mystery man. Or boy. Alex, how is he doing?"

"Out of the hospital tomorrow," said Alex. "Once he regained consciousness, it was fairly smooth sailing. He doesn't remember the events of what his lawyer will call the "alleged" attack on Dylan on the seventeenth green. But that's to be expected with head injuries. He does remember Uncle Fergus and he started talking even when I was present. Right, Mike?"

"My lips are sealed," said Mike. "Except to say that he's been talking to the prosecutor since Sherry is very anxious he be tried as a juvenile."

"I can say from what I heard," put in Alex, "that Matt on that foggy afternoon apparently was transporting stolen bike parts in empty fertilizer bags to one of the storage sheds—a temporary stash, I suppose. And he found Uncle Fergus breaking open a bag with his niblick and decided something had to be done fast. The police guess that Matt nailed Fergus on the back of the neck with his fist, knocked him down, then grabbed the niblick and finished the job. George intimated to me without coming right out and saying it that Uncle Fergus's blood type, microscopic tissue particles showed up in the smear on the face of the club. And that a "prime suspect's" fingerprints were still detectable on the leather grip, even after wiping it down. Apparently the whole business of clubbing Uncle Fergus and then exchanging niblicks was a solo job by this 'prime suspect.' " By the way, Sarah, Dylan's bike, your sneakers, and Dylan's were found in the basement of the greenhouse. With Moseby family fingerprints showing up clear as could be. They can be collected at the station."

"Okay, that's that," said Sarah. "But getting back to Uncle

Fergus, I suppose Matt felt he had to kill him on the chance the old man had had a good look at stolen bike parts. And there was Fergus's own golf club ready to use. And Matt, after he'd dug the body into the sand trap, knew how to get into the Pro Shop after hours, switch the niblicks, and throw the clean one away in the pond. He probably thought that no one would notice a change in the display of old golf clubs. And he was right. Even Pete Salieri missed the switch."

"How could he exchange the clubs without being seen going into the Pro Shop, even if it was after hours?" asked Elspeth incredulously.

"That afternoon and evening were wild," said Alex. "Heavy fog, the search for Dylan, Sarah and I bringing Dylan home, the search for Fergus. Finding his body. No one was watching the Pro Shop."

"Those Moseby guys had quite an industry going," said Mike, leaning back in his canvas chair, which teetered perilously on the edge of the deck. "Bikes are big business, and as we've all said a thousand times, expensive, easy to steal and package. Whole or in parts."

"I suppose," said Elspeth wistfully, "that's what happened to my bicycle, because it hasn't turned up. But why ship them out of the country? Why not just out West? Or out of New England?"

"You're not thinking big," said Alex. "U.S. made bikes may be too expensive to sell profitably in Europe, Asia, South America. For the European market certainly Italian, French, British, Asian bikes will always be a better buy."

"I don't follow," said Elspeth frowning.

"Easy," said Mike. "Legitimate U.S bikes are expensive when sold overseas. Foreign bikes may be less expensive, but stolen bikes are the cheapest of all. The Moseby Bike Consortium—my name for the operation—could undersell any foreign bike because all they have to do is to pay for the shipping and distribution. Someone else paid for the manufacturing. They can take an import, say a French bike, steal it here in the U.S., then ship and sell it to a buyer in France. For peanuts. Well, almost for peanuts."

"And Nick Moseby and Thomas Schmidt were the salesmen?" asked Sarah.

"Seems like it," said Mike. "They were legitimate bike racers but on this trip they were working on sales. Hitting some of the bike-race people in France."

Elspeth clasped her hands over her caftan. "Please tell me that Naomi Foxglove was masterminding the European end. She's a perfect agent. A female dealer with her designer outfits and soft little ways. Who'd suspect her?"

"We don't," said Mike. "Sorry, Elspeth. With Naomi Foxglove, what you see is what you get. The perfect hostess, the efficient facilitator. Wonder woman in person. A brilliant African American, Native American, part-Oriental woman. She's the cornerstone of Manager Martinelli's 'Ocean Tide Embraces the World' program. She and Carly Thompson should run as a team for the presidency."

"I am disappointed," said Elspeth, running a hand through her white hair. "I was so sure. And she would have been so good at it. When she finishes here maybe the CIA can use her. All I did in Provence was make a fool of myself trailing her around. I will find her and try to make amends."

"Actually, you confirmed what Naomi told us. She'd been gripped by the idea that the two boys were up to something, and acted on it. On impulse which wasn't like Naomi at all. And here's another bit of news. George finally found out that young Nick left Yale at the beginning of the winter term. Nick's future apparently didn't include academics."

There was a thoughtful silence all round broken only by the crunching of chips and carrot sticks. Then Elspeth said without much hope, "I suppose Joseph Martinelli is in the clear? Not running an international bike scam? Papa, the head cheese. Capo di capo. Il duce."

"You and George Fitts. Ever since he found out that Joseph Martinelli played golf he's been hoping against hope. Even pointing out that Joseph reminded him of Marlon Brando. But it didn't work that way."

"But not all of the Moseby's were involved," Sarah pointed out.

"Not quite," said Mike. "Young Tim and Sherry are clean as far as we know."

"But what on earth is going to happen to the poor things?" asked Sarah. "The father and two boys ending up in prison."

"Hello, hello, hello," said a voice. A heavy step. A perspiring presence. John McKenzie. But a smiling John. He threw himself into a wicker armchair and reached for a glass. Maybe, Sarah thought looking over at him, golf has finally worked its magic.

"I'm about ruined," said John cheerfully. "I hooked or sliced or shanked every ball I hit. Pete Salieri says it's going to take months to turn me into a beginner golfer. I told him we leave for Weymouth Island in a week. No golf on the island so my links career is on hold." He turned to Elspeth. "I suppose you've been squeezing Mike about what's left in the murder cases? And Mike has been indiscreet."

"Never indiscreet and always off the record," said Mike, standing up. "But I have to be on my way. It's crime time."

"I'll walk you out," offered Alex.

"You're not just being the perfect host, you want something," Mike said as they came to the end of the little brick walk.

"Right," said Alex. "You owe me. Tell me for God's sake how Jason and Ned Colley figure in this. Why were they killed? Had they been sticking their noses where they didn't belong?"

"Alex, you know I can't—"

"I know you can. You're speaking to one of the county's medical examiners. The next time you want me to look at a ten-day-old body that's been lying out the sun, I may be much too busy. Hospital rounds to make."

"Okay, but you didn't hear it from me."

"You heard it from Matt, didn't you? When he was trying to get an A plus for cooperating with police."

Mike looked around as if expecting to see George Fitts lurking in the lilac bush on the front lawn. "I'll make it quick. In the beginning, like in the winter when Ocean Tide was barely open, the bike scam was hatched. Nick Moseby's idea, actually, but Daddy was all for it and Matt was gung-ho. Now, Matt was an off-and-on buddy of Jason Colley, who was foot-loose, up to not much good, and out of cash. Jason was added to the team, given money to buy that expensive new bike as a come-on, insurance that he'd stay the course."

"So what happened? Did Jason get cold feet?"

"Matt thinks maybe. Or maybe Jason decided to go out on his own. Whatever. Seems he ran into his father, and talked about it. Ned took an interest in the project. May have suggested that father and son could run their own scam. We'll never know. But the result was that Jason had a sort of confrontation with big daddy Al Moseby, somewhere behind one of the Route One parking lots. Jason said he'd been thinking it over and wanted out. Which was too late, Jason knew too much. As did Ned Colley, for that matter. Result, Al strangled Jason with that bicycle-lock chain, the one in the plastic sheath—forensic confirmation—hauled the body over across Route One past the hiking and mountain bike trails, and dumped it into the long grass off the third practice hole. Where it stayed for almost a week."

"But Ned Colley?" objected Alex. "Wasn't he on the look-out for something bad when Jason disappeared?"

"Your premise is that Ned was a proper father. No way. Didn't stay in touch that closely. Probably went off on a five-day drunk. But we guess he decided he wanted to know more about the Moseby business. Went looking for Al or Matt or Nick. Maybe blackmail. Maybe for a partnership. Maybe to find out if they had anything to do with Jason disappearing. And he got knocked on the head for his trouble. Very stupid of Ned

Colley, who should have realized something was up. Nick did the dirty work, whacked him on the head with one of the gardener's spades—we found it buried under the toolshed—Matt transported the body along with the fertilizer bags. Perfect way to hide a body in that rig. End of story," said Mike. "Now that you've pumped me, I have to be going. Maine Midcoast crime never lets up. Now it's motorcycles. Two antique Harleys lifted from the Wal-Mart parking lot."

Alex, his head churning with too much poorly digested information, returned to the deck and settled back in a chair and reached for his now warm beer. Then John, who had been impatiently tapping his foot and fiddling with his glass, turned to his wife. "Have you told them?"

"Told them what?" demanded Alex.

"You mean us?" said Sarah.

"Right. You two. The first in the family to hear our news," said John. "Tell them, Elspeth, so I can take a shower. I'm not fit for company."

Elspeth bit her lip, straightened her shoulders, put down her glass. "It's hard to know how to put this. You see, your father and I . . ."

Sarah opened her eyes. Was this going to be a divorce announcement? A separation in the works? Because John had turned into such a bear.

". . . have had a very serious talk. Because it's a serious step."

Sarah couldn't stand it. "You're not leaving John, are you? Or going to a lawyer. Separating? Have you seen anyone? How about counseling?"

"Okay, Mother," said Alex. "Let's hear the worst. If it is the worst. Is it?" he asked his mother. "Is Sarah making sense?"

"Oh, ye of little faith," said John. "Don't be ridiculous. Go on, Elspeth."

"Of course," Elspeth began, "with Uncle Fergus gone, we've canceled the big party. And we're going to be very busy.

We're picking up stakes. Moving out. Number Seven Alder Way is going on the block."

"Back to Cambridge?" said Alex, staring.

"Of course not. Cambridge is history," said Elspeth briskly. "It all came clear as a bell on my flight home. We made a mistake. We're square pegs in round holes and nothing Manager Martinelli can do will change it."

"Actually," said John, "I'm the squarest peg."

"Very true," agreed Elspeth. "But now we've made an offer on some property near Fallen Tree Pond in Union. And it was accepted. It has about ten acres and a fair-sized farmhouse on one end and another smaller house at the other."

"But," sputtered Sarah, "you don't want two houses. And the upkeep. The snow. All that shoveling. Mowing the grass. Cleaning the gutters. And farmhouses, if they're anything like ours, will cost a mint to put back together. Do the houses even have inside plumbing?"

"They do need work," said John complacently. "But so do I. Need work, that is. As I keep telling everyone, I'm not ready for the assisted-living scene. Not yet. Maybe sometime. But not this year. I'm getting a little tractor with a lawn mower and a snow blower attachment. And any fool can build bookshelves and chop kindling. Do simple plumbing."

"But the second house on the property? Will you sell that?"

Elspeth smiled broadly. "It's all arranged," she said. "The largest house will have Betty Colley, her mother, Rose, Dylan and his younger brother, Brian. And, because this is the only good solution to a terrible situation, Sherry Moseby and young Tim Moseby will move in with them. Betty said she wants her boys—particularly Dylan—to start over in familiar territory with some space around it. She wants a proper vegetable garden, perhaps keep a few hens. Room for three dogs. And she says that her mother, Rose, has been out of sorts ever since they moved here."

"And I've been out of sorts," said John. "Even with Elspeth

doing her best to be a good Ocean Tide citizen and make me one. But now the dawn is breaking and the sun will be shining, Elspeth will get a new bicycle, and even if I break my hip slipping on the ice or catch my foot in the snow blower, it will be worth it. We'll make a bike trail around the property, and besides, I've always wanted a tractor."

Alex and Sarah drew in deep breaths, looked at each other, then got to their feet, and held their glasses high.

"Cheers, and mud in your eye," said Sarah.

"Bottoms up," said Alex.

"Happy days," cried Elspeth.

"Olé!" shouted John McKenzie.


Thus it was that in the middle of September that year, the troubled waters of Ocean Tide became smooth, the Harvest Festival Gala, through the efforts of Carly Thompson and Naomi Foxglove, topped all previous events in its "fun for all ages" format, and Manager Joseph Martinelli, his kingdom by the sea restored to his control, said a thankful good-bye to a number of his most troublesome residents, and the next day welcomed three replacement families with baskets of fruit and large arrangements of autumn flowers.